perfect for readers who love to escape with empowered heroines and arrogant alphas who are too sexy for their own good. When not writing, you'll find her wrangling her four children, three cats, two goldfish and one dog… and snuggled in a heap on the sofa with her husband at the end of the day. Follow her at natalie-anderson.com.

Millie Adams has always loved books. She considers herself a mix of Anne Shirley—loquacious, but charming, and willing to break a slate over a boy's head if need be—and Charlotte Doyle—a lady at heart, but with the spirit to become a mutineer should the occasion arise. Millie lives in a small house on the edge of the woods, which she finds allows her to escape in the way she loves best: in the pages of a book. She loves intense alpha heroes and the women who dare to go toe-to-toe with them. Or break a slate over their heads…

THE NIGHT
THE KING
CLAIMED HER

NATALIE ANDERSON

THE
BILLIONAIRE'S
BABY
NEGOTIATION

MILLIE ADAMS

MILLS & BOON

First published in Great Britain 2022
by Mills & Boon, an imprint of HarperCollins*Publishers* Ltd,
1 London Bridge Street, London, SE1 9GF

www.harpercollins.co.uk

HarperCollins*Publishers*
1st Floor, Watermarque Building,
Ringsend Road, Dublin 4, Ireland

The Night the King Claimed Her © 2022 Natalie Anderson

The Billionaire's Baby Negotiation © 2022 Millie Adams

ISBN: 978-0-263-30090-1

07/22

MIX
Paper from
responsible sources
FSC™ C007454

This book is produced from independently certified FSC™ paper
to ensure responsible forest management.
For more information visit www.harpercollins.co.uk/green.

Printed and Bound in Spain using 100% Renewable Electricity
at CPI Black Print, Barcelona

THE NIGHT
THE KING
CLAIMED HER

NATALIE ANDERSON

MILLS & BOON

For Barb, Iona and Janet,
aka my sorority of wise, wonderful, writerly women.

You guys are central to a support system like no other
and I am so grateful to have you in my life.

CHAPTER ONE

Friday, 4.05 p.m.

'LEAVE. NOW!'

A warning alarm beeped, emphasising the urgency of the harsh whisper. Elsie Wynter crunched her eyes more tightly and hunched lower in her seat. She didn't want to leave. Not again.

'Miss?' Someone spoke right above her. Someone different—a woman—not *him*. 'Miss? Please lift the window shade and ensure your safety belt is fastened.'

Elsie blinked and realised reality and nightmare had merged. She was in a plane and she *was* going somewhere new. Only they were landing far sooner than she'd expected.

'Please, miss.' The air steward shot her an authoritative glance. 'Your safety belt.'

'Of course.' Elsie followed the orders.

She always followed orders. Especially those given so seriously. But as she checked her belt she glanced at the middle-aged man across the aisle from her. 'Are we already in Spain?'

'We've been diverted,' he said softly. 'A woman on board needs medical care.'

'Oh—'

'She's having a baby a bit early but they seem to have it under control.' The man shrugged his shoulders.

'The poor woman must be scared,' Elsie murmured.

She slid the window shade up. Their plane was moving swiftly over a vast expanse of sapphire water and a large island was rapidly coming into view. Smaller islands were visible in the distance beyond it but that main island soon swallowed the window space. Beautiful stone villas were built in the crannies of the cliffs, while to the north the island narrowed. A palace rose imposingly from the rocks at the end of the spit—like a fortress, it was a powerfully hewn beacon of strength, impervious to the ravages of weather or time or the changing needs of the world. It stood as it had for centuries. Part fortress, part palace, part medieval torture prison.

Elsie's heart pounded. She'd recognised it immediately but couldn't help asking, hoping she was wrong. Surely fate couldn't be so cruel. 'Where are we landing?'

'Silvabon.' The man peered past her. 'Beautiful, isn't it?'

Heartbreakingly beautiful, yes. She'd been here before. And in one day, one meeting—one person—had changed *everything*.

'Apparently there's a dungeon beneath that palace,' the man said. 'And treasure everywhere.'

Silvabon was a Mediterranean paradise—resplendent and timeless, a literal treasure in a vast sea. Blessed with abundant natural resources, the kingdom had skilfully fostered strategic alliances for security—in centuries past through marriage with other royal families in the region, and in more recent times through business alliances and access to its prized shipping routes. Elsie had known they'd be flying near as they travelled from Athens to Madrid, but she'd not realised they would come this close to the illustrious kingdom—let alone be diverted directly to it.

A memory flickered—a firm step, a teasing laugh, a long look. A whisper about that dungeon. Hot hurt crescendoed as the recollection solidified. She breathed deliberately slowly to ride the worst out—humiliation and ostracism weren't strangers to her. But she'd worked too hard to let just one thought of him diminish her peace. But more than one thought of him impinged now. Elsie had spent over two months here in the glorious sunshine and luxurious atmosphere until she'd been unceremoniously evicted.

Leave. Now!

That order had come from the King himself. At the time she'd been stupidly confused why his tone had been so cruel, so urgent. She'd been more than stupid because for a second she'd thought he might actually—

No. His actions after that order had been unequivocal and utterly humiliating. So she'd not needed to be told twice and she'd vowed never to return. But now, she rationalised with purposefully even breaths, she *wasn't* returning. Their plane was landing only to drop off the patient. The rest of the passengers—including her—wouldn't disembark. They'd simply take off again. There was no reason to be anxious.

But as they came in to land, her pulse went off beat. An army of private jets was perfectly lined up on the tarmac like a flotilla of bragging billionaire toys. Banners hung from the airport terminal and surrounding buildings. She stared at the midnight blue, black and gold—the colours of Silvabon emblazoned every possible edifice in celebration. The flags weren't fluttering. There was no wind to lift them. Because the weather was perfect. *Everything* was perfect. She knew exactly why. The mourning period for his grandfather was over and King Felipe Roca de Silva y Zafiro's official coronation was less than twenty-four hours away.

An ambulance raced to meet their plane, flanked by two fire appliances. It took only a few minutes for the distressed woman onboard to be transported away. King Felipe's people were incomparably efficient— *especially* his security team.

'Thank you for your patience and I apologise for the interruption to our journey.' The pilot spoke over the intercom. 'Unfortunately there will be further delay.'

Elsie's lungs tightened.

'We were granted permission to land only because of the medical emergency onboard. Silvabon's skies are closed for King Felipe's coronation this weekend. Because of this,' the pilot continued, 'we must remain grounded until the ceremony concludes tomorrow.'

A collective groan echoed around the plane but Elsie couldn't utter a sound.

'Can't we just take off again now?' someone called out.

'You'll be accommodated at a hotel here at the airport.' The pilot kept talking. 'Once again we apologise for the inconvenience. If you need to rebook an onward journey, our ground staff are in the terminal ready to assist.'

Elsie didn't have another plane after this one was meant to land in Madrid. She'd planned to spend the last of summer in Spain. Greece had been okay but the islands reminded her too much of Silvabon. She wanted a large city in which to become anonymous—with no views of sapphire waters. She'd find another job in another café and continue to save so she could eventually settle somewhere completely new. England, her original home, wasn't an option—there were too many desperately sad, awfully bad memories attached. But now she was back in the place she'd briefly believed to be perfect. Until the country's charmless royal had ruined everything.

Instinct urged her to hide, but surely he wouldn't find her. He wouldn't have given her a second thought after he'd booted her out of his precious country. She hadn't even said goodbye to Amalia, the one true friend she'd made here. But Amalia was the King's stepsister and after what he'd done? There'd been no chance. And that *hurt*. He'd taken too much away from her.

Elsie focused inward, calming the surging anxiety. One

night in an airport hotel would be fine. No one from the palace would ever know she was here.

'Your Majesty. We have a problem.'

Not the words King Felipe wanted to hear from Major Garcia, his ageing security chief. Preparations for this wretched coronation had taken up far too much of his time already. But this was it—in less than twenty-four hours he would give his nation its ultimate royal spectacle. Pomp, ceremony, publicity. It was the first celebration in just over a decade and down to him once more. But this would be the *last* time.

'If this is the flight with the woman in preterm labour onboard, Ortiz already requested permission,' he said. 'I thought it had landed.'

'It has, Your Majesty.'

Felipe glanced up from the paperwork on his desk. 'Then what? Were the medical team unable to—?'

'She's being cared for now. The baby is premature, but all signs indicate a positive outcome.'

'Good.' Felipe looked back at the draft trade agreement he'd been perusing. 'So…'

'The other passengers onboard must stay on Silvabon until after your coronation. We could open the skies only briefly for the plane to land.'

Felipe refrained from rolling his eyes. His security was always ridiculously excessive, but they were ludicrously stringent at the moment because Felipe had not yet declared an heir. All his advisors were antsy—should Felipe meet an untimely demise they feared a war of succession as there was no close relative to take the crown. But Felipe had no intention of meeting an untimely demise and though the succession declaration rested with him, right now he was resisting it. Of course, having children of his own would provide a natural succession plan but he wasn't just resisting that. He point-blank refused. He had an alternative plan. He just needed to get through tomorrow's coronation before revealing it. The coronation had precedence over everything. So while it was unfortunate for that plane's occupants, he wasn't about to cause more stress to his team. Changing security agreements at this stage would be difficult, given so many VIPs from other countries were here. It had been a monstrous undertaking to ensure everyone's needs were met and Felipe well knew accepting inconvenience was part of palace life.

'Fortunately the flight wasn't full and we're able to accommodate the remaining passengers at a hotel,' the Major added. 'We're providing complete service for them, of course.'

Felipe nodded.

Major Garcia cleared his throat. 'Naturally we checked the passenger manifest to be sure this wasn't a possible Trojan attack.'

Felipe smothered a rueful smile. Yes, Garcia was particularly thorough at the moment. Silvabon was a constitutional monarchy but even with elected representatives forming a parliament the King—Felipe—had substantial discretionary powers far greater than similar monarchies in other countries. And poor old Garcia had already lost one royal under his watch.

'I assume no one was onboard with the intention of disrupting the coronation?' Felipe asked.

There was a momentary pause.

Felipe lifted his head to read his major's body language. The man stood unusually stiff, even for him. 'You found something?'

Wariness entered the man's eyes. 'Elsie Bailey is onboard.'

Felipe froze.

'Otherwise known as Elsie Wynter.' Garcia cleared his throat. 'She's the woman Amalia—'

'I know who she is,' Felipe clipped. His blood rushed everywhere except where he needed it most. *Elsie Wynter?*

A flash of dirty-blonde hair. A heartbeat of husky laughter. A blink of unnervingly pale blue eyes.

'She was on the flight but the plane wasn't supposed to land here?' He gritted his teeth at his roughened voice.

Garcia nodded. 'The flight was bound for Madrid.'

Felipe couldn't move. He shouldn't be bothered by Elsie Wynter's unscheduled, unintentional arrival. She wasn't here for any reason other than fate. He'd ignore it.

'Is she travelling alone?' Why had he asked that? Why did it matter?

'Yes, sir.'

His gut tightened, squeezing something cold and undeniable.

'Bring her to the palace,' he said curtly.

'Sir?'

'I want her brought to the palace. Immediately.'

The words were out before he could stop them. And they felt good.

I want her—

Fury swamped him. No. *That* wasn't why.

Elsie Wynter wouldn't escape the emotional harm she'd caused. She'd *explain*. He wanted to hear it from her damnably beautiful mouth. Why she'd vanished, why she'd let down his vulnerable stepsister, why she'd lied.

Felipe loathed liars as much as he loathed people who turned their backs on their responsibilities and *left*. Invariably those who did one, did both. Both his parents had. He wasn't having Amalia's life blighted by the same even on this minor level. She'd lost enough.

'Your Majesty—'

'High security. No drama. No witnesses,' Felipe added uncompromisingly. 'Put Ortiz on it. Understood?'

He'd look into Elsie Wynter's cool eyes again, but he'd not be blinded by their beauty this time. It was his job to protect his young stepsister. Because of this woman, he'd failed.

For that, she would pay.

CHAPTER TWO

Three months earlier, morning

'SHE COULD BE *a security risk.*'

Felipe stiffened. He'd forgotten Ortiz, his best body-guard, was at his side and expecting orders. Felipe resented the intrusion yet immediately castigated himself for his own distraction. He was meant to have been assessing the scene. Only in seconds he'd become entranced by the soft strumming music. He'd been straining to listen harder to that lilting voice with the husky edge that made him—

He gritted his teeth, biting back the response surging within. But now it had been acknowledged, that response became emboldened. Felipe named it with self-mockery. Desire. The woman wasn't what he'd imagined at all. She was far more—

'You really think so?' he muttered shortly.

He focused on reducing his ridiculous tension, but he'd been inadequately prepared for her beauty. Her blue and white floral dress highlighted her pale blue eyes. Slightly messy silky blonde hair framed her sweet heart-shaped face.

She looked delectable, not dangerous.

In truth Felipe's security team were too cautious. His father's disappearance years ago had resulted in a deeply engrained overzealous protection plan. Now Felipe barely listened to his bodyguards' mutterings. If he did, then everyone and everything would be a security risk and he'd be unable to even breathe. That was why he'd put Ortiz on Amalia. The guy was a little less over the top. Yet now they were here. Frankly it was hard to see how and why this woman could be a threat. Except just looking at her tightened every muscle in his body. Jaw aching, he forced his attention to the person sitting beside her.

Becoming sole guardian of a thirteen-year-old he'd never before met hadn't been easy. Nor was it optional. Felipe had brought his stepsister Amalia to Silvabon six months ago. Quiet and listless, she wasn't anything like he imagined a normal young teen should be. But she was still recovering from injuries, still grieving her parents. She'd suffered too much for someone her age. As this was the first social contact she'd initiated, he needed to tread carefully. Amalia wasn't royal, she didn't have the obligations and shouldn't suffer the penalties of palace life. But while she was young and vulnerable, while she was under his protection, he had to check out who she was gravitating to. His gaze drifted back. What did this woman offer Amalia?

'She usually works alone. She bakes, updates the menu sign. The café is small but popular. Her boss turns up later to help,' Ortiz briefed him quietly. 'Her lemon cakes are really good.'

Oh? For some reason the thought of Ortiz tasting her food scraped Felipe's bones. He glanced at the menu board. The specials of the day were written with swirling artistic streaks. A multi-talented creative, this petite blonde leaning close to his stepsister.

For almost the last fortnight Amalia had come to the café for at least an hour, sometimes longer. Felipe had thought it might be a boy she was meeting. But no, it was this shrimp of a woman with a canvas apron covering her billowy sundress. Her chunky work boots looked incongruous against *that floaty fabric and an assortment of silverwork adorned her ears. The earrings sparkled in the morning sun and made him stare harder, longer. Which in turn made him notice the length of her pretty neck.*

So not appropriate. *He made himself count for four—slow and controlled as if he were diving down in deep water.*

They were seated out the back of the café but still in public view, strumming chords on a weird-shaped, undersized guitar. Safe enough surely. But seeing Amalia bent close to the blonde put him on edge. It shouldn't. All she was doing was showing Amalia which frets to put her fingers on.

'She's been in Silvabon almost three months. Amalia's been visiting these last ten days. I have some details but haven't run a comprehensive security check yet,' *Ortiz said.* 'Shall I do that now, sir?'

Felipe watched her smile at Amalia in encouragement as the girl plucked the thin metal strings. 'No. Not yet. I'll find out.'

He strode forward. As Amalia's 'bossy, overbearing' *stepbrother, he couldn't do a thing right. Interfering with her new routine was hardly going to help. Too bad. His number one priority was ensuring her safety.*

'Amalia.' *He watched her blonde companion as he spoke.* 'Aren't you going to introduce me to your friend?'

He could easily ignore Amalia's resentful expression, but the shock on the woman's face was an immediate alert. Wariness widened her eyes, furthermore fierce colour swept into her cheeks. Felipe was used to people reacting to his appearance—blushing, yes; stammering, absolutely; smiling and being unable to meet his eyes, often... But this was different. She was different. Because even though her skin flushed she held his gaze—coolly, completely. Maybe Ortiz was right.

'As if you don't know who she is already,' Amalia said. 'I saw you talking with Captain Ortiz. I'm not stupid.'

No. Just sullen and impossible to engage with, let alone make happy. Felipe tensed all over again. Being a young teen stuck in Silvabon palace? He knew all about the resentment that could bloom if there was no release... But he didn't know how to make it better for Amalia and she had to understand there were risks with her new position as a palace resident.

'Does she know who you are?' he asked.

Amalia's expression turned stony. 'Are you saying she only wants to spend time with me because I'm related to you? Because she doesn't know.'

'She knows. Everyone in this city knows who you are.'

'Well, she didn't until her boss told her and we were already friends by then.'

A spark of sympathetic amusement lit the woman's face as she glanced at Amalia. 'Guys, I'm sitting right here.' She turned those blue eyes back to him. 'I'm Elsie Wynter. And you're King Felipe, Amalia's stepbrother.'

She didn't stand in his presence as she ought. So there was no curtsey. No Your Majesty. No Pleased to meet you. No fear in those stunning eyes either.

But there was a slightly mocking edge to her self-introduction. For a moment he gazed at her. She gazed right back—measure for measure. He wondered what she was thinking—whether she liked what she saw of him. Suddenly there was a dragging sensation deep in his gut, pulling him towards her. But he didn't move an inch. He'd met many beautiful women in his life, he wasn't about to lose his equanimity here. Instead he watched and he waited. And then he saw it—the resignation flickering in her eyes. She didn't drop her gaze, but the defiant strength of it? That flatlined.

She expected him to dismiss her from Amalia's life—

because she thought he knew something about her, that he'd had a security briefing? If she thought that, then there must be an element of threat. His curiosity spiked—what, why, and how?

'Amalia's been spending time with you.' He gritted his teeth, annoyingly aware he sounded like a puffed-up, over-protective older brother. Which, admittedly, was what he was. He had to be.

'I'm sitting right here, Felipe.' Amalia rolled her eyes as she echoed Elsie Wynter's light sass.

'And it's time you weren't,' he replied coolly. 'You're late for your physio. It's rude to keep your therapist waiting.'

Amalia sighed. 'So you've come to drag me back to prison?'

'Prison?' Elsie interrupted Amalia's escalating tone with a laugh. 'No, don't destroy my dreams about what living in a palace is really like.'

Amalia's eyes widened and she almost smiled.

Felipe paused, absorbing his stepsister's reaction with slight shock. He hadn't seen Amalia smile much since she'd arrived. And that she saw the palace as a prison? Not good.

But now Elsie glanced up at him with that cool defiance again. 'I'm sorry, we lost track of time.'

'Amalia didn't. She ignored the messages on her phone.' He glanced pointedly at the expensive phone placed face down on the table.

'She put it on silent at my request.'

Felipe tensed. Why didn't she want Amalia using her phone?

'We didn't want to break concentration.' Elsie seemed to read his mind.

'So her tardiness truly is your fault?'

'Sure.' A shrug of her slim shoulders exposed a soup-çon more skin.

He had the strongest urge to reach out and touch it and see if it was as warm and as soft as it looked.

'No—'

'It's all right, Amalia.' Felipe interrupted his stepsister. 'I understand.'

Amalia passed the instrument back to Elsie and stood up from the wooden chair with another dramatic sigh. 'He's going to warn you away now,' she said to Elsie. 'Please ignore him. We're not really even related.'

Amalia indignantly stomped past, her limp prominent. She'd recently taken to wearing her long hair down, but it didn't hide the scarlet filling her face.

Felipe gritted his teeth, unaccustomed to failure. But he was inexperienced in a relationship like this. He'd not had a sibling before. Nor had Amalia. And he was more guardian now than brother. The girl had no companions anywhere near her own age. And this woman? She was nearer his age than Amalia's.

He wanted to protect his stepsister from...well, everything. Which, he realised, made him very similar to his own security team. Fundamentally he simply wanted what was best for her. But he had no idea what that even was, let alone how to achieve it.

'She's definitely not stupid.' Elsie's smile was wry. 'Knows how to strike, doesn't she?'

Felipe tried to ignore the woman's creamy skin and instead got caught up in her ice-blue eyes. Her pupils widened—not from fear. She clearly wasn't intimidated by him so the unconscious response was based in something else.

'She's more vulnerable than she thinks,' he said with an honesty more blunt than usual.

Elsie nodded regretfully. 'If you don't think I know that already, then you must think I'm stupid.'

'Jury's out,' he muttered, prodding to see what other reaction he'd receive.

Sparks flashed. 'Jury?' she echoed. 'Is impartial justice actually a possibility here? I thought you were the instant judge type.'

'No.' Unable to resist, he took the seat Amalia had vacated. 'That appears to be your forte.'

Now he was closer, something gnawing within him was soothed. He caught a hint of lemon scent and his mouth watered. He clamped his jaw shut. While her eyes were glacier blue, they weren't cold. The narrowed atmosphere between them crackled.

'Who are you, Elsie Wynter?' he eventually asked. 'Why are you in Silvabon?'

'As if you haven't had me checked out already?' She nodded her chin towards the tall man standing a few metres behind him. And the other beyond.

Yes, with wires in their ears and guns under their jackets, his plain-clothes security detail were as obvious as his fully uniformed soldiers standing guard at the palace.

'I'm checking *you out now,' he murmured.*

He couldn't resist. He studied her far too intently for far too long. The faint mottling on her skin and the slight parting of her full lips gave her away but she defiantly held his gaze. This electricity? She felt it too.

'So what have you learned?' she asked.

That she was more beautiful than he'd have believed. That something in her attitude made him tense. Yet at the same time he felt an impossible urge to trust her. And he wanted to learn her secrets, her past, her future, what drew her laughter or tears. And her taste. The desire to discover her taste gnawed deep. None *of which he could say.*

But during his hesitation she paled and swallowed. Hard. His curiosity only deepened.

'I'm not going to be in the country permanently,' she suddenly said before he could answer. 'Amalia heard me playing at the back of the café on my break. She asked me

to show her my mandolin. I said yes before I knew who she was.'

So it was a mandolin? He nodded. But he found it most interesting that her priority was to inform him that she wasn't sticking around. Was she a threat? One part of him most definitely thought so. 'But you know who she is now.'

'My boss told me the other day when he arrived early. Until then we'd been alone,' she acknowledged. 'We sit out the back early, when it's quiet. She's less visible. She has an officer with her, you know. In fact, she has three.'

'I do. I also know she's been visiting daily. That's why I'm here now.'

Unmistakable resentment flared in her eyes. 'Because her meeting with me is a problem?'

'That's what I'm here to decide.' He drew a breath. Personal information wasn't something he ever shared but this was different. 'Amalia's parents died in a train crash seven months ago. She was with them and was injured too. Badly.'

'Yes. She told me.'

'She did?' As far as he was aware Amalia hadn't spoken to anyone about the accident that had killed her mother and stepfather and left her with a limp that might be life-long. Certainly not him—their interactions had begun as stilted and degenerated into simply uncommunicative. So he'd engaged a tutor and a therapist. But Amalia hadn't confided in either of those or any other palace staff. Elsie was the only person he'd seen her engage with much at all.

Elsie looked at him. 'I'm sorry for your loss.'

Her voice had that edge he'd heard when she'd sung before—a fragment of the tune echoed in his head and made him think of grace and sanctuary. He tensed.

His loss.

Her acknowledgement was an unexpected balm on an old wound and an irritant to it at the same time. He pushed the sympathy away. Carlos might have been his father, but

Felipe hadn't seen him in more than a decade. He'd chosen to leave and Felipe had chosen not to think of him. Because Carlos had run away with his lover and her daughter to Canada and they'd never returned to Silvabon. While Felipe's mother—shamed and blamed by his grandfather, King Javier, for the marriage breakdown—had also left the palace, emotionally broken.

Felipe had become heir to the throne and recipient of his grandfather's deep focus and iron-fisted instruction. Now Amalia was as alone in the palace as he'd once been and he didn't want her to suffer the—

Felipe mentally counted to ten, slowly, deliberately, pushing all that back. But he regarded Elsie Wynter as he did. Because he couldn't turn away.

She'd paused; the emotion in her clear eyes was now concern. But there was more than that empathy. There was an echo of grief that he recognised. She'd lost someone too. He wondered who and when and how and again that desire to know her almost consumed him. This sudden fascination? Not normal for him. Not okay.

Yet she was still, exuding a quiet serenity that encouraged confidences. He lowered his gaze to avoid the startling clarity of hers but got caught by her mouth. It was slightly wide and her lips were pillowy and he suddenly thought of mussed-up sheets and husky laughter. It was a thought so out of place that he flinched.

Felipe never flinched. Ever. That was when he knew Ortiz was right. She was a security risk. To his peace of mind. To his mastery over his own body. And he had to leave.

'She wants to keep learning the mandolin,' Elsie said softly, slaying his intention to go in a millisecond. 'She's extremely musical. But I'm sure you know that already.'

Actually he didn't. He'd had no idea she was even interested. When he'd first met Amalia, having flown her pri-

vately from Canada a few days after the accident, she'd been in hospital. She'd missed the rest of the school year recovering. This summer she was catching up on her studies with a private tutor and still working on her physical strength.

'You could get a music teacher to come to the palace if you don't want her out here,' Elsie suggested.

'Why can't you come?' he said before thinking.

The 'thinking' took only another millisecond anyway. Amalia needed distraction. She'd chosen Elsie, chosen this interest. Music was fine—wholesome even. If they were in the palace grounds then his overzealous security team could relax. And besides—

Elsie's lips parted, colour stained her cheeks, and the look in her eyes?

Yes. He might be puffed up and overprotective, but he could still stun a woman into silence. He glanced at the café roster on the kitchen wall and absorbed the information with satisfaction.

'I don't—'

'The palace is not a prison,' he said coolly, daring her to deny him. 'You can see if your dreams are remotely accurate.'

'I—'

'You will be met at the gate at two p.m. Don't be late.'

'But—'

'Don't disappoint her.'

Her chin lifted, mutiny flaring in her stunningly pale eyes. 'Or?'

A ripple of something stronger than satisfaction shimmered through him now. Temptation in all its colours.

'Or you'll have to answer to me.' He couldn't resist leaning a little closer as he stood. 'Personally.'

CHAPTER THREE

Friday, 4.48 p.m.

'Ms WYNTER?'

Elsie glanced up and stiffened. It was one of the elite force who protected King Felipe.

'Do you mind if I have a quiet word?' the guard asked. He had an earpiece and no doubt a gun concealed beneath that black jacket.

She glanced at the other passengers patiently waiting in the airport arrivals lounge and tightened her grip on her mandolin case as she recognised another plain-clothes guard a short distance away. The last thing she wanted was to attract attention. Better to answer softly, as if this weren't a worry at all. 'What about?'

'If you'll follow me, there's an office…'

Conscious of an audience, Elsie nodded and followed him. Nerves proliferated. But she wasn't about to create a scene. She'd suffered too many in the past. Public humiliation? Scorn? Rejection? She'd checked those boxes in the past and she wasn't about to tick them again in front of all these people. But the moment she got in private with this guard? Her words weren't going to be quiet.

He'd referred to her as Elsie Wynter. But on her official documents she was still Elsie Bailey. Clearly someone had done their homework. But she knew that already. It was why she'd been banished the last time she was here.

The guard led her through a door marked 'airport security'. Nerves exploded now. Was he taking her to the strip-search room? But they turned left, went through another door, then another and were suddenly out on the tarmac again. The warmth of the late afternoon was balmy but Elsie shivered. Anxiety did that to a person.

A large black vehicle was parked only a foot from the door, which meant there was no way to go around it. Another 'casually' dressed guard held the rear passenger door open.

She stared. 'Where are you—?'

'Please, Ms Wynter. I assure you, you'll be kept safe.'

Kept safe? From *what*?

'It'll only take a few minutes,' he added.

Elsie saw the sideways glances from the few airport staff still on the tarmac. Holding tight to her case, she climbed in the car. Was someone else already in there? No. The back seat was all hers. Behind her the door closed. Less than a second later the car moved. Elsie put her case down and automatically fastened her seat belt. It was less than two minutes since the first guard had approached her and now she was being driven who knew where? Only her pulse skidded because she knew already. They were on the road that led straight to the palace.

Why? That was the real question.

Celebratory banners hung above the picture-postcard cobbled streets but she couldn't appreciate the beautiful villas of the abundantly wealthy nation. Not when she could see the palace looming large. It had begun its life several centuries ago, built as a fortress to protect the rulers and to imprison those who threatened their power. Over time various additions had been made until it reached peak glorious palace. But there was no getting away from its foundations—it wasn't just a prison, but a *dungeon*.

They drove through the gleaming gates. She'd never thought she'd come back, let alone be all but kidnapped like this. Her anger built at the high-handed treatment. There was only one person to blame.

'If you'll follow me,' the guard said when he opened the door.

Despite her loose-fitting jeans and cotton cropped jumper, Elsie felt hot and sticky. She blew a stray strand of hair from her face as the guard led her along the snaking passage. In the menacing, oppressive silence her temper rose. She'd not done *anything* wrong.

The guard opened the door and stood aside for her to enter. 'Please wait in here.'

Next second she was suddenly utterly alone in a vast room designed to intimidate. On her previous visit she'd been in relatively public rooms with light, luxurious decor and all modern amenities. In this room there weren't even any windows. There were high vaulted ceilings, tapestries on the walls and uncomfortable-looking wooden furniture. There were sconces for candles though the room was currently lit by that marvel of modernity, *electricity*—but it might as well be three hundred years ago when the rights of women were non-existent and one man could order everyone to do whatever he wanted. It might as well be a prison cell. In fact, Elsie decided it was one step away from a medieval torture room.

The heavy door opened again as if by magic. It wasn't. It was one of the two armed guards waiting outside. But then…

King Felipe Roca de Silva y Zafiro swept in.

The door shut. Silence. She wanted to berate him but she wasn't just frozen, she was transfixed. Bereft of brain, her body was immobile. She couldn't look away and she *really* needed to.

He wore a black suit like his security agents but, where theirs hung slightly loose to hide weapons and allow movement, his perfectly hugged the sleek lines of his fit body. His jawline was sculpted—all sharp edges. And she'd forgotten how tall he was. Tall, tense, *furious*. And staring right back at her. Through her. The intense expression in his eyes was unrelenting, unforgiving, unyielding.

Breathing got tougher. The air was hotter, thicker, and this massive room now felt small and smoky. Every emotion bubbled to the surface. Upset. Hurt. Isolation. Longing. *All* of them slipped from her control. But the worst reaction was the utterly forbidden, uncontrollable *want*. King Felipe was the most handsome man she'd ever met. Not just handsome. Handsome she could cope with. He was *compelling*—the *only* man to stir her into temptation. Not just temptation. He'd roused the kind of selfish greed that had destroyed her family. He terrified her. And *she* was furious about it.

Elsie watched as he walked too close before he stopped. But she didn't step back. She wasn't a citizen of this country. He wasn't *her* king. And she point-blank refused to be intimated. *Not this time.*

His gaze bored into her. His eyes were the deepest brown and she'd spent too long trying to decipher what he might be thinking. She'd got it wrong. Now she knew the man wasn't just impossible to read, he was very likely thinking the exact *opposite* of how he appeared. He silently scoured her for every visible detail. She was conscious she'd been in her clothes for hours, having got up early to get to the airport. Ugh—why should she care about her appearance before him? She didn't want to *care* at all.

He still didn't break the silence—too focused on scrutinising her with serious displeasure. A tremor ran through her—a visceral response to his attention.

Elsie didn't have affairs, didn't have boyfriends, didn't feel lust, let alone act on it. But the moment she'd met Felipe?

'What do you want from me?' she muttered.

It wasn't what she'd meant to ask. Certainly not with a husky whisper.

His jaw tightened.

'Am I being arrested?' She stiffened, hating that her voice was still scratchy. 'Why have I been detained and dragged before you, *Your Majesty*?'

He'd not liked her calling him that before. He'd acted as if he wanted her to be 'on the same level' as Amalia, and by extension him. As if.

'You were on the flight diverted here.'

'Yes.' She lifted her chin. 'But I didn't cause some poor woman to go into labour early. It was no plot of mine, if that's what you're thinking.'

'That's not what I'm thinking.'

'Then what?'

She needed him to stop staring at her as if she were guilty of something terrible. The condemnation felt hot and prickly and rubbed everything raw. Shame hurt. She hated that he had the power to hurt her. But he was a two-faced hypocrite. He'd acted friendly and understanding and she'd actually liked him. For a second there she'd thought she might even be able to *stay*. But behind her back he'd betrayed her, revealing his clinically cold heart.

'Your armed muscle men wouldn't even tell me why I was abducted from the airport in broad daylight.'

'They didn't know why,' he explained coolly. 'They were simply following orders.'

'*Blindly* following orders. Indulging the whims of a spoilt royal.' She glared at him. 'Being frogmarched through the airport isn't my idea of a good time.'

'Did they really cause a great scene?' His eyebrows lifted.

'Of course, they didn't. They were ruthlessly efficient in their armed *Men in Black* style.'

'And you didn't resist?' he said softly.

She hadn't resisted at all. And she hadn't exactly been frogmarched. She'd quietly followed the guy. Right now she really regretted that. But Felipe's question picked at her wounds. 'Why should that surprise you? I've done *nothing* wrong. In fact, I've only done what I was told. But you don't trust me.'

His eyes narrowed but he didn't deny it.

'Are you going to search my case in case I've a surface-to-air rocket launcher in there?' She stiffened as he edged nearer.

He took the mandolin case from her fingers and set it on the table to his side. 'My men already know what's in here. It went through an X-ray scan. So did you. You're not armed.'

Just with words. With anger.

'Elsie.'

She froze. It hurt to hear her name on his lips. As if there were an intimacy they'd shared? There *wasn't*. That was the point. He'd been charming and she'd thought he'd not just trusted her but welcomed her. Then he'd gone behind her back and wrecked her life without a second thought. Because he was used to getting anything and everything he wanted. He did as he liked without any concern for anyone else.

'How did you know I was on board?' she asked.

'It was an unusual diversion at an unusual time and the manifest was cross-checked by my security.'

'And my name was flagged?' She was hurt. Did he really regard her as such a threat? He'd asked her to leave and she had, but he'd gone ahead to wreck the rest of her life anyway.

Elsie *Wynter* wasn't listed. Elsie Bailey was. The legal name she'd never given him yet he knew anyway. Thanks to that security team again, right? Had they ripped through the tawdry secrets and shame of her past? The humiliation of the family that she'd once thought perfect, but she'd been such a sheltered *fool*—

'Has anyone else been hauled before you, or just lucky little me?' she asked bitterly.

There was a pause. 'Just lucky little you.'

'Well, as honoured as I am,' she said coldly, 'I'd like to *leave. Now.*'

CHAPTER FOUR

Three months earlier, afternoon

ELSIE MARCHED TO the imposing gates, carrying her pride and her mandolin. Who did he think he was, demanding she appear at the palace at two p.m. on the dot? All *Don't be late... Don't disappoint...*

The King, duh.

When he'd walked up to their table at the café this morning Elsie should've stood and curtseyed but she'd been unable to. Literally unable to. Her legs had become wet noodles. She'd been so unprepared—even though she'd seen his photos, of course. You couldn't live on Silvabon and not know the super-popular King's face. He was like a deity who could do no wrong and the population were all stupid proud of him. Her boss had been giddy with excitement when he'd learned Amalia was now a regular customer and he'd instructed Elsie to take extra special care of her.

Of course, Elsie took care of her. But Amalia's relationship to King Felipe wasn't why.

Only in meeting him today she'd discovered he had the deepest, dreamiest brown eyes. Tall, lean, so handsome she'd been unable to stop herself staring. But there was more than physical beauty. He'd compelled every ounce of

*her attention and the way he'd assessed her had made her
feel as if she were the only person on the planet.*

*No. She couldn't be that foolish. To develop a crush on
the one king she'd ever met? The world's most popular
one? Especially when she'd then seen that the guy was a
bossy, overprotective control freak.*

*Only that was a little harsh too, wasn't it? Because she'd
caught a glimpse of human beneath his stuffy layers. He
cared about Amalia. The girl had been loyal, careful not
to betray her stepbrother by complaining overtly to Elsie,
and Elsie respected her for that. But Amalia was obviously
grieving, clearly lonely and lost in a new place, knowing
almost no one—least of all her stepbrother, apparently.
But it seemed Felipe was worried about her. So, of course,
he made demands. And doubtless he got his way in everything. It was his normal.*

*But she didn't expect him to be there waiting for her in-
side the palace gatehouse.*

*'Security needs to process you.' His gaze lingered on
her mandolin case.*

*She battled the disappointment that he'd not directly
looked into her eyes. When he had earlier she'd felt a surge
of energy—something hot and strong that had given her the
courage to gaze right back at him. And in doing so, she'd
simply taken in more. He'd been like a personal charger—a
bolt of vitality that could easily become addictive. But that
was so fanciful, so impossible, she had to rebel against her
own wayward imagination.*

'Are you security this afternoon?' she asked shortly.

*In his black trousers and white shirt he'd almost fit the
part—except the fabric was too fine, too perfectly tailored
to his body.*

'Apparently so. Supervising.'

*Supervising no one. They were alone. But the palace
had more security machines than any international airport.*

Now he met her cool look with a challenge in his eyes and took the mandolin case from her.

She clenched her empty fist as she felt that surge inside. 'Do you want fingerprints and a DNA sample?' she asked. 'Haven't you done a full background check already?' Her heart thudded. Surely he had.

His gaze narrowed slightly. 'Maybe we'll get onto that later.'

'If you think I'm a danger, why are you letting me in the door?'

'I don't necessarily think you're a danger.'

'Are you worried I'll be a bad influence on her?' She shook her head. 'Because Amalia is an independent thinker.'

'I'm aware. Believe it or not, I want to encourage that. I don't have a problem if she stands up to me.'

Elsie couldn't help a sceptical laugh.

He shot her a look. 'You think I would have a problem with that?'

'I think you're used to getting your own way. Everybody does what you tell them to.'

'Judging me so soon on so little?' He suddenly smiled. 'You're right, of course. But it's the birthright, I can't help it.'

Elsie was too stunned to reply—his smile? Heart-stopping. Another glimpse of the human hiding within the perfection.

'Tell me,' he invited. 'In what way might I think you'll be a bad influence on her?'

She shrugged, mainly to cover her inner trembling at his smile. 'Too many earrings?'

He studied them and she regretted the silly joke because he took too long and his focus was too intent. Her neck felt exposed and vulnerable and suddenly hot and she shivered at the imaginary kiss she saw in his eyes...

Dear heaven, she was going mad. She hurriedly lifted her shoulder bag onto the X-ray machine's conveyor belt. She was reading all kinds of impossible into nothing.

King Felipe lifted her mandolin case onto the conveyor behind her bag. 'This has seen better days.'

Lots of things she owned had seen better days, but she appreciated the care with which Felipe had lifted it. She had to brace her heart every time she looked at that battered case. Her father had almost destroyed it, now she kept it together only with duct tape and string. She'd get a new one eventually but finding cases the right size was almost impossible and she didn't have the funds to have one made. And all that really mattered was that the mandolin itself—which had belonged to her mother—had survived. 'It still does the job.'

'Barely.' He glanced at her. 'If you're going to tutor Amalia in the mandolin, we need to pay you.'

Elsie paused, instinctive rejection halting her heart. She did not want to be his employee. 'I'm not taking your money.'

'You wouldn't be,' he said equably, but implacably. 'You'd be being paid for your skills and expertise.'

'No, thanks, I'm here doing a favour for a friend.'

'I don't accept favours. I don't do them either.'

She shot him a death look. 'I'm not talking about you. I mean Amalia.'

'I won't owe anyone anything,' he said firmly. 'Nor will she.'

She deliberately breathed out, wondering why he was so determinedly independent. 'So every relationship is reduced to a financial transaction? Wow. That explains a lot.'

'We're not taking advantage of our status to underpay people. Or not pay them at all.'

She inhaled sharply. 'I'm not here for money.'

Not from him. The context felt false and forced and with

the fraud of her father? No. She would never accept money from Felipe.

'Your time is valuable,' he said. 'You could be working right now.'

'As I believe you're aware, I've finished my shift for the day so my time is my own. I chose to spend a little of it with Amalia. Unfortunately I didn't realise the invitation included spending time with you.'

His smile flashed. 'Had enough of me already?'

'More than enough.'

His low chuckle only aggravated her more. Honestly? The sparkling sexual attraction was something she'd never experienced and it was so inappropriate. It was all in her head, right? She was embarrassingly inexperienced and couldn't be sure of what she thought she saw in his expression. He was polite, a little caustic, but that look in his eyes...

She really wanted an ocular translation app.

Never had she ever imagined she'd meet someone royal and be so irritated by them. Or that she would talk back so sharply. She didn't ever do that. She was too busy trying to stay under the radar, hoping people wouldn't bother with her enough to ask about her past, her family...because when they found out?

'Where will I find Amalia?' she asked him hurriedly.

'She should be in the music room. I'll take you to her.' He took her mandolin case before she could, but again he lifted it carefully. Somehow that made it worse—that he was careful with something so precious to her?

Floored by her response to him, she followed him almost blindly. The intensity of this attraction? It was so awkward. She needed to escape, yet that was the last thing she wanted. She wanted nearer.

She realised they were passing through seemingly never-ending palace corridors. She blinked and looked about, try-

ing not to be overwhelmed by the high vaulted ceilings, the light frescoes and gleaming antique furniture. And what he led her to wasn't a music room, it was a full-scale concert hall and there was a gleaming grand piano centre stage.

Amalia was waiting restlessly in the wide doorway. She had her hair pulled back from her face for the first time in a few days and as she turned to face them Elsie caught a flash of sterling silver in her ears.

'Nice earrings.' Elsie smiled at her. 'They look—'

'New, Amalia?' Felipe interrupted blandly. Too blandly.

Elsie stilled as she realised with burgeoning nerves that the girl had got them pierced—just like Elsie's—and she was only just showing them to her stepbrother, her guardian, her king. Just showing them now, when Elsie was there.

Elsie glanced at Felipe warily.

'Yes. New.' Amalia stood stiffly and didn't quite meet his eyes. 'It doesn't bother you?'

Felipe shrugged. 'Not at all.'

Yet Amalia didn't seem relieved by his unperturbed reaction. 'Could I get a tattoo, then? You'd be cool with it?'

'That would be illegal at this point because you're too young.' Felipe's expression turned solemn. 'But when you're older? It's your body, Amalia. Your rules.'

Elsie's heart thudded.

Amalia stared at him for a second. 'You're so annoying.'

She turned and stomped across the room towards the stage.

Elsie couldn't suppress a sympathetic smile as Felipe watched her go with a mystified expression. Then he glanced at Elsie.

'It wouldn't have mattered what you said,' she said softly. 'She's thirteen. And she's had a hard time. It's normal to push back.'

He didn't reply and for a moment she thought she'd overstepped the mark.

But then he sighed. *'I don't want to be anyone's gaoler.'*

Something tightened within Elsie. 'You're the ultimate authority figure around here, pretty hard to avoid that.'

He glanced up at the ceiling for a second and there it was again, the glimpse of conflict and confusion, of human.

Elsie couldn't resist unbending. 'For what it's worth, boundaries are good. And I thought yours was a good response.'

'She ambushed you too, didn't she? I saw your face.' He suddenly smiled. 'You thought I was going to blame you for the earrings, but she hadn't confided in you. Which puts you in the overprotective adult camp with me.'

He was irritatingly astute and she didn't want to be bracketed with him in any kind of camp. 'What's your tattoo, then?'

He shot her a startled look.

'If it's your body, your rules...' She leaned a little closer. 'What have you got—a quote? Your favourite animal?'

'There's no tattoo.'

'No? Not even someplace private? No piercings either?' She blinked at him innocently. 'Because?'

The muscle in his jaw flexed. 'I think you know the answer already.'

'Because you're the King?' *she mocked, enjoying herself immensely. 'So serious, so important. So there's one set of rules for Amalia and another for you?'*

'Absolutely. But I'm the last who'll live by those rules here. Amalia doesn't. She gets her liberty.'

'But not you?' She cocked her head. 'Why can't you have the same freedom of self-expression? Don't you get to be a man—or are you only a king?'

He stepped close and she suddenly realised what a challenge she'd issued. Magnetised, she struggled to read the swirl of emotion in his eyes—aggravation? Amusement?

'*What's yours?*' *he asked too softly.* '*More to the point, where's yours? Someplace* very *private?*'

He was so close he stole all the oxygen and she couldn't think to answer anything but honestly. '*I don't have one.*'

'*So you're all talk.*' *He laughed—a breath of light amusement.* '*Barely a rebel at all.*'

That was very *true.* '*Amalia was right,*' *Elsie muttered weakly.* '*You're* so *annoying.*'

She followed Amalia's flounce across the room.

By the time she braved a quick glance back the doorway was empty and her heart—no. She couldn't be disappointed by his disappearance. She definitely didn't feel it as a loss.

She turned to Amalia, who was seated at the magnificent piano. '*You must be here all day every day.*'

'*I didn't know this room even existed until lunchtime today. Felipe instructed the staff to prepare it after he came to the café.*'

'*Oh?*' *Elsie drew breath, unable to get her head around the size of the labyrinthine palace.*

'*Felipe said he'd get any other instruments I want. I just have to let him know.*'

That was pretty damn amazing of Felipe, but Elsie frowned. '*Then what have you been playing on up till now?*' *From their conversations at the café she knew Amalia played piano and clarinet at least.*

'*I haven't.*' *A sheen muted Amalia's eyes.* '*Not for ages.*'

Not since the accident?

'*And Felipe didn't know you play at all?*'

Amalia just shrugged.

Not until today, then.

Elsie's heart ached. The girl was so isolated. And this explained her minor explosion at Felipe just before. These see-sawing emotions were grief-based. Because music was inextricably entwined with memory and she knew Amalia's mother had been her music teacher. And to sit at a piano for the first time now? It would bring so many memories back for her. And Elsie empathised with that so very personally. Amalia sat in a tight bundle with her hands knotted in her lap. Elsie sat beside her.

'I didn't play for a long, long time after my mother died,' she admitted quietly.

There were additional reasons for that. Ones she wouldn't ever tell Amalia. But she knew grief stole joy. And she didn't want Amalia to lose her musical expression as well. It would be another grief—one too much to bear when in fact the release might help her.

'But it heals even as it hurts, I think, sometimes,' Elsie added as she got her mandolin out of the old case and tuned it to the piano. 'Why don't we start with something simple? Just a few bars. I'll join in with you, or I'll pick something?' She drew in a steadying breath and plucked a few notes of an old folk song. 'It's been a while for me too.'

It had been for ever. She didn't want that for Amalia.

But Amalia put her hands on the keys and tested a couple of chords. Then she began. Elsie accompanied her for a little bit but after several bars she stopped and simply listened to the girl. Lost for words. Lost in the music. It was something Elsie hadn't experienced in so, so long.

'You have huge talent,' Elsie whispered, utterly awed, when Amalia stopped, meaning it completely. 'I can't teach you anything.'

Because there was natural talent and there was skill and technique. There was hard work and there was a natural feel for musical expression. Amalia had it all. Every bit.

'Don't ever stop,' Elsie whispered. 'It's too important for you.'

A wan smile bloomed through Amalia's silent tears. 'It feels better.'

But it still hurt. Elsie got that. And the only thing she could do was keep Amalia company and play alongside her. As they did—as they breathed, paused, and played, the emotions veered, passed, changed. They giggled then in almost giddy relief with that hurdle of starting now overcome. Now they could savour it. Be silly with it. Love it. And go so deeply into it the tears stung again.

'You'll stay for dinner, right?' Amalia smiled as she'd finished the repetition of a piece Elsie had adored.

'Dinner?' Elsie gaped. Was it that late already?

'Naturally she will,' Felipe said from directly behind them.

Elsie spun in fright—having an emotional explosion of her own. She glared first at his feet. The man was wearing boots, yet she'd not heard him arrive. 'You shouldn't sneak up on people.' She raised her stare, attempting to laser his too-handsome face with visual disapproval. 'How long have you been listening?'

His brown eyes were intensely full of unreadable emotion. 'Dinner is the least we can offer.' He avoided her question yet made it very clear he wasn't taking no for an answer.

That new-to-her defiance rippled through her. 'I thought you were determined to pay me so you don't have to "owe me" anything.'

He sighed. 'Demonstrate some manners for once, will you? Especially in front of the teen.'

Amalia squeaked but Elsie was too far gone on the rebellious reaction he provoked within her.

'Then try asking nicely instead of answering on my behalf.' Elsie smiled not so sweetly.

He stepped forward, out of Amalia's sightline, and fixed Elsie with such a hot stare that her brain fried. It seemed she wasn't the only one having the emotional explosion.

And in the official 'devastating stare tournament' the score read: Felipe one, Elsie nil.

'Dine with us tonight, Elsie...' His smile of very adult triumph made her shiver.

Elsie gritted her teeth. She was saying no. No.

'Please,' he added.

And at that? She simply couldn't stop herself. 'I'd be delighted to, thank you.'

CHAPTER FIVE

Friday, 5.26 p.m.

ELSIE STARED AT FELIPE. Instinct warned her to run. He was a threat to *her*. But she could only watch for his reaction to her request to *leave, now*. Would he remember?

Yeah. His pupils blew. His eyes grew impossibly darker, deeper and dangerous to anyone's peace of mind. On hers there was a catastrophic impact.

'You can't leave,' he said roughly, reinforcing the fact. 'The skies are closed. There are no flights until after to-morrow's coronation. There are too many VIP guests in town. Your plane was only allowed in as a mercy mission.'

Where was the mercy for *her*? Hadn't he done enough to her already?

'So you're making an entire planeload of people stay here for *twenty-four* hours?' She glared at him. 'You don't think that's excessive? It's like being imprisoned for no reason. Or is their time and liberty not as important as yours?'

'It's a matter of security,' he said stiffly. 'Not just mine.'

'Wouldn't it be more secure if they *left*?'

'It's the advice not just of my security general, but that of my counterparts gracing me with their presence for the coronation. They will not deviate from the plan.'

'Heaven forbid one should *deviate from the plan*.' She threw her hand in the air. 'Couldn't possibly do *that*. Even when the plan inconveniences literally *everyone* else. But we commoners simply don't matter, do we?'

But as she stared at him memories slammed her. And the breathless *yearning*? The childish fantasies she'd wrought that *one* day three months ago? That she'd allowed only one day to influence her so hugely?

He was a liar. She loathed those. She would leave and this time it would be all her own idea.

'On the contrary, you all matter very much. I've been assured everyone else who was onboard is very happy with their accommodation,' he said.

'They probably wouldn't dare say otherwise for fear of retribution.'

'Fear of retribution?' he drawled. 'It's a five-star hotel. They're paying for nothing and will have a celebratory dinner tonight.'

'Wow,' she muttered sarcastically. 'Celebrating your existence, are they? When can I get back there? I won't say no to a free dinner.'

He regarded her intently, the way a cat did a mouse. A very big cat focused on a very stunned mouse who felt she'd made a wrong move. 'Oh?'

His gaze raked down her body again. Her jeans-and-cropped-cotton-jumper combo felt too hot while the chunky boots she always wore while travelling didn't give her height enough boost. She was still too short to stare him straight in the eye. Doubtless her hair was a flat mess. It had been in a ponytail but there were loose bits falling about her face, which also felt stupidly hot. She did *not* want to feel this awkward and self-conscious. And it was *his* fault.

'Why did you make me come here?' she blurted.

He stood so still—so *coiled*—that she forgot to breathe. His eye deepened in colour—darker than midnight. She drank the sight of him in—his black hair was cropped not too long, not too short. The 'perfect' king who never broke his rules, never even bent them. Consummately reliable. Dependable. Dutiful. And extremely annoying. Because he was also rigid and inflexible and once he'd decided upon a course of action? There was no changing from the plan.

He was *spoilt*.

She'd taken one look at him—*one*—and her body had decided it wanted to be his. It was so embarrassing. Resisting the temptation to lean closer was a constant battle. Humiliating given that he'd *banished* her.

He was rhythmically tapping his fingers very slightly against his trousers. One, two, three, four… She realised he was *counting*—striving for *control*? He saw the direction of her gaze and stopped.

'Aren't you going to ask after Amalia?' he asked shortly.

She sucked in a breath because that *hurt*. She'd thought about Amalia every damned day since she'd been forced to leave this country. 'Of course. How is she?'

'You walked out on her without even saying goodbye. You made a commitment to come back and didn't.'

'Of *course*, I didn't. I *couldn't*.'

She blinked back the sudden burn of tears. She didn't care who he was, he didn't get to judge her. She'd been judged by too many already and invariably they concluded she was in the wrong. But how could he accuse her of heartlessness when it was *his* doing? She would never, ever have left Amalia the way she had if it hadn't been for him.

'Why did you leave?' he asked.

'Are you kidding?' Had he forgotten what he'd said? *How* he'd said it? She glared at him. 'You *told* me to.'

His jaw tightened. 'You took that as an order to leave the country?'

'It *was* an order.'

'You know I only meant you had to leave at that moment.'

'Or?' she challenged him.

He watched her and she felt it—that pull towards him. But it was *false*.

A muscle ticced in his jaw. 'I meant then and you know it.'

He was such a liar. 'No, you didn't. Because you made sure I wouldn't come back.' She laughed bitterly. 'You followed through.'

He frowned. 'What?'

'How was I supposed to stay here when I'd been *fired*? Some of us have to work for a living. We're not all born with palaces and crowns and pots of gold.'

'What do you mean, "fired"?'

She stared at him. '*Every* decision you make impacts on other people's lives.'

'Elsie. As far as I'm aware you just disappeared. You didn't show up when you said you would. Security then informed Amalia that you'd left the country.'

Informed Amalia. Because *Felipe* already knew. Because she wasn't going to stay, not just where she wasn't wanted, where she was doubted, but where she could no longer even work. Her boss had thought he'd found out her past and her secrets and instantly judged her. It didn't matter that she'd worked hard for him for those two months already. All those days and all that effort she'd put in had meant nothing as soon as suspicion had been raised in his mind.

'Of course, I had. You cost me my job.'

'Then you should have come to me,' he said.

'Oh, would you have fixed everything?' She narrowed her gaze on him. 'You were the one who told him! Would you have bullied my boss into taking me back? Or paid me off? No, thanks.' She shook her head. He didn't get it. He never would. The audacity of the man to blame her when he'd been the one to interfere. 'You asked about my references. They found that video.'

That hurt the most.

'*What* video?' He pinched the bridge of his nose. 'I assure you I didn't tell anyone anything.'

'*You* didn't?' And that made everything worse. 'Of course. That would be inconvenient for you to do personally.' Too minor. 'You just let your team do your dirty work for you.'

He was the very definition of spoilt and entitled, privileged and utterly uninformed.

'Look, Elsie, I don't know what video you're talking about and I did *not* have you fired.' He huffed a breath.

He was so emphatic she almost believed him.

'What's the video even of?' he demanded.

Elsie froze. He really didn't know? He really hadn't seen it? Oh. *No.*

'Forget it.' She shut down.

She could see him thinking through all kinds of possibilities. None of which would be right, but she wasn't about to open that box. Some things were too personal. Too painful. Too *precious.*

'If my men raised doubt in your employer's mind then I apologise,' he said carefully. 'And if they did, it wasn't on my instruction.'

He'd wrecked her life and didn't even realise. He'd assumed she'd skipped out with no concern for Amalia. Which told her all she needed to know that he thought about her.

She didn't know what was worse—thinking he'd had her fired or realising that he was so little interested in her he hadn't bothered finding out what had really happened. She'd just disappeared and he didn't particularly care. He was only angry on behalf of his stepsister.

She nodded. 'Okay. Well, now that's sorted, can I leave?'

'No. This misunderstanding is...' His frown was massive as he stared at her. 'You must be hungry. Airline food isn't fantastic.'

'As if you've ever flown commercial.'

'And apparently you wouldn't say no to a free dinner.' He ignored her mutter. 'So, please, attend tonight's banquet.'

She stared at him. 'Pardon?'

'You lost your job as a consequence of your association with Amalia and me. As recompense, please attend tonight's banquet.'

'Sorry, what?' Her jaw dropped. 'You think that's going to make everything better?'

'Small things can have large consequences.' He actually smiled. 'What better way to restore your reputation on Silvabon than as a guest of the royal family?'

'You mean approval by association?' What if it backfired and he was found guilty by associating with *her*? No, thank you.

'I'm not interested in restoring my reputation,' she said stiffly. Hot humiliation flooded her cheeks—that was an *impossibility*. 'I don't want anyone to know I'm here.'

His gaze narrowed. 'What happened to not saying no to a free dinner?'

'I don't think this one will be free. I think there'll be another kind of payment attached,' she said bluntly.

His voice was velvety soft. 'Does that scare you, Elsie?'

Her pulse suddenly tripled its pace. 'Absolutely. I'll likely have my head on a spike before the night is over.'

His smile flashed again. 'But I'll be there.'

'To slay the dragons for me?' She shook her head. 'Don't you understand *you're* the dragon.'

He stepped closer. Dangerously close. 'Should I breathe fire, Elsie? Is it threats you want?'

As he walked forward, she stepped back and both kept going until she was in a very small corner of the very large room. At that point she tossed her head and stared him down. Anger—energy—blooming.

'What'll you do if I say no, Felipe? Will you lock me in

this dungeon of a room and throw away the key?' She half hoped he would as long as she was alone—*away* from him.

But wicked vitality gleamed in his gaze. 'Don't tempt me.'

Tempt *him*?

'Prison doesn't scare me,' she said defiantly.

'Prison?'

'You don't know my past, so you don't know *what* you're inviting into your precious banquet.' She shook her head. 'Bet you regret not reading the security report on me now...'

'On the contrary, I'm happy not to have. It means I get to investigate you all on my own. I'll skip the banquet too. I'll stay here and find out exactly what the hell is going on with you.'

'Why do you care?'

He shrugged. 'I want to know. Everything. What's on that video, Elsie?'

No. That was an infinitely worse proposition. She didn't want to open up to him in that way. She didn't open up to anyone.

'You're bored,' she said scathingly. 'It's the eve of your coronation and you're *bored*.'

'Maybe I am. Spoilt royal, at your service.' He mock-bowed. 'So, come to the banquet. Let us apologise and make amends. For the loss of your job. For "dragging" you from the airport. Plus, you can catch up with Amalia and I know you want to do that.'

His words smote her heart because, yes, *that* was the sucker punch and he knew it. She *had* felt for Amalia. She'd felt the loneliness and grief and uncertainty. And while there'd been little she'd been able to say to make anything better, they had been able to spend time in the moment with their music. But still, self-preservation sank in. And practicalities.

'It's a ridiculous notion,' she growled. 'All the seating

arrangements will be done already. You can't do that to your staff.'

He really had no idea of the impact of his capricious whims.

'They're supremely capable and finding space for lucky little you will be a breeze. They won't bat an eyelid.'

'When I walk in dressed like this?' She gestured at her baggy jeans and cropped cotton jersey.

'Your luggage will arrive shortly.'

'As if I have an evening gown stuffed in there?' Didn't he realise how ridiculous his insistence she attend was? How unnecessary? 'We are *not* from the same planet, Felipe.'

His lips twitched. 'It'll be no problem to find you a suitable dress.'

'Suitable?'

'Amalia will sort you out.'

Elsie gaped. The man had *no* idea. 'Amalia's *thirteen*. While I'm only a few inches taller than her, there are other parts that—'

'She'll find you a dressmaker.' He interrupted. 'I didn't mean for you to wear one of her dresses.' He compressed his lips.

He thought this was funny?

'It would be a good distraction for her,' he added.

'So I'm a distraction?'

He drew a sharp breath. 'She would love to see you. She's been miserable.' He glanced down to the floor and then back up. 'I'm asking for your help.'

'You call this asking? I call it abduction.'

He released a growl of a laugh as he stepped closer. 'How nicely do you need me to ask, Elsie?'

How *nicely*? He was so close she could feel his heat. It was like—

No. Don't think about it. But nothing had changed. Together they bounced between antagonism and amusement and attraction. Such *attraction*. And that was the problem.

Her heart was attempting to bash through her ribs and a wall of heat enveloped her—as her stupid, foolish body quivered at its own interpretation of what he really meant.

He leaned so close it was almost a kiss. 'Say *yes*.'

CHAPTER SIX

Three months earlier, evening

FELIPE STOOD BENEATH the streaming shower jets and spun the tap to cold. Ideally he'd have taken a quick swim but he didn't have time. Cool down, get back in control, carry on.

He dressed for dinner as always. The expectation had been enforced by his grandfather and they'd maintained the routine in recent years to try to stave off his decline. Since his passing, Felipe had continued it. Structure and stability mattered. He didn't put on a suit though. Fresh shirt, trousers—no jacket, no tie. It was as casual as he got with guests.

But his temperature climbed again just at the thought of her. There was a reason he'd left the music room. But for the same reason he'd kept listening. He'd leaned against the wall just outside, eavesdropping. His curiosity was too strong to resist. He'd not heard the words clearly but he'd felt their tone—the gentle encouragement of husky-voiced Elsie.

Then there'd been the revelation and he couldn't have moved even if he'd tried. He'd been blown away by Amalia. Her talent and skill? Guilt had swiftly followed. He'd had no idea. All these months and he'd not known, not understood something that was such a huge part of her. But *of course he should have known. Her mother had been a musician, far more than the 'floozy showgirl' his grandfather—and the media—had dismissed her as.*

Amalia's immediate future was his responsibility. He'd wanted to give her time to recover from her injuries here in seclusion but now he knew he'd failed her. He owed it to her to ensure she had the training, the education to fulfil the potential, the promise and the passion she clearly felt for her music. And she needed to do that away from here where they still ran articles dismissing her mother and his father. He couldn't let them compare her to them. He wouldn't let her down again.

And the supportive tones of her five-foot-two, blue-eyed, dirty-blonde companion had devastated him. Elsie's laughter? He'd not heard laughter like that in the palace walls. Ever. Nor the singing. He'd fought to resist walking back in there, knowing they'd stop if he did. So he'd closed his eyes and listened in pure torment as the place had shimmered to life. What had Elsie drawn from Amalia?

From him *too. There wasn't the distance between King and commoner that there should be. Somehow she'd stolen in and he'd dispensed with all proper protocol. He never should have teased her, never let her ask him any personal questions. But from the moment they'd met formality hadn't bothered to show up. Because something else was already there—something addictive and irresistible. She'd challenged, he'd sparked. Hell, even he'd laughed and he hadn't laughed in an age either.*

In all these years he'd been sure he wasn't jealous of Amalia—for his father Carlos choosing her and her mother over him. For her having that time with him and that freedom far from the palace. Felipe was fine with it. He had a privileged life and a job to do and he honestly loved his palace and his place in it even though it wasn't always perfect... But right now?

Right now he truly envied his stepsister. He wanted Elsie's attention too.

But he couldn't have it. Not how he really wanted it. So he squared his shoulders and reached for a tie.

Elsie was conscious of the eagle-eyed palace footmen as they set out the dinner dishes. Didn't Amalia and Felipe often have dinner guests? Given how stilted and awkward the initial atmosphere was, she wasn't even sure they dined together much. Elsie looked again at Felipe. He'd got changed for dinner. He was freshly shaved and his hair was still slightly damp, his shirt crisp and his tie sharp. Immaculate. Urbane. Buttoned up. And so stunning it made her grip on the cutlery weak.

She desperately focused on the food so she didn't simply stare at him. But her appetite was pathetic—even though the soup was light and delicious, the salads fresh, the steak perfectly cooked. She kept conversation Amalia-centric. It was easiest and safest that way.

'This is amazing.' She complimented the indulgent individual molten-centred chocolate cake served for dessert.

'Not as good as your lemon cake,' Amalia said loyally.

Elsie chuckled. 'That's very kind, but untrue.'

'Do you enjoy working at the café?' Felipe suddenly asked.

He'd been quiet through dinner, only occasionally commenting as she and Amalia chatted about favourite songs.

'Very much.'

'You don't worry that working with knives you'll cut your hand and not be able to play?' Felipe asked. 'I've met other musicians who wouldn't even keep sharp knives in their home.'

'I can understand that, but it's not like I have a choice.' She laughed. 'I need to earn money.'

He looked at her steadily. 'Why not do that with your music?'

'That's flattering of you to think I could, but no.' She paused. 'I don't want pressure. I'd rather peel a sack of potatoes for my pennies and then be able to make music just for me. But Amalia's different. She's gifted.'

He nodded thoughtfully and turned to Amalia. 'After the coronation you'll return to school, Amalia. I was thinking we should find one with a strong music programme. There are a few on the continent I can think of that might be good.'

'School?' Amalia's eyed widened, then she frowned. Heavily.

'A specialist music school would be amazing, Amalia,' Elsie said softly. 'You could learn every instrument there is.'

Amalia shook her head. 'I don't want to go back to school.'

Felipe shrugged. 'We all must do things we don't want to. That's life.'

Amalia's frown turned into a glare. 'Like you having to marry after your coronation?'

Elsie suddenly couldn't breathe. She stared at Felipe, waiting for him to laugh it off. But he didn't. He stilled.

'Who told you about that?' he asked Amalia.

'Carlos said King Javier was furious with him and now you have to marry the woman he chose for you.'

Elsie kept looking at him, hoping he'd deny it. But he was focused on Amalia, who kept eating her chocolate cake, unaware of the arrested expression in Felipe's eyes.

'He told you that?' he prompted.

Amalia nodded and reached for her glass of water. 'He said you were the only person with the strength to handle Javier's expectations.'

Something raw flashed on Felipe's face before he dropped his gaze to the table. Elsie's heart raced silly fast. Amalia hadn't realised the profound effect of her words and not only on Felipe. It was none of her business. His future had nothing to do with her. Yet she couldn't stop herself asking him.

'You really have to get married?'

He glanced at her. Now the expression in his brown eyes was sombre and steadfast.

'To a princess.' Amalia added.

A princess? Seriously?

His gaze remained locked on hers. Something sparked, swiftly suppressed.

'Like a fairy tale?' Elsie tried to tease but it didn't feel funny. 'Or a nightmare?'

'She's already been picked,' Amalia said.

Of course he'd have to marry a princess. No doubt he'd go on to have baby princes and princesses too—securing the future of Silvabon's royal family.

Felipe inclined his head. 'I made my grandfather a promise. Several, in fact.'

'And you keep your promises?' Elsie asked, battling the horrible hot feeling inside at the thought of it all.

'Of course.'

Elsie's lungs constricted. 'Does the princess in question get any say in this? Or was the decision just made for her too?'

The corner of his mouth quirked. 'You feel sorry for her?'

'Utterly.'

'But you don't feel sorry for me?' he inferred.

Elsie forced a smile. 'Why would we feel sorry for you?'

He spread his hands. 'Not getting to choose who I marry.'

'You made the promise to your grandfather. That was the choice you made.'

'Have you never wanted to please your family?'

This time Elsie stilled, trying not to show the hit the query had. 'Some things are super impossible.'

He waited, obviously trying to read her expression but Elsie tried to stay stony and not give anything away. Somehow he still saw too much.

And suddenly his demeanour softened. 'They don't like all your earrings?'

She knew he'd deliberately lightened his tone because he'd seen her inward flinch. But she was inexplicably melancholic and not for herself. The prospect of his arranged marriage seemed cold and unromantic and even though it really had nothing to do with her she couldn't seem to let it go.

'You're really going to marry for duty? Even though your grandfather's gone?' she asked. 'He wouldn't even know if you did or didn't. You're the King now.'

'Exactly.' Felipe's expression shuttered and he sat back. 'There's no separation of the personal and the professional for me. What I am is who I am. It impacts on every area of my life. Every decision I make.'

'Yet you don't seem to have been the one to decide the detail.'

'King Javier wanted what's best for me and for the country. He knows the kind of person needed to take on this mantle.'

'This mantle? As if you're Atlas balancing the world on your shoulders?' She shook her head. 'The King thing is just a title. You're actually just a man. You should be just a man.'

'Arranged marriages are successful around the world.'

The blunt, emotionless assessment didn't suit him. Yet she knew he meant it, that he believed it.

'Plenty of love matches fail,' he added. 'My parents' marriage, for example.' He sent Amalia a small smile.

'Don't worry, they were long out of love before my father met your mother.' He turned back to Elsie. 'But you disagree?'

She regarded him sadly, taking in this determined facet of him. 'Perhaps it will suit you. The two of you will do and say and wear the right things. It'll be perfect.'

His eyes narrowed slightly and she saw the flex of his jaw.

'I'm never getting married,' Amalia said with feeling.

'Not for at least a decade.' Felipe suddenly smiled and the whole world lifted. 'Then we'll see.'

Amalia shot him an outraged look.

'Just for that she'll elope at sixteen,' Elsie said slyly.

'Don't put ideas in her head,' he admonished her with an arched eyebrow. 'I knew I shouldn't have let you in the gates.'

Elsie chuckled. 'Bad influence at your service.'

'If I really thought that you wouldn't be here.'

'Stop trying to be reasonable,' she called him out, enjoying the burst back into banter. 'You're spoiling Amalia's and my need-to-rebel narrative. We already know you're an autocrat.'

Amalia giggled.

'Why do you need to rebel, Elsie?' Felipe asked.

She met his challenging stare and the brief hit of levity evaporated. The intensity was back and bigger than ever.

Truthfully, she didn't need to rebel. Truthfully, she wanted to fit in and be accepted like most people. But when new acquaintances or colleagues learned about her family's behaviour, they then expected the worst from her. So when they found out, she left. Living in fear of that constant judgement was like waiting for the axe to fall. It was only a matter of time. But her response to Felipe was different all over again. Absolutely—incomprehensibly—she *instinctively rebelled against* him. *She was flint, he stone. Sparks were guaranteed. 'I don't like being told what to do.'*

'Is that right?' he muttered as if he didn't quite believe her—as if he could prove her wrong.

And with horrible hot awareness she realised he could. That there were some very specific things she would do if he told her to.

Kiss me. Touch me. Spread for me.

Heat engulfed her at that shocking last instruction— what was with her suddenly rabid imagination? What was with this awful inappropriate reaction? He would never, ever...and she wouldn't, couldn't—

She cleared her throat and turned to Amalia, trying to think of an innocuous question to get them back to safety. But she saw darkening smudges beneath Amalia's eyes— emotional shadows loomed and lingered.

'You look tired, Amalia,' Elsie said, suddenly sorry. 'I'd better get home and let you rest.'

It had been a big day for the girl. Honestly, it had been a big day for Elsie too. Bigger than she'd ever intended. The consequences of meeting Felipe?

'I'm okay,' Amalia said.

But Felipe immediately stood, a frown gathering in his eyes as he nodded to a waiting footman. 'Amalia, your maid is waiting for you.' He turned to Elsie. 'I'll escort you to the gatehouse. You'll return tomorrow afternoon. I'm not telling you,' he added with a meaningful emphasis. 'That was an invitation.'

'You call that an invitation?'

The smallest mocking smile softened his sudden solemnity. 'Please.'

Elsie quickly hugged Amalia and then walked with Felipe. Swift and serious, he stayed close to her side. While that was disturbing, she was also relieved because the palace was insanely huge.

'How do you find your way around here?' Elsie muttered, unable to contain her edginess. She was still off-kilter knowing he was going to marry some princess, and shocked by her fevered reactions to him. 'Don't you get lost all the time?'

'You want a GPS tracker?' Felipe's drawl had both light and dark edges and that madness flared within her again.

'I feel like you'd use it as an electronic tag on me,' she said acidly. 'I wouldn't want to take a wrong turn and end up in the dungeon.'

'That would take a little more than a wrong turn.'

'Are the rumours true, then?' she asked, diverted. 'There really are dungeons in the basement?'

His smile flashed. 'No one who sees the torture chambers lives to tell anyone about them...'

'So prisoners really were shipped off in the middle of the night, never to be seen again?' She parroted one of the stories spun in the tourist shops in the city centre.

'That hasn't happened for at least a hundred years. Though that's not to say it still couldn't happen now.'

She only half laughed—because the thought of being bailed up in Felipe's dungeon? It was a shockingly fascinating idea.

The route took them through a large portrait hall, part of the public wing of the palace. Each enormous painting depicted various members of the royal family. Elsie slowed as they came to the more modern paintings and she couldn't resist stopping at the last and studying it. 'When?'

'It was my investiture. A formal ceremony to recognise me as heir to the Crown after my father left,' he explained.

She glanced back at the previous few frames. 'There aren't any pictures of him.'

'He abdicated.'

'So that means he's not part of the family any more?' She gazed at the previous portrait and recognised his grandfa-

ther, King Javier. 'There are none of your mother either. Doesn't she live here?'

'She hasn't set foot in the palace since my father left her for Amalia's mother.'

Elsie was shocked. 'Not at all?'

'She didn't want to shoulder the burden of my grandfather's disappointment.'

It sounded as though his grandfather was more tyrant than king. To have banished people? For their images to have been literally scrubbed from the palace? It was punitive and surely must have marked Felipe deeply. 'But what about you?'

'I guess she thought I was old enough to handle it.'

She looked again at that portrait of him in a fearsomely ceremonial robe standing alone. 'How old were you at your investiture?'

'Seventeen.'

'Young.'

'Young adult,' he amended.

'Still young to have to take on adult concerns and responsibilities.'

'You think?'

'Yeah.' She didn't just think, she knew. 'I was seventeen when my mother got her diagnosis.' And as old as she'd believed she was when she was seventeen, it wasn't old enough to handle that...and maybe not things like heavy robes and crowns and the weight of a nation either.

'Ah.' He nodded. 'I'm sorry.'

In some ways Elsie wasn't. Caring for her mother through her illness had been a privilege and she'd never ever regretted the time she'd had with her. But it had been hard. Her father had absented himself—supposedly unable to cope. Her brother had avoided it too—staying away at university. Leaving Elsie alone until almost the end when—

She breathed in. So, yeah, in some ways she felt for Felipe.

'It's not easy to lose a parent at any age,' she said huskily. It was something the three of them had in common. 'Amalia's lucky to have you now.'

His gaze dropped and he cleared his throat. 'That's the most engaged and animated I've seen her since she came to Silvabon. Thank you.'

Elsie shrugged, suddenly shy. 'Music soothes the soul.'

'It wasn't the music.'

Heat slid across her body. Inappropriate, awkward, because surely that wasn't how he'd meant the compliment. She was an over-imaginative fool.

It was a few more minutes before they got to the security room at the gatehouse. There were no guards present again. She went to the door—her escape back to the real world. But she didn't open it.

She glanced up at him. 'Amalia doesn't seem enthused about going back to school.'

'The music focus will help. I'd not known how good she is. I'd not known anything about it, honestly. But boarding school in Europe will be excellent.'

Elsie's skin prickled. 'Why boarding school?'

'I don't want her to stay here.'

His bluntness shocked her. 'Why not? She's all alone. You're all she has.'

'I'm not...' His shoulders stiffened. 'This isn't the best place for her. She'll be better off away.'

Elsie wasn't so sure. 'Were you better off?'

His expression shuttered. 'I was educated here. I only had one term at boarding school in France.'

She shouldn't pry, it wasn't her business, but she couldn't resist. 'Why only one term?'

'I was needed here. I had things to learn—more than the core subjects.'

'Crowd control? How to wave politely?' She tried to joke but it wasn't that funny because she understood all

those other things had really meant the loss of any carefree youth. To have such big responsibilities so young... Pressures like that shaped a person's growth.

'Boarding school will give Amalia some freedoms she won't have here. Plus she'll have people her own age around her.'

'Not random café workers with too many earrings.' Elsie half smiled. 'But I get it, you don't want her to be burdened.'

'She's already had enough to deal with.'

He'd dealt with a lot too when he was young. All the royal stuff for a start, let alone the marriage break-up and an authoritarian grandfather King.

'I'd better get back, it's getting late.' She told herself as much as she was telling him. She put one hand on the door—about to open it. To leave. But it was as if there were an unseen cord between them that she didn't want to sever. Not yet.

And he didn't move out of her way, nor did his intense gaze leave her face. 'You're sure you don't want me to summon a car?'

'It's a gorgeous evening, too nice not to walk.'

He nodded almost robotically, and she realised he had no idea.

'You don't get to do that, do you?' she said slowly. 'You can't walk along the city streets without security guards on either side of you and the whole world staring.'

His mouth curved. 'Are you finally feeling sorry for me?'

'You don't want my pity.'

That beautiful smile faded. 'No, I don't.'

'What do you want?'

There was a long silence. She hadn't meant it provocatively. Not consciously at least. But she had provoked. She had pulled back the veil to reveal—

'Elsie...'

His huskiness emboldened her, charging that inner rebel. 'Yes, Your Majesty?'

He stepped closer. 'Since when do you bother with my title?'

Since he stood this close. Since he made her blood sing with simply a smile. Since she'd learned he belonged to someone else and suddenly she was so angry—because this lust was nothing more than a fever dream. It wasn't real.

Only he leaned in. 'Are you putting me in my place?'

His place? His place here, close to her, felt so right. Yet it was wrong. Because he did belong to someone else, even though Elsie knew to her bones that was wrong too. But even if his betrothal princess didn't exist this thing between them would still be wrong. Because if he knew about her family? He obviously didn't because he wouldn't be anywhere near her if he did. But his nearness now unlocked the yearning that had been building all of the damned day.

'As if you'd stay there,' she breathed. 'You're used to doing whatever you want.'

He cocked his head. 'What I want?'

The echo. The emphasis. The ache.

She couldn't turn away from him. The storm in his eyes and tension in his body mirrored her own. It wasn't a dream. Fever, yes. But real and inescapable. It was that match—fire with fire. His breath was ragged and her heart burst. This need within her was more than skin-deep, it burned through to bone. She needed him so much closer. And there was only this—one moment where anything—the ultimate—was possible. All could be hers—

'Felipe?'

His gaze drilled into her and she was pinned in place. There was no wall at her back, no arms holding her, but it was as if she were chained. She clutched her battered mandolin case tightly. It was the last barrier between them but she couldn't drop it. For a long moment he branded her with the heat in his gaze, the steel in his stance. And then—

'You have to go,' he snapped harshly. His words scored into her skin—raking her raw like hot claws. 'You have to leave.'

The rejection was sudden and absolute and vicious. Elsie was so stunned she couldn't answer, let alone move. Her heart stopped—swollen and vulnerable and almost bursting. He swore and when he stepped closer again that tortured expression in his eyes flared.

What she saw—what she felt—terrified her.

And he told her again. 'Leave. Now!'

CHAPTER SEVEN

Friday, 5.38 p.m.

ELSIE GLARED UP into Felipe's eyes. 'Why are you so determined I go to your stuffy banquet? I'm not some Cinderella.' She refused to say yes to him. 'Or is this just some
way for you to assuage your guilt—giving lucky little me
a make-over and a special trip to the zoo as if you're my
fairy godmother?'

'The zoo?' He laughed. 'You might be right about that
but I'm *not* your fairy godmother.'

'No?' Unable to maintain her ground against him, Elsie
rested a little weight against the wall. 'Because from where
I'm standing that's a lot how it seems.'

'Oh?' He lifted his arms and placed his hands either
side, bracketing her in place, and leaned closer still. 'How
does it seem now?'

Elsie's heart hammered as she battled the temptation to
melt against him. It was the very urge she'd run from months
ago. The one she'd not wanted to remember.

Because of him she'd been sent away again, when she
was the happiest she'd been in years. She'd finally found a
place where people didn't know her past. Who only knew
her as she was *now*. Until he'd ruined everything. Yet *he*
was everything. That one day had been the most thrilling

of her life. Meeting him. Discovering her *weakness* for him. The weakness she needed to resist now.

'This isn't appropriate.' Elsie swallowed. 'You're supposed to be a king. A moral leader, right?'

'You don't think kings are power-hungry selfish types who do whatever they want without consideration for anyone else?'

'You said different.' She struck where she was sure he'd feel it. 'But you're not using me to cheat on your fiancée.'

But he merely smiled. And that made her angry.

'Did you think I'd forgotten that you're engaged?' she asked.

He was marrying that beautiful princess from some Alpine country in Europe. Not that she'd searched it up in a moment of weakness or anything. It hadn't been officially confirmed but there'd been a mass of speculation in a zillion articles.

'I'm touched you remember that conversation.' He leaned closer.

She remembered *every* word from that one day.

He lifted his hand and brushed back a loose strand of her hair. 'But if I was engaged to someone else I wouldn't even be talking to you right now.'

'You're never going to speak to another woman?'

'Any other woman would be fine. Just not you.' His pupils dilated. 'But as it happens, you can relax. I'm not engaged.'

Relax? Her heart hammered and her mind spun out. She tried to focus. She'd got the archaic terminology wrong. 'Betrothed, then. Are you using semantics to wriggle out of this?'

'Not engaged. Not betrothed. Not getting married.' His expression tightened. 'Princess Sofia and I have decided not to ratify the betrothal once agreed upon by her father and my grandfather.'

She didn't want to believe him. Didn't want to feel a sudden effervescence and a head-to-toe shiver. 'What a convenient excuse to dream up when you're pinning me to the wall like this.'

His lips curved. 'You don't believe me?'

'It hasn't been reported on.'

That princess had been mentioned in the paper at the airport just today. There'd been speculation as to whether she'd be at the coronation and whether there would be an announcement regarding any imminent wedding.

'You've been reading the press about me?'

'No,' she lied.

'I'm waiting until after the coronation before letting all know there'll be no wedding. I don't want it to be a distraction from the coronation.'

Elsie struggled to absorb what he'd said. 'So she didn't want to marry you? I can't imagine why.'

'Can't you? Your amazement flatters me.' Something softened in his eyes. 'But now you know, I'm neither your fairy godmother, nor am I someone else's fiancé.'

'But you *are* the king of an excessively wealthy island nation. You're about to be crowned and celebrated as such. Everyone has to pay homage to you.'

'Don't fret.' His lips twisted. 'I have little desire to *force* you to kneel before me.'

She paused, thrown by the thought of being on her knees before him. The terrible thing was it was a totally tempting prospect that made parts of her tighten in anticipation. She couldn't say no to him. That was the problem. It had been the problem all along. He made her want all the wicked things.

He smiled knowingly and, heaven help her, she loved seeing those cracks in the facade of the very serious King. She'd seen them before when she'd last been here in his kingdom.

He shifted and took her hand in his. Three months ago

they'd not touched. He'd kept his distance. She'd kept hers. Until that last moment when even then there'd only been a heartbeat of closeness, a breath of agony expressed. Somehow she'd known if skin struck skin, sparks would fly. Turned out it wasn't sparks—it was a complete detonation and it was impossible to stifle her shiver of excitement. Of anticipation. She'd *dreamed* of him touching her like this. But the gasp she'd just released? It was mortifying.

'Felipe…' It was meant to be a warning growl. It was more of a pleading whisper.

Triumph fired his eyes yet there was a hint of a deeper storminess. A hesitation that she knew went beyond them both.

She ached. How could she have missed him so much? She barely knew him. But that one day had changed everything. The intensity of his magnetism had terrified her. It did again now—and it ripped away the facade of blame she'd cast upon him. The fact was while he'd told her to leave, she'd had no choice but to run regardless. The truth was she'd *wanted* to flee every bit as much as he'd wanted to fling her from the palace. And she'd used his words as her excuse. That unfairness of her boss's assumption was the final thing she'd used to save herself.

'I'm only going to ask one last time, Elsie. Please come to the banquet tonight.' The quiet question melted the last of her weak resistance.

'Yes,' she whispered. 'I'll come to your wretched banquet.'

'Good.'

Felipe had to release her. He had to loosen his fingers and let her go. She wasn't saying yes to what he really wanted—*yes*, she'd follow him to his personal quarters this instant and, *yes*, together they'd forget everything for a few blissful moments. Not appropriate. Not an option. But he felt a strength of satisfaction out of all proportion to what she'd agreed to. For the first time in weeks, a sore spot was soothed.

She would come to the banquet.

'Amalia will be pleased to see you,' he said mechanically. 'And my staff will make the arrangements.'

His staff were probably going to pass out in shock. Too bad.

But the second he'd heard her name this afternoon his blood had lit. The lust hadn't burned out, it had remained simmering in the background all this time while he'd tried to ignore it. He'd been so furious when she'd disappeared that he'd not been able to bring himself to ask his team where she'd gone. Why she'd gone. He'd not wanted to admit to anyone, let alone himself, how much it had bothered him. And whether it had been because of him.

Of course it had. But not quite in the way he'd thought.

He'd shut down Amalia's questions. He'd been gruff and impatient. But he'd only needed Elsie's name on a breath to be cast back into utter captivation. And now he'd seen her again, he was lost in lust like never before. Stepping away from her was impossible. He cursed the animal drive. He'd hoped it had been scarlet-tinted glasses maxing out the attraction in hindsight. But seeing the heated challenge in her ice-blue eyes, hearing her anger? It was worse than before.

Maybe she was right and he was simply bored—or taking a second to avoid what was to come tomorrow. Maybe this was one wishful hint of rebellion before making those vows. Because it couldn't be the one thing he refused to feel—not complete lust for a woman that would make him renege on *every* other promise he'd made. He would never do that. He was not his father—not a man who would walk out on everything he was born to do, for a woman.

Tomorrow he would honour his promise to serve his people, country, duty before anything else. Any*one* else. The truth was he already did. His life hadn't been wholly his own for a long time and despite the ceremony tomorrow not much would actually change. It was a formality, a celebration of the fundamentals that had been in place since his accession to the throne the second his grandfather had passed. This was a thing his people wanted and he couldn't deny the economic benefits of this weekend. This pinnacle positive event of the decade was going to be streamed so anyone in the world could watch. And as there was never going to be a wedding, he needed to step up for this one. He would do so with all the loyalty and love he felt towards his country and the people within.

But tonight's banquet was the 'private' event. There'd be no cameras other than those permitted in the atrium and he'd ensure no photos were taken of Amalia or her companion. He'd apologised to Elsie. He'd now ensure she was cared for tonight. And that didn't mean her ending up in his bed.

Not an option.

Because while he'd been furious that she'd walked out, he'd also been relieved. Felipe didn't often have affairs. It was difficult to maintain privacy here on Silvabon and his former betrothal had come in handy as deflection from women who wanted to get too serious. But the trigger for his final rejection of that betrothal was standing right in front of him. He couldn't consider a political alliance once he'd realised how badly he could want someone else. And while he'd once wanted to do his duty for his grandfather, he'd realised that the sacrifice wasn't only his to bear.

None of it would have been fair on Princess Sofia.

Finally he'd realised he would never ask *anyone* to move to Silvabon for him. Palace life had broken his mother. It had also broken his father—a man who'd been born into the life and had every preparation and support but who still hadn't been able to make it.

So Felipe wasn't asking anyone to take it on. Not ever.

Yet a thread of rebellion tightened within him. He'd been

so good for so long—he'd done everything demanded of him. Now he wanted something for himself. Because despite Elsie's little digs to the contrary, he wasn't completely spoilt. The orders he made were invariably for the benefit of others. They were the 'right thing to do'. He wanted to do the wrong thing for once. With her.

And she knew it. He felt her pulse hammering against his fingers and his body tightened. She'd been bothered by his supposed betrothal. *Jealous?* He knew the feeling.

'What's the video?' he asked, unable to resist his curiosity.

Her blue eyes shimmered. 'You really don't know?'

'I really don't.'

'What sort of security team have you got?'

'A very good one. But I haven't read the report they compiled on you.'

'You weren't interested?'

He couldn't answer that.

Her gaze dropped. 'Please don't look at it.'

His muscles were so tense they ached. Whatever it was clearly mortified her and he carefully considered his words. 'Did someone take advantage of you?'

He wanted to know if someone *hurt* her. Because if that were the case he'd grind their bones. His imagination was going overtime but he didn't want to hurt her more.

She swallowed. 'Not in the way you're thinking.'

He breathed out. 'I'm sorry that happened. I won't look for it.'

She nodded but he had the feeling she didn't quite believe him. Which meant people had made promises to her in the past only to break them. Having one's trust violated hurt, deeply. He knew that too.

Guilt rose. She'd lost her job and he hadn't known because he'd been too angry to bother finding out the truth. He should have looked for her. Instead he'd decided not to purely because he was bothered about how much she'd bothered him. Now he had to move because there was too little time. He wanted her to at least have some fun tonight. And not the horizontal sort.

A 'trip to the zoo'. Her acerbic retort made him smile. He had a quixotic desire to see her enjoying the celebrations. He pulled out his phone.

'Your Majesty?'

'Send Callie to Amalia's suite in ten minutes.'

'Of course, sir.'

He carried the mandolin case and led Elsie through the back corridors, aware of the curiosity of the palace guards but none dared meet his eyes or ask questions.

Amalia's face lit up the second she saw Elsie.

'It's my fault Elsie left.' Felipe spoke smoothly before Elsie could. 'My security team were invasive and Elsie's employer got the wrong idea. They let her go. That's why she couldn't return to the palace. She had to leave Silvabon the next day.'

The colour was building in Elsie's cheeks. Hadn't she expected him to tell his stepsister the truth?

'That's *terrible*.' Amalia's eyes widened.

'It is,' he agreed. 'I've apologised—profusely—and asked her to join us tonight.'

'You're coming to the boring banquet?' Amalia spun towards Elsie. 'I didn't want to go but if you're coming—'

'Callie's on her way,' Felipe said to Amalia. 'Can you help her find something for Elsie? You have good taste and you know the kind of thing required, right?'

Amalia stood a little taller. 'I think so.'

'Is that okay with you, Elsie?' He finally faced her fully again.

There was a glint in her eyes but she didn't argue.

'Great.'

Felipe left them to it, unable to stand being in Elsie's

company any longer. But he was aware that Amalia had suddenly looked livelier than she had in months. She was lonely. He needed to do better for her and once this time-sucking ceremony was over he'd take her to investigate those schools properly.

He walked into his office and five people froze. They were already aware of his instructions and invitation regarding Elsie and it was as if he'd dropped a bomb on them. Maybe he had. Felipe had always done everything expected of him. Today an air of the unexpected infiltrated. He found he quite liked it.

'Everything's in hand, right?' he asked mildly.

His PA glanced around and was the one who stepped forward first. 'Some of the Europeans have asked if you'd like a meeting—'

'Not today.' Felipe didn't let him finish. 'I need to focus on the coronation.' Actually he needed to focus on *regaining* his focus. 'Please assure them that in the coming weeks I'll make time for them and I'll greet everyone tonight at the banquet.'

Everyone stilled again. Yes, that wasn't the answer they'd expected. Ordinarily he'd make a meeting if requested. But trade talks could wait. He had very few personal moments left before the ceremony.

'The passengers who are stuck at the airport,' he said thoughtfully.

'Sir?'

'Is there any way we could give them a tour or something in the morning? So they don't feel imprisoned in that hotel for the full twenty-four hours?' He rolled his shoulders, trying to think of something—anything—but Elsie. 'A bus tour? A walk around the vineyard at the other side of the island? Then back to watch the coronation on the big screen at the airport before they leave?'

His assistant looked hesitant. 'It would be a logistical challenge.'

'But one I know you're capable of pulling off. It would a gesture of goodwill for the inconvenience they're suffering—something to alleviate the impact we've had on their time and liberty.'

'Of course.'

'Your Majesty.' Garcia stepped forward. 'Someone's been in touch about Ms Wynter.'

Felipe paused. He needed to talk to Garcia about what had happened. 'Clear the room.'

Stillness again, then a sudden exodus.

Felipe eyed Garcia. 'Who?'

'One of the passengers on her flight asked airport security.' Major Garcia avoided his gaze and read from the tablet he held in front of him. 'Peter Sainz was seated across the aisle from Ms Wynter in the plane. A financier from Barcelona, he was concerned that she'd disappeared from the terminal.'

So Ms Wynter raised protective instincts in other people? Felipe's own possessiveness tightened. 'You can let him know she's safe and will return for the flight tomorrow.'

Garcia stiffened. 'Will she attend the coronation as well, sir?'

'No.' It was an instant, gut-instinct answer. 'The plane will depart immediately after the ceremony. She'll be at the airport ready to board with the other passengers at that time.' She'd be gone from his life for good then.

Major Garcia didn't step away.

'You have thoughts on that, Major?' Felipe regarded the man who'd been Head of Security for the last twenty years. His grandfather's iron fist. The man who'd spectacularly failed once and who'd worked excessively hard to make up for it ever since.

'Did you ever read my report on Ms Wynter, sir?'

'I wasn't aware I requested a report from you.' He allowed his voice to drop to an icy whisper. 'Major Garcia?'

Garcia's nostrils flared. Yeah. It was time to remember who the King was in the room.

'When Ms Wynter came to the palace I thought it would be prudent to check her background more comprehensively.'

Felipe's anger grew. 'And you did that immediately?'

'Sir.' Garcia nodded.

'You went to the café while she was at the palace and asked her employers about her?'

'Sir.'

'Without my instruction.'

Garcia stiffened. 'It is my remit to protect you and your family from any threats.'

'You didn't trust the work Ortiz had already done?'

'With respect, it wasn't detailed enough.'

Possibly true but beside the point. 'I had told him to hold off on a full check.'

Garcia stood his ground. 'Would you like to see the report, sir?'

'No.'

'But—'

'No.' Felipe straightened. 'I appreciate your concern, Garcia. And I respect that you need to do your job but in this instance you overstepped the mark. Furthermore, you were *not* discreet. The resulting impact on Ms Wynter was unacceptable. It damages the monarchy's reputation that she was dismissed because of palace interference. Can you imagine the media headlines if that were to get out?'

Garcia swallowed.

'The fact it *hasn't* been leaked is a credit to Ms Wynter.'

'But—'

'But nothing. I trust that your team has the entire island at maximum security. You may be assured Ms Wynter is no threat to me, Amalia or any of the dignitaries here for the coronation. Tonight's banquet is a sealed occasion and she will depart the palace tomorrow and the country moments after the coronation, which she will *not* attend. I am confident you will be able to keep her identity and attendance tonight under wraps. Am I clear?'

'Of course, Your Majesty.'

'Thank you. That will be all.'

He didn't want to read the report. He didn't want to watch the video.

What he wanted was so much worse than that.

Elsie was amazed at the efficiency of Felipe's staff. They'd had a selection of dresses delivered in less than an hour—during which a trio of stylists had descended to begin work on her hair and nails. It was only in this brief moment that she and Amalia were actually alone and even then Amalia was burrowing through the rack of dresses.

'I'm sorry you had to leave so suddenly.' Amalia smiled awkwardly at Elsie. 'Felipe shouldn't have done that.'

'I don't think it was necessarily his fault,' Elsie said slowly, realising she'd actually believed him when he'd said he hadn't known his team were going to investigate her.

'We could skip the banquet altogether,' Amalia suggested. 'I could say I have a rash and we could just stay up here and play music.'

Elsie laughed. 'As nice as that idea is, I don't think we can do that.'

'Why not? He won't even notice if I'm not there.'

'I think he would, actually,' Elsie said softly. 'I know he's very busy but he's concerned for you. I think he doesn't want you to be alone. So…let's go together.'

'Okay, then, what about this one?' Amalia held up a scarlet dress, her eyes sparkling.

'Oh, um. I think that might make me stand out too much.' Honestly, she was terrified.

Amalia looked curious. 'You don't want to stand out?'

'Definitely not.' Elsie laughed. 'I don't really fit in here, Amalia. And I definitely don't think I can wear something like *that*.'

'I don't really fit in here either.' But Amalia suddenly smiled. 'We can not fit in together.'

'Discreetly.' Elsie nodded.

'You want discreet.' Amalia shook her head. 'That's disappointing.'

Elsie didn't just want discreet. She wanted wallpaper—something in which she'd melt into the background. She had no desire to be Cinderella and make everyone stop and stare and wonder who she was. She wanted to enjoy the evening with anonymity.

Just over half an hour later Elsie wriggled her toes. 'It'll be fun. She said. It'll be quick. She said.'

She shot Amalia a look from the chair in which she was being very, very still so the hairdresser and make-up artist and nail technician could all work miracles. 'I'm super glad I am not a princess.'

'Me too.' Amalia chuckled. 'But you have to admit this is a little bit fun.'

Yeah, Elsie hadn't really meant it. Because the secret pleasure of having people wash and comb out her hair, paint her nails and make her feel pretty? It was lovely. She'd apologised a billion times because she hadn't had a trim in for ever, but the hairdresser had brushed aside her murmurings with a smile.

'The dress is perfect,' Amalia added, looking pleased.

Amalia had helped her choose a column dress the deep navy of Silvabon. The fact it was both sleeveless and strapless had been a sticking point, but it was the best of the bunch in terms of subtlety and that was what she wanted. Inoffensive and not eye-catching. Elsie didn't want to breathe in case it slipped. Amalia assured her it wouldn't and the seamstress had supplied her with tape.

'Which shoes?' Amalia danced in front of the five pairs Callie had set out.

'I can't do heels that high,' Elsie shook her head at the stunning black stilettos with the red sole.

'Satin ballet slippers?' Amalia held some up.

'Mmm, not going to make me any taller.'

'What did you want, stilts?' An amused voice came from behind them.

Elsie spun around and Amalia smothered her giggle.

'I've told you before not to sneak up on people,' she said bluntly. 'Especially when they're still getting *dressed*.'

'You look dressed to me.' His gaze dropped down her body.

Fiery awareness flickered across her skin as he took in her appearance, but she hadn't exactly rendered him speechless. Whereas now *she'd* taken a second to see him? She almost swallowed her tongue.

He was wearing a tuxedo with a navy sash that had gold trim and an insignia. Not full royal regalia but enough to remind all who he was. The star of the show. Her pulse skipped infuriatingly. Her reaction in secret places? Mortifying.

'Are you wearing that bathrobe tonight, Amalia?' Felipe asked idly.

'Two minutes.' Amalia dashed to her dressing room.

Without another word, the assistants cleared the room.

Elsie stared as the door closed behind them and then turned to look at him. 'Does it take them long to master the mind-reading thing?'

He chuckled. 'You didn't see my signal.'

'You literally just lift your little finger? Is that so you don't tire your voice?'

He ignored her and scooped up a pair of shoes. 'These would be good.'

She ground her teeth, not wanting to give him the points for picking the best pair. Mid-level heel but with pretty straps. 'You're not putting them on me.'

'So that's a yes?' He smiled.

She awkwardly took the shoes from his hand. 'Thank you, fairy god—'

'I will silence you with my little finger, Elsie,' he said huskily. 'Or better yet, make you scream.'

She froze at the shockingly sexually tinged threat. Then bent to hide the scorching blush on her skin. *With just his little finger?*

'I'm pleased,' he murmured as she strapped on the shoes. 'Generally you manage to ignore most things I suggest.'

'Was it a *suggestion*?' she echoed. 'I thought it was another of your orders. You being the King and all.'

He chuckled. 'As a guest of Silvabon you are required to abide by the laws of the country. Including the orders of the King. But tonight I waive that requirement—just for lucky little you, you understand.'

'Wow.' She straightened.

He regarded her, suddenly serious. 'I vow, I won't order you to do anything. Not tonight. I'm not a king. For you, Elsie, I'll be just a man.'

She couldn't move. His words? The way he was gazing at her?

She was suddenly so self-conscious.

'Amalia said this dress would be suitable,' she stammered.

Why was she seeking his approval? It didn't matter what he thought. But her mouth was dry and that moment kept flashing in her mind—when he'd told her to leave, when it had looked as if that was the *last* thing he'd wanted her to do, when he'd almost kissed her. The look in his eyes now matched that. As if a storm were raging—a war between want and denial.

'You look immaculate.'

'Are you sure about this?' she asked.

'People will be informed that you're here as a guest of Amalia's.'

'Like her music tutor?' She nodded. 'That could definitely work.'

'Music tutor it is.'

'They won't know my full name, will they? And I won't be seated near you, will I?'

A half-smile quirked his lips. 'This inferiority complex you've got going…we're equal, are we not? I thought I'd just made that clear.'

'No. We're not. You know we're not.'

Before he could reply Amalia appeared. But there was a look in his eye that promised they'd continue the conversation later. But that wasn't happening. It couldn't.

'You look stunning, Amalia,' he said.

'I'm only doing this for her,' Elsie whispered as they followed Amalia along the corridor.

'You can think that if it makes you feel better.'

CHAPTER EIGHT

Friday, 7.03 p.m.

ELSIE'S NERVES TIGHTENED, but Felipe didn't take her straight to the ballroom. Instead they stopped at a small chamber not far from Amalia's suite. A selection of velvet boxes had been set out on the table.

'I know you appreciate and enjoy jewellery.' He gestured for Amalia to step forward. 'You may choose something to wear tonight.'

Amalia's eyes rounded. 'Are you sure?'

'Of course,' he said. 'Take your time. You can try them all.'

The waiting maid showed Amalia earrings, necklaces, jewelled hair combs, even a couple of miniature tiaras. After a moment Felipe walked over to where Elsie was quietly marvelling.

'Your skin is also bare.' He pulled something from his pocket. 'Perhaps you would like to wear this?'

Elsie's skin rippled with goosebumps as he held it for her to inspect. A narrow rope of glistening diamonds set in gold. It sparkled brilliantly, making her think of an unbreakable chain that would undeniably *tie* her to him. She stared into his eyes for a smouldering moment, shocked by her thoughts…at the temptation at the thought of being so *linked* to him.

'It's a bracelet,' he explained slowly as if she'd suddenly become brainless.

Which apparently she had because now a vision rose—of herself clad in nothing but this diamond chain on her wrist and with Felipe bracing above her, the wickedest of smiles on his face. A ball of heat exploded low in her belly.

'No.' She shook her head, clearing the shocking image. 'No.'

'It's just a bracelet. Just for tonight.'

'What happened to "my body my rules"? Adornment?' she asked, desperate to escape her own overactive imagination. 'You said you weren't my fairy godmother, but you want to dress me up to fit in with your world.'

'It's not that. You'll never fit into my world.'

The truth stung.

He gripped her wrist and stopped her from stepping away. 'That's a good thing, Elsie.'

'If it's good, then don't ask me to pretend to be someone I'm not.'

'Can you not be someone who wears pretty things? Or expensive things? Do you think you're not worthy in some way?'

His perception angered her. She needed to stop him. To shock him. And there was nothing more shocking than the truth. As he'd just demonstrated. 'My father is in prison.'

He stilled. 'Your father is not you.'

She felt the prickle of tears and blinked rapidly, resisting the overwhelming emotion. It seemed more truth might be required. Things she never spoke of. She needed to push him away from her. 'My brother was in prison too.'

'But *you're* not.' He hesitated. 'Have you ever been?'

She slowly shook her head.

His eyes were very deep and dark and he regarded her steadily. 'And your mother's gone. I'm sorry, Elsie.'

It hadn't worked. He hadn't withdrawn. Now he actually stepped closer, lifting the bracelet in his hand.

'Please, Felipe.' She shook her head again. He could tempt her into wearing it. Part of her desperately wanted to—to be accepted, to pretend for just a little while. Another part wanted to snatch it from his hand and *never* give it back. 'It's not mine. It's not something I earned and I paid for. It's not appropriate.'

'It's only to borrow, not keep,' he argued. 'Amalia told me you didn't want to stand out. Unadorned you will. I imagine Sofia will be wearing so many kilos of jewels she'll barely be able to stand beneath the weight of them.'

Startled, a horrible hot sensation rolled through her stomach. 'She's going to be here tonight?'

'Are you jealous of my ex?'

Her gaze flew back to him. 'Is that what she is?'

'Not really.' His intensity sharpened and his voice dropped. 'We didn't sleep together.'

Embarrassment burned, yet relief swamped her. 'You didn't need to tell me that.'

'No?'

'You wouldn't have slept with her until you were married.'

He looked at her quizzically, then began to laugh. 'Virgin princesses are the stuff of fairy tales, Elsie.'

She burned worse now. 'You've slept with other princesses?'

He puffed out a breath. 'None of my former lovers will be present tonight.'

'This information is too personal to be relevant to me,' she gritted.

He merely laughed harder—but the warmth in his gaze?

'You sure you want to trust me with this?' She tried to shoot him down.

'You've not told anyone about your time in the palace all

those months ago and you could have. You wouldn't expose Amalia. You wouldn't hurt me either.'

'Not even if someone paid me pots of money?'

'You could have sold your story weeks ago and you didn't. Your integrity matters too much to you.'

Just like that he stole her breath for good.

'I trust you, Elsie. I wouldn't invite you to wear this if I didn't.'

Tears prickled. That he trusted her *mattered* intensely and it meant so very much. But it suddenly saddened her. He was one of the few people to believe in her and he was so far from her reach. It was the most bittersweet feeling.

'Thank you for the offer. I'm honoured,' she said simply. 'But no. The dress is enough. I'm her music tutor,' she said. 'No one expects me to be dripping with diamonds.'

He gazed into her eyes solemnly. 'As you wish.' He put the fistful of jewels back into his pocket and called to Amalia. 'Are you ready?'

The girl turned. She'd chosen a pretty pearl necklet that was just gorgeous.

'Silvabon pearls.' Felipe nodded. 'Nice choice, Amalia. Several in that piece were found off one of the smaller islands many years ago.'

Amalia fingered the necklet gently. 'Is it true you used to go diving for them?'

Felipe's eyebrows lifted. 'You heard about that?'

'Carlos said that one time you were free diving and you went under for so long the bodyguards all jumped in fully clothed to rescue you. But then you surfaced and you laughed so hard. Carlos said you'd found an amazing pearl.'

Felipe blinked. 'He told you that story?'

'He talked about you all the time,' Amalia said. 'He said you found lots.'

There was a flash on Felipe's face that made Elsie instinctively step closer to him.

But Amalia hadn't noticed. 'He said the old King banned you from diving again after that.'

There was a beat before Felipe answered. Where Elsie realised he'd taken a moment to count himself down. He glanced at her and his shoulders squared because, yes, she'd seen.

'He might've made a *suggestion* along those lines.' Felipe shot her one of those devastating stares.

'But you dived anyway,' Elsie surmised wryly, understanding he needed a moment of levity. 'And there we all thought you *kept* your promises…'

'I didn't promise him I wouldn't dive.' Felipe winked. 'He suggested that I refrained from it. I chose not to listen.'

'Carlos said you have more courage than anyone.' Amalia nodded, oblivious to the charged undercurrent that returned at her words. 'Do you still find them?'

This time Felipe didn't reply.

'Felipe?' Elsie said softly.

'I haven't had much time to dive there recently.' He didn't look at either of them.

'I wish I could try,' Amalia said wistfully. 'But I can't swim well.'

Felipe cleared his throat. 'We all have different strengths. I can't play the piano at all.'

Amalia touched the necklet again and suddenly lifted her chin. 'I'll teach you a tune if you teach me to dive.'

For another silent moment both step-siblings stood frozen. Elsie desperately sought Felipe's gaze, and as he glanced towards her she stared at him meaningfully.

Say yes to her. Please.

That muscle in his jaw flicked. 'Okay.' He nodded briskly at Amalia. 'Sure. Later in summer when your leg is stronger.'

Elsie's heart pounded. She was stupidly relieved because the two of them could be closer and that would be good for them both.

'Good motivation to do your physio exercises.' She smiled at Amalia. 'You look so pretty. The pearls are perfect.'

Felipe walked with them through the labyrinthine corridors towards the reception room. Just as they arrived, he dropped husky words in her ear. 'By the way, did you really think you wouldn't stand out in that dress?'

She smiled, his tease soothing her nerves and assuring her he'd recovered from that moment. Of course he had. He was a king and had consummate control of everything. 'I was hoping to blend in with the banners.'

He shook his head and peeled away from them.

'Felipe said we don't have to do the greeting line, we go in another entrance,' Amalia said. 'I don't know how he remembers everyone's names. There are hundreds of them.'

Elsie watched him, trying to be surreptitious and totally failing. It didn't matter; no one was paying attention to her. He stood at the opposite end of the banquet hall, ready to greet his guests, tall and strong and obviously comfortable. But he was also isolated. Even with courtiers and government ministers waiting with him, he was set apart. It wasn't just that air of command, that he was full-fleshed authority to the bone, the one from whom all sought approval. Everyone in this vast room ached to impress him yet there was no one at his side. No partner. No family. Not even his mother. He was starkly alone. And that, she realised, was how he wanted it.

He'd never wanted to marry that princess. He'd not wanted Amalia to suffer through the boredom of the reception line. He saw this all as solely *his* duty—as he stood beneath the portrait of his steely-eyed grandfather. Given any image of his father had been scrubbed long ago, only Felipe remained now. It was down to him. And that was how he'd keep it.

As she studied him, he turned. Unerringly his gaze met hers. There was a moment when she felt the intensity as if he were standing but a breath from her. A moment later liveried guards swung the wide oak door open and the procession of guests began. In minutes there were several princesses in the room. Their dresses were sleek and glamorous. She and Amalia amused themselves in admiring them, then Elsie had to focus on enjoying the musicians' skill because she was inordinately jealous of the women talking to Felipe. She'd recognised the princess he wasn't marrying. She was wearing a golden dress and looked like a goddess.

'I want to learn the drums,' Amalia said.

Yeah, Elsie had the urge to bash loud things with heavy sticks this second.

More princes. Kings. Prime ministers. Presidents. Security was obvious and tight. Elsie understood why the skies had been closed. There was a detail on Amalia. She saw the men from the café watching at a discreet distance.

Like every guest there, she was hyper aware of where Felipe was. Who he was talking to. He was an absolute professional—greeting every guest by name, circulating, allowing everyone moments of his attention. The thing they all craved most.

The air of excitement and celebration was palpable. The banquet hall glittered with polished silver and chandeliers. The food was sublime but Elsie found she couldn't eat much. She smiled politely as nearby guests talked to Amalia about places to visit in Europe. She considered them all like customers, inquiring politely, admiring something. Her introduction as Amalia's music assistant was accepted without question. After the feast they headed to the ballroom. She and Amalia were left more to themselves.

Felipe needed to stop staring at her, but *not* staring at her felt even more obvious. He couldn't find the balance. It was stupid and in overthinking it he found his gaze drifting towards her again. With nothing around her neck, no jewel to distract the eye, there was no escaping the beauty of her smooth skin, the desperately tempting line of her collarbones. He couldn't get enough of the stunning scope of her bare skin. He wanted to see more—everything that lay beneath that demure neckline of the dress. Her hair was highlighted and gleaming like a halo. She didn't need a tiara for people to take notice of her.

At her side Amalia was laughing, while Elsie was more circumspect. But her glacial blue eyes burned like the hottest flames whenever her gaze clashed with his.

Why had he wanted to adorn her? Why when she couldn't sparkle any more than she currently did? The bracelet was still in his pocket. He'd imagined it sparkling on her wrist as she played her mandolin. A hint of perspiration popped at the thought of her curled on his bed wearing nothing but those diamonds, waiting for him to pet her. What was with the dominant fantasies? He'd never explored that kind of play before. But he ached for her complete submission to him. Not as a king, but as a man. As the lover to whom she would allow absolute access—to every inch of her skin, to those secrets in her soul. He wanted complete *possession*. And equally he ached to fall to his knees before her and feel the honour of her touch, her caress.

The power she could wield over him was startling in its intensity and the dominance in his thinking. He could never allow lust to bring him—and the monarchy—to its knees.

She *was* a threat. He hadn't known that members of her family were in prison. He ought to know why already. But he'd ignored Garcia's warnings. Hell, he was turning into his father—turning his back on duty to indulge in lust. And the worst thing was he didn't care. But he did feel a qualm of guilt for *her*. She didn't want exposure. She wasn't part of this world. She'd never faced paparazzi, never should.

It was too late to banish her from the palace again, but she would leave tomorrow and he would never see her again. She would be safe.

Right this second he wanted to turn back the clock and return to medieval times when a king had concubines and kept chosen mistresses in court, ready for his attention. He wanted to send everyone packing with a finger snap. He wanted *all* the freedoms, *all* the time and he wanted it *all* with her.

He tried to maintain polite conversation. Tried to ensure that he worked his way around all the dignitaries so he didn't unintentionally offend anyone. Honestly, the greeting line had been endless, even for a royal of his experience…

Now Elsie glanced over. He had to stay very still so he didn't give away his unguarded rushing response. He was unwilling, unable to release her gaze… Until the prime minister spoke to him and directed him to another dignitary who'd been waiting. No, he couldn't speak to her yet. He'd not allow himself near until he'd controlled his desire to touch her.

People danced in the ballroom. He didn't. He never did—never favoured anyone in public at any rate. A few more minutes passed and he'd lost sight of them.

'Where are they?' He frowned at Ortiz. 'Why aren't you with them?'

'They're secure within the private wing, Your Majesty.' Ortiz replied. 'They left about twenty minutes ago.'

Yeah, he knew exactly how many minutes it was since he'd been able to see her. She'd left the banquet before the King gave his consent? No one did that. Amalia was only allowed given her age. Except he'd given Elsie a reprieve tonight, hadn't he? He was not her king. But had she really thought she could leave him again without saying goodbye?

Not this time.

CHAPTER NINE

Friday, 11.27 p.m.

ELSIE WALKED DOWN the long corridor, hoping it would lead to the guest wing. She should've asked Amalia's maid to show her but hadn't wanted to be a pain. It was so quiet this far from the ballroom she felt as if she were the only person in some magical realm.

'You didn't even make it to midnight before running away.' A tall shadow stepped from a corner.

'Felipe?' Her jump-scare switched to jump-sizzle as he moved closer until he was right in front of her.

She could hardly look at him in that sharp suit with the glimmer of stubble on his sculpted jaw and the smouldering ferocity in his eyes.

'Amalia is over it,' Elsie nervously explained. 'She's just gone to bed.'

'I'm over it too,' he muttered.

Elsie couldn't think about *him* going to bed. 'What about your guests?'

'I've talked with all of them.' His stormy gaze pierced her. 'Except you.'

'I'm not your guest, though. I'm—'

'Here under sufferance?' he interjected huskily.

'Here for Amalia,' she corrected softly.

'No, you're not.'

Her pulse flicked into double time. Amalia had been one reason he'd demanded her presence tonight. But there was another—stronger one.

Take a breath.

It was impossible. Hot and tense, she needed to get away from him.

'I'm going to my room.' Her voice wobbled worse than an opera diva's.

'Is it satisfactory?'

She hadn't actually seen it yet. She'd got ready in Amalia's room, where they'd provided literally everything for her. Dress, shoes...*panties*. But before she could answer him, he frowned heavily.

'It's in the guest wing,' he growled.

'Speaking of guests,' she answered awkwardly. 'You really should get back to them.'

'I don't want to.'

She couldn't help a smile. 'You do sullen far better than your teenage stepsister.'

'I'm not sure it's wise to provoke me right now, Elsie.'

Her mouth dried.

'I've let it be known I've retired to reflect before tomorrow,' he said.

Tomorrow was too close already. Time was ticking—trickling away.

'To reflect?' She reached for a smile but failed.

At midday tomorrow he would be the sole focus of millions of people. She couldn't imagine the pressure that came with that level of scrutiny.

He shrugged. 'The banquet ends at midnight anyway, so the guests may be fully rested before the coronation.'

'But you can't miss the fireworks.'

A wicked smile glimmered in his eyes as he leaned too close and whispered, 'I don't intend to.'

Adrenalin raced, setting off a raucous, wicked temptation.

'What about you?' he added. 'You're all dressed up and it's not even midnight and you're running away.'

She wasn't—she was fixed to the spot when she should be running through the castle—running from *him*. But she couldn't pull herself free of his mesmerising presence.

'You didn't dance.' His eyes were full of regret and his voice was so quiet she was unsure he even meant her to hear. 'I wanted to dance with you. But I couldn't.'

'Couldn't or wouldn't?'

'They'd eat you alive. I can't let that happen.'

A last barrier melted inside her. 'You're trying to protect me?' Was that why he'd kept at such a disappointing distance all evening? It wasn't that he'd forgotten about her.

'Their pursuit would be relentless.'

He was so close her mind spun and she lost control. That dangerous part of her spilled free. 'What about your pursuit?' she asked huskily. 'Would that be relentless?'

His eyes widened. He stood still before her but his fingers touched hers. So lightly. So carefully. 'Are you flirting with me? Finally?'

Only a very little. 'You don't need to protect me from anyone,' she said. 'I'm leaving tomorrow and I'm not coming back.'

His fingers interlinked with hers—the softest, most fragile of connections. Electricity surged—striking a chord deep within her.

'Dance with me.' There was a thread of steel in his voice now.

'Here? We can't even hear the music.'

'You're musical. Hum something.'

'Any other orders?' she asked with an arch of her brows.

'So many, I'm struggling to hold them all back.'

She couldn't suppress the shiver of sensual intrigue. 'Is that so?'

His jaw locked. 'Temptress.'

Was she? 'I thought I was Cinderella. But I'm not—that's you.'

Genuine surprise flickered on his face, then amusement. *'Me?'*

'You're trapped in a palace, doing all the work—cleaning up the messes your family left. You ensure everyone has everything they need...'

'Then don't say no. Dance with me,' he said simply. 'Just once.'

It felt so much more than a mere invitation to dance.

'Because you ask so nicely?' she teased.

'Please.' He stepped back and held his hand out to her.

It was such an old-fashioned formal gesture it made her smile. She put her hand in his, half expecting—hoping—he'd haul her to him, but he kept a courteous distance. His posture was ballroom-dancer perfect. She rested her hand lightly on his shoulder. She could feel the rigidity of his muscles. There was no softening into an embrace. He stared into her eyes, watching, waiting.

There was always that pause, the beat before the music began when one was supposed to take a breath. But Elsie couldn't breathe at all.

'Elsie?' He nodded, a gorgeous encouragement. 'Make some music.'

She barely hummed and only for long enough to establish the rhythm. He picked it up and led her into a waltz—intimate yet constrained.

They were in a bubble of their own. The atmosphere thickened, heated. Touching him? Finally feeling the breadth of his shoulders, the leashed strength in his achingly near body, unlocked something that had long been caged. Something she hadn't wanted to admit existed, let alone allow out. It was a part of her she'd wanted to hide. *Greed.*

She couldn't hum anything any more, but the rhythm between them pulsed regardless and they slowly danced down the darkening corridor. As they passed each low burning light, she caught the gleam in his eyes—the considering look, the curve of his lips.

'Where are you taking me?' She was breathless—as if they'd been dancing a foxtrot, not a carefully controlled waltz.

'Somewhere secret.'

He released her to open a door. A flick made lights illuminate the room.

She paused and took in the glittering space. 'You have a whole other ballroom?'

It was smaller than the one downstairs currently filled with visiting dignitaries from nations around the world, but equally stunning—if not more. This one was gold—figurines and frescoes—cherubs and smiling nymphs all in suggestive scenes.

'This is a salon for private performances,' he explained.

'*Private* performances?' She shot him a look. 'What sort of performances?'

'Not the sort you're thinking. At least, not in the last decade or two. Maybe last century it was for—'

'Orgies?'

'Perhaps my forefathers enjoyed personal dances here.' He held out his hand, inviting her to dance again, only this time in this gorgeous small ballroom.

So easily she slid back into temptation—where all that mattered was his touch, his movement, his nearness, his damned breath. Could she let his seduction happen so easily?

'I think Amalia enjoyed tonight,' she muttered, desperately trying to distract herself for just a second.

His shoulder tightened. 'It'll be better for her at boarding school.'

'Do you think?' Elsie's heart ached. 'Is it not a fairy tale to be rescued by a brother who's a king—taken to an idyllic island in the middle of the Mediterranean? To live in a palace and not have to worry?'

'It's no fairy tale.' His expression twisted. 'She lacks friends her own age and normal freedoms.'

Yeah, Elsie had been aware of the girl's isolation when she'd first met her at the café. 'You still don't want her to stay here?'

'The press were beyond cruel to Amalia's mother and to my own. I want to protect Amalia from that future. The only reason she's not already at boarding school is because she needed time to recover, not just from her own injuries, but from the loss of her parents.'

Had Felipe recovered? It was his father who'd died too. In fact, Elsie realised, Felipe had lost his father twice—years ago when he'd abdicated, then again when he'd died in the accident. How had he adjusted to that? And to his mother vowing never to return to the palace?

Elsie had been older than him when she'd lost her mother. And then she'd been ostracised by everyone. People she'd considered close hadn't believed in her innocence. It had been so easy for them to think the worst, so easy for them to cast her out alone. Alone sucked. Alone was hard. Elsie didn't want either Amalia or Felipe to be alone and they didn't need to be. They could have each other. Amalia had reached out already tonight when she'd asked about the pearls. If Felipe allowed it...

'But she's okay here, Felipe,' she said nervously.

'Tonight she smiled for the first time in weeks. Thank you for that.'

'It *wasn't* me.' It had been *him*.

His gaze intensified. 'You don't think?'

In the distance a clock chimed. By unspoken agreement they stilled, counting the beats. Twelve. Midnight. As the last chime resonated through the room, there was a sudden volley of bangs like gunfire. She jumped in fright. Only this time he had hold of her. And this time he pulled her closer.

'Fireworks,' he murmured.

The explosions echoed even through the thick walls. But Elsie was safe, pressed against his solid, hot body—in an embrace that was so secure she shivered.

Cinderella was all wrong. The magic didn't *end* at midnight, it was only then that it *began*. Secret, wonderful things could only happen under cover of darkness when everyone else was asleep. When no one would see. Now was *her* time.

'The next time that clock strikes twelve your time will be up. You'll be crowned.' She smiled at him a little sadly. 'My poor Cinder-fella, stuck in a life of duty.'

'Cinder-fella?' He rolled his eyes.

She'd giggle if she didn't actually feel sorry for him.

'The coronation is a formality, Elsie. It's not as bad as you think. Fundamentally, nothing will change.'

No? But she saw resignation smothering restlessness in his eyes. Cemented, regimented, he was bracing for a constrained future.

'A very public formality,' she said.

His expression grew stormy. He didn't want her pity. Just as she didn't want his. They didn't have the time to waste on it.

'Be careful, I'll take advantage of your compassion.' He backed her into a corner. 'And I'll ask for things you shouldn't give me.'

'Such as?' she breathed.

'Everything.' He cupped her jaw—holding her in place. With her lips upturned to his, this was a prelude to a kiss. 'Say no to me.'

His breath skimmed over her mouth, making her shiver, but she stayed silent.

'Say *no* to me,' he repeated—urgent and imperious. But his eyes asked another question altogether.

She still didn't answer. He was the merest breath from her now.

'Say no, damn it.' His tone splintered.

So did her temper. Why should she make it easy for him? Why should *she* have to bear the burden of doing the right thing? She'd done that before and it had hurt her badly. What was the point in trying to be good? She'd still lost—everything. And this once she wanted something for herself.

She lifted her chin as anger and desire overwhelmed her. *'No.'*

His mouth parted and he froze, but before he could snap away from her she hooked her arm around his neck and held him close. His eyes were blown—as black as midnight, as endless, as aching.

'Not what you wanted to hear after all?' she jeered, but her voice shook. So did her body. She arched towards him like a tulip leaning towards the sun. Craving. Yielding. His mere nearness unleashed the part of her that wanted to take all and damn the consequences. The greedy, selfish, reckless part and she didn't care any more. Her energy was bursting at her seams. She wanted him to release it. She didn't want him to be anything but honest and raw. Now.

'What do you *really* want?' she asked, angry and aching. 'Tell me the truth.' It was an order of her own.

His hands dropped to her waist. He closed the gap completely and the weight of him pressed the breath from her body.

'You. Bed. Mine,' he snarled. *'Mine.'*

'Yours.' She murmured her assent and melted. There was nowhere she could go. Nowhere else she'd rather be.

He pressed her harder against the wall and held her gaze before nipping her lower lip—so lightly, so gently, so quick, she gasped. It was intimate. Dominant. Playful. And a promise. In a blink he was back with the gentlest of kisses. Elsie shuddered—aching, accepting, surrendering it all.

This man had everything. He stood at the apex of the world, ruler of an entire country, an island of riches and beauty. He was a man who apparently had everything. Yet he had so very little for *himself*. And he wanted her.

Sensations exploded—taste and scent and touch. Felipe was everywhere and everything—seeking her very soul with a sublime kiss. His tongue stroked and his lips pressed and it was so heady she was lost. Any last space between them was gone as they sealed together. His hardness pressed against her belly and she pressed back. She gave but he wanted more and the more she gave, the more he wanted. But it was the same for her. Wedged between him and the wall was the best. Breathless, crushed. Every cell sang. It was a line call between laughter and tears as she unashamedly rubbed against him with a mewl of pure agony, pure delight.

At that he tore free and stared into her eyes. The torture in his made her freeze.

'Elsie, I don't...' He huffed a breath. 'I don't want...'

He'd stopped. He *wanted* to stop. He was conflicted about this, which meant there was a problem. *She* was the problem.

Heat churned into anger—the only acceptable release for it because she couldn't let him see how much she hurt. How could he stop so easily? Why wasn't he as crazed with lust as she was? The one time she'd given into the urge to *take* what she wanted—to be greedy and selfish like her family—she'd been denied. She couldn't win whichever way she tried.

'Aren't you going to ask what I want? Are you making this decision without asking me?' she asked fiercely.

Why had he offered something she wanted so much only to snatch it away from her at the last second? Did he not want it as much as her after all?

Something flickered in his gaze. 'I'm trying to do the right thing.'

But how was this wrong? Here—just here, just now— was the right thing, wasn't it? That part of her that didn't care was released. The greedy, naughty part she'd tried to suppress for years. 'Stop trying to do the right thing and do what you *want* for once in your life,' she snapped.

'And damn the consequences?'

'What consequences? Why will there be any? Nothing bad's going to happen because we both know...' She shook her head in frustration. 'This is it. This is the *one* time we can do what *feels* right, not what we *think* is right. Not what we should do. We have minutes, Felipe. Only minutes.'

This was the one time they had. The *only* time she'd ever *wanted* to. No one would know. No one would judge. Here in his palace they had the safest, most secure, most secret, most solitary of chances.

'Elsie.' A tic in his jaw flicked.

'Why would it be *bad*?' She was unable to stifle her stark honesty, the avaricious need within overruling her usual caution. 'You're not a king to me, Felipe. You're just a man I want.'

It would be a brief crossover in lives that were so very different. But he stared at her—still locked against her. As slow seconds ticked by, shame slithered in.

What was she doing? Basically begging the guy to take her to bed? He clearly didn't want to. She was making a fool of herself. She felt ripped open and *unwanted*.

'Forget it.' Overwhelmed, she pushed hard against his chest.

He stepped back.

And she *was* such a fool. She ducked out from him. 'I'm going to my room.'

Three paces towards the door she realised she had no idea

how to find the wretched thing. She stopped. 'I'm afraid you need to show me the way.'

She didn't want to look at him but her eyes wouldn't obey her brain. He was standing where she'd left him. Still and frowning at her. And so handsome she wanted to throw something at him. He'd made her want him, so quickly, so easily, so completely. He was her impossible.

'The way?' he echoed.

'I haven't even been to the guest wing.' She put her hands on her hips in a fake gesture of confidence and glared at him. 'You know this place is a rabbit warren. Full of secret corridors that all look the same and lead to…' It was beyond embarrassing now and she growled at him. 'Could you just flick your fingers and have one of your staff magically appear?'

He finally moved. 'I'll show you.'

'*You* don't have to.'

He walked over to where she stood, ignoring her deliberately defiant pose to step in too close and press his hand against her mouth. The gentlest laughter gleamed in his eyes. 'Who's the sulky one now?'

CHAPTER TEN

Saturday, 12.24 a.m.

FELIPE DIDN'T LEAD her back down the corridor but took her deeper into the medieval part of the palace that had once been an impregnable stone fortress. It still was. As the path narrowed he battled his conscience. He wanted her. But that there would be no consequences?

'Is this a short cut?'

Her impatience and defiance made him want to kiss her—to soothe the hurt he knew he'd inflicted. But he couldn't. Yet. 'No.'

He'd tried to resist. But touching her was all he could think about. Dancing had made it worse. He'd asked her to say no, fearing that if she said yes, he wouldn't cope. He hadn't. That kiss had destroyed him. He'd almost taken her hard, against the wall, all control gone. He'd had to slam on the brakes because he was a damned runaway train and he had to make sure she was on board with him. But he'd phrased it poorly. She'd thought he was pulling back. Another miscommunication. When she'd first blown, he'd been awed by her spirit—her fight for him. But her hurt had turned inward, he'd seen the snap in her eyes. He knew she'd felt unworthy and unwanted, which was the absolute opposite of his intention and his truth. She'd stopped mid-fight as if she'd suddenly remembered she had no right to ask for anything. That *wasn't* the surrender he wanted. Giving up? No. She had every right to ask for what she wanted. He wanted to hear it, wanted to enact her demands… His own desire shocked him.

Surely the intensity was a reaction to the relentless preparation and coronation pressures. He just needed a release valve. And they'd had this physical attraction from first sight.

Two silent minutes later she stopped, forcing him to turn and face her.

'Where are you taking me? The dungeon?'

Heat blasted, short-circuiting his brain, and he stepped back into her space. 'Why do I get the feeling you'd like that, Elsie?'

Her eyes widened. *Oh, she would.* With that one flash of desire she damned any lingering good intentions to hell. There was no way he wasn't having her tonight. For all her flightiness, her flashes of temper at his demanding nature, she also craved the dominance he offered. And it worked both ways—the fact was they were imprisoned together by desire. He watched her lift her chin in that show of strength. But they were in thrall to each other. He ached for her submission every bit as much as he ached for her to take him in hand and school him. Released from hesitation and doubt, he knew she'd give him both.

'I'm taking you to my room,' he informed her bluntly. 'Once there, I'm going to kiss you. Only this time I'll not stop until you ask me to.'

Her eyes glazed. A haze of heated colour washed over every inch of her skin that was visible. 'Promise?'

The husky command almost felled him. He wanted nothing more than to satisfy her. 'I promise.'

He took her hand and led her for another minute along the winding corridor—deliberately taking this route to avoid any courtiers. There was an inevitability about this. He pressed his palm to the security system and opened the door. He released her hand, watching with amusement for her reaction as she stepped into the suite. The sight of Elsie trying to conceal her very obvious emotions brought him immense pleasure. She couldn't, of course; he could see the response in her expressive eyes. She didn't try to hide usually, but this time—was she trying to be polite? Aiming to spare his feelings?

'This is your bedroom?' She turned on the spot, taking it all in until her gaze eventually settled on the large bed. 'Did you decorate it yourself?'

'No,' he replied softly. 'It's been like this for the last century or so.'

She wrinkled her nose. 'Those curtains are over a hundred years old?'

'They've been refurbished, but the decor is as it was originally designed by my many greats grandmother.'

'Was she a performer?' She shot him a look, her smile bubbling when she saw his amusement. 'Honestly, that's like a proscenium arch at the back of the bed. And what's with all the curtains?'

He leaned back against the door and laughed. Elsie's expression was everything. He studied the surroundings—trying to imagine seeing it for the first time. The room was dressed in navy, black, gold—the colours of Silvabon. Twin candelabras stood either side of the massive bed, making the ornately carved, gilded headboard gleam. Heavy velvet curtains in midnight blue hung behind in gold-fringed swathes. Layers upon layers of the things. Another large crystal chandelier was suspended above them while beneath their feet was thick, intricately woven carpet.

'Has it always been your bedroom?' Elsie murmured.

'It was the most convenient room to take when Grandfather became unwell.'

Right now only the candelabras were lit—with warm

bulbs; candles had been phased out a half-century ago. But the effect was undeniably theatrical and lush. For the first time he truly appreciated it because Elsie, dressed in that navy column dress that hugged her curves, fitted perfectly in the centre of the vast, darkened space—like a pearl nestled in an iridescent shell. He wanted to keep her here. Her head was tilted back, exposing the luscious pale skin of her neck as she studied the balcony that ran around the top third of the room.

'Is that for the audience?' she asked. 'Did the royal couple have to…have to do it in front of people to make sure the pregnancy was legitimate or something?'

He watched the colour building in her cheeks. There was a hint of shyness in her stumble over the words, a bigger hint of sensuality in her response to the thought.

'You think they were exhibitionists?' He glanced at the curved wooden staircase that led up to that small mezzanine walkway. 'I've never thought about it. I've never brought a lover back to this room.'

He didn't know why that admission had felt so imperative. No one but his valet came in here. He didn't pay much attention to the room—it was as it had always been. But now as he took in the carved elements of the bed and the balcony, infinite tempting possibilities stirred in his mind.

'You haven't?' Her pale eyes widened. 'Why now?'

It took him a moment to parse the reasons that were bound so tightly with the bare drive of desire. 'It's the safest place we can be together tonight. The room assigned to you is on a relatively busy wing. There's the danger we'd be seen there.'

'And we can't possibly be seen.'

'That's in your best interests.'

'Very concerned for my best interests, aren't you?'

Touched by the wistful vulnerability in her soft mouth

and shy eyes, he pushed away from the door and strolled towards her—immediately gratified by the sensual wariness that smouldered more every step he took.

'I'm very concerned for you, full stop,' he said honestly. 'But I'm willing to do whatever you want me to.'

Rebellion tightened his muscles. His natural instincts were at war. He conceded power to no one, but for Elsie tonight he'd give it in order to take it. One and the same. Everything they both wanted.

'Even if it's *wrong*?'

'I'm yours, Elsie.' He reminded himself of the boundaries to ease his tension. 'Yours until dawn.'

Her eyes sparked with a gleam of something he wasn't sure he could handle.

'Where do you usually take your lovers if not here?' she asked, the colour in her cheeks betraying her. 'You do have lovers, right?'

'Not often.'

'No?' Her eyes glittered.

He chuckled. 'Does that worry you?'

She shook her head and her gaze dropped. 'I hope I'll…'

He clamped his jaw as a hot shaft of possessiveness flooded him. She brushed a stray lock of hair from her face and he saw the tremble in her fingers.

'Tonight is it. All there'll ever be,' he said.

Not because she wasn't worthy. But because he refused to have her endure everything else that came with him. Lovers of princes and kings weren't treated well by the rest of the world, even in this supposedly modern and permissive age. This was a symbolic last moment of freedom. Of choice. Because she wasn't a choice he could make after tomorrow. And that was for her benefit, not his. Tomorrow she'd be gone for good.

'Are you taking a vow of celibacy tomorrow too?' she asked.

He didn't know how it was going to work. An occasional discreet lover here and there. He hadn't considered it until now and, honestly, he didn't care. As long as he had her. Tonight. Now.

She ran her tongue along her lips. 'I think you should stop wasting time...'

For all the bravado she was emotional, maybe even a little nervous. He was going to take care with her. Gentle, savage care. He'd wanted her the moment he'd seen her and she was so close to being his.

Who knew desire could be so total and destructive—tearing reason and rational thought into confetti and scattering it on a storm of lust? But this wasn't just sexual desire. He was drawn to her strength and vulnerability, her humour and earnestness, sassiness and sweetness. He knew her past hindered her and he almost didn't want to know why. It didn't matter what it was because there could be no future between them anyway. He'd watched her in that café and knew she needed her freedom. He'd never allow someone so beautiful to wither as a prisoner here and that was what would happen. He planned to be the last King of Silvabon and it was a path he had to take alone.

But tonight? As she'd said. He was merely a man. And he couldn't resist her a second longer.

Elsie couldn't believe she was in a vast room so ornate it ought to be monstrous. Yet it wasn't. It was rich and lush and, despite the size, incredibly intimate. That Felipe was so accustomed to such a literally gilded life? He had no idea how uncommon this decadent atmosphere was. But she forgot about the intricately carved wooden crests and glittering crystal chandeliers that made the gold glow because he cupped her face and kissed her—lips, cheekbones, jaw. He leisurely trailed along the base of her neck, gifting her a collar of kisses, licking the pulse of pleasure, exposing her vulnerability and responsiveness to his touch. Delight swirled, building a stronger need. She wanted more. She sank her full weight against him and let him into her mouth, her body…licking him back. She ached for him to take it all. He dropped a hand to stroke her backside and rocked her closer still against him. The rhythm maddened her, pushed her closer to an edge that she couldn't quite grasp. Now she would feel him, have him. Now she would escape this terrible tension. Because it would flow, then ebb, right? Unleashed, it would be explored and then expunged. It had to be, because she was wound so tight she wanted to scream. And he knew. He held her, strong and sure and hard, against his arousal. Her feet parted a little and she pressed again, seeking another rush of pleasure. That pressing need for release bore down on her. Sudden and urgent.

'Elsie.' He felt it. Of course he felt it. 'You want me? Don't be silent.'

He slid his hand to that aching part at the apex of her thighs. It didn't matter that she still wore her dress and panties—that his fingers were blocked by two layers of fabric. But his touch was scorching.

She was so hot, so desperate she was almost in tears. 'Please.'

'Elsie.' His low voice was strained but forceful. 'Take pleasure from me, Elsie.'

She shouldn't have needed his command—his permission—but she did. She'd never let anyone this close. Never *allowed* herself to be this vulnerable, this exposed. She'd never had someone hold her and kiss her and touch her until she lost her mind. She bit her lip, hard.

'I've got you,' he promised.

She let go—a keening high-pitched cry of release as he held her tighter still and slid another luscious drag of his tongue inside her lips. She fell. But he had her. His grip on her tight and sure as she shuddered and bucked against the hot cage of his body. Bolts of pleasure fired through in an orgasm so quick and hard but that left her impossibly hungrier still. And when she opened her eyes and saw his? She felt both a qualm and a resurgence of excitement. He looked as wild as she felt—as tortured by this heat and need. But they were here, now, and he would hold nothing back. That he felt this hunger? That, beneath his perfect royal facade, the man who was dutiful and good was greedy too? That made her breathless and giddy.

He kissed her again and she instantly yielded. She would let him do anything in that moment and he knew it. His sudden smile said it all. He stepped back and she realised he'd unzipped her dress while kissing her senseless. She grabbed the front of the frock before it slithered to the ground. Where a second ago she'd wanted to be naked, now she verged on embarrassment. She'd never been naked in front of *anyone*. But as he lowered his gaze the hunger in his face burnished her returning confidence.

'Drop the dress, Elsie.'

His order fired her blood. 'Pardon?'

'My dauntless rebel.' His smile broadened. 'Drop the damn dress.'

'I'm not going to obey your every command,' she said, resisting the urge to do exactly that. Knowing that his instructions were intended only to please her.

'Oh, but I think you are.' He tugged the front of her dress playfully. 'Just as I'm going to obey yours.'

'Really?' A fierce longing trammelled through her and she couldn't resist testing him. 'Take off your clothes.'

His gaze shot back to hers. 'All of them?'

'Yes.' She swallowed as he stepped back.

She watched, transfixed, as he stripped. A resurgence of arousal struck—she was so close, just from watching him obey her...and the revelation of his beauty? A dangerous smile played around his lips as he unfastened his shirt, then his trousers. He arched his brows as he removed each item—displaying such wicked charm as he laughed in the face of her fierce blushing silence.

He didn't laugh enough—she liked the sound. She wanted to hear it more. But now she drank in the show until he stood before her—naked, strong, proud, fearless. Hers. Everything she *ever* could have wanted. A lithe, strong body—muscular and gleaming and utterly perfect.

'Elsie?' There was a thread of laughter in the steel. 'I think it's your turn.'

She dropped her dress. She was shaking, now clad in nothing but a tiny pair of navy silk knickers and her breasts full and tight and aching for his touch. He flinched and locked his muscles—maximising their already thrilling definition.

She couldn't actually stand any more. He caught her as she trembled.

'Time for bed, sweetheart.' A warning. An order. A release. He stared into her eyes as he lifted her into the centre of his massive bed. His mouth lifted in another lazy smile. 'Time for me.'

Her panties were already damp from the orgasm he'd wrought from her so easily earlier but with just his words, his expression, her body grew slick and ripe, ready for the possession of his. But it wasn't enough for him, she realised, because he set about kissing every inch of her. He wanted more.

'The scent of you drives me crazy.' Feral hunger sounded in his husky tone. 'I want to taste you too.'

Like an animal. He peeled her panties off and gently stroked her, exposing her to his touch, his tongue, his whole hot, wicked mouth. Gasping, she reached out, caressing the parts of him she could. But he moved down the bed—down her—and licked and nuzzled every centimetre.

'I want to hear you again.' His rhythm was unrelenting, his words driving her wild. 'I want to hear you lose it, Elsie.'

Overwhelmed by the onslaught, she spread her legs wider and arched, exposed in an ultimate invitation. And he ate all she offered. His hands gripped, holding her still as she writhed uncontrollably. Panting and moaning and utterly out of control, she didn't care that she was begging as she came hard for him.

'Now we're here, we have all the time in the world,' he growled.

'We really don't.' Exhausted yet elated, sated yet somehow still starving for more. 'Don't make me wait any longer.'

There was an emptiness inside her. A literal emptiness that she needed him to fill. She wanted him in her arms.

His expression both softened and flickered with satisfaction and amusement. He stroked her hair back from her flushed face. 'I couldn't take my eyes off you that day at the café,' he admitted with a laugh. 'I wanted you here, behind the palace walls.'

He reached in his drawer and pulled out protection.

'You destroyed me before you even spoke,' she mumbled as she watched him prepare himself to take her. 'Before you made me mad. Before you made me laugh. I wanted you and I knew I wasn't going to have you.'

'You can have me now, sweetheart.' He parted her legs so he could push between them. 'And I can have you.'

The hunger in his voice and his gaze made her shiver, made her excitement tighten again. 'Yes. Please.'

The wanton luxuriousness in this most secret of hours made her fearless and bold.

Braced above her, he grazed his knuckles down her body and tested the cleft between her legs once more. 'You're so hot for me,' he groaned.

'Yes.'

He dropped his hips and she felt the first intimate press of him. She was unaccustomed to the weight of any man, let alone a man as tall and muscular as he, but she loved the sense of security—of being pinned in place by him—right at her core. The searing invasion of his rigid body was too slow. She sighed achingly. She wanted him to hold her so close that she couldn't escape. So tight that no one could take her from him. So completely that no one could send her away. Ever. She cried out because that wish was so close—but ultimately impossible.

'Elsie? You with me?' He paused at this most pivotal of moments, his muscles bunching with tension.

'Yes.' The breathiest of whispers as she blinked through the shock and the intensity of her emotions. 'Take me. *Please.*' A raw cry of need.

With a thrust he fully breached both her physical and emotional barriers. She cried out again at the intense, ferocious reality of his possession. He was *hers.* 'Yes,' she sobbed. 'Yes.'

'Elsie.' He huffed a growl as she arched her hips to let him slide that bit further, easier inside her.

He kissed her and moved slowly, taking such care in his caresses, testing her response to his touch, so attuned he adjusted his timing, the depth and intensity of each thrust to make her savour each moment of this discovery…until he aroused her to the point of madness. And he knew—because it was at that exact moment that he grinned at her.

'This what you wanted?' His playfulness returned.

Her heart sang. She wanted to provoke him. In part to hide the emotional intensity of sharing herself with him. She'd not expected this to mean so much. But it did. And she wanted it to be like that for him too. Instinctively she nipped his lower lip the way he'd nipped hers earlier.

'You want it harder?' His eyes sparkled.

'I want *you* out of control.' She was beyond eager to see that, to feel it, to be the cause.

'Be careful what you wish for, Elsie.' A low growl, a glittering tease.

'What are you going to do?' she challenged. 'Tie me down and touch me till I scream?'

He thrust deep inside her and stilled—his eyes drilled as deep as his body. He let his full weight drop on her so she couldn't move. With heart-shuddering ease he clamped his hands around both her wrists and lifted them above her head. There he pinioned them together in the one hand and held them firmly to the mattress. Now she really could barely move.

'I can feel you getting hotter,' he growled. 'And tighter...' He half choked. 'Shouldn't be possible but...*oh*.' He groaned as Elsie quivered with another of those pre-orgasmic clenches she couldn't control.

The slip in his facade when she did that? She realised it was the key to *his* loss of control. She rocked her hips— the slight amount she could—and squeezed on him again.

'Elsie.' A warning this time.

One she was utterly thrilled to ignore. Because while he had her wrists pinned, making her his very willing prisoner, she now lifted her legs and locked them around his hips. And she wasn't letting him go either. He swore with such barely contained savagery, it heated her more. She rocked, using muscles she'd not worked much before, driving him until he took over completely. Lost to the rhythm and the most basic of urges, they pounded together. Her gaze was locked on his, watching the gorgeous agony as he fought to delay the delicious inevitable drowning of reason. Sensation pummelled her as he rolled his hips, pushing harder and deeper and rubbing her right where she needed. As she screamed he released her wrists and hauled her closer. His body shook as his orgasm surged and electrified her own. Hands released, she clutched him so hard she'd leave scratches on his back. But his breath was in her ears. His words. Her name. Over and over.

CHAPTER ELEVEN

Saturday, 02.27 a.m.

ELSIE KEPT HER eyes tightly closed. She didn't want this to end. She didn't want him to lift off her. Her breathlessness wasn't from this weight but the mind-blowing intensity of what she'd just experienced. But she shivered and he immediately moved and reached to pull a covering over them. Only he suddenly stopped.

'Elsie?' A soft query.

She *really* didn't want to open her eyes.

'Elsie.' He sounded uncharacteristically uncertain. 'You bled.'

She'd read that not every woman did the first time they had sex. She'd hoped that would be her, but it seemed luck wasn't on her side this second. 'Please let's not make a big deal of it,' she whispered.

'So…' He drew an audible breath. 'Was that…?' A sigh this time—one that merged with a muttered imprecation. 'Elsie, was that your first time?'

She was mortified. This was a conversation she'd hoped to avoid. She'd hoped he wouldn't have noticed. 'Please don't make it matter more than it does.'

Please don't be angry with me. Please don't ruin what has been so perfect.

'Look at me.' He put a hand on her shoulder, a firm one.

She opened her eyes and saw the burdens he carried—wariness and concern—back in his gaze.

'How much does it matter?' he asked, clearly confused. And determined to understand. 'How much does it matter to *you*?'

Her heart thudded. 'What matters,' she replied softly, 'is that you just gave me the most amazing experience of my life.' She wasn't afraid for him to know that truth. 'And I'll treasure it always.'

'I could have—'

She covered his mouth with her hand and shook her head. 'It was perfect. I didn't want you to stop. Please don't be mad.'

He blinked and pulled her hand away, keeping a tight hold of it in his. 'I'm not mad. I'm just…' He drew in a jagged breath. 'I'm sorry you didn't trust me enough to tell me.'

'I trusted you not to hurt me. To take care with me. And I was right. But personal things…'

'You think what just happened wasn't personal?' he countered. 'Why did you give me this? Why for only a few hours, when I can offer you so little in return?'

'Other people do.'

'Other people haven't saved themselves—' He frowned as if she were a puzzle. 'No boyfriend ever, Elsie?'

His surprise made her smile. 'Did you think I'd been having flings all over the continent?'

'Other people do,' he echoed.

'Yeah, well…' She shrugged.

He gazed at her for another long moment. 'Don't you think you're worth an actual relationship?' He tightened his hold as she tried to tug her hand free of his. 'You don't have them, do you? Even friendships. You move places so frequently I don't think it's possible. You won't put down roots. You won't fight to stay in one place. Why?' He gazed right into her eyes. 'You can tell me anything...you know that, right?'

She knew he meant it. But she shook her head. 'I told you, I trust you with my body, Felipe. But my secrets? My thoughts? What's precious to me in here?' She pressed her hand to her heart. 'I don't trust anyone with any of that.'

'Who broke your trust, Elsie?'

She smiled sadly. 'I'd have to trust you to tell you.'

'I won't tell anyone. I won't see you again past sunrise. What's the risk in telling me?'

'What's the reason to?'

He shifted and leaned back against the headboard. 'Because carrying a heavy burden is hard. It's lonely sometimes.'

The throb in his voice she recognised; they were two lonely, isolated people.

'Maybe sharing it might lighten it,' he muttered. 'Even for a little while.'

Her heart ached. 'As if you ever do that?'

A glimmer of an acknowledgement as he smiled. 'Then let's trade.'

She turned to him. 'You're going to trust me with one of your secrets?'

'You know I trust you.' He wrapped his arms around her and drew her back to rest against his chest.

'Even though you didn't read that security check on me?' she asked, stupidly saddened by that realisation. 'Grab your phone. Do it now. You hardly need detective skills—it's all there in a simple search. Type in my name and it pops up like it happened yesterday. It's never going to go away.'

'I'm not going to do that. I'd rather you told me,' he said huskily. 'Start small. Tell me one little thing.'

She laughed. 'You're never going to stop at wanting just one.'

He brushed his hand through her hair. 'One thing and I'll give you a kiss.'

She leaned into the touch. 'Are you *seducing* me into giving up my secrets?'

'Absolutely.' He kissed the base of her neck.

She pulled back and shot him a look. 'One secret. One orgasm.'

'There's my Elsie, raising the bar. Not afraid to challenge me.' A serious glint entered his eye. 'So why didn't you do that the morning you lost your job?'

Elsie stiffened but Felipe tightened his grip on her ever so slightly and pressed.

'Why didn't you march back to the palace and demand to see me? I know you liked it here. I know you were genuinely fond of Amalia. Why didn't you come and tell me and my interfering security team where to go?'

'Because of *you*.' All that low-burning shame bubbled up. 'I had to leave because of you.'

'Because I—'

'Belonged to someone else.' That possessive fire in her belly had raged so intensely it had been scary.

It was so unlike her. She *wasn't* possessive and she certainly had no right to be possessive of him. Yet there it was. An emotion so strong that she couldn't ignore it—not then, not now. But she'd given him so much already tonight, and he had treated it—her—with infinite care. Which suddenly made it too easy to confess everything.

'If I'd stayed, I would've behaved badly and I wouldn't have cared,' she admitted rawly. Her desire for him made her want to do something wrong and she never wanted to become that person. 'I would have *cheated*. I would have hurt someone else. I *never* wanted to be that person. I always promised I'd never be like—' She broke off and breathed out. 'But the temptation of you?'

He'd made her want to be everything she'd fought hard

not to be. Meeting him had unleashed the part within her that didn't give a damn—that was selfish and hungry and uncaring of anything other than getting what she wanted. Like her father and her brother. People who took what they wanted without any scruples.

'So you left without saying goodbye, without fighting. Because you would've become my lover even though you thought I was engaged to someone else?' His chest rose and fell rapidly.

She closed her eyes, mortified. It was a truth she'd not admitted even to herself until now. 'I didn't even know if you wanted—'

'You know I did.' A husky breath. 'I wanted you desperately but I couldn't, and not because of that damned betrothal. But because of the risk to you. I come with a whole country. Paparazzi and a life so public you can never reclaim your privacy. My mother. Amalia's mother. It was terrible for them both. I don't want that for anyone and certainly not you.' He sighed. 'But this now? You deserve so much more than a few hours…'

'I don't. I really don't.'

'Why do you say that? What happened that was so awful?' He watched her for a moment before asking carefully. 'Can you tell me what's on the video?'

She looked at the suppressed concern in his eyes and realised she had to put him at ease. 'It's not…it's not any kind of sex tape and I wasn't physically hurt or anything… It was a personal moment but not *that* kind of personal.'

He released a long, careful breath.

'I played the mandolin for my mother,' she said simply.

His gaze narrowed but he didn't realise what she'd told him. What it meant. She smiled at him. 'I learned the violin for years, but I found the mandolin in her wardrobe one day when I was clearing it out. It belonged to her great-grandmother.'

'It's old, then.'

She nodded. 'I don't know how she put up with me picking out tunes by ear painfully slowly when I first started. I guess it was a distraction.'

'Because she was sick.'

'Cancer, yes. It took a long time.'

'That must have been hard.'

She hadn't spoken of this in so long. But Felipe was quiet and never going to tell. He trusted her, which allowed her to trust him. 'I looked after her. I was happy to. I dropped out of the course I was studying, lost touch with most of my friends. But I did my creative projects at home while caring for her. I loved music, art, baking...silly stuff.'

'Not silly.'

She smiled at him gratefully. 'It's something we shared.'

'Where was your father? Your brother?' He frowned. 'Were they—?'

'My brother, Caleb, was at university. He's older by a couple of years. My father worked. He struggled. Was absent.' She frowned. 'Actually he wasn't great. He cheated on Mum. He promised me it was a one-off thing. That he'd been stressed. I'd thought it was just...he was lonely and it was hard with Mum having been sick for so long. But it wasn't one lapse. There were times earlier I'd just been too young and naive to be aware of them. My mother protected me from all that. I'd thought that everything was fine. But he was a cheat in every way possible.'

Felipe was still.

'Mum's illness worsened. There was this new medication she could have but it was expensive. My brother set up a crowdfunding page, you know? I made some things even to sell to raise the money. And we got some in. Quite a bit. But one day right near the end...' She closed her eyes. 'I'd written a song for Mum. It was just for her. From me to her. She was so frail and I didn't know...'

He stiffened. 'Elsie?'

'I didn't know Caleb secretly recorded me the first time I played it for her,' she whispered. The only time. 'He uploaded it to the site—to solicit more donations. It got attention. It got a lot of money. Really quickly. Far more than we needed because by then…' It had come too late for her mother. Elsie still felt so cold, so hurt to think of it. 'Dad and Caleb said they were setting up a foundation to raise more money for other sufferers. I believed them—Caleb was studying accounting, you know? But next thing Caleb arrives in an expensive new car. My dad has a new watch… and Mum had died.'

'Oh, Elsie.' His arms tightened about her.

'I finally figured it out. I went to the police. Testified against them. They faced fraud charges and were sentenced to prison. Caleb's out now. Turned out Dad had been embezzling from his business as well so he's still in there.'

'And you'd lost not only your mother.' He gazed into her eyes. 'But your music.'

'I couldn't play at all for a long time. It was only…'

'Here.'

Yes, on Silvabon. In the sunshine, sitting at the back of the café on a break, looking at the sapphire-blue water. She'd finally begun to defrost and to hear fragments of melody in her mind. Her music had returned. Some of it, at least. And then Amalia had appeared and she'd needed it too.

'I can't play that song at all any more,' Elsie whispered.

It had been taken from her. The precious moment between her and her mother hadn't just been commoditised, it had been used to *con* people out of their money. And as a result, *she'd* been abused in more than one way. Something that had been secret and special had been exposed for public scrutiny and, ultimately, mockery. The glowing compliments had turned as the truth of the money funnelling had emerged. Critics of her composition had shredded her. But it hadn't been intended for anyone else. She wasn't a performer like that. Maybe it had been a little sweet, but not 'falsely saccharine'—like the scathing assessments.

Calculated to pluck your heart strings and open your purse.

'I didn't know he'd recorded it.' She blinked fiercely. 'I didn't know he was going to use it like that.'

'That was the violation of your trust, Elsie,' Felipe said roughly. 'That was the betrayal right there.'

Shame filled her when she thought of it. Shame and such devastation.

'They stole that moment from you,' he muttered. 'I'm so sorry.'

She swiped away the tear. 'Please don't watch it.'

'I won't.'

'Promise?'

'Yes.'

The online pile-on had been horrific and the face-to-face vitriol? Even from people she'd thought were friends. People she'd thought would have her back and believe her. It had made her so wary of other people now. Because it was still there—online, as fresh as the day it had been posted. It would be there for ever.

'I turned my own father and my own brother in, but other people didn't believe that I didn't know. They all doubted me. And my father was so angry when he'd found out I'd gone to the police. He tried to smash my mandolin. That's why the case is broken. He didn't know I'd taken the instrument out and that was only by chance. That's the only reason it survived.'

He'd tried to destroy the last thing she had of her mother's. The thing most precious to her. All in a vitriolic rage.

'We'd never had much money and suddenly people were giving buckets of it. Dad was so greedy. He thought it was a way of getting more without having to work for it. By lying to people.'

'He lied to you too.'

Yeah. He'd monetised what should have been a bitter-sweet, heart-rending but precious memory. Put it out there for people to judge and mock.

'It didn't matter that I'd been honest. Everyone had judged me anyway. Sometimes I think it would have been easier to say nothing.'

'Doing the right thing takes courage.'

'Was it the right thing though? Was it worth all that upheaval? It didn't make anything better. It didn't mean those people were *repaid*.' She was mortified that they'd lost money.

'But they saw that justice was done. That matters. We need to see that. We need to know there are good people in the world.' Felipe regarded her solemnly. 'But you always worry how they'll react if, when, they find out?'

'No one likes a nark, right?' She glanced at him. 'No one believes that I couldn't have known sooner. How could I not have known? I even made things to auction for the fund-raiser. I was so *stupid*.'

'Not stupid. Sweet and sincere. And you are not respon-sible for the choices your father and brother made.'

'Family sticks together. Family doesn't rat each other out. They disowned me completely,' she said. 'My father's family won't forgive me.'

'There's nothing to forgive, Elsie. You did the right thing. You shouldn't be paying for their mistakes.'

But she was. 'My mother was an only child so there's no one there. And all my old friends didn't just doubt me, they didn't believe me. I don't belong to anyone or to any place. Not any more.'

'So now you're alone and now you don't trust anyone.' He swept his hand through her hair. 'I won't let you down.'

'There's no time for that to happen.' She tried to smile but found she couldn't.

His arm around her waist tightened. 'There's nothing wrong with wanting touch and connection. You shouldn't ever feel as if you shouldn't have that.' He sighed. 'And you should have so much more than this.'

'I'm scared I'd want *too* much,' she whispered harshly. 'If I let it go, let it consume me? I could be the most jealous witch.' She already was. 'That's what scares me—being as selfish and as greedy as them.'

'You wouldn't. That fear is from the threat of losing it, right? That it was going to be taken away from you. Another time, another place, another...' He whistled in a raspy breath. 'You'll find the security that you deserve. You're nothing like your father Elsie. You're not dishonest. You're not a cheat. You didn't. And you wouldn't ever. You need to forgive yourself. You did nothing wrong. They let you down and they shouldn't have. But you shouldn't suffer any punishment. You should have a home and a job and a family—whatever you want, with someone you want. You should have it all.'

But not with him. With some other guy some other time. And that thought? *No.*

She was exposed and she needed—*escape*. She appreciated Felipe's sentiment. She didn't even regret telling him about her family, but she slid from the bed, taking the top sheet with her. Because she couldn't stay in his arms telling him all her secrets. Soon she'd be begging him never to let her go. This wasn't that and never would be.

'Where are you going?' he asked.

'I'm annoyed with you.'

He sat up, startled. 'Why?'

'You should have it all too.' She shot him a look. 'You think that's possible for me, but not for yourself.'

His jaw compressed. 'I'm not in the same position as

most people, Elsie. Not even most other royals. There's *only* me.'

'Is that what your grandfather said?' Honestly, she didn't much like the sound of the old man.

'I'm the last one.'

She snorted. 'That's impossible. The King is dead, long live the King, right?'

He drew a breath. 'Not yet. There's no clear successor. It's on me to declare one.'

'Or have an heir of your own—your own children.'

'Not happening.'

She looked back at him, realising he was utterly serious. 'So when you die…'

'The monarchy will become extinct. Our elected representatives will have full power. We'll become a democratic republic.'

She gaped. 'But Silvabon loves its monarchy.' They loved *him*. 'They won't let it happen. Won't let some distant cousin crawl out of the woodwork, claim the crown and cause all sorts of chaos.'

'Not if I say there's no crown anymore. Not if I've relinquished the excessive power the Crown currently has.'

That was what he planned to do? Elsie was shocked. 'But you could choose to appoint someone—'

'No.' He flashed a tight smile. 'I'm not declaring a successor.'

No children? No successor? 'Because you think it's a poisoned chalice?' She frowned, not understanding him at all. 'But you're so popular. Everyone loves you and you do *all* those things.' She'd seen it in all the coverage—the effort he went to for his country, promoting his people, the causes. 'You *love* it here.'

'I do,' he said simply. 'I want nothing but the best for Silvabon. And I will do nothing but my best *for* it.'

'Then to leave the country without a monarch when it's

such a part of...?' She slowly shook her head. 'Can nobody better *you*, Felipe?'

A husky, bitter laugh. 'You don't agree with my plan?'

'No. I don't.' She slowly climbed the curling wooden staircase. 'You're so arrogant, Felipe. Can no one else help you? No one keep you company to help shoulder the burden and keep you warm?'

'I have too much power.' His gaze narrowed. 'You don't understand what—'

'Oh, I understand. The great King Felipe. Determined to be an isolated martyr to the end...'

His jaw dropped and she laughed at the expression in his eyes.

'Lie there and listen to the truth, Felipe. If you're so trapped, I guess you're stuck there?'

She was suddenly angry with *both* of their circumstances and she didn't want to waste any more of their precious minutes dwelling on things that couldn't—or wouldn't—be changed. She could have it *all* tonight but *only* tonight. And it seemed it was the same for him.

Felipe stared in shock as this *nymph* ascended the curling wooden staircase with a dramatic flair he should've anticipated sooner. His body was hard and his heart? Racing.

'King Felipe,' she said softly. 'The man who sacrifices everything for his country.'

'What are you *doing*?' His heart wouldn't stop pounding and her fiery reaction was confusing the hell out of him.

'I've had enough *talking*.'

Oh. But he was hurt for her—for what her family had done. For her losses. But now? Now she'd flipped on him and she was full of fury and strength and he wanted her. 'Then come back down here.'

He'd been the one to scoff at virgin princess brides, yet she'd been innocent and her naive assumption revealed she was a believer in fairy tales. This wasn't going to be one. But he also knew she understood that. Hence, *this*.

Now she'd hit the balcony and she peeked over the railing. Her skin flushed. 'Oh. Okay.'

'What?'

'It's a really great view.'

'Is it?' He couldn't resist stretching out on the bed for her.

'Are you putting on a show for me?'

Amusement lit him up all over. 'Would you like me to?'

She glanced down his body. 'I think that could be pretty good.'

'Then absolutely, I will give you a show.' He stretched wide then ran his hands across his chest before sliding them south, massaging his thighs, then…

'Maybe you should stop…' Her voice wobbled.

'Not sure I can.' He could see she was excited. Hell, *he* was excited. To teach her more. To make it better. In this one way, this one night maybe he could…but how could it get better than what they'd shared just before?

'You'd better,' she called down to him.

'Or what?'

'Or…' She bit her lip, a gesture not of wariness but of sensuality. 'I'll have to make you pay.'

He was absolute toast. She was going to toy with him and he was going to let her. She watched, fascinated, as he slowly stretched his hand back onto the mattress.

'Good.' She stood at the top of the staircase and slowly let the sheet fall from her body until she was as naked as he.

She was watching him with a fixated, glazed look and he knew she was dreaming of what she was about to do to him.

'I think you'd better get ready for me,' she said.

Felipe could hardly don protection, his fingers were trembling so much.

She sashayed down the stairs, back to him. She didn't ask with words, but discovered with her hands his most sensitive places. He liked it when she made the decisions, had liked it when she'd lain back and let him decide everything too. He was used to people paying attention to him—waiting for his command, seeking his advice, doing his bidding. But this was different. This was Elsie taking time to know him. Taking what she wanted. Their push and pull, give and take were intoxicating. He could boss her in a way he'd not dared with another only because she liked to flip and push it back on him. So he let it happen now—let her tease him. Her concentration was the sexiest thing he'd ever seen. There was an almost gauche generosity to her actions. But she was doing this not only to please him but to sate her own curiosity as well. Not because she thought she had to pleasure him, but because she truly wanted to. He felt utterly honoured and it was a gift he didn't take for granted. He wanted to gift her more in return and he couldn't hold back any more. He reached for her.

'For once in your life, let someone else take charge,' she hissed at him. 'Hold onto the headboard.'

He stared at her. 'Is that an order?'

'Absolutely.'

His muscles sharpened. 'You know I'll get you back for this.'

'I'm aware. And I'll accept that as my due reward.' A sweet, sweet whisper.

He could hardly breathe, and he couldn't release the board above his head now. If he did, he'd clutch her so hard he'd bruise her. His need for her was white-hot and blinding. His arms burned. His whole body was tense—as if he were on the damned rack and being stretched—just waiting for her to claim him.

Elsie stared down at him. Felipe was a beautiful, beautiful man and tonight he was hers. She released everything—the kind of hunger she'd never allowed to flow. That truly she'd never felt before. All-consuming, yet so playful.

'Hold on,' she muttered, while holding *him* her prisoner by straddling his powerful thighs. But she didn't take him yet. She teased and took him in her hands.

'I am,' he gritted. 'I will.'

She felt liberated and free and giddy with desire.

'Elsie,' he groaned. 'What are you doing?'

'I'm playing you. Do you like it?'

'Your fingers are magical.'

She giggled breathlessly. 'Hardly.'

'Trust me, they're amazing.'

'You want me to play you some more?'

'Mmm-hmm.' He strained into her hand.

'Oh.' Pleased, she shimmied closer. 'What other pretty sounds can we extract from you?'

'Pretty sounds?' he gasped with mock outrage. A groan swiftly followed.

She laughed. The power of this, the play, was everything. The smile he sent her, the growls of delight, another groan of exquisite agony. She loved it all.

'Elsie.'

That was what she liked best. His desperate, helpless muttering of her name. She blew on his hot skin, gently exploring him. He was her perfect instrument, big and strong, and he bent to her touch and arched into her hands, making her feel all-powerful. She liked it so much she hummed her own pleasure in seeking out his.

'You're killing me.'

'I think you're very much alive, Felipe.'

'Ride me.' He swore again and thrust his hips upwards. 'Ride me.'

An order, but she chose to take it as a plea. Slowly she sank onto him—adoring the glazed look in his eyes as he stared from her flushed face, down her body.

'Not sore?' He gasped desperately.

'I'm fine,' she assured him. 'More than fine.'

His obvious relief made her bolder and sink deeper, even more pleasurably. That was when he struck. He released the headboard and sat up swiftly. Clasping her to his chest, he kissed her and kissed her and he didn't let her go. Not until she'd come again. And again. Not even when she finally collapsed and succumbed to sleep.

CHAPTER TWELVE

Saturday, 04.37 a.m.

FELIPE WOKE, TENSION rippling through his body as he realised how many hours they'd lost. He needed time to stop.
He didn't want his valet arriving in an hour. He didn't want
to send her away. He wasn't ready.

'I fell asleep,' he muttered. 'Damn.'

She lifted her head from where it was nestled in the side
of his neck and drowsily smiled. 'You needed it. You have
a big day ahead. You don't want to be so tired you're slur-
ring your words in front of the world.'

He didn't want to think about the world right now. But
there was no stopping the reality speeding towards them.

'Your fellow plane passengers are going on a tour at
nine,' he said, trying to lighten his own mood. 'So I'm not
totally wasting their precious time with my unreasonable
detainment of them.'

Her ice-blue eyes softened. 'A tour?'

'I'll have you know we got a one hundred per cent strike
rate on the offer.'

'I bet you did. I would've said yes to a tour like that.'

'I'll give you a private tour right now if you like,' he said
huskily. 'The best Silvabon has to offer.'

Her eyebrows arched. 'The best?'

'The *very* best.' He threw back the sheet and forced himself out of bed. 'And just so you know, I'm *never* redecorating this room.' He lifted his finger. 'That viewing balcony stays. In fact, I can think of some enhancements.'

'Enhancements?' She laughed. 'And are you going to impregnate your wife in front of an audience like the good old days?'

He shot her a look. 'You know I'm not going to have a wife to impregnate.'

She shook her head disbelievingly.

'Stop trying to marry me off,' he said. 'I'll release most of the power the Crown currently has over the next few years. Then I'll grow old and slowly become nothing more than a figurehead. After I'm gone this place will become a museum.'

'It should never be a museum. It should be filled with life and footsteps and laughter.' She slapped down the plans he'd taken so long to prepare. 'Why not become a figurehead *family*, doing positive things for the country?'

Oh, she did still believe in fairy tales. 'The personal cost is too great,' he said honestly.

'And your decision to remain alone isn't a personal cost?'

'It's not for *me*.' He smiled now. 'I've known no different.'

She stared into his eyes. 'Your children would know no different from the royal life you create for them.'

'I'm *never* having…' He stiffened. 'I'm not doing that to them—being born into such a burden? That's not fair.'

'Yet that's what happened to you and you're still here and you even told me you love it. So why wouldn't they?'

Because no one else *had* stayed. Because he couldn't take the risk of their unhappiness.

'Maybe if there was a solid support structure?' Elsie offered tentatively. 'Maybe, yeah, release some power so they were more free to do the work they're passionate about? Maybe then it could be okay?'

'It's not that easy.'

'Nothing great ever is. But wouldn't it be worth trying? To have a family flourish in this crazy huge palace? How wonderful would that be…? Surely you could insist on more balance? Royals in other places seem to.'

Seem to was the thing, but protocol was ingrained and *people* were too complicated and couldn't be stretched too far. *He* couldn't do balanced—it wasn't in his genes. They were all or nothing and he couldn't put anyone else through it or ask them to make such sacrifice.

'Real life isn't that simple.' He drew breath, desperate to end the fantasy she was tempting him with. 'Come on, hurry up.'

They were losing too much time.

'I'm not sure if this has registered with you, but I'm naked right now.'

'It has registered, actually.' He grinned. 'I like it.'

'Yeah, well, if you want us to sneak around the palace like rebellious teenagers, then you might want to find us something to wear. I'll probably get caught on the security cameras and I don't need any more unflattering footage up on the Internet.'

With an exasperated growl he went into his dressing room and returned wearing black shorts and holding a white tee shirt. He ripped the tag off it and handed it to her.

'You have a wardrobe full of new clothes?'

'You already know I'm spoilt. No need to judge harder.'

'I'm not. I'm delighted. It's very handy this second.' She slid the tee on; it hung on her like a dress.

He stared at her. 'You can make literally anything look good.'

She flushed. 'Stop charming me.'

The only thing he wanted to stop right now was time and that was impossible even for him. 'Let's go.'

'Where?'

'There are over a thousand rooms in this castle, did you know that?' He winked at her. 'That's not counting the secret ones.'

'A *thousand* rooms and you choose that theatre to sleep in?' She laughed as she followed him down the corridor. 'Honestly, Felipe.'

'You have to admit it has its benefits…'

'Your *enhancements* should include silk ropes. You could hang them from the balcony railing,' she provoked him slyly. 'Work on a naked aerial circus act…'

Silk ropes? He turned back and saw the playful gleam in her eyes. 'That's a stunning idea.'

'Thank you.' Elsie almost had to run to keep up with him. The corridor was narrow and barely lit and had lost all the luxury palace feel. This part was pure hand-hewn stone. He paused by an oak door.

'What's this?' she asked, aware of the vitality and anticipation in his gorgeous eyes.

'My secret. It was a trade, right? I'm looking forward to my reward orgasm already.' He opened the door.

'Your—' She broke off and stared at the view he'd just exposed. The door led to a ledge on the edge of a cliff. The sapphire sea gleamed metres below. 'Don't tell me you—'

'Cliff-jump? Absolutely.'

Her heart raced. 'I thought you weren't a risk taker. You're jumping into the open sea and have to avoid those rocks.' She glanced down at the water and then back at him worriedly. 'They're big rocks, Felipe.'

'And I've managed to avoid them every day for the last decade. Trust me. It looks harder and scarier than it is. It's actually easy. You game?'

She really wasn't. But she wasn't going to say no. This was their one night—and it was barely light. She could have a few more moments. 'Are there sharks?'

He chuckled. 'Hold my hand, I'll get us into the right spot.'

She held his hand. Hard. The water was a shock and she let go of him, gasping as she surfaced.

'I didn't think it would be this *cold*!' She glared at him indignantly when he laughed. 'I thought it would be like a bath. The beach is so much warmer than this.'

'Because the water here is deeper.' He swam towards her with energy and a huge smile. 'And it's very early. And you were hot from being in bed.'

'I'm not hot now.'

'Sure you are. That shirt has gone devastatingly transparent.' He stretched out his arm and tugged her nearer. 'This way.'

They swam a short distance past the rock and she realised there was a cave entrance tucked below where they'd jumped.

Felipe put both palms on the rock and vaulted from the water, turning to extend a hand to help her out. 'Come on, Elsie, welcome to my dungeon.'

'Oh. *Wow.*'

There were worn stone stairs and as she climbed them the hidden cave's interior fully came into view. And when he flicked a switch?

'Wow!'

How was there electricity down here? She wriggled her toes. How were there large smooth marble tiles beneath her feet that were warm? And was that round pool built into the back of the small cave *steaming*?

'The thermal water is piped to give the cave some heat.'

She knew there were hot springs on other parts of the island and a public facility in the centre of the city, but to have his private pool?

'From here the palace has private access to the open sea—as long as you know how to get past those big rocks,' he explained. 'Originally it was rumoured the King's treats were smuggled in under cover of darkness—straight from the sea.'

'Treats? You mean like cigars and brandy? *Women?*'

'It's never been verified.' He smiled. 'Then they started the story that the dungeons were down here. That there are torture chambers and that people disappeared from here. It was a plan to keep people afraid and away. But, in fact, only the King's most trusted warriors were permitted in. This was their place to heal battle wounds—to rest and re-cuperate in privacy and hewn comfort.'

She touched the stone. 'So it's really old.'

'The worn mosaics didn't give it away?' He laughed. 'It was abandoned for a long time. I came here as a kid. Then after my father left, I got it cleaned up. Put in some lighting.'

'Because you have a spare chandelier or two lying round,' she teased lightly. 'Not to mention a few nice rugs and fancy cushions.'

'We added in a fridge and a little oven as well.'

'You can use an oven? You amaze me.' She chuckled. But the thought of him restoring this place intrigued her. When there were over a thousand rooms to choose from in that palace, he'd still wanted his own space. 'Your grandfather didn't know you jumped off that cliff, did he?'

'No.'

'Free-diving for pearls, cliff-jumping to access caves. You love the water. Rebel Felipe.'

He shrugged slightly. 'Only my valet and my top secu-rity men know. And now you.'

She was incredibly touched about that—too touched. She needed to deflect the emotion that suddenly surged. 'They helped carry the fridge?'

He laughed softly. 'Yeah.'

She studied the bookcase that was tucked beside the clev-erly concealed fridge and oven. 'It's literally your man cave.'

But there were no giant screens. Just books and an exercise area on the other side of the pool. This revealed such a secret side to him that she couldn't resist exploring. The books were fiction mostly—crime and fantasy, witches and dragons and great battles. Several looked as if they'd fallen into that great big bath more than once. It seemed he appreciated imagination—and she knew he had a playful one of his own. This place was his private escape.

'You bathe here every morning?'

'Sometimes in the evening as well.'

Alone. Because he was locked in his palace—a young king burdened by responsibility, expectation and isolation. It saddened her. 'You never had wild teen parties down here?'

'No orgies either, before you ask. And I know you were going to ask.'

'Then what's with the massage oil?' She picked up a small bottle and waggled it at him.

'That's from when I had a sore calf from running too much once.' He lifted a shoulder. 'The water has healing properties. The trick is alternating the cold sea with the thermal spring. Which we need to do now because you're shivering.'

Shivering not just from cold, but from deepening heartache. She turned to hide it and climbed the curling stairs into the perfect pool tucked at the back of the cave. The warm water soothed her sensitive skin. She studied the beautiful veined patterns on the ancient marble tiles as the chandelier cast a golden glow in the gloomy space. The bubbling of the endless spring echoed softly against the rocky walls. She knew the islands cradled a wealth of natural resources but this was pure magic.

She glanced over and saw he was watching her with a softly wicked smile.

'Do you like my torture chamber, my darling?' he teased.

Like it? She never wanted to leave it. But she couldn't

admit that. 'It's not bad, though I think you've wrecked the vibe with those kettle-bell weights.'

Felipe chuckled and pulled her towards him. 'Down here no one can hear you scream.'

But she couldn't scream because he was kissing her. And when he kissed her, time stopped. She *never* wanted him to stop kissing her.

Somehow they were out of that pool. She lay in a tumble of soft cushions and he massaged her with the oil and she was thankful he'd brought protection in his swim shorts. The scent of cedar and sandalwood and bay filled her— earthy and fresh and heated. Afterwards, warmth from the heated stone rose through the rug where she lay sleepily. But through the rocky fissure masking the cave's entrance she saw the glimpse of sky lighten and the sea begin to sparkle.

Time threatened. 'Thank you for sharing your secret place with me,' she said.

She was beautiful, lying on his rug, gleaming in the golden light. Felipe wanted to demand she stay for ever. His secret treat, hidden down here for always. But that was impossible and he couldn't stop time any more than he could stop that thermal spring or those waves hitting the cliffs.

'You're frowning.' She smoothed his forehead. 'Are you nervous for the coronation?'

He shook his head. 'I'm used to it.'

'But this is really big.'

'Are you trying to *make* me nervous?' He laughed.

But she turned those eyes on him. 'Don't you ever wish you could just get in a boat and head out of here?'

'Disappear in the middle of the night?' He glanced to that gap where he could see the sea. 'No. I would never do that to Silvabon. Not after my father.'

The truth of his abdication was a long-kept secret but now his father and grandfather were gone. There was no need to protect them any more. Felipe was tired of protecting them. 'We woke up one morning and he was missing. That's why my security chief is so paranoid now. He missed my father's escape. Grandfather was apoplectic that he could've left without anyone knowing.'

'You mean he literally ran away? Like, "escaped the dungeon" sort of ran away?'

Felipe nodded. 'He left a two-line apology on a piece of palace paper. He didn't want to be stuck here. Both Grandfather and my mother knew he was restless, it wasn't a complete surprise to them—only that he got out with such secrecy and skill.'

'Was it a surprise to you?'

He stilled. 'I knew they weren't happy. I didn't know about her.'

'Amalia's mother?'

'She was a musician at a club in town. A single woman with a baby. You can imagine how that went down with my grandfather. And the media made it so much worse. They ignored her talent, belittling her as a trampy showgirl. She was vilified. As was my mother—the frigid wife who couldn't satisfy her husband. They're always particularly harsh on women. I don't want that for Amalia. Or anyone.'

'Where's Amalia's father?'

'Long gone. Apparently he didn't want to be a dad and left before she was born.'

'So Amalia understands what it's like to be abandoned too.'

Felipe's heart puckered at the realisation. 'Yeah, I guess she does.'

He had more in common with his stepsister than he'd ever have imagined.

Elsie nodded. 'I didn't know your father just disappeared.'

'My grandfather kept the story quiet while he tried to

bully him into coming home.' He sighed. 'But that didn't work. My father had got far enough away to make his escape complete. And when everyone found out? The news cycle fed off it for months—demanding answers that were never given. They still bring it up regularly.'

'And your mother?'

Was destroyed. 'Went to one of the smaller islands.'

'Did you go with her?'

'I was needed here. I was now next in line to the Crown and Grandfather had a lot to teach me. They decided the investiture was the best way to change the narrative from the runaway royal escaping the tyrant King...'

She looked troubled. 'You were separated from both your parents.'

'That's not as miserable as it might sound. They were wrapped up in their own affairs.' He felt bitterness flicker. 'I couldn't console my mother anyway.'

'You shouldn't have had to. She should have been here for you.'

'Grandfather blamed her for not keeping my father happy. She couldn't handle his anger and she's never got over it.' She'd been betrayed so publicly, blamed by his grandfather, rejected. Felipe had hidden his own anxiety, loneliness, heartache from her. 'I was old enough to handle it. Besides, I wasn't the target of his anger. I was his hope for the future.'

'But she's not coming to your coronation today?'

'I told you, she vowed never to set foot in the palace again.'

'Not at all—when you were younger?' Elsie asked. 'Not even now your grandfather is dead?'

'She can't live in the public eye, Elsie,' he said firmly. 'Her nerves can't take it and I don't expect her to. We talk on the phone. I visit her...'

'You do all the work for everyone. All the caretaking.

Even for the country itself,' Elsie murmured. 'Did your father ever return?'

'He wasn't allowed. He'd made his choice. It wasn't here.' It wasn't him. 'They went to Canada. The three of them built a new life. A private one.'

'So he didn't come back.' She leaned closer. 'Did you ever visit them?'

He glanced down. 'That would have been a security risk. Plus, Grandfather didn't want my father influencing me away from my duty.'

Her eyes widened. 'You never saw your father again?'

'Not in person. No.' Felipe watched the small patch of sky beyond the rocks brighten with a sinking feeling. 'I think he was happy over there. That's why it's hard for me to have brought Amalia here. I know this isn't what they'd have wanted for her.'

'It sounds like he missed you,' Elsie said. 'He obviously talked to Amalia about you a lot.'

Yeah. He was still getting his head around that. It felt both good and bitter and just…sad.

'That's why I won't give her an honorary title or make her a princess. It's important she knows she can do anything, be anything, go anywhere once she's of age.'

'But you'll still teach her to dive, right?'

Honestly, he was still a little thrown by that request.

'She obviously chose those pearls last night because she'd heard about them—and you—from your dad,' Elsie said. 'You must have missed him too.'

He bent his head. He did not want to think about this, let alone *feel*.

'I know you feel an immense duty to protect her,' Elsie said. 'But she also needs family, Felipe. *Everyone* does.'

'Family isn't always awesome. You know that.'

'But *you're* pretty awesome. And you and Amalia could

be a small but strong family, right? Can't families be fixed sometimes?' she said wistfully. 'Can't we rebuild them?'

It was too late. And it was too complicated. Because there were elements in his life that no one else should have to shoulder. He'd seen how much it damaged those who didn't have the desire to handle it.

'I'm sorry, Felipe. They weren't here for you. None of them. Not for *you*.' She sighed, her frown deepening as she tried to understand. 'Your parents' marriage wasn't arranged, was it?'

'No, it was a love match that didn't last. That's why my grandfather was so keen for me to keep the betrothal with Sofia. He thought a political alliance between two professional royals would be better.'

'And you kept it up to keep him happy. Until?' She pressed her lips together.

'Until I realised it wasn't fair on Sofia or anyone else. Not even me.' He was better off on his own.

'Not going to lie, Felipe, the Javier dude doesn't sound like he was all that great.'

Felipe tried to laugh. Tried to explain. 'He wasn't that bad, you know? For a long time he was a good king. And he wanted what was best for everyone. For the country. But then he got older and he was more sick than we realised, I guess. He was losing his grip on his mind so he tightened his grip elsewhere even more. He got really difficult in the final years. Some parts of his mind faded, while he fixated on certain things.' On lineage. On the Crown. On Felipe. 'The courtiers wanted to keep his cognitive decline under wraps for as long as possible because of my age and the risk of political instability. If others thought the King was incapacitated in any way…' It was why he was going to clear the bulk of the King's power and change the constitution. 'I took on most of the public engagements. It's why I'm in that ridiculous bedroom. That historic wing of the palace was the easiest to make most secure. We converted his rooms into a full facility hospital suite and created an enrichment area to try to slow the advancing dementia...'

'You cared for him.'

'Of course. I had to stay here for him. I was the only one left who could. And he was a good man. Things were just different. He'd had a happy marriage. His wife had died young and he wanted stability for the family and he didn't get it. He didn't understand my father. Honestly, I didn't either...'

'How old were you when he got ill?'

'Almost twenty.'

'So soon after your father left? You were so young. And you were trapped here.' She gazed at him. 'Not just by duty and obligation. You were *literally* trapped.'

No, he wasn't. 'I was being *protected*. And then I was protecting him. And my country.'

'Felipe.' She shook her head. 'No. What they did to you?' She drew in a shaky breath. 'When did you last leave—last take a holiday?'

'It's not possible to leave for any length of time. I couldn't let them down. They need me to be here.' Defensiveness rose. He'd never allowed himself to consider leaving for longer.

'Is that what they said?'

His aides, sure. Over and over. 'I was the strong one who had what it took. I was the only one left. Grandfather was counting on me. Not just Grandfather. The whole country.'

'But they left you alone to face everything—including him. Alone, Felipe. They made you become this...'

He stiffened. 'This *what*?'

'Isolated guy. You've had to be so strong. And silent.' She shook her head. 'I don't think anyone should be forced to stay somewhere. Or forced to leave. You should have had *choices*—the freedom to come and go as you wished. To become the person you wanted to be. To have *all* the things. Not just the palace and the power and the people who run at the lift of your little finger. But you should have the family support—the *fun*, companionship, the fulfilment of private and personal dreams…'

He tried to smile at her—to lighten this because it was too intense. Private and personal dreams? 'Don't pity me, Elsie. I already warned you.'

'That you'll use it to ask all the things of me?' She leaned forward. 'Then do it, Felipe. Ask me anything. I would do anything for you. Not because you're the King—because it's *you*.'

He froze, overcome by a desire so strong, so impossible. 'Don't…'

He didn't mean to mutter it. Didn't mean to show how much her words affected him. How much he couldn't handle this. Her sweet generosity? Didn't she know he would take *everything* if he could? Not just sex. She was afraid of being selfish, she had nothing on *his* latent greed.

She read his tension. 'You can tell me *anything* you like. The best. The worst. Just tell me the truth.'

'It wasn't that awful, Elsie.'

'Wasn't it? Are you not *alone*, Felipe?'

He heard the note in her voice. Yeah, she knew how hard that could be—not all the time, but sometimes in those moments when he wasn't quite strong enough… It could be so hard.

'I'm not someone else you have to be strong for and take care of,' she said earnestly. 'Not someone you have to protect.'

'Is that what you think I do?' He tried to pull together some anger. Some humour. Anything to hide from the raw honesty he'd accidentally revealed.

'You did for your grandfather. And your father—you took on his burden, allowing him to escape. And your mother too. Now Amalia. You don't need to be that person for me as well. I mean it. I've been through fire and out the other side. I'm burnished. Tough. I can survive anything. You don't need to protect me. Certainly not here. Definitely not now. So I repeat, you don't need to be strong for me.'

'What should I be, then?'

'You don't have to be *anything* for me. You can just be. You. As you are.'

As you are. He stretched out a hand and ran his finger along the base of her beautiful neck, feeling the delicate notch between her collarbones.

She leaned into his touch, letting him feel her vulnerability and her vitality. 'I mean it.'

'I know you do.' His chest ached. 'Then let's just be.'

No pressure. No expectation. No. It was impossible. And there was no point in talking. It wasn't going to change anything. It was only wasting the precious little time they had left. Only making him feel unsettled.

He kissed her, desperately seeking the mindlessness of physical pleasure. Only it wasn't mindless. There was still thought. Still feeling that went so much deeper than skin on skin. She offered something that couldn't co-exist in his world—a fantasy that could never be real. His country was in his blood. Work was everything and was utterly inextricable from who he was. *What* he was was *who* he was. There was no separating the royal from the man. The duty from the body. But he would never be able to come down here again without thinking of her. Without remembering her silken heat. Without reliving this—the last time they'd made love.

She was shaking but he was too. Both were desperate to go fast, to go slow, to conquer time. They would go back inside the palace. He'd get into his robes and she would leave for good. But right now the emotion in her eyes? He couldn't stand seeing the emotion in her eyes.

'Stop thinking,' he ordered. 'Stop feeling sorry for me.'
Stop feeling anything for me. Suddenly—too late—he
realised just what a mistake he'd made.

'How do I do that?' Elsie asked brokenly, torn apart by the
sensual, emotional onslaught.

How could she possibly stop thinking? How could she
hide her heartbreak knowing, breathing…this was the last
time she would hold him? How could she convey everything she was feeling?

It was only so intense because it was the last time, right?
She tried to rationalise the ache in her heart. It couldn't
happen again.

But it wasn't that. It was more.

Only she couldn't tell him. He'd just told her not to. He
wouldn't accept it. And he was far more vulnerable than she
ever could've imagined. His father had left him. So had his
mother. While his grandfather pressed the weight of a nation's future onto his shoulders—and then became an additional burden on Felipe himself.

He growled, frustration evident in the lines bracketing
his mouth, in the tension in his limbs. They kissed with
such longing. So close there was no room left any more for
thought. Only feeling. Only letting him in—so deeply, intensely, her heart soared. If there was only this, this was
complete. She wrapped around him. She never wanted him
to let her go. She never wanted to let *him* go.

There was no more talking. Then there was no more time.

Silently he stood and held his hand out to help her up.
The robe he fetched was huge on her and clearly his.

He wrapped a towel around his waist and rubbed his
forehead. 'Elsie—'

'I need you to get me to my room,' she muttered.

'I'll get you there but you can't leave the palace yet.' He
shot her an apologetic look. 'Media crews are already in

place. You'll be driven out in the convoy of the other VIPS and dignitaries. Ortiz will get you to the airport safely.'

Her throat was growing tighter and tighter. 'Do I have to scale that cliff?'

'There's a secret passageway from here.'

She silently followed him through a long narrow corridor until he paused at a doorway.

'Go through, yours is the second on the left. I'll stay in here.'

This was it. Would he give her a goodbye kiss as he moved from one stage of his life to the next?

No. He remained standing at a distance, stared at her hard, resolute.

If he asked she would stay. Here. Hidden. His. She would stay in this secret part of the palace. She would do anything for him. Always.

But he didn't ask. And she didn't ask either. Neither said goodbye. She couldn't make a sound. She took the step and heard the door close behind her. And then she realised what she'd done.

She'd left him. Just like everyone else.

CHAPTER THIRTEEN

Saturday, 09.42 a.m.

ELSIE PACED IN her suite. Her heart thudded, trying to escape her ribcage. She had to get out of here but she couldn't. When she'd snuck in early this morning, she'd found her meagre luggage in the corner. Her mandolin had been brought from Amalia's room. She'd showered. Dressed. A footman had delivered a breakfast tray that she'd not touched. There'd been a note from Security informing her when she'd be taken to the airport. She was to remain in her suite until then. Her bedroom, bathroom, lounge—all had views overlooking the sparkling sea. She couldn't see the city—and none of those gathering crowds could see her either.

Her heart beat so hard but she couldn't believe its warning. She couldn't *trust* her feelings.

Surely it was loneliness making her respond so intensely to his attention? He'd trusted her, he'd let her in. It was flattery and infatuation and gratitude. It was the impossibility of anything more. They'd had such a short time to be together of course it was going to feel *perfect*—and as if it would be so for ever. It wouldn't. There would come a point where they didn't want each other this desperately any more. It was just sex. It would pass. The frantic panic of her own pulse was a fraud. Trusting her instincts? No. She couldn't.

Now she wanted the minutes to fly.

Someone knocked on her door and she spun towards it.

'Elsie?' A whisper from behind the wood. 'It's Amalia.'

Elsie sucked in some courage to stabilise her emotions and managed to open the door and smile.

'Have you had breakfast?' Amalia looked at her curiously as she walked in with Callie, the assistant at her side. 'You're very pale.'

'I'm not used to late nights at palace parties.' Elsie tried to joke.

'This is for you, Ms Wynter.' Callie put a large parcel on the writing table and then left.

'From you?' Elsie asked Amalia.

'No.' Amalia shrugged. 'Maybe Felipe?'

Elsie's heart quaked. The parcel was *massive*. She didn't want a gift. She certainly didn't want to open it in front of Amalia. But Felipe wouldn't have sent it with her if it was inappropriate…

'Aren't you going to open it?' Amalia looked intrigued.

She didn't want any kind of recompense for her 'time'. But she couldn't resist tearing the paper. It was a box. And within that box? A custom-made mandolin case. She slowly, reverently opened it. Navy velvet, a gold protective cloth, black silk straps…the colours of Silvabon.

She blinked back tears. How had he got it so *quickly*? She was beyond touched.

'Elsie, it's gorgeous.' Amalia was awed.

'It is.' She put her mandolin into it carefully, taking the time to recover from the explosion of emotion. 'I'm heading to the airport soon.' She made herself speak. 'Before all the crowds line the streets and make it impossible for anyone to move.'

'Don't you want to stay for the coronation? You could stay for longer. Fly later.'

Elsie's heart ached. 'I have to go, Amalia. But I'll email.'

'The ceremony's going to be so boring anyway.'

Elsie looked over at her. 'You're the only family he has who's able to be there.'

Amalia's expression pinched. 'I'm not really family. He wants to send me away.'

'He wants what's best for you.'

'Maybe I want to stay here. But he won't let me.'

Yeah, Elsie had figured that. 'Have you tried telling him how you feel?'

'I don't think he'll listen. He's already decided.'

'Maybe try anyway?' Elsie suggested.

At least she would feel better for having tried.

There was another knock at the door and Callie's voice called for Amalia.

'I'd better get ready,' Amalia said.

'I'm really glad I got to see you again,' Elsie said. 'I'm so sorry I couldn't say goodbye properly last time.'

Amalia nodded and turned but Elsie hurried to the door and pulled the girl into a hug. For a split second Amalia stiffened and Elsie wondered if she'd done the wrong thing. But then Amalia hugged her back, her grip tight.

'Travel safe, Elsie,' Amalia mumbled.

'I will,' Elsie promised. 'And I'll be in touch. I have your personal email now.'

Amalia chuckled. But Elsie meant it. She wasn't letting Amalia down again. Even though she'd end up hearing about Felipe and that would hurt. But she could never avoid all news about him and Amalia was too important.

Moments later, alone again, she touched the mandolin case with trembling fingers. It was so precious, so thoughtful of him. And it said everything, didn't it? How special *he* was. *All* those emotions flooded her.

Could only one day change everything? Could it change her?

One *moment* could change everything. One moment

could mean life, or death. Bigger things happened in less time. Trusting this? Trusting her own instincts? Believing in what she felt? She owed herself that. She owed him too. She had to do the right thing. For herself and for him. Which meant she had to take her own advice and *try telling him*.

She had to speak the truth and not hold back. Holding back meant misunderstandings and loneliness. At the very least he would know and she would've released it from her own hold. Keeping secrets. Staying silent for fear of rejection? She was so over that. Saying what she needed to say *mattered*—there was freedom in that even if rejection was inevitable. She would process the emotion eventually, but not if she didn't recognise it, acknowledge it, appreciate it. She had nothing else to lose and she wanted to gift it to him. She wanted *him* to know *he* was loved.

But it was too late. She was stuck in her suite in his palace. Their time had passed. She couldn't break into his private wing.

She would never see him again.

CHAPTER FOURTEEN

Saturday, 11.01 a.m.

IT WAS LESS than an hour until the coronation procession and Felipe needed a smack in the head to pull back his focus. *Do not think about Elsie.* He'd showered, shaved, and dressed entirely on automatic. *Do not dream about Elsie.* He had to concentrate on his country and he was finally almost ready. *Do not ache for Elsie.*

'Sir—'

'I said I didn't want to be interrupted.' He turned to glare at the man who'd walked in unannounced. But Garcia was grey and sweating.

Felipe's blood chilled. 'What is it?'

He held out his hand for the tablet Garcia was holding. It took two seconds to scan the headline and a summary of 'facts'.

Fraudster family breaches palace.

Acid burned the back of his throat. He didn't want her reading this rubbish.

'Someone noticed her last night,' Garcia muttered nervously.

The article shifted the focus from the coronation to his vulnerable stepsister. To Elsie. The threat of something this

salacious overshadowing the coronation? His grandfather
would be rolling in the family crypt. But his grandfather
was dead. And Elsie?

Everything she'd not wanted had been dug up and it
would destroy her.

He had done this. By not staying away—not curbing his
urges—he'd failed to protect *both* Amalia and Elsie. And
how did he recover this now? There was no stopping what
people would say. They could only shield themselves—try
not to read it? Run away from it?

Impossible.

Rage gripped him. He never should have touched her.
Never invited her into his private chambers. She should
never have to pay the price for his greed.

'They haven't published it yet,' Garcia said. 'They're asking for exclusive comment before they do.'

Protocol was never to comment on media stories—to
'rise above it', to pretend it wasn't happening. Like the mystery of his father's disappearance.

*Don't explain. Suppress emotion. Curiosity will die and
we will all carry on.*

But it didn't die.

King Javier had insisted it would all be smoothed over by
a single abdication announcement weeks after the fact. No
one had fronted to answer questions… Only the questions
hadn't eased, they had been rehashed every day for weeks
until finally his grandfather had fed them Felipe's investiture. Creating a great 'celebration of a new heir!' Seventeen
and alone, Felipe had walked into the cathedral in front of
his entire country…

But he'd been okay. He'd had the protection of the palace walls. He'd had the sea to dive deep into. And of course
there were times when it was hard but he loved his place
here.

But his father had only been okay because he'd gone to

live a quiet life in Canada where he hadn't seen the drama mentioned every few months in the Silvabon press. His mother, too, had gone—to a quiet existence on an outer island. And the judgement had never really gone away. It never would.

Felipe refused to let anyone else become the target. He hoped to ensure Amalia would be okay by getting her to a secluded school. But Elsie?

If she escaped the country quickly they might not be able to track her down. Which meant they needed to bring her departure forward. She couldn't wait for that flight this afternoon. She certainly couldn't travel with all those people if this story had broken—they'd stare, harass, worse. Feeling afraid? Being judged? This was her nightmare. Her life would be wrecked again, this time because of him. He had to buy her time. Then he'd come up with a decoy. He had no idea what yet, but he'd think of something.

'Tell them if they print it I'll sue,' he said roughly.

'Pardon?'

'Threaten them. They'll hold it at least until we get her out of here.'

He scrolled down past the first paragraph. There was a video embedded in the article. He didn't have to click on it—it played automatically.

Stop watching.

He couldn't. Even as guilt swallowed him.

She asked you not to watch.

He couldn't stop. His eyes stung and his heart raced. Her hair was in a ponytail and she was in jeans and a tee. She looked achingly familiar. Just younger. Sadder. Her husky voice broke his heart. It would break any one *human's* heart. The look shared between mother and daughter? It was so intimate, so deeply personal.

He closed his eyes. But he still saw it—burned in his

brain. Such a private moment that should never have been made public.

He knew she had strength now. She'd been forged in fire. But that sweet, vulnerable woman was still inside. She *cared*, despite her determined armour. It was only a thin covering. That was why she didn't stick around, right? Because she could be pierced too easily.

She'd been recorded unknowingly—by someone she trusted invading her privacy. Taking the preciousness of that memory, taking advantage of her for monetary gain. And the dark side of that exposure? Elsie had been turned on by everyone, including her family. The absolute isolation she'd suffered… And that was when he read some of the comments that had been posted online. The shredding of her music, her voice, her very being.

The bitterest bile rose. He couldn't let it happen again.

He utterly understood the loss of privacy, the invasion of deeply personal moments and he felt sharp-edged resignation as they were put forward for public consumption. Funerals. Weddings. Coronations. Even a simple walk around a park or a visit to a café… He intimately knew how it felt to have such private moments put on display and he was always guarded to ensure his deepest feelings remained known only to himself. To protect himself from things like this.

But this had been so much worse than that. This had been a deeply personal moment between a dying mother and her daughter that never should have been witnessed by anyone let alone stolen. Used. And then *scorned*.

So unfairly. So unjustly.

So she shouldn't have to bear the scrutiny and judgement of this damned article now. She shouldn't have her family's past raked over, repeatedly. And it would be repeatedly. Once her name was publicly linked with his, anyone who'd met her in their travels would now sell their stories. It would also be relentless. The exposure was too much for anyone but those hardened to it. Who had the skills to handle it. That wasn't her. She moved on as soon as the whispers began—choosing fresh start after fresh start.

He couldn't blame her for that. His mother had been miserable in public life. His father had simply run away from it. Felipe had to do better for Amalia and heaven knew he was trying. But he'd made a promise to his grandfather. He needed to be the one who stayed and stood fast.

But he needed to get Elsie far away so she would be safe and free. She should have security and love—a family of her own. Children? He was never bringing children into the palace. He couldn't protect them.

He had to fix this. Because he couldn't stand to watch her wither beneath the glare of those cameras and phones. He had to get her out. He had to see her himself and ensure she understood the urgency.

He brushed past Garcia. 'I'll be back—'

'But, sir—'

He glanced at his watch. Had she left already?

CHAPTER FIFTEEN

Saturday, 11.06 a.m.

SEEKING ONLY ONE THING, Felipe swept past the guards, through the guest wing, straight to Elsie's suite. He opened the door without knocking and slammed it behind him. She was there and he was so relieved he had to put his hand on the wall to brace himself.

'Felipe?' Elsie stifled a scream of surprise.

She was wearing the white and blue billowy dress from that day at the café months ago. Demure yet sexy with that scooped neckline that drew his eye to her lovely neck. Her hair was swept into a messy topknot. Those chunky boots gave her an extra inch in height but not enough for her to be able to look him directly in the eye. That didn't stop her trying.

'You shouldn't be here.' A frantic whisper. 'This is the guest wing. Other people might see you.'

He didn't answer. He couldn't even remember to count to calm down.

'I was getting ready to leave.' Her chest rose and fell as she stared at him. 'Look at you…'

Her gaze brushed over his body. He felt it as if her fingers really were fluttering over his skin. He'd forgotten he was in his uniform—all gold buttons and braid and starch. He stalked towards her—unable to maintain his distance, unable to deny the urge to reach for her and pull her close to ease the ache. Oh, God, he was sorry. He was so, so sorry.

But she stepped to the side. 'Did you do this?' She gestured to the mandolin case open on the writing table behind her. Her voice was husky and sweet and she smiled at him tremulously.

His thundering heart raced faster and faster. Because that look?

Her eyes shimmered with emotion. 'You got a new case so I don't have to strap my old one together every time I want to go somewhere.' She touched the velvet lining gently. 'How did you get the right size so quickly? It's an old instrument—most modern cases aren't the right size.'

'I ordered it a while back.' His voice barely worked.

She blinked. 'A while back?'

'That night you came to the palace.'

'That night?' She licked her lips as if they were parched. 'You ordered this *after* you'd told me to leave?'

'I didn't want you to leave for good.' Not then. His shoulders lifted and he moved to stand beside her. 'I don't want you awkwardly lugging it round in a broken case. It's precious to you and needs better protection.'

Her fingers curled in the soft cloth used to wrap the instrument in. 'How did you get the right size?'

'While we were at dinner—I got my man to measure up.'

'And had it made specially.' Her eyes glistened. 'That was really thoughtful.'

'So this is a gift you can accept?' Unlike the bracelet that was still in his pocket.

'It's the nicest thing anyone's done for me in a really long time,' she said softly.

Silence fell. He knew she was wondering why he was here. He didn't want to tell her. He didn't want to see her expression change. He liked her like this, beautiful and glowing, and he couldn't bear to move.

'You should go.' She cupped his cheek.

He drew a breath in shock and caught the lingering scent of his oil on her skin. His temperature skyrocketed.

'You should be on the way to the procession already.' She swallowed.

He grabbed her wrist, holding her palm to his jaw. 'I'm fully aware of what I should do. It's just that I don't want to do it.'

She gazed into his soul, emotional but unwavering. 'What do you want to do, then?'

Elsie waited for his response, but he was too silent, too rigid—which meant something was wrong.

He was in full regalia for the coronation. The navy fabric hugged his powerful thighs while the braid emphasised his broad shoulders. He looked as if he'd stepped out of a poem from the past—a glorious, vital, virile king. In his prime—powerful and intense, he'd let nothing stand in the way of what he wanted.

'Your Majesty?' She dared him. She couldn't resist.

He wrapped an arm around her waist and she was trapped between him and the table. She read agony in his eyes, but as he slid his other hand beneath the hem of her dress she widened her legs. A growl emerged as he skated a fingertip across her panties.

'You're ready for me,' he muttered.

'From the moment you walked in.' She wanted the wildness. She wanted to soothe the man constrained inside that uniform. She wanted to embrace the feeling he had for her.

It took a mere moment to unzip him. For him to step forward. He gazed into her eyes.

'Take pleasure from me, Felipe.' She tossed his words at him.

The permission he'd once given, she gave back to him. And he took it. Took her. Right there, upright against the table. She hooked her leg around his, her arms around his shoulders, and clung as he thrust.

'Don't let go of me,' she begged, barely balanced in his arms. 'Don't let go.'

His mouth was hers—hard and passionate—his possession complete and unbridled. He locked into her, driving closer and closer and she went soft—so willing. In seconds his passion sent her over the edge and he cried out in feral agony as he followed.

Shockingly hard. Shockingly quick. Shockingly over.

His hands bit her waist. He ensured her feet had found the floor then stepped back. Her dress dropped into place.

'Elsie…' He was pale and she saw his fingers trembled as he fixed his trousers. There was such regret in his tone.

Both dressed. Both undone.

Felipe couldn't look at her as his brain came back online and his horror grew. 'I apologise.'

He did not lose it like that. Ever. He did not put his entire future at risk. Or *hers*.

'That shouldn't have happened.' He cleared his throat.

None of this should have happened. He couldn't even blame alcohol or a hangover—he hadn't touched anything all evening save three mouthfuls of champagne at last night's dinner. Utterly sober, he'd been drunk on desire, on desperation. High on the heat of her. He'd been so dutiful his entire life and suddenly he'd been so damned out of control.

He swore. 'I didn't use protection. I'm so sorry.'

He loathed himself that second.

She watched him warily. 'Don't worry about that, I'm on the pill. It's easier when I'm travelling.' She swallowed. 'You haven't just got me pregnant.'

He stared at her, trying to process what had just happened, what she'd just said. His horror deepened as he realised he was feeling a flicker of *disappointment*. Because if there had been a chance of her being pregnant he could have stopped her from leaving. She would've had to stay. Only until she'd seen a doctor. But then he could have stopped her from seeing a doctor...

The escalating thoughts horrified him. The train of imaginings—of *making* her stay? That wasn't just selfish and controlling, it would be ruthless and *insane*. The absolute spoilt whim of a dictator used to getting everything he wanted. Everything his own way—like his grandfather after all.

'It still shouldn't have happened,' he said hoarsely. Because he hadn't known she was covered. He'd gone ahead and taken the risk—without even thinking about it. Without giving a damn.

'Don't regret it.' Her eyes flashed. 'Please don't say that was a mistake.'

'It was.' He swallowed.

Heaven help him, he wanted it again. He wanted to pull her into his arms and rest against her. He wanted to turn his back on the world and forget about everything else in his damned life. So right now he *was* his father. So selfish he'd ignore all other responsibility. When right now, just beyond these palace walls, crowds of people were depending on him, waiting for him. How could he want to forget them all and give everything up just for a woman? For sex. For the best ride of his life.

It was so *weak*. He'd be betraying his country. Breaking the word he'd given to his grandfather. Becoming everything he'd vowed he'd never be...

He *wouldn't*. He couldn't. 'This whole thing was a mistake.'

Elsie paled, her anger obviously mounting. He didn't blame her. She should be angry with him. He was angry with himself. That he'd been momentarily tempted to do *everything* wrong to keep her with him? To cheat and lie and do whatever it took? He loathed the man he could devolve into. Out of control. Selfish. Possessive. Utterly uncaring of everything else. And she would become so miserable.

He could never let it happen.

CHAPTER SIXTEEN

Saturday, 11.18 a.m.

OVERTIRED, OVER-EXPOSED, over-stimulated and overwhelmed by *everything*, Elsie stared. Her eyes were scratchy and dry, her skin felt flayed, while her heart felt as if it had been whipped until raw and bleeding. She'd seen the flash before he'd turned away. She was struggling to recover from that intensity and the fall from ecstasy couldn't have been more sharp or more sudden.

Now he stood with his back to her, his head bowed, and he was walking already. 'I have to leave.'

Without another word? Without even *facing* her?

'What *was* that, Felipe?' she called as he reached the door.

His shoulders straightened. 'I'm sorry. I shouldn't have taken advantage of you.'

He thought he'd taken advantage of her? As if she hadn't been involved, hadn't been *taking* every bit as much as he had? As if she hadn't been *giving*?

'I've never let you take advantage of me,' she said proudly. 'I've taken what I wanted. What did you want? Why did you just come in here?' she asked. 'Was it for one last quickie? To take the edge off before your big show? Is that what this was?'

He turned, his back to the door, anger reeking from his

rigid stance. 'I came to tell you—' He inhaled sharply. 'My private jet is ready. It has clearance to leave as soon as you're onboard.'

She stilled. 'You want me to leave now?'

'Yes.'

'Not on the commercial flight later? Not after your coronation? Now?'

'Now. Yes.'

'What about all the other royals and their security? Isn't this problematic?'

Why was he so desperate to get rid of her that he was bending all the damn rules?

'Not at all,' he clipped.

So she could request a flyover of the damn cathedral in which his coronation would be happening—make such a noise he couldn't ignore her? Why wait for some jet when she could do *that* now?

Because what those last few minutes had proven more than anything, was how human he was. How deeply he too needed connection. Needed love. Of *course* she'd fallen in love with him. He wasn't perfect. He was as flawed as she, in as much need of play, laughter and love. She needed to be honest with him. And now she had her chance.

'No.'

'No?' He stared at her. 'What do you mean no?'

'Not used to hearing that word, are you?' She tried to smile but failed. 'You try not to be, but you're still spoilt in some ways, Felipe. You still expect to get whatever you want, whenever you want.'

He paled. 'I just said I was sorry—'

'I'm not talking about what just happened. I wanted that too. We both know that,' she interrupted. 'I'm talking about the rest of your damned life.'

He stared at her.

'You've carved out time in these last twenty-four hours.

They should have been the busiest yet, but you got yourself out of it. Meetings with advisers that you blew off? You did that to see *me*. Why can't you do that the rest of the time? Your life doesn't have to be completely conscripted. You could have the time and space for a personal life. I think you *choose* not to because it's *easier* for you not to.'

'Easier?' A scoffing snort.

'Putting yourself first sometimes isn't a crime, Felipe. You're allowed to want things for yourself. You're allowed to want me. Maybe even for more than one day.'

She bit her lip. She wanted him to more than *want* her. She wanted him to need her, to love her. And she had to speak her own truth.

But he shut down. 'You need to go, Elsie. Now. This is over.'

She summoned all her courage. 'I don't think it is.'

He regarded her solemnly but then his gaze slid from hers and he actually fidgeted.

Warily she watched him. 'What aren't you telling me?'

'Someone at the dinner last night must have tipped off the press. I've seen an article they want to publish. They've done their digging.'

'About me.'

He nodded curtly. 'I've managed to delay its release. You can get safely away from here before it lands.'

She braced against her instinctive shudder. She could handle this. 'It doesn't matter.' She squared her shoulders. 'I've been through it before. There's actually *nothing* worse than what I've already been through.'

His jaw tensed. 'You don't understand. You can't handle what they're going to throw at you, Elsie. Whatever online hate you had before, it'll be nothing on this.'

'You're underestimating me. You, the one person I thought actually gave me a chance, now think I'm not up to it?'

'I don't want you to be hurt,' he said grimly.

'It's not any media that will hurt me, Felipe. Real hurt is far more personal than that.'

He stiffened. '*This* isn't real,' he said. 'This will never be real, Elsie.'

He was shutting them down before they had the chance to really explore it.

'Not if you remain so completely closed to the possibility that it *could* be more,' she argued. 'You'd decided that from the start. I'm just your convenient distraction, a final fling in the countdown to the all-important coronation.'

'Is that so awful? Is it so wrong to have something fun for myself?' he asked. 'You're the one who just said I needed that. And *you* said yes. You agreed it could only be this one night.'

'So I did. Now I'm just telling you the rest of the truth. You don't want *me* to be hurt? *You* don't want to hurt anyone? Too bad. Life doesn't work like that. We all hurt people. Especially those we care about. Making mistakes is part of being human.'

'So you finally agree this has been a mistake?'

'Never. I will never regret this.'

'Even though I used you.'

She reeled at the sudden flex. 'Don't cheapen what's happened between us.'

'Sex, Elsie. What's happened is a lot of *sex*.'

'*No.*' She would not let him reframe this that way.

'It's been less than a day,' he said shortly. 'Let me assure you, whatever you think you feel, it's *not* real.'

'Are you denying what I have to say? What I feel? Won't you listen?'

'Elsie—'

'You trusted me and believed in me only last night when I told you about my father. You took me at face value months ago, took my word then. But not in *this*?' She frowned at him. Why—what was so different? Her heart ached. 'Wow, so the one thing you can't believe *isn't* the worst of me, it's that I could want more from you?' She stared at him as the truth dawned. 'You don't want to be loved.'

He bristled. 'I have too much else to do to be responsible for keeping you happy.'

She breathed out at the hit—keeping her *happy*? 'You don't have to keep me happy. That's not what letting yourself love me—love anyone—would mean.'

Did he equate all love with duty? As a burden of care and responsibility?

Because he'd spent his life trying to keep people happy. His grandfather. His mother. Now Amalia. He'd carried the burden of other people who had torments, illnesses, griefs of their own. And he didn't want to shoulder any more—because he didn't believe he was enough for any of them. For anyone.

It turned out her spoilt king was the ultimate people-pleaser. And he never really took time to please himself personally.

'You wouldn't have to do any of that for me,' she said. 'All I'd want is to be in your life. To *share* things *with* you—the good and the bad. To be as honest with you as we've been this last night. With truth there's trust, right?'

He was very still. 'There are things you'll want to do in your life that you couldn't do if you stayed here.'

'Maybe but maybe not. I know you're the King, I know there are expectations that you will always meet because you love Silvabon and you love the people here and you love the palace even though you've had heartache here. I would never want you to renounce your duty or your crown.' Her heart raced. 'The thought of a public element to my life scares me a little but I know you'd help me. And maybe I could then even help *you* with it? I could help others too, couldn't I? I could find something...' She trailed off as she saw the tension in his face, but she couldn't stop herself from fighting for him. He was so worth it. 'You don't have to be alone in everything, Felipe. You could have it all—the crown, yes, and a wife, and children. And with us all together, supporting each other, it could be okay…?'

'I've seen people try, remember?' he said harshly, denying her. 'They all fail.'

She stared at him so determinedly standing alone and implacable. 'You're like a rock in the centre of a fast-flowing river. All the water is swirling around but you're always there, always anchoring others. Steadfast and dependable, right? But you need your own strength replenished. You can't keep holding on for everyone else for ever. That's not fair.'

'Life isn't fair.'

'But you don't have to be *alone*. You don't have to sacrifice everything for everyone else. You can have your dreams. Your person. You could have me.' She inhaled shakily and confessed it all. '*I* would love you. I've *already* fallen in love with you. Felipe…'

Felipe stood so still—not hearing, not believing. He had to stop her from talking. From confusing him and making every cell inside him ache for something so much more than physical. He was shaking on the inside and he had to stop her from saying *that*.

'I watched the video,' he muttered harshly.

'You…what?' She stared at him, clearly derailed. *'What?'*

'It's embedded in the article they've written. It played automatically.'

'Why didn't you stop it?'

Because he couldn't breathe. Because she was beautiful. Because once it had started he simply couldn't do anything.

'I asked you not to,' she whispered. 'You said you wouldn't.'

She was truly hurt now. Pinched and pale and shocked.

She'd not believed he'd have ever done that. But he had. Maybe he shouldn't have told her, but he couldn't not. He felt too awful not to be honest with her. And now he had to hurt her more. He was being cruel to be kind. He had to push her away. He had to make her run. Because he couldn't cope with what she was saying. Not now. Not ever.

Her eyes shimmered with reproach. 'You broke your promise to me.'

'Yes.' His throat tightened. Never had he regretted anything more.

He'd betrayed her. And now she shut down in front of him. He saw it—the change, the defiance blooming in her eyes. He leaned against the door—stopping himself from leaning into her.

'So the thought of this becoming anything more—' She looked at him directly and asked sadly, 'That's a hard no?'

He couldn't answer that.

'You only had to let me in,' she said. 'Only let me love you. You only had to be there for me.'

No. That wasn't right. 'You should have so much more than that, Elsie. You should have someone love you too. I can't be the man who does. I don't have—' He shook his head. 'Can't.'

'Won't,' she said brokenly. 'You won't. There's a difference.'

'Can't.' He couldn't bear to see her wither. People didn't thrive at the palace.

His mother had faded. His father had run away. His grandfather had become like stone—unyielding, uncompromising. And suddenly he was furious with her for not believing him. He'd *seen* it, lived it and he could *not* see her suffer. She'd want to leave eventually. And when she did? It would destroy him. So she had to go now. Before the damage to them both was irreparable. And he was so angry he could scarcely see straight.

Only *her* anger propelled her forward. She marched up to him and planted her feet so she stood right in front of him. He couldn't escape. He could only push.

'Was I just someone convenient who you wanted only because you knew you couldn't have me for long? The thrill of the challenge? The fun of deception and claiming someone completely inappropriate for your status?' Elsie did *not* want to believe that. But she didn't know what to believe now.

He'd seen it. The one person she didn't want to. It was something so private that had been so shredded and he'd *promised*...

And now here he was telling her he needed her to leave. He didn't have the energy for her. She wasn't worth the effort. And the rejection hurt. The denial of her feelings, of her value, sliced so deep, creating a wound like none before. She'd thought he understood her—that they'd understood each other. And now she was angry because, not only was she unwanted, she felt a fool. All over again. She'd had no idea of the ugly truth—just as she'd believed her father had been genuine in that crowdfunding effort when it had been just a scam to get more of what he'd wanted. This was a scam too—Felipe had made her fall with his charm and his assurances. Only he'd lied.

'I thought you were strong, but you don't even know what strong is.' She stepped forward, unable to hold back from blasting her feelings at him. 'Strong is standing up for change. Strong is saying this is me, this is what I want. Strong is taking charge of your own life. Strong is saying no to an impossible pressure. Strong is making personal needs a priority. Strong is accepting people into your life when you've been hurt before.'

Finally she realised the problem. The burden of the crown was his *excuse* to cut himself off. What he *feared* was people leaving him again. The people he'd loved had left. And he didn't trust anyone to stay. That was why he wouldn't open his heart to anyone. Why he didn't want children. It broke her heart. But made her angry too. He was so terrified of loss he couldn't even *try*.

'And are you so very strong?' he taunted harshly. 'You run away like a wounded animal every time you think someone might think less of you. You don't ride out any storms. You're petrified of rejection. You're the one who won't follow dreams.'

'What am I doing *right now*, Felipe?' she yelled at him. 'Putting myself so far *over* the line. Strong is trying to make change and not giving up even when it's an ongoing struggle. You won't even redecorate your Elizabethan-orgy-style bedroom because you're so constrained by *duty*.'

He sucked in a shocked breath. 'I *cannot* do this right now, Elsie. I have my bloody coronation.'

'You cannot do this *ever*. You *won't*.' She was so hurt by his denial. 'You made me trust you. When you gave me a chance with Amalia, when you believed me when I told you everything. You gave me hope and made me think that maybe…' She paused to pull herself together—and failed. 'But *I'm* not enough for you to get past it completely.'

And that devastated her.

Her only *mistake* had been in thinking there was nothing worse for her to suffer. There was so much worse. Because before it had been the past that had been picked apart. Her choices, her actions—she'd been crucified for them. She'd been rejected—cast out to be alone. But this was the *future*. This was *hope*. He'd given her all of that only to then destroy it. So suddenly, so completely. And she damned him for it.

'I can't be ashamed of my family for the rest of my life,' she said. 'They made such bad choices, but those choices weren't *mine*. I won't suffer that punishment any more. I'm worth someone's trust and *I* can *keep* trust. I'm worth someone's love and I have value to give. It might not be palaces and gold and jewels and an army, but I have other more important things. I have a *heart*. I'm not no one. I'm not nothing.' She stared at him. 'You don't want to *make* someone have to stay with you, but maybe they'd *choose* to. It's the height of arrogance to assume that no one else could understand your world. That no one else could handle it. That you couldn't make the changes necessary if you really wanted to.'

'Elsie—'

'Reject *me*, fine, but don't do that to Amalia. She likes it here. She feels safe here. Talk to her. You managed that for me once, do it for her. She deserves that. Don't send her away.'

'I'm not. She—'

'Have you actually *asked* her whether she wants to go?'

He jerked his head. 'I want her to have her freedom.'

'Freedom is when you *know* you're loved,' she argued. 'That family is there for you. That, no matter what, your people have your back. And that even if you make a mistake, if you're sorry, they'll forgive you if you ask.' She lifted her head. 'I would have forgiven my father, Felipe. My brother. But they didn't want that from me. They didn't want me. They don't love me. I would have forgiven you too—if you'd asked. But you don't want my forgiveness. You're *not* sorry. And you don't want me either.' She got it now. 'So no, thank you, I don't want your damned private jet. I don't want any special treatment. I'm not some *mistake* you can just kick out of your precious country. I am not something to be ashamed of.'

She was so hurt.

'I'm doing this for you—'

'You are *not*. I don't give a damn what they write about me, don't you get that? I've had it all. Worse already. And I survived. I'll survive again. I am so much stronger than you'll ever let yourself believe. But none of that matters because I'm still never going to be good enough for you. *You're* the one who cares what they think.'

'I know how they can destroy you.'

'The only person destroying part of me right now is *you*.' She shook. 'It was never about what everyone else—what *random strangers*—said. It was that the people who I loved…*they* didn't believe in me. They didn't have my back or even try to understand. That's what hurt. And that's *you* now.'

He'd let her down and he didn't care. Because if he did, he wouldn't have done it. But he really did want her to go.

He closed his eyes briefly. 'I never meant to hurt you.'

She laughed bitterly. 'You think you're so honourable? So dutiful. But in less than a day, you betrayed me. Maybe you did use me. Did you scare yourself, Felipe? Wanting me so badly you risked being unsafe with me? Were you finally vulnerable? Did that frighten you?'

His eyes flashed.

'I'm not the one who has anything to hide, am I?' she realised scornfully. 'Being abandoned hurts. And you won't let anyone close enough again. That's why you're sending Amalia away. And me. You can't risk your own heart. You're not willing to even try. You're a coward.' She was so hurt. 'It's all an excuse, to stop *yourself* being hurt.'

He was shaking too. 'I'm trying to protect *you*.'

'You're protecting yourself. Go right ahead. Be as rigid as your grandfather, as emotionally unavailable as both of your parents. Be an isolated island of a king, Felipe. Be lonely always. Because *I* won't. I've handled so much I'll even get over you.'

'Elsie—'

'I'm not ashamed of anything I've done these last twenty-four hours. Or indeed any of my life. I'm *not* hiding any more. So go and do your damned duty. You—' She broke off and drew breath. 'Leave. *Now*.'

CHAPTER SEVENTEEN

Saturday, 12.01 p.m.

FELIPE WALKED SLOWLY, leading his stallion. His head was bare beneath the burning sun and he was alone for this part of the procession—walking as an unadorned, humble man—to be crowned King. In the cathedral he would be robed, handed a sceptre, an orb, and finally crowned. The throngs of people lining each side of his path were silent, as was custom. The only thing he could hear was the beat inside his head. He counted, keeping it slow, keeping himself calm. It wasn't working. He couldn't focus.

He'd *made* her leave. He'd *lied* to her. When she valued truth so deeply.

I used you.

But he'd protected her—hadn't he? It was all he'd really wanted to do.

He swallowed back bitterness as he recalled her accusations and the deeply buried vat of hurt she'd ripped open. His father had left him. So had his mother. His grandfather had burdened him with so much that *wasn't* personal. He'd emphasised his duty—rules, regulations, requirements. So if he didn't do this now—who would he be then? Who would he be without the crown?

No one. Anyone.

And part of him was tempted. Because he wanted everything he didn't think he could have as long as he had the crown on his head. He wanted *her*.

He had never ever been tempted to walk away from it all. Until now he'd been unable to understand his father. He'd thought it weak that Carlos had abdicated and left in the dead of night. And yes, maybe it wasn't the best way he'd gone about it, but he appreciated now that it had taken his father a courage of his own. Maybe Carlos hadn't been able to figure out a compromise with King Javier... Yeah, compromise hadn't existed in the old man's mind. And the way Amalia's mother had been vilified in the press? Hell, she *still* was even after she'd died, which was why Felipe felt so protective towards Amalia.

Finally Felipe totally understood why Carlos would've wanted to get the woman he loved far away from here. But *here* was also amazing. The media was only one minor element and he *couldn't* let them win. He couldn't stop this walk any more than he could stop breathing. This was his home. His soul. *His* crown. He didn't want to turn his back on his country. But he wanted to keep Elsie close. And safe. And yet she didn't want him to turn his back on his country either—not at *all*.

The temptation of her offer called to him.

I would do anything for you.

The wickedness rose. He wanted her to live in the castle as his concubine. To secretly swim with him every morning and be there in his room for him at night to return to. She could live in a different room every day for three years and still have more to explore. She'd be his secret. It was pure fantasy and it was appalling how tantalising it was.

She could work in the café still, during the day. He'd build another secret tunnel so she could get there. But secrets escaped. And for her to be some secret as if he were ashamed? She'd grow pale and miserable and lonely. He couldn't let that happen. She deserved so much more than that.

She'd been destroyed once. But she'd risen from the ashes like a phoenix, hadn't she? Stunning and strong, beautiful and proud. She'd been so proud when she'd stood in front of him today. Regal in her slaying of his doubts and shattering his defences. She'd believed in him more than he believed in himself. She'd expected more from him. Yet she'd accepted everything.

His failure. His heartache. And hers.

He slowly mounted the steps of the cathedral, aware of the absolute silence of the crowds around him. For so many people to be so quiet and focused?

His entire country was watching, waiting for him. Millions more were watching around the world. He couldn't expect them to wait longer by putting his personal interests ahead of the gift they'd given him in attending the ceremony today. This was about far *more* than him. Now wasn't the time. He would not fail them.

He made his promises, clearly, honestly, meaning every word.

The crown was placed on his head. It was heavy. So was the cloak. And his hands were full with the sceptre and the orb. Everything was real and weighing a tonne. A literal burden. But as music played in celebration? That was when his mind wandered again.

Don't let go of me.

She wanted a home. Someone to *want* her to stay. He remembered her smoky eyes and her excitement at the lightest of restraint plays. She'd wanted him to make it *impossible* for her to leave. She didn't want to be released. She wanted to be *kept*. Not as a possession. Not as a thing. But safe and secure.

Maybe she'd wanted to be held because she'd been afraid of asking him if she could stay. But in the end she *had* asked. She'd opened up and told him how she felt. She'd been vulnerable and brave in admitting that she wanted to be a permanent, living fixture in his heart.

Which was exactly where she was already.

Only he hadn't told her. He hadn't realised—until right now. Right now when he was in front of millions and unbearably lonely without her. He wanted her *beside* him. Not watching from the palace. Not waiting in some secret chamber. But walking *alongside* him. He would be so proud to have her with him. And he didn't want to do it without her. And he didn't give a damn what anyone would have to say about it. Somehow he would shut down any rogue reporting. Or maybe he would just rise above it with her. Because being with her gave his heart wings.

But would she stay here in Silvabon?

Have you actually asked her?

Elsie had been referring to Amalia. And he hadn't asked her either. He'd made a unilateral decision—as if he knew best. An autocratic dictator. His grandfather all over—trying to do what was best, yes, but not understanding everything. It was so much more nuanced than that. He'd been such a fool. Because yes, he'd been afraid.

He had to ask Elsie. He'd never asked her. He should have given her the *choice*. But she needed to know his feelings first and right now he had to let her go. There wasn't time. Too many people were counting on him to be here *now*. She was counting on him too. Not to betray her to the public. Not to turn that spotlight on her. Not without even the limited protections he could put in place first. They needed time alone and that was hardly about to happen. But he'd let her believe he didn't care. He'd let her think *he* didn't believe her. He'd belittled her feelings. And he couldn't let that stand. He had to tell her how he felt.

He could envisage it. He'd get to the airport. Halt her plane. Board it if she had already. Otherwise he'd corner her in the terminal. He could make a public declaration—

an invitation, a proposal. But it would be one she wouldn't want because she wouldn't be able to answer with complete honesty. Not with the world watching. And they would be. Everything was up for consumption. Weddings. Funerals. Coronations. Dates. Proposals. All picked over and commented upon. The lack of privacy was insufferable—even that balcony in his own damned bedroom was a relic of public consumption from years gone by and all that had happened since was that the audience was even bigger. Everything personal could be live-streamed to anyone who bothered to click the link and he refused to have what was between them shared to anyone. It was too precious.

But if he let her go now, if she got on that plane without him stopping her, she wouldn't come back. She'd made her stand. She'd offered everything he'd wanted and he'd rejected her. She wouldn't return to make the offer again. She was too hurt. Which meant he couldn't let her go without telling her how he really felt. And how did that happen away from this audience of millions?

There wasn't any time. Not now. He had to be here for his people. He'd never let them down. He would do this properly—to the very best that he could. So he didn't mount his horse as he was supposed to. He gestured to his waiting groom to hold for a moment and stepped forward alone, deciding on an impromptu walkabout. He saw Garcia's fierce look but ignored it. These people had been waiting for hours to get a glimpse of him and to be part of these celebrations. He walked towards the crowd. They were not silent now. They'd swiftly settled in a chant.

'Felipe! Felipe! Felipe!'

He could imagine Elsie teasing him about the size of his head. He smiled at the thought and the cheering crescendoed to deafening decibel levels. Hell, he wished she were with him. Because he loved Silvabon. The people. The palace. The city, sea, sky. He would give *anything* in his country's best interests. It had his heart completely. But so did she. And it was only now that he realised his heart was so much bigger than he'd ever known. It could hold it *all*—most especially her.

'Thank you.' He bowed to the group of people nearest the railing. Their cameras flashed but their smiles were brighter.

'You're the King.'

'Yes.'

He didn't often talk to children but this one was being held up by her father. And Felipe couldn't help thinking of that shocking dismay from earlier when Elsie had said he couldn't have just got her pregnant. Both the disappointment and the desire still lingered. He'd sworn he wasn't going to have children—that he didn't want them to be heirs to all that was the Crown. But Elsie had called him out on that too, hadn't she? He could alter the weight of it. He could build in choices. He'd been too wary—too rigid—to give that full consideration before. But now? Now he ached for *everything*—especially children. *Her* children. The laughter he could imagine…the footsteps…the music.

'Where's your queen?' The little girl gave him a smile.

'I don't have one yet,' he said huskily.

'Can I be the Queen?'

A ripple of laughter went around the surrounding crowd.

'Unfortunately not at this time,' he informed her gravely.

'Is it because I'm not a princess?'

'No, I think anyone can be a queen' he replied. 'But you're a little young.'

The little girl frowned, apparently considering his words. 'You need to find someone else. You'd better hurry up.'

Out of the mouths of babes. 'You're right. I'll see what I can do.'

With a smile at her parents, he stepped back and signalled to his groom. A moment later he swung up onto his horse. As the crowd cheered, he saluted them. This was good for Silvabon. For the promotion of alliances, for tourism. But his heart still ached. He did need his Queen.

He made himself maintain the slow trot and not gallop back to the palace as if he were racing for the moon. He smiled, occasionally waved, nodded in appreciation of their attention. He'd been rehearsing for this moment all his life. He knew exactly what to do. And he wanted to do it. It felt right.

He would be their king. But he would also be a man. And men made mistakes. Men weren't perfect. Sometimes they had to be strong and face their fears. And ask for forgiveness.

Back inside the palace, he strode through the private wing. He hardly had any time.

'Is everything okay?' Amalia asked as he swept past her. 'You look pale.'

'I need to make a call.' But he hurriedly swivelled back to face her. 'You know, you don't have to go to boarding school if you don't want to.'

She stared at him.

'You can go to a local school here in Silvabon. Live in the palace. We can get additional music tutors. Or you could go to summer camps for music or something…' He watched the colour wash into her face. 'I thought you'd hate it here, but if you don't.' He cleared his throat. 'If you'd rather stay…' He drew a breath and realised another powerful truth. 'I'd like you to stay.'

She stared at him for a moment.

'That's if—'

'I want to stay,' she said quickly. 'I want to go to school here.'

'Really?' Relief then a small bit of happiness hit—maybe he could have a little family. But he wanted so much more. He wanted *Elsie*. 'Okay. Talk more later.'

Amalia nodded. 'Thank you, Felipe.' Her smile was shy.

As if he were a kind and benevolent king? He shook his head. 'I should have asked what you wanted sooner. I'm sorry.' He glanced at his watch and his heart stopped.

'Are you sure you're okay?' Amalia asked.

'Yeah.' He flashed his sister an appreciative smile and hoped like hell he would be.

Adrenalin flowed in his veins and he ran up the stairs three at a time. He knew what he needed to do. And he needed to do it *now*.

'It's time for the balcony appearance.' His aide was reading his tablet as he walked into the antechamber. 'The flyover is four minutes out.'

'No. I need a brief break.'

'*Sir?*' His aide froze. Only his eyeballs swivelled, giving a side-eye that would've been funny if Felipe weren't so frantic.

Elsie's flight couldn't leave until after the flyover. Which meant he had only minutes to contact her. Four minutes wasn't going to be enough. 'I need to make a phone call. Stall the flyover. Give me a phone.'

He hadn't had one on him for the ceremony. This action was so unsophisticated. So simple. So desperate. But it was all he could think to do.

'Sir, we *can't*.' The poor aide was having conniptions.

'We can and we will. Adapt and get used to it.' He shot the guy a twisted smile. 'Some things are going to have to change.'

CHAPTER EIGHTEEN

Saturday, 03.38 p.m.

'WE HAVE TO wait for the flyover, then you'll be able to board the plane.'

Elsie nodded as Captain Ortiz reminded her of the plan. No one else in the waiting lounge seemed to mind the delay but it was sending Elsie's blood pressure to the stratosphere. Everywhere she turned there was another screen. There'd been no avoiding any of the coronation—from the procession to the cathedral, to the service inside, to the procession back to the palace again. Everyone wanted to watch the entire thing. Weren't they tired of staring at him? Apparently not.

She'd been driven in a car as part of the guest procession as he'd planned. They'd gone across the palace esplanade, towards the cathedral in the centre of the city. Then they'd taken a left when everyone else continued straight ahead. Under cover of a bridge there'd been a rendezvous and a change of car. Again with fully tinted windows. Felipe hadn't been joking when he'd told her his security team was intense. But maybe they'd been right to be. The streets had been lined with citizens. Most were dressed in the country's colours—that deep navy and gold. They were all bright smiles. The hum of excitement breached the bulletproof glass and low rumble of her car. They loved their king. His honour and duty to his country was appreciated. He was a good guy. Spoilt, yes. But still good. But right now she wanted to hate him.

Even though he'd believed in her, that he knew she did the right thing, he didn't want her. He didn't want to fight or make an effort for her or make whatever changes might need to happen. *She* was lacking and unlovable in some way. And while that hurt, she had to believe that he was using her own vulnerability as a convenient excuse as well. In truth *no* woman was ever going to be good enough for him. She felt sorry for that gorgeous betrothal princess who he'd refused. That *she* wasn't good enough? It was an impossible pedestal to mount and he didn't want to put any woman up for that kind of scrutiny.

But more than that, he didn't believe *he* was good enough. That was why he wouldn't fight. His mother had been devastated by the very public break-up of her marriage. His father hadn't been able to cope with the pressures of palace life and had left with his lover. Now Felipe was trying to protect Amalia from feeling the same by sending her away from it for periods of time. And he? He'd built such defences he wouldn't let anyone in. He wouldn't let anyone *stay*.

Predictably, Ortiz hadn't just dropped her at the airport. Apparently he'd been assigned as a protection officer for her. But she knew he was Felipe's main protection, which meant he wasn't doing the job he was meant to on this most important public and presumably most risky of days.

'You should be with the King,' she said.

'I'm where His Majesty needs me to be.'

She knew there were other guards watching her from a greater distance. It was so unnecessary. Even if that media story was going to run it wouldn't be until after the coronation. So she shouldn't be the priority today. 'Are you going to board the plane with me?'

'Yes.'

She was surprised. 'How long are you going to be guarding me?'

'My next orders will come through once we land.'

A wave of misery hit. She didn't want that. She needed to be free of him to heal. The possibility of drawn-out links to Felipe gave her false hope that he wanted to ensure more than her safety. Maybe he wanted to know where she was? Maybe he would come after her?

She shivered. Dreams like those were self-destructive. She needed to end it completely and she would once she'd landed elsewhere. She just needed to get through the last of this day.

She'd picked a chair that faced away from the giant TV screen but had still been able to hear the nauseating official commentary.

'He's paused at the top of the stairs. His head bowed. The weight of a nation on his shoulders, the eyes of the world upon him right now...'

But it had been the endlessly pro-Felipe indulgent opinions of the other plane passengers that had destroyed her thin emotional control.

'He looks very alone. Why wouldn't his mother come to the coronation?'

'She's never returned to the palace since Prince Carlos left her, isn't that awful?'

'She left Felipe alone with King Javier?'

Yeah. No wonder Felipe was so defensive of his heart. His mother couldn't overcome her own hurt or grief to be there for her son and Elsie knew he'd tried to reach out to her. But his mother hadn't seen that he could have used her support as well as offering her his. His father hadn't been able to face the burden of the Crown and the judgement against his lover. They'd both abandoned him to face everything alone. Elsie couldn't blame him if he was angry with his parents for that. If he was wary of others doing the same.

'That's Princess Sofia of Charlemeux. I don't think she's right for him.'

Elsie had shrivelled inwardly as the cameras had panned through the audience pointing out all those presidents, princes, princesses to the millions watching on the live stream. Amalia was in the front row. There had been a rippling murmur of support for the way he'd become guardian to his stepsister.

'It's not her fault her mother was such a—'

At that point Elsie had resorted to staring at the floor. She'd wished her headphones weren't lost somewhere in the bottom of her bag. Her original plan had been to go to Madrid, find work, carry on as usual. Only she didn't want the usual few months here, months there any more. She was *tired*. She didn't want to be moving all the time. She wanted a permanent home. She wanted to build a career, build a network of friends, maybe even build herself a family one day. She'd go home to England. She'd have her own café. She'd have a quiet, fulfilling life. She'd be okay.

That news about her being in the palace might break but news would blow over. It had before. And that news—that *notoriety*—wasn't the true cause of her heartache.

She'd watched him walk back down that long aisle, the crown heavy, the sword at his side, the sceptre and orb in his hands and she'd still felt a flicker of pride for him. Strong and dutiful. He'd been a lone figure in front of his soldiers but he'd done what he was born to do. Now he had another celebratory dinner ahead of him. More fireworks. He was caught fast in his world and all she could hope was that one day he'd meet a woman who'd love him the way he ought to be loved. Just for himself. Someone who he loved enough to lower his barriers. Someone who would play with him, with whom he could laugh and laze about within those rare moments he allowed. She wanted him to be happy.

But yeah, right now she still hated him. She hated how much she felt for him.

'How much longer until that flyover?' she asked Ortiz anxiously.

'Apologies Ms Wynter.' Ortiz looked tense as he glanced at his watch. 'It should be any moment. But it will take a few minutes, I'm sorry.'

She really didn't want his pity.

'You missed a great tour this morning.'

She turned at the voice. It was the man who'd sat across the aisle from her on the flight in.

'It was a real treat,' he added. 'I'm going to bring my wife here for our next holiday.'

She smiled. 'That's great.'

Whereas she was never, *ever* coming back here.

'Ms Wynter?'

She turned. Ortiz was looking ridiculously expression-less, which *really* made her worry.

'Is something wrong?' She stepped nearer.

'I have a call for you.'

She realised he was holding a phone to his chest.

'If you'll follow me, there's a private room.'

She remembered what had happened the last time she'd followed this guy—abduction to the palace. Her heart thun-dered. But this time Ortiz really did lead her to a nearby room and then left her in there alone with that phone.

'Hello?'

'Elsie.' Felipe, sounding rough and rushed. 'We need to talk.'

Her legs hollowed out but she paced around the small room. 'You're supposed to be stepping onto the palace bal-cony overlooking the esplanade right now. The whole world is waiting.'

'They can wait another couple of minutes.'

'You're holding up a plane full of people too. We can't board until after the flyby.'

'The flyby won't happen until this call ends. So it's your choice, Elsie.'

Her choice? She stilled.

'You can get on that plane or you could come back to the palace so we can speak,' he explained. 'But know this: if you get on the plane, I will follow. As soon as the formalities are over here, I'll come to you. The world will know and there'll be drama and all that if you want.'

She really didn't want that. But she wanted him. She yearned for him. And all she could do was grip the phone more tightly and listen.

'Or...' He drew an audible breath. 'You can get back into the car with Ortiz and come back to the palace so we can talk face to face as soon as this show is over.'

'We don't have anything to talk about, Felipe.'

'There's something I need to tell you.' His voice caught.

Her heart ached as she heard the break in him. 'You can't tell me now?'

'Elsie...'

She closed her eyes because suddenly hope soared and she couldn't handle it. 'Don't do this, Felipe.'

'Don't leave, Elsie.' The softest breath. 'Please don't leave me.'

At the precise moment every citizen and guest in Silvabon was looking skyward, King Felipe was looking in the middle distance. He was beyond tense and couldn't even count. Then he caught it—the slow progression of a sleek black car through the back streets where the crowds weren't gathered. It made its way towards the tunnel that would take it to the palace's underground entrance. Another ten minutes and she would be within the room.

He lifted his gaze and finally breathed. The aerial display

was impressive. Their pilots were few in number but elite in skill. Streams of colour flowed from the planes—the navy and gold of Silvabon. He raised his hand. Braved a smile.

The fact was he was more nervous than he'd never been in his life.

Ten minutes later he swept along the corridor. He'd inwardly debated where he'd wanted Ortiz to bring her. His bedroom was the first place that sprang to mind. Then the cave. Neither were appropriate. They needed privacy but she also needed to know she wasn't a prisoner. That was him.

He'd settled on his private library. No guests would see her and the windows gave the room a light and airy feel and she'd not been in there. They had no history in that room.

She was already there, still wearing the blue and white, sweet and sexy dress. Her face was pale and her gaze wide and his heart stopped. It took everything not to take her into his arms and dispense with words altogether. But she needed words. He needed to figure them out.

'I'm sorry.' Simple. True.

She was so still.

He took a step forward. Then stopped.

'Do you know what I want?' He shook his head, starting the wrong way already. 'You said I was spoilt. I'm *worse* than spoilt. I'm possessive and selfish. I want you for me. You're mine. No one else's. Not even Amalia's. I want you in my bed, waiting for me. My secret pleasure. I don't want to share you at all. And I don't ever want this—' he gestured around the room and all its gilded features '—to change what we have. It changed my mother. My father. Amalia even maybe. It changes everyone. Never for the better. I don't want *this*, this joy between us, to end. Ever.'

Her whole body shook. 'This joy?' A whisper, an echo.

His heart burst and his secrets spilled. 'So I have this fantasy about keeping you in the palace in secret. But I can't. You deserve so much more than that. I didn't want kids because I thought I shouldn't and then today I'm desperate to hold onto you and I forget…and then I imagine your children—*our* children—and suddenly I've never wanted anything more and I want to change things up all differently so we can keep them safe and happy and free and I don't know who I am any more,' he growled. 'And it terrifies me. And what you said to me earlier? I couldn't listen. I couldn't *stand* to listen.'

And he couldn't stand now because he was tired—tired of fighting it, tired of holding back, tired of being strong, of being afraid. He was so damn tired he sank right where he was. And then he was just a man on his knees—all but hopeless as he tried to make her understand the things he could hardly make sense of himself.

'But at the same time it's the only thing I want to hear,' he mumbled. 'And I want to hear it again and again because it will never be enough.' The yawning void in him couldn't ever be filled and how had he handled the delight of her? By pushing her away. He was the master of his own devastation and he was furious with himself. 'I lied to you. And I hurt you and I am so sorry. And too late I realised that what terrifies me more than anything is the thought of you leaving me. I don't want you to leave me. Ever. So if you stay, know that I couldn't…that for me it's for ever. That's what I want. For ever. With you.'

Helpless, he watched a tear trickle down her cheek and his own throat choked up.

'You just appeared and you lit everything up,' he admitted, so sad to see her so upset. 'You made me laugh. You make me want to play. You gave me a sense of freedom to the point that I didn't care about the crown and that scares me too.'

Everything scared him. But mostly this. Mostly seeing her pale and silent and wiping away her tears. But then she moved. She walked towards him.

'Of course you still care about it.' Compassion shone from those blue eyes and he really didn't deserve it. 'You just stood through three hours of pomp and ceremony. You can be both things, Felipe—king and man. You can be *all* the things. Lover and tease,' she whispered softly. 'Maybe husband and father even.'

His breathing roughened and he still couldn't steady his own heart. 'I don't know how to work it out. I don't know how to…'

'Maybe you don't have to. Not alone, not any more,' she said. 'Maybe we can figure it out together.'

He paused and his insides twisted. So did his lips in the slightest of smiles. 'Right. Together.'

'I don't expect you to have all the answers, Felipe. You might be a king, but you're not some kind of god.'

He'd have chuckled if he weren't still so terrified.

'You're just a man to me.' She stepped closer. 'But I do want you to be *my* man.'

'I am. You know I am.'

Elsie was beginning to know that, yes. Suddenly his arms snaked out and he pulled her close. For a long moment he crushed her to him. His face hard against her belly, his arms shaking with the strength to hold her as tight, as close as he could.

And feeling his surging emotion? She braced, her hands on his shoulders as a tumult of relief tore the loneliness apart. She was home and he was never letting her go.

'Elsie…'

'Can I help you with this?' She took hold of his crown and tugged it up.

'Oh. Yeah.' He'd clearly forgotten he even had the thing on. 'Thanks.'

She lifted it carefully and put it on the nearest table. When she turned back he was still on his knees, rubbing his temple where the crown had left a mark.

'What?' He registered her frown and a self-mocking expression crossed his face. 'Is the hat hair bad?'

'No. But that thing is horrendously heavy.'

'Real jewels,' he muttered.

'Yes.' Standing before him again, she gently ran her hands through his hair to ruffle it. He leaned in, closing his eyes when she pressed a little harder to massage his scalp.

'Better?' she asked softly.

'Yeah.' He caught her hand and drew the inside of her wrist to his mouth. His head still bowed, he stroked her skin so gently.

'You're so beautiful,' he said. 'Watching you play the mandolin in the café that day. It sounded so delicate, almost ethereal and you were like an angel come to make us feel...' He trailed off. 'And then last night I wanted to find something delicate but strong, something that shone as brilliantly as you so that when I had to watch you from far away, when I couldn't stand beside you, I would see it even from that distance. And I'd know that I'd offered and that you'd accepted something from me. That you'd chosen me.'

Her heart melted. The bracelet.

'It was too beautiful,' she muttered. 'And I was scared, Felipe. I didn't know how to handle it.'

'I can relate.' A flash of a smile, then he hesitated. 'Would you still say no?'

Never. Not now she knew just what he'd meant. And how much he'd meant it.

He reached into his pocket with his free hand. He still had it with him... Her blood scurried as he fastened the gleaming coil around her wrist—an unbreakable rope of diamonds linking her to him.

He looked at it for a moment and then lifted his gaze. She smiled tremulously as she read the shy pleasure in his eyes that she'd accepted his gift. This, a man who had everything, hadn't had the joy of giving before.

'I love you, Elsie. And I'd love you to stay. Please.'

'I have nothing to give you,' she said softly. 'Only me.'

'That's everything and all I'll ever need.'

He meant it. She saw how much he meant it in the shimmering depths of his glistening eyes. Her legs gave out and she dropped to her knees to join him.

'I love you,' she whispered.

The kiss was messy and the tears wet and the laughter full of hiccups. But their hearts bloomed and the heat took over.

'How does this jacket even work?' She growled in frustration at the time taking to get to his skin.

He laughed a little and leaned back to divest himself of the jacket and everything else. Right there on the floor he stripped her too. And when she was naked and arching her hips he braced over her, locking her into the most delightful of cages.

'I know this is crazy quick,' he muttered. 'But I have no intention of rushing *this*. Not now.'

She trembled with the pleasure of being in his arms again. Of seeing the way he looked at her—with that adoration, relief, *joy* in his eyes.

'I didn't think I would ever have this again.' She gasped. 'You. Holding me.'

Tears then tumbled again, even in this sweetest, hottest of moments. But it was so intense. So desperately *wanted*. He held her through the storm, kissing her gently, staying with her—alongside her, inside her—as she released the last of that aching loss. And then he pressed closer, claiming his place in her body, her heart. And giving her his.

'Repeat after me,' he whispered. 'I belong to Felipe. And Felipe belongs to me.'

She smiled tremulously. 'I belong…'

Her eyes filled again and she couldn't finish it.

'I'm yours, Elsie,' he promised raggedly. 'And I'm never letting you go.'

'I never want you to,' she sobbed and clutched him closer still. 'I love you.'

They remained locked together for a long, long time after the searing cries of relief and of joy and of love had faded. It was an embrace she would never forget and never wanted to leave.

But eventually the worry machine that was her brain flicked back on.

'What are you thinking?' Felipe had felt her growing tension.

'They're going to say awful things about me,' she mumbled. 'Are you going to be able to handle it?'

'You're worried about me?'

She nodded. 'You—'

'Will not let them destroy anything.' He breathed in deeply. 'Nothing more of mine. I'm not losing you.'

'You won't,' she assured him. 'We can have time out. We can go down to the cave.'

His smile flashed. 'You like it?'

'Love it.'

'Me too.' He inhaled deeply. 'We'll get through it together. All of us.'

'All?'

'I talked to Amalia. You were right, I should have done that properly so much sooner. She would like to stay and go to school here in Silvabon.'

'And what would you like?'

'For her to stay.' He nodded.

'I'm so glad.'

Now his smile was sweet. 'So am I.'

There was a cautious knock on the door and an oddly high-pitched voice called, 'Your Majesty?'

Felipe groaned at the reminder, then laughed as he

glanced at their total disarray. 'My aide is both frantic and terrified.'

'Your guests are waiting for you,' she said.

He nodded. 'I could send them all home?'

'No. You can't.' But she appreciated the offer. 'You need to go to the dinner.'

'Do you want to come with me?'

'Not this time. Not yet. Maybe I could have a tray in your room?' she suggested. 'I can wait for you there. Maybe I could stay a secret for a little while longer? Just while we...'

He gazed at her intensely. 'Are you okay with that?'

'Sure.' She suddenly grinned up at him. 'I might find some things to play with in there. I could shred your sheets and make a trapeze to swing from that balcony.'

He laughed. 'I'll be done with dinner in ten seconds.'

'No.' She turned serious again. 'They need time to celebrate with you. I get that you have a job to do. I'll be here and I'll figure out my own. With you. We have time on our side now, right?'

'We do.' His gaze turned smoky but he swiftly stood then held out his hand to help her up. 'Come on, I'll take you to my room now. I have to shower and change. Will you keep me company for that? I don't want to leave you even for a moment.'

'Is there a secret corridor to get from here to there?'

He flicked his eyebrows. 'Of course.'

Elsie smothered a giggle as she walked with her dishevelled, half-dressed king of a man along the curling, quiet corridor.

It had been barely one day—one day in which they'd found each other again, in which they'd felt and they'd fallen...

But now they had all the time in the world to be together. They had for ever.

CHAPTER NINETEEN

Two years later, 10.18 p.m.

TWENTY-FOUR HOURS COULD be a surprisingly long time. In twenty-four hours a man could fall in love. He could make life-changing vows. He could be driven crazy by the need to be alone with the love of his life and not be stuck in front of cameras live-streaming his every move to an audience of millions.

There'd been so *many* cameras. So many moments when he'd just wanted to tell the officiants to hurry the hell up. But there'd been protocols to follow, expectations to meet, and Felipe Roca de Silva y Zafiro was still working on that tricky thing known as work-life balance. But *now* time was his. And it was almost twenty-four hours since they'd last been alone. The wait had nearly killed him. And his new wife knew it.

Tightly gripping her hand, he led a softly chuckling Elsie along the narrowing tunnel. There was only one place he wanted to be and the fast route wasn't an option tonight. If she jumped into the ocean in that dress—and with the additional weight of the jewels in her necklace, earrings and tiara—she'd drown in seconds. He wasn't letting that happen.

'Spoilsport.'

She was still salty about it. Elsie had become quite the accomplished cliff jumper.

'You just want me to strip you sooner,' he countered playfully. 'Sorry, sweetheart, you're going to need just a little more patience.'

She shot him a sizzling look. Yeah, he knew her very well. Right now she was itching for him to undo the bajillion and one teeny tiny pearl buttons that fastened the demure lace back of her wedding gown. He was too—and she knew it. Which was why she was provoking him. He had, once again, left a ballroom of presidents and princes to party without him. Their wedding celebrations were still in full swing but he didn't give a damn. He was having his wedding night *now*. He'd waited long enough. And he definitely didn't have the patience for one button at a time.

'Felipe…'

She'd stopped just inside the secret doorway. He'd instructed his valet to make a few adjustments to their cave for the evening and it was worth it to see the look on her face the second she saw it.

More cushions, more rugs, scented candles as well—not just the chandeliers. There was food too—a spread of sumptuous delicacies in platters on a low table, easily accessible from the bed. Yes, there was an actual bed, swathed in soft white luxury linen. It was a four-poster and he had plans for those posts. And beside the bed there was a large ornately carved box. He'd put that there himself.

'What's in the box?'

He smiled, loving that it was the first thing she'd noticed. 'Silk ropes.'

'Silk…?' Her eyes went very round.

'And some other little things I think you might like.'

The colour in her cheeks was now very rosy. 'How long are you planning for us to stay down here?'

He pulled her close. 'At least twenty-four hours.'

Twenty-four hours could be a shockingly *long* time.

Elsie felt as if it had been for ever since she'd had Felipe alone and all to herself. She had something to tell him. Something important—she'd only found out herself late last night and because tradition dictated she couldn't see him again before the wedding she'd had to wait. But the wretched man distracted her—making her so mindless she couldn't even speak.

'Did you just rip the back of my wedding dress?' She gasped, giddy with excitement as he hauled her closer against his extremely hard body. 'Isn't it supposed to go on show in the palace later?'

'I'm sure someone can fix it,' he muttered.

He was fully a careless, spoilt king at that moment and she loved him for it. He knew what he wanted and he wanted it now. So did she.

'It's beautiful, by the way,' he growled. 'But can we get you out of it now?'

'Fel—'

Too late, he'd kissed her again and she was too far gone to remember her own name, let alone anything else. All she wanted was all of him. Their love-making was always pure energy, pure magic. But in this place—in his secret lair with its steaming mineral bath, on this, their wedding day—it was pure *heaven*.

'We're keeping the bed here,' he mused later when he'd recovered enough breath to speak. 'I can't believe I didn't think of it sooner.'

She rested her head on his chest, linking her fingers through his, and lifted their hands, admiring the way their wedding bands glinted in the light and her bracelet sparkled. 'Best honeymoon destination ever.'

He chuckled.

They'd weathered the storm of public scrutiny and judgement. He'd stood alongside her when the press had run story after story about her family. Felipe had kept her hand in his, kept her by his side, kept her head high and her heart full. And as he was the King who could do no wrong—they couldn't help noticing... *She obviously makes him happy.*

And she'd found her *own* focus—a deeply personal campaign of caring for the carers. She'd made under-the-radar visits to the local hospices, preparing food in the family accommodation for those supporting loved ones in hospitals, finding other ways to help them. Word had leaked—not from the palace—and while there'd been some nasty elements online, Elsie had kept up her visits and in fact done yet more. She wasn't going to let what people might say stop her from doing something that mattered so much to her. In this she *could* make a difference. A couple of patients' families had spoken out on her behalf, but it was the people she met personally who showed their appreciation. And that meant everything. As people on the street stood up for her, slowly the media opinion swivelled her way. Honestly that fact pleased Felipe more than it did her, but that he was so relieved for her? That made her smile.

'Amalia did such a great job today,' she murmured happily.

'Did you see some of the commentary online about her? She's just a child,' he grumbled.

'Felipe, she's almost sixteen.' Elsie chuckled. 'Don't let her hear you say that.' But Amalia had turned heads in her pretty bridesmaid's dress. 'They'll leave her alone while she's studying, won't they?'

'I'd like to hope so.' He sighed. 'It's good they've eased off on you.'

Amalia was attending her school locally, but she now had her heart set on attending a music conservatory abroad later. Composition was her jam—she was fulfilling her artist's need to create. Elsie was creating something else entirely. She had to tell him. Now.

'Elsie?' He eased out from beneath her and rolled to his side so he could see her face. 'What are you thinking about?'

'That we're about to cause more scandal.'

'Oh?' He skimmed teasing fingertips across her belly.

'Correction.' She looked at him with a nervous smile. '*I* am about to cause more scandal.'

'Why, Elsie?' He pressed his mouth to the sensitive skin just beneath her belly button. 'What have you done?'

She shivered. Not from his kiss but because she was suddenly serious. Suddenly scared. 'The trolls are going to say I trapped you into marriage.'

'Trapped me? How?'

Elsie swallowed and lay very still. 'With the baby.'

He lifted his head. His eyes had darkened. And his palm was warm against her lower belly. 'Baby?'

'Yes.' Her eyes filled.

But his smile spread wide. 'Baby.'

'I think it was when we went on that secret trip to Italy and I told you I'd forgotten to bring my pills and that we needed to be careful.'

'But I wasn't careful.' He sounded so proud and so *smug* and he looked so gorgeously satisfied.

Suddenly her heart flew and her humour bubbled up with it. 'You were so *reckless* we were almost caught by that ferry full of tourists!'

'And didn't that turn you on even more?' He laughed delightedly. 'Oh, Elsie!'

He was kissing her and she couldn't speak again. She could only cling to him as her own excitement and joy fought to find a way out of her limbs and into his.

'Given the wedding preparations have taken more than a year, I don't think the trolls' arguments will have any teeth. If they only knew the truth…' he muttered between kisses. 'If only, if only…'

'The truth?'

He ran his hand down her body with the surest, most possessive touch yet. 'That I'm the one who's trapped you. That here I am holding you prisoner in my personal dungeon and I even plan to tether you to my bed.'

Her breathing shortened. '*Tether* me?'

'Right now, as it happens.'

'Now?' She wriggled in an automatic response to the surge of electricity his words had charged within her.

'So you can't distract me while I show you just how much I love you. So you can't escape from the truth of how much you've changed my life. I'm going to thank you, Elsie. I'm going to please you.' He pulled a strip of silk from that ornate box at the side of the bed. 'Is that okay with you?'

'Uh...' Breathless already, she licked her lips. 'Yes. But *I'm* going to explore that box later...'

'I hope so.' He carefully wrapped the silks around her wrists, his smile tender and possessive. 'I can't wait to meet our baby.' His voice quietened as he worked. As he was honest and vulnerable with her. 'Part of me is terrified. I'm desperate to protect her. But I know that with you...we can do this. Together.'

'Yes.'

Felipe had pushed forward with relinquishing some of the Crown's more substantial powers and he'd formulated a new succession plan that had been put to a public vote. His people had supported him entirely. So now their little prince or princess would become heir to the Crown only when old enough to understand the decision. There would be *choice* and more privacy in their children's lives.

His gaze down her body was intense and brooding and so, so fierce. 'I want this baby with you,' he breathed. 'I want lots of babies with you. I want everything with you.'

'Especially more holidays, right?'

'Yes.' He chuckled. 'Holidays and babies and laughter and you always with me on public engagements and so much time alone together down here. I love you, Elsie. Don't ever leave me.'

'I love you,' Elsie whispered, every bit as fierce and emotional and honest. 'And I never will.'

She was locked in his love and he in hers.

If they'd been looking they might've glimpsed the bright flashes of colour from the celebratory fireworks through the narrow gap in the rocks. But they weren't looking.

They were too busy detonating fireworks of their own.

* * * * *

THE BILLIONAIRE'S BABY NEGOTIATION

MILLIE ADAMS

MILLS & BOON

CHAPTER ONE

THERE MUST BE a German word for that near unendurable feeling of wanting to punch someone and make out with them at the same time.

At least, Olive Monroe felt there *should* be. She had a passable understanding of German and had never heard that word though. Neither was it in English, Japanese, Chinese or any of the other languages she'd learned to foster her career in business.

It was what she felt every time she looked at Gunnar Magnusson.

Billionaire, philanthropist, possibly part-time Viking, and full-time pain in her ass from the first moment she could remember.

Gunnar being an impediment was an early childhood memory.

The first time she'd seen him, she'd been six, he'd been sixteen.

Their fathers had been locked in competitive negotiations, and she'd been sitting outside on a bench, just outside the conference room. There had been a spread of goodies on the table, and her father had warned her not to touch anything. But she was certain it did not include a chocolate cupcake that were sitting out there for anyone to take.

But just as she'd steeled up her confidence to take it, a tall, blond man had walked into the room—at the time she'd thought he was a man—and had eaten the cupcake in one bite.

He'd turned and looked at her then and there had been something like embarrassment in his blue eyes, which had quickly turned to haughty disdain.

It was later she would find out that he was the only son of her father's greatest business rival.

Gunnar Magnusson, son of Magnus Ragnarson, the most hated man in the Monroe household. And he had eaten her cupcake.

It had been a *very* disappointing birthday.

It could be argued perhaps that her father had contributed at least in some part to the disappointment of the birthday, given that she had spent it sitting outside of his tense negotiations.

Her mother had died when Olive was only a baby, the love of her father's life, gone. And rather than leave her with nannies, he had taken her into his world. He had never acted like she should be a boy, or like he would have been better off without her. He treated her like she was an integral part of this world—his company, which had been his one true love before meeting her mother, before having her.

She knew he didn't mean to give her a bad birthday. He meant to give her a birthday with him. And he had taken her for sushi after, so that had been nice.

Her father was all she had. If she felt disappointment about not having a birthday party with other children, a pretty cake and pony rides, it didn't matter. It was easier to make Gunnar the bad object.

It wasn't as if he took any great care to avoid irritating her. No. They had clashed constantly over the years.

It was the trouble of their fathers being in the same industry. Constantly competing for the same tech contracts.

There had been a space of time when she'd had some relief from Gunnar. When he'd been eighteen he'd gone off on his own and started his own corporation in manufacturing and had been absent from her sphere other than industry events, which he'd often come to, dressed in tuxedos and wreaking havoc on her sanity.

She could remember—vividly—the time she'd been fifteen and he'd showed up at a charity event. He'd walked into the highly polished hotel and everything had seemed to stop.

Most men looked tamed in a tuxedo. It was the fashion of the sleek and sophisticated. But Gunnar, all broad shoulders, chest and muscular arms, slim waist and hips, looked all the more dangerous.

And Olive had fallen into a potted plant.

To her horror, it was Gunnar who appeared to lift her out, his large, warm hand, so rough and masculine, wrapping itself entirely around hers and making her feel small and fragile. Red, and hot.

Very like he had eaten her cupcake all over again, except there was something different too.

She was not fifteen now, she knew what it was now. She was just thankful fifteen-year-old Olive hadn't known, because the poor thing had already been overcome by shame at her graceless tumble into the greenery.

She hadn't needed to know she was experiencing sexual attraction for the first time in her life on top of everything else.

When she had been seventeen, Gunnar's father had died.

"We must go to the funeral, Olive."

She'd looked at her father in confusion. *"But you hated him."*

"He was my rival. Iron sharpens iron. Having him as an adversary made me better."

It was then she realized the complex nature of such relationships. And she'd been somewhat relieved. That maybe her feelings for Gunnar were something along those lines.

Because it wasn't a rivalry where you wanted your enemy to die in a fire.

You needed an opponent to race against to be your fastest.

A skilled opponent was a good thing.

That was when Gunnar had assumed control of Magnum Enterprises. And he'd come back into her life in a much more regular space.

And her feelings for him had only grown more and more tangled. Because he was the one going into those meeting rooms, and she was still sitting outside.

"Someday," her father had said, *"you'll go toe-to-toe with him. And you'll win. Maybe you'll win."*

He'd smiled at her sadly.

"I don't think I have that kind of time. But you...you're a brilliant mind, Olive, and you can do it. But you must remember. Compete without mercy. Never let emotion cloud your judgment. Give no quarter."

She carried those words with her now. Because now she was the one who went into the boardroom. It was her battle now.

And Gunnar was her opponent.

They were the same. Locked in negotiations, all day every day sometimes, to secure the best and highest paying contracts.

But this… This was the big one. Her father's baby. The one he'd worked on for years, the one he'd died before finishing.

Getting their touchscreen system, their operating system, into the largest fleet of electric cars in the world, and it would bother him so much if she won.

Gunnar Magnusson had been a vanguard of green energy for years. And while Ambient was slightly behind on that, Olive was making up for lost time. Her father had been a stickler for tradition. For doing things the way they had always been done. Not that Magnus had been any different. It was only that Gunnar had taken over Magnum Enterprises a decade ago, and Olive had only been running Ambient six months, taking over her father's unfinished projects and working as hard as she could to fulfill his goals, to be what he'd trained her to be.

And if not for what had happened after her father's funeral, she wouldn't have felt at all guilty about the way in which she had gone about gaining her info for today's meeting.

It was a bit of corporate espionage. But this contract would see her business tied up for the next decade. Constantly innovating and pushing the new technology in green energy vehicles forward, and she wouldn't have to see Gunnar for… Well, it would at least be ten years.

Because she wouldn't be able to compete for another contract on this level with everything existing that she had. They had been playing a chess game for years. Magnum's technology was ubiquitous in the corporate world. Ambient was for artists. Ambient had the most successful phone.

Magnum provided the GUI and back-end software for most things that ran on computer chips. Including a massive contract with the largest airline to use their microchips to keep the planes in the sky.

It was all global domination, and the more computerized vehicles became… The more competitive that all was.

Anyway. Ambient was just better for something like that. It needed to be slick, visuals based and artistic. Clean. In her opinion, everything that Magnum did was dull. It was corporate. And it showed.

But she would save that for the pitch, rather than hyping herself up on her own achievements in the corridor.

Twenty minutes until the meeting. And her mouth was watering.

Because she wanted a chocolate cupcake.

Damn him.

This was why she needed distance. Her father might have been able to see Magnus as iron sharpening his iron, but Gunnar wasn't iron for her. He didn't make her sharp.

He made her soft.

She'd done this to prove it didn't have to be that way. Done it to be who her dad had raised her to be.

She needed to be iron.

She couldn't do that with Gunnar around her all the time.

And just then, she heard heavy footsteps in the corridor. And looked. And there he was, striding toward her in a navy-blue suit custom-fit to conform to his hulkingly masculine figure. He was large, blond, with a beard and piercing blue eyes that she was certain could see right beneath her black turtleneck.

She didn't do suits.

"Little Olive," he said. "How nice to see you."

As he always called her.

He'd said it at her father's funeral too.

"Little Olive. How are you?"

And it had broken her. To see him, not in a business meeting, not in a highly visible charity event. But in the quiet after the funeral. With his blue eyes different than she'd ever seen them. They didn't hold a challenge.

There was concern.

And she'd wept.

And he'd held her.

She hardened herself against that memory now.

"Hello, Gunnar. Not raiding any villages and carting women off against their will today?"

He arched a pale brow. "The pillaging must cease sometimes."

"Must it? For here you are."

"Is it pillaging, or is it business? I know you like to

pretend to be very victimized by needing to compete with the best."

"But see, I win half the time. So I'm not certain how you can maintain that you're the best."

"Because some people prefer form over function."

"No. It's just that some companies are capable of providing both. Some of us think outside the suit," she said, taking a step toward him and tugging the lapel of his jacket. She regretted it in an instant. Heat arced between them.

And she tried, she really tried, to remember the times they'd clashed over the years. Not the time he'd pulled her out of the potted plant.

Not the time he'd taken her back to her empty family home after that very worst day of her life, when she'd said goodbye to her father and felt more alone than ever.

Not when he'd sat across from her in that living room and looked at her with sympathy. Let her cry and talk and share memories. Had wrapped her in a blanket and carried her upstairs.

And when he'd set her down in front of her bedroom door, all disheveled and her eyes stinging from tears, she'd put her hand on his chest and felt his heart beating hard.

He'd taken his jacket off downstairs and was wearing just a white shirt, unbuttoned at the throat and she'd wanted him.

She wasn't fifteen and she knew how she wanted him now.

So she'd stretched up on her toes, her mouth a breath from his.

"No, Olive."

The refusal stung, even now.

"Go to sleep. You're tired and grieving. And you would not thank me in the morning."

He'd hurt her. Broken her with that refusal, even as he'd knit her emotions together with his concern earlier.

And when she'd seen him again at a business function he'd acted as if the night hadn't happened.

She'd been outraged and relieved all at once.

Outraged she was still affected by him. Relieved he wasn't going to humiliate her by bringing up her attempt at kissing him.

But sadly, she still wasn't cured. Which had fueled her need to win this contract. It now held the weight of so many of her needs.

To see her father's dreams come to fruition. To be as strong and ruthless as he'd wanted her to be.

To get Gunnar out of her life so she could be free of this tangle of feelings.

Because even now there was heat. All these months there had been heat.

For far longer than that. For years, her late-night fantasies were of being carried away by a Viking and tied up as his prisoner in his longhouse…

Well. No one had to know that. And no one ever needed to see her stack of medieval Viking romance novels.

There was a particularly interesting Caitlin Crews on the subject that had occupied the last few nights.

It was probably *not* the best reading material just before heading in to see Gunnar. But being totally truthful, it didn't matter if she read the books just before seeing him or not. He owned that part of her. He was tangled up in so many things. In formative ideas about fantasy, sex and romance.

It was easy for her to tell herself she'd never had a romantic life because she'd been so busy training to take over Ambient.

But the truth was a lot more specific. A lot more Icelandic.

A lot more…him.

"Very avant-garde. Nobody has ever done this…" He gestured over her outfit. "I have simply never seen it."

"I'm not trying to be *original*, I'm trying not to take up my time with ridiculous details that have nothing to do with innovation."

"I brought you something."

She knew that he had. He reached into his briefcase, and pulled out a chocolate cupcake. Oh, she despised him. Because it was like Pavlov's dog, and she had a feeling that he knew it.

He had taken to bringing her a chocolate cupcake at each and every one of these pitch meetings. Which only became more and more heated.

They never spoke to the person whose contract they were competing for separately. No. They always did it together. Their fights over who would win these wars had become legendary, and people wanted a front row seat.

He claimed, and she did not believe him, that the cupcake was a peace offering. She thought that it was just to make her angry. But the problem was, she was now conditioned to need a chocolate cupcake prior to these events.

And if she refused, she felt that he would know it.

"Thank you," she said taking the cupcake in hand.

Her stomach growled. And she just grinned past it. She began to delicately lick at the frosting, and when she looked up, she saw that there was heat in his blue eyes.

Yes. This was not one-sided.

"You know. Whoever wins this contract will be tied up for so long… I daresay we won't be seeing each other for quite some time."

"Indeed," he said.

She twirled the cupcake in a circle as she licked at the chocolate butter cream. Making eye contact with him. "I'll miss you. Or maybe I'll just miss the cupcakes."

"I'll get you a subscription to a bakery service. Cake of the month."

She put her hand on her chest and looked at him with

what she hoped was mournful sadness. "That would help ease the pain."

"What will be next for you," she said, "when you don't get this contract? Will you fade off into the distance and focus all of your attention on your other endeavors?"

"I won't lose," he said.

"Oh, Gunnar. You are going to lose. You're gonna lose bad." She smiled at him.

He curled his upper lip, almost as if in a sneer, and then tapped his blindingly white front tooth. "You have chocolate. Just there."

"Of course I do, dumbass," she said, closing her mouth and running her tongue quickly along her teeth. "I'm eating a chocolate cupcake."

"Still. You might want to sort that out before the meeting starts."

"I'll just be a moment."

She stopped in the bathroom and made sure that everything with her teeth looked good, and by the time she was finished it was time to step into the meeting.

Poor Gunnar. She almost felt sorry for him. Because she had seen his entire presentation. Months ago. And she had tailored her projected technology accordingly. He would simply never know what hit him.

And being so confident in her position allowed her to sit back during his presentation and focus on his hands. The way they caressed the different visuals. The prototypes. The sharpness in his consonants, the masculine set of his broad shoulders... Yes. It was so easy to imagine him as a Viking marauder.

She really didn't understand how you can hate a person so much, and also have that same person exclusively be the one man you ever wanted to go to bed with. Olive wasn't a prude. Her reading material proved that.

But she was busy, and she had decided a long time ago

that there was no point pursuing anything with a man who didn't make her half as excited as a new piece of technology… Or Gunnar Magnusson.

Because if a man she disliked could make her entire body ache in inappropriate places… A man she liked should be able to do just as much with one look. And she had never felt compelled to experiment physically. She had kissed a couple of men. And again, the issue was that one withering glare from Gunnar gave her weeks more fantasy fodder than any of those kisses had.

That moment in the hall at her family home…when she'd been able to breathe him in, when she'd been so close to him she could feel his heat…

It haunted her, even now as they pretended that evening of tenderness, of connection had never happened, it haunted her.

So what was the point?

What was the point.

If she couldn't get away from him, there would never be anyone else.

Not ever.

And Gunnar was finished. And it was her turn.

"Thank you. That was very interesting, Mr. Magnusson. I think, though, Mr. Yamamoto, that you will find this to be the most compelling direction." And she laid out a thorough a assassination for Gunnar's system. She had identified every flaw in his design, and she had tweaked and reflected her own in response. She had set about making a system that annihilated his. And in her—not her words, but profiles that had been done on her—engaging and down-to-earth style that made technology so accessible anyone could understand, she laid out her plan for the fleet.

And in the end, she was the one who got the handshake.

"Congratulations, Miss Monroe. Ambient is the clear choice to be fulfilling the need for our fleet."

Gunnar didn't react. This wasn't the first time he had lost to her. But it was his biggest loss. He shook Mr. Yamamoto's hand gamely, and smiled. "Perhaps we could do work together in the future."

"You never know," said Mr. Yamamoto.

And after that, she and Gunnar left, at the same time. And began walking down the hall together quickly.

"It will be such a shame not to see you for the next ten years. But I'm booked."

"It was a valiant win," he said. "Your product is brilliant. Anyone can see that."

"Even you. What an incredible, astonishing concession."

"Fair is fair. Best is best. Do you have any plans while you're here in Tokyo?"

"Not really." *Sushi in my hotel room and more of my book.*

"I see. And where are you staying?"

"Down the street."

They got in the elevator together, and the doors closed. He looked at her, and she looked at him. She smiled. "How are my teeth?"

"Sharp," he said.

"Good. All the better to eat you with and all that."

"And truly, decisively, you have."

"I hope you don't take it too hard."

"All's fair in business."

She grinned. "Indeed."

She doubted that he would think her efforts with her mole on the inside of his corporation for the last few months was fair, but she didn't care. She had killed two birds with one stone. Not only did she have the contract, Gunnar would be out of her life. She could stop obsessing. She could stop waking up drenched in sweat, panting and shaking from a climax she'd had in her sleep because of dream sex with him.

Yeah. She was feeling pretty pleased.

She was hungry for this kind of happiness.

I did it, Dad. I guess you were right, iron did sharpen iron. But it's not him. You sharpened me, and you can be proud of me.

"Where are you staying?"

"I believe we're in the same building," he said.

"Of course we are. It is the nicest hotel within walking distance," she said.

That was one of the many problems with Gunnar. He often employed the same logic she did. There was understanding your enemy, and then there was knowing them just a little bit too well.

They walked into the busy, polished lobby and continued walking across the room together.

"Top floor."

"I'm the same."

They stepped onto another elevator in tandem, and the doors closed. And this time, she could hear her heart beating in her ears.

"Care to have a celebratory drink?" he asked.

"I would," she said.

"Wonderful."

And there was something, something building inside of her. In anticipation, and a feeling. And when the doors opened to the abbreviated hallway that housed the penthouse rooms, he led her down the opposite direction from her own room, his phone granting access to the room immediately.

"After you," he said.

"Thank you."

His penthouse seemed entirely different than hers. This one was all black. A high shine floor, with curved modern art everywhere. All black.

And the large windows that looked out over the city gave

a view of the madness below while keeping the occupant at a distance.

"I love Tokyo," she said.

"I prefer the top of the mountain. But as cities go."

She turned, and saw that he was standing in front of the kitchen counter, his hands flat on the glossy dark surface.

Such beautiful hands.

"Yes. But on a mountain you're probably alone."

"I elect to have solitude. I quite like it."

"Not me," she said. "A business meeting. A party, with networking… I love all of it."

Of course, her surrounding life was completely empty. But that was a choice. Because her father had taught her how to network, how to connect in ways that benefitted and suited you, but he'd impressed upon her the importance of guarding herself.

It was like she lived in a constant state of tension with her emotions.

Be friendly, but not known.

It was why she often went so soft after a business event or negotiation.

You could not go as hard as she did in these situations and then not decompress somehow. Usually, a warm bath and a book.

She shouldn't have thought about baths. Not standing there in front of him. Or maybe…

Something changed between them. The quality of the air.

No. She couldn't let her guard down, but she could feel it. Could feel it falling away, and it was too soon.

It was safe to read romance novels alone. Safe to cry alone. Safe to feel alone.

But not in front of him.

They had nothing to discuss. So what was the real reason she was here?

You know why you're here. You came for this.

This was going to be her last interaction with Gunnar Magnusson for a very long time. Maybe they would never compete for the same contract ever again. Their companies were in divergent spaces. And this may have been truly the last and most decisive competition.

This was the moment.

She had been sixteen the first time she thought about kissing him.

It had been a fever dream. Something that had hit her when he had treated her to a derisive smile while he had prepared to go into battle with her father, the first time he had been at the helm of Magnum in a negotiation.

He'd won. And she had spent the flight home feeling guilty, shame filled and confused. Her fantasies had steadily grown more and more adult.

But time, animosity and common sense had not dimmed them.

She'd wanted him six months ago and he'd denied her.

But she wasn't weeping now. She wasn't sad.

She'd just defeated him, so whatever his excuses about her being vulnerable...

He couldn't cling to them now.

And maybe he would still reject her. But she wouldn't have to face him after, so what did it matter?

This was her moment. And she would take it.

"I know my turtlenecks are not to your taste. Maybe I should just..." And without thinking, she grabbed the hem of her shirt and pulled it up over her head.

CHAPTER TWO

OLIVE WATCHED GUNNAR's expression closely, trying to gauge a response. She had a simple black bra beneath her turtleneck, but honestly, she hadn't planned this, even though now she could see…

There had never been another end point.

Not for her. She had to have this, or try to have it, anyway.

She had given and given to this life, to this dream of her father's—she wanted to give to it. Out of loyalty and love.

But this was something she wanted to take for herself.

Needed to take for herself.

But she couldn't see if it was the same for him. She had no idea what he was thinking. So she stared.

Would he reject her again?

She didn't know what she had expected. For him to laugh. For him to suddenly transform into a charmer of some kind?

Gunnar had quite the reputation as a lover. He was not a playboy, in fact, he did not flaunt his physical relationships at all. But there were whispers. Of his prowess. Of his particular…assets. And of the intensity.

Not that she had looked in online forums for rumors about what it was like to have sex with him.

No. Couldn't be her. At least, she hadn't done it in a while.

He did not smile. He did not put her at ease. But he most

certainly didn't laugh. Instead, he reached up and began loosening his tie, stalking toward her, his blue eyes intense, like a predator.

And all the breath in her body whooshed out.

"Oh," she said.

It was the last thing she said before he gathered her up in his arms, and brought his mouth down on to hers in a raging torrent of pent-up passion that threatened to destroy them both.

Finally. Finally. He was kissing her. And it had been worth the wait. Because it was everything. Beyond. It was the pages of every romance novel. The kind where tension and lust burned from the pages and left her weak with wanting. He was a conqueror.

And he plundered her mouth.

It was hot and slick, and even though she hadn't done this before, she had read enough to have an idea. She parted her lips, met each thrust of his tongue with her own. She was ready.

Physically, she might be innocent, but she had a treasure trove of fantasies, and they were not tentative. And they all centered on him.

She wrenched his tie the rest of the way free, pulling it off and throwing it down onto the floor.

"Thank you for being such a gracious loser," she said, wrenching at his shirt, pulling it open and letting buttons fly everywhere.

His chest.

Dear God. That chest.

She ran her hands over it, hungry. Excitement building between her thighs.

Rough golden hair covered tawny skin, the muscles there thick and well defined.

He was everything she had ever fantasized about.

He was more.

He was…

He growled and leaned in, biting her neck. "It was always going to end here, Olive."

Relief swamped her.

He felt it too.

He did.

But the years of learning to guard herself, against him and everything, pushed her to be spiky in return.

"I am not an inevitability," she said.

Except she knew she was. This was. It had been set in stone perhaps since the dawn of time.

Her body was trained to respond only to Gunnar Magnusson, whether it made sense or not. And it didn't. Because he was the antithesis of all that she should want.

Except… She was a smart, ambitious woman, and she could not accept a man who was any less of those things than her. So of course… The modern-day Viking raider who wore a suit with ease, but also looked like he could wield an axe, was all she wanted.

Anything else would be a compromise.

And Olive had never been taught how to compromise.

Conquer. Destroy. Dominate.

The word made her knees feel weak.

Because the truth of it was…

She thrilled at the idea of a man strong enough to dominate her.

A man that she would want to submit to. To let him make her feel the kinds of pleasure he dictated.

And that, well that, was exactly why Gunnar appealed to her, even while driving her crazy.

"For me you are."

And that was when he pushed his hand down beneath the waistband of her pants, her panties, his big, rough fingers sliding between that damp cleft there, finding her wet and ready. "Is this not inevitable, Olive?"

And it was the strain in his voice that nearly sent her over the edge.

The way the ferocity in his gaze stood as an admission to his own desire.

That she wasn't simply claiming this for herself, but that he was claiming it for him too.

Which made it theirs.

Oh, this fire was theirs and that drove her higher, faster.

He stroked her, rubbing her sensitized flesh with the pad of his finger, before thrusting it deep inside of her.

She gasped, grabbing hold of his broad shoulders. "Gunnar."

"It feels inevitable to me. You're so wet for me. This cannot be the first time you've ever thought of giving yourself to me. You must think about it. Often. Not just that night you tried to kiss me."

And she wanted to admit it. That he was the only man she'd ever wanted. That she'd dreamed of him for years. That when she'd turned eighteen she had a fevered fantasy of sneaking to see him—another birthday that she had in office buildings, because of her father's business dealings. Another time when Gunnar had been in a hotel room close to hers.

And she had thought… She was legally an adult, and could go to his bed if she wanted to.

In the end, she had been too afraid to do it.

She'd been too afraid of his rejection.

And she would have him now, in honor of eighteen-year-old Olive. She would not tell him that she had fantasized about him. She would not tell him how long she'd wanted him.

And she would not allow him to believe that they were inevitable.

She'd been taught to guard her feelings all of her life, and she could see the benefit to that now.

She felt shaken and vulnerable already. Guarding the deepest part of herself was necessary.

He could believe in the attraction. The physical aspect of it. But she couldn't expose her sweet, girlish fantasies of him. Couldn't let him know about that soft, secret part of herself.

Except then he pushed a second finger inside of her, his blue eyes boring into hers as he thrust them in and out of her willing body.

"You are enjoying this," he growled.

She moved her hand to cup the front of his pants. "So are you."

It was an effort, not to react to what she found there. Hard and so large that the virginal nerves she didn't think she possessed rose up hard.

He moved his hand away from her, and she felt bereft when he left her body. But then, he reached around and undid her bra, and there was something about finally being exposed to him like this that only amped up her arousal.

She pushed his jacket from his shoulders, then his shirt. Then she moved away from him, kicking off her shoes, and pushing her pants and underwear down her hips, relieved. That finally she was naked in front of him.

Finally.

She sat on the black, velvet couch in the living area, in that perfect, ladylike manner she had been instructed to sit in charm school. And it amused her. To act prim even now.

His lips curved into a smile, his hands going to his belt. And every part of her went liquid at the sight. He undid it slowly, moving the belt through his palms, and snapping it, the sound sending a jolt of anticipation and desire through her body.

"You are something, aren't you?" he asked.

"How long have *you* fantasized about me?" she asked, because he was happy to try and force her to admit that this was a long-held desire, so why shouldn't she push for the same?

"Probably not a good question to ask."

He began to undo the closure on his pants. Kicked off his shoes and socks, and stripped off everything else.

His erection was thick and long, and while she had been absolutely certain that nothing about the man would be diminutive—plus there had been those online rumors—she wasn't certain she had been prepared for him to be quite so... Much.

"Spread your legs," he said.

She met his gaze, because she was never one to back away from a challenge, most especially a challenge issued by Gunnar.

She sat poised on the edge of the couch, and opened herself for him. He stood there, devouring her with his eyes, and even though he was not touching her... She felt that blue lightning as if he were stroking her.

She moved her hand, ready to ease the ache herself.

"No," he said, and that stopped her midmotion.

"You will not come until I say you can."

"That's quite misogynistic," she said.

"I think some people call it a game, Olive. If you play games with me, you follow rules. Do you understand?"

She was shivering now. Uncontrollably. Because this really was her every fantasy. Every dark, shameful need brought to the surface, bright and sharp.

He walked toward her, every inch the conqueror, and reached out and took hold of her chin. Then he leaned down, and he kissed her.

It was hot, deep and dirty. A pantomime of what he would do to other parts of her body, that hot tongue thrusting deep, creating havoc in her core.

Still poised on the edge of the couch, he kept her head

tilted up as he stood, and then he moved forward, fisting his large erection, and guiding it toward her lips.

She parted them eagerly. Greedily, and took the shiny head of him inside. And then he canted his hips forward, pushing himself deeper into her mouth.

She sucked him greedily, wrapping her fingers around the base of his shaft and squeezing tight as she took in as much of him as she could.

This was her fantasy. From the submissive position, making this man weak with desire.

She had thought of it so many times. And while it felt new, while it felt like a first time, it also felt as if she had some idea of what to do.

She had read about the act, described explicitly, and her own mind had run wild with scenarios where she might end up in a position to do this to him. In a limousine. Shared on the way to a conference, for some reason. Beneath the boardroom table. After a tense negotiation. Yes. Her mind had well and truly been over this territory before. She was lost in it. In the rhythm. In the dark magic of it all.

And then suddenly he drew away from her. "Enough. It's my turn."

And he knelt down, lifting her up by the waist and sitting her atop the arm of the couch. He guided her to use her arm to brace herself on the back of it, and to use the other hand to grip the edge. Then he roughly parted her legs, one propped up on the couch, the other on the floor. And he wrapped his hands around, cupping her ass as he leaned forward and began to eat her.

It was not tentative. He devoured her like a beast, sucking her clitoris into his mouth, before pushing two fingers inside of her to create a hypnotic rhythm, lips and tongue working in tandem with his magic hands.

She writhed against his mouth, his beard rough on her inner thighs. His tongue hot and obscene.

"Gunnar," she moaned, fisting his hair and rocking her hips in time with his thrusts.

"You can come now," he said, sliding the flat of his tongue over that sensitized bundle of nerves, and making her world shatter behind her eyelids.

She couldn't stop. Wave after wave of desire crashing over her. And when she was done, holding that same position, he shifted and pressed his arousal between her legs, teasing her as he rubbed the glossy head over where she needed him most.

"Please," she whimpered. "Please."

"What?"

"Take me, you monster," she said, the words coming out random.

"Oh. That's what you want from me, little Olive? You want me to take you and make this all go away?"

"Yes," she moaned.

And then, he was right there, sinking into her, filling her. It was tight, but it was glorious.

And she let her head fall back. Her keening cry so loud it should've embarrassed her. But she couldn't be embarrassed. All she could do was feel.

"It will never go away," he whispered against her mouth. "You will want me. Always. You will never be free of this." He began to rock his hips forward, going deeper, deeper still. And his thrusts became hard, erratic, and she thought she was going to die from the wave of pleasure that threatened to capsize her.

Then he lifted her up off the couch, still buried deep inside of her, and walked them both out of the room. He separated from her a moment, to lay her down on the bed, where she knew she was open and glistening and obvious to him, and she didn't even care.

Then he was on her, over her, thrusting hard back inside of her and making them both cry out with the glory of it.

"You'll think about me," she whispered. "You'll think about me forever. I promise you."

"Then give me everything now," he said.

And she found herself breaking apart again, shivering and shaking, this climax deeper, different than the first. And then, he snapped. He growled, fierce and like the Viking raider she knew he was in his soul, as he spilled himself deep inside of her.

It was done.

She had done it. It should be a thick, permanent line drawn beneath them.

Why then, did she shiver? Why was she trembling from the inside out? Why did she feel like weeping?

Why did she feel lost?

"Congratulations," he said. And then he got up off the bed and went into the bathroom. She lay there for a long moment, and then stood slowly, making her way back into the living room and collecting her clothes.

She felt rocked. Scraped raw, but she forced a smile on her face.

She had won. In every way she had won.

She had the contract. She wouldn't have to see Gunnar again.

She would not indulge this pain in her chest telling her she had lost something.

And before she had cut ties, she had finally lived her deepest fantasy. And it had been everything… Everything. And now when she went to bed alone… She would have the real thing to think about. And not just wild fantasies based on fiction.

And of course, she had always known that she and Gunnar could never have more than one night. It was impossible.

But this night had been everything she needed it to be.

She didn't need any more.

CHAPTER THREE

WHEN HE SAW Olive Monroe's name come across his desk two months later, he was almost certain that it was a hallucination.

She had been haunting him, like a ghost, so it seemed in keeping with everything else. He woke up at night, tangled in his sheets, slick with sweat.

Gunnar did not do unsatisfied desire.

When he wanted something, he got it. Whether it was a chocolate cupcake or a woman. But thus was the longstanding issue of Olive Monroe.

There was no other person on the planet he understood quite so well.

And none who was buried so deeply beneath his skin.

Were he another sort of man, he might have called it… love.

But he was not that man, so he called it fascination, or even just protective.

From the time she'd been a beautiful eighteen-year-old girl, looking at him with hungry eyes and uncertain desire.

Because yes, he took what he wanted, but within the bonds of moral certainty. Women who knew what they wanted, and who wanted him. And who well knew the desires and needs of their own bodies.

He'd known what her desire was for. What it meant. He could have shown her then, but he'd…

He'd made his life a pursuit of being nothing like Magnus Ragnarson.

His father had been a bastard of the highest order, and the only thing worse than the man's actions, had been the years Gunnar had spent idolizing him. Not realizing the manner of man he truly was.

It was his desire to be nothing like the kind of man who used and discarded young women, who engaged in morally bankrupt business practices that destroyed the environment, displaced families and paid workers piteous wages to work in dangerous factories, that had held him back from ever touching Olive.

And yet it had done nothing to dampen his desire for her.

His obsession.

He did not spar with her because he needed to indulge the public spectacle. He had no use for such things. He sparred with her because he enjoyed it.

He sparred with her because it was better than sex with anyone else.

Turning her away the night of her father's funeral had been a feat of unhuman strength. Certainly, it had fueled a sense of moral superiority in him that had nearly been consolation enough for not tasting her sweet mouth.

He'd given in now, though.

And he'd considered calling her many times over the last two months. Why should they not have an affair?

Self-denial had so long been his virtue when it came to her that he'd resisted it out of habit.

But his body wanted a particular woman. And that was another thing about Gunnar. He did not take second. When he wanted something, he would have the *first* of it. The best of it. Or he would have none of it.

And so his lust had remained thoroughly unsated these past two months, because all his body wanted was Olive.

But no. It was not a hallucination. Olive's name truly was

on this memo, and his assistant was standing there fidgeting, the man looking utterly ill at ease.

"All of the information is here in this written memo," he said. "But I feel also that I need to speak to you."

"Make it quick."

"Do you know how Olive was able to win the auto contract?"

It was no mystery to Gunnar. The simple truth was… Olive had destroyed his presentation. Hers had been better in every way. Her product was better. He had been… fiercely proud of her.

"I am always happy to receive a bit of insight," he said.

"She had seen your products. And your presentation."

Something in him went still. "That is impossible."

"It isn't," the man said. "Because… Because she paid me. To feed her the information."

It was as if the world had been turned on its axis. Gunnar was immobilized. He prided himself on his read of people. For being wrong about someone had destroyed his world, and the lives of the people he had loved most, and he had learned that he could not afford to make such mistakes again, not ever.

And here he was now, faced with the betrayal of his assistant, and…

Olive.

Olive, who he'd long wanted to protect. To save.

Olive who he…

In his mind was a montage of every time he'd brought her a cupcake. Every time they'd sparred. Of the time he'd lifted her from a potted plant when she'd been an ungainly teenage girl—long before he'd wanted her.

Of the first moment he'd realized he did want her. And of the strange mix of pride and competition he'd always felt when watching her work.

He'd always found her brilliant. A much brighter mind than her father. And he'd believed her to be…good.

But she was no different than all these men who played games to line their pockets. Than those who disadvantaged others to elevate themselves.

Little Olive, who he had always believed to be singular, was nothing more than a common thief.

Everything in him turned to ice. "So, you've been working for her?"

"Yes," Jason said.

"I would venture to say you are not coming clean now because of a guilty conscience." Clearly neither Jason nor Olive had a conscience at all.

"No," the other man said, hesitating.

"Then why?" Gunnar pressed.

"Because I don't feel her company is the future. There are issues… There are issues at the moment. Vulnerabilities."

"In what sense," Gunnar asked, his voice hard.

"She hasn't been herself. Everyone on her team has noticed. She has been at work less, coming in late. One wonders if she's slid into the sorts of traps that many people her age might in this position."

"What are you saying?"

"Maybe a drinking problem? Partying? I'm not certain. All I know is it's becoming clear she may not be the future of the company I initially believed."

Even now, he wanted to defend Olive. She was young and saddled with an incredible burden.

She isn't who you thought.

He cast his mind back to the night of her father's funeral. How she'd wept. How soft she'd been.

That had been a lie like everything else. Because how could that woman who had betrayed him also be that soft creature who'd tilted her face up to him in silent demand for a kiss?

"What is it you want?" Gunnar asked.

"I want a position secured at the company. I can provide proof she earned the contract nefariously, and you can get her out of the way and secure a contract with Yamamoto yourself."

Gunnar laughed. And laughed.

"I do not negotiate with traitors who have no honor. Clean out your desk."

Olive was wretched. She had been feeling sick for weeks, and she was in utter denial about why. She simply couldn't handle the potential truth. And she had avoided thinking about it. Completely. It made her feel like she was shaking apart.

She didn't think it was a mystery as to why she hadn't had her period two months in a row. It wasn't a mystery why she was feeling groggy and tired and sick in the mornings. Not when you considered she had sex for the first time in her life, and it had been *decidedly* unprotected.

She and Gunnar were two of the greatest minds in technology, and they were also two idiots who'd had sex without a condom.

She blamed him. Really.

She had been a virgin. He ought to know better. And all right, maybe she ought to know better too. But she made a terrible choice. They had made a terrible choice. And now, the consequences were…

Well, the consequences were particularly and potentially dire.

She'd…ruined everything. She was supposed to be the guiding light for this company and she was barely able to sit up straight at her desk. She wasn't a pillar of leadership. She'd been fuzzy and disorganized for weeks, her brain a total mess.

She'd gotten herself pregnant with the enemy's baby.

Her father would be…

He wouldn't be proud. Not of this.

She was slumped behind her desk, but nobody was here. So it didn't matter.

She took a sleeve of saltines from the top drawer and brought it down, holding it close to her chest. This was really just awful.

She was feeling wretched. And terrified. She had come out on top when it came to the contract, but when it came to everything else…

She had not gotten him out of her system, not if what she suspected was true. If what she suspected was true was, in fact, true then… He was quite a bit more in her system than she had anticipated him ever being.

The idea made her want to throw up then and there.

And suddenly, she heard a commotion outside, a scuffling and then commotion.

And suddenly, the door to her office swung open.

She popped her head up like a meerkat coming up from underground, and then she saw him, and shrank down slightly, so that she was certain only her eyes were visible over the top of her desk.

"Olive," he said, her name on his lips a warning.

"What's going on, bestie?" she asked, trying her best to paste a bright and convincing smile on her face.

She had a feeling it looked more like a grimace.

He rounded the desk, and she scrabbled downward, pulling her knees up to her chest, the sleeve of saltines held tightly against them.

"Did you think that you could get away with this?"

Terror streaked through her. How could he know? She didn't even *know*.

"I don't know what you're talking about," she whispered.

"Your unfortunate foray into corporate espionage."

She was almost relieved to hear him say that. And how

ridiculous was that? Except the company didn't seem like the important thing, not right now. Not between them.

So she tried her best to look and sound casual, even while she was shaking apart.

"Oh. That. All's fair," she said, brushing some crumbs off of her knee. And suddenly, his blue eyes sharpened.

"What exactly are you doing?"

"I am having a sick day," she said.

"You're in the office," he pointed out.

She shrugged her shoulders and took a saltine out of the cracker tube, because really, there was no pretending this wasn't happening. He had caught her in an inglorious position and she refused to scramble out of it, which in her mind would be giving in. Bending to the pressure of his presence, and she refused to do that.

"If there's work to be done, I'm here. Just with crackers."

"You are on the floor."

"Yeah. They did a study? In Sweden. It was very obscure. You probably haven't heard of it. But it was about the increase of workflow when you sit in unconventional spaces. Something about the freedom to shape your body how you feel you ought to."

"Olive," he said, harder this time.

And just then, the absurdity of all of it crashed over her. He was her mortal enemy in many ways, always had been. Trained up from the time they were children, essentially. And in other ways, he was the person she knew best left in all this world. Her father was gone, and aching grief that hadn't eased up even once in the last six months, and she had never had time to have friends. As far as she knew, Gunnar didn't have friends either.

He had lovers.

Which she supposed she was now among. But they actually did know each other. And right now, she wanted to confide her woes in him, except he was the source of them, and he could never know.

He made her feel guilty for having double-crossed him, and that was ridiculous.

His father had certainly taught him the same values as hers. When it came to business, nothing was off the table, her dad had been clear on that. And that Magnus had acted in the same fashion.

"Well. If all is fair, then you will appreciate what comes next," he said.

He crouched down in front of her, and she felt her stomach get tight.

He grabbed the edge of the cracker packet, and tugged it out of her hands. "I shall need you paying attention. And not eating crackers."

"I didn't eat crackers in bed," she said. "You can't be too annoyed by the crackers."

"You did not eat crackers in bed, you did not stay long enough to have a snack."

"I wasn't aware snacks were on the table, so to speak."

His eyes flashed with ice. "They weren't."

"See. There was no point bringing it up, then," she said weakly.

"You were the one that mentioned bed."

"So I did."

And he just sort of looked at her, those blue eyes piercing deeper than she would like.

"I'm going to ruin you."

He said it conversationally. As he had said everything else since he had walked in.

"What?"

"You know, what you did is illegal. In many jurisdictions."

"Well, you're going to have trouble figuring out which jurisdiction exactly I did it in. We both travel all over the world, we have corporate offices all over the world." She was terrified, her heart beating so hard she felt dizzy.

And worse, she felt guilty.

Because Gunnar was angry, and that she had expected. But there was a sense she'd…disappointed him.

And she hated it.

But she couldn't do anything but brazen it out now. Her dad hadn't taught her how to back down. He'd only taught her to dig in.

And right now, defending herself had never been more important.

Because it was quite possible she contained a life.

"I know that at least at one point you were somewhere where it was illegal. As it was Jason committing the espionage, and he is my assistant."

"That little weasel. He ratted me out didn't he?"

"Can a weasel rat something? Or is it… A weaseling?"

"I don't know, and I don't care," she returned, ferociously. She leaned forward and snatched her crackers out of his hand, and stood up. But all at once, the blood left her head, and she felt woozy.

"Gunnar?" It was the last thing she said, and his face was the last thing she saw, before she collapsed into his arms.

CHAPTER FOUR

GUNNAR HAD NEVER taken Olive for being weak. She had always seemed strong and plucky and well able to dish out and take the same.

But here she was, collapsed into his arms, fainted dead away, and he knew that it wasn't a ruse. Because there was no way that she could contrive to have her lips turn that worryingly bluish tint.

And there was no question that he must take action.

Gunnar lifted her up, carrying her out of the front of the office.

And everybody outside looked up at him as if he had murdered her.

"She fainted," he said, growled. "Does anyone have water?"

"I…" The woman behind the counter looked nervous.

And no one was jumping to attention. No one was making movements—frantic or otherwise—to see to the health of their clearly unwell boss.

A drinking problem, Jason had said, but this was not alcohol.

She was ill.

"Ridiculous," he said, striding down the hall, holding Olive to his chest. He was furious with her. For not being what he'd believed her to be.

That realization caught hard in his chest.

He had been on the verge of strangling her, and then, he had found her crouched in a corner eating crackers.

Something wasn't right about this, and he knew that.

But then, something wasn't right about any of this. It was that damned woman. The way that she had gotten him to let his guard down. He had to wonder if she had been running a long con all this time. Had gotten him to see her as someone formidable, but ultimately fluffy. Someone he wanted to protect as much as he wanted to spar with her.

He had brought her cupcakes, and it had started as a joke, and then he had been amused by the fact that she expected them.

But he wondered if somewhere in there, he had allowed her to get between a crack in the wall.

He had begun to feel for her. Deeply.

And now…

She had betrayed him. And it burned.

He had set about to live a life that needed no one. That was not dependent on others to be good or true or right, because he knew he could not trust them to be.

But somewhere along the way he'd grown complacent about her, and too confident in his own ability to discern who was right and good.

He had let her get beneath his defenses.

Never again.

Even now, while he felt obligated to see to her health, he hardened himself against her. Against those feelings.

An interesting question to ask himself as he carried her limp form through the lobby of her high-rise office building, and out the revolving doors. His driver pulled up to the curb. "Take me to the nearest private doctor. I will pay whatever expense, but I don't know what is the matter with her."

"Did you poison her?" the driver asked.

Everyone knew about his rivalry with Olive. It was legendary. A thing written about in the press. Their competition for contracts was a highly sought out show.

And sometimes he thought that people reviewed both of their work simply to see them in action.

He had thought—many times—about farming that part of the business out, but...

You like sparring with her. You like being with her.

It was so raw, so much an apparent weakness now, that it shamed him.

Now he needed to get her to a doctor. What he liked or didn't like about sparring with her was immaterial.

He carried her limp form up to the edge of the sidewalk, and jerked open the passenger door, sitting her inside and scooting her across the seat. Then he got in beside her. He shut the door behind him, and for the first time, she stirred.

His driver took off, melting into the New York traffic.

"What?"

"Oh," she said. "I feel sick."

"If you throw up in my car, there will be a steep cleaning deposit."

"What about if I throw up in your lap?" she asked.

"I don't know. No one has ever done it. I would imagine the consequences would be interesting."

"Oh," she said. "I feel like I'm going to die."

And this made his heart twist, because no matter his anger, whenever he saw a bit of vulnerability in Olive it called to the Viking warrior within him, who wanted to shield her from all danger.

Including himself.

"Are you?" he asked.

"Am I what?"

"Going to die."

"That depends on if you're going to kill me," she said.

"I said *ruin*. Not kill."

She was half lying in the seat, her hand pressed against

her forehead. And suddenly, it was as if she had taken in her surroundings for the first time.

"Where are we going?"

"I'm taking you to a doctor, you silly woman. You are clearly unwell."

"No," she said, suddenly scrambling into a sitting position. "I don't need to go to a doctor. Dump me in the gutter with the rest of the traitorous gutter weasels. You want revenge, right? Leave me out in the cold!"

"You collapsed into my arms in your office. I found you on the floor eating a sleeve of crackers. You may be dehydrated. It's likely that you need an infusion of liquid."

"I think I fainted because of my shock at seeing you. And your threats. If you take me to a doctor, I might well just have you arrested for assault."

He lifted one brow. "Will you?"

"A doctor can prove that I was under duress because of you and your words."

"Somehow, I do not think that the doctor will find that I am the cause of your duress."

She laughed. And laughed and laughed. And he had no idea why. "That's just... That's just a hoot. Really. High art. Great comedy."

"I do not understand you."

"No. That's fine." She seemed to curl up into a ball then, as he had found her at the desk.

"Olive," he said, his tone terse now. "What is going on?"

"You're the one that knows everything. Why don't you tell me? Why don't you tell me everything? Including how you plan to ruin me."

"Oh. It is very simple. I want Ambient to become a subsidiary of Magnum."

Because one thing was clear, even as part of him wanted to protect her. There was only one true punishment for this transgression.

"You want to buy me out?"

"Yes."

"I feel like that violates multiple antitrust laws, Gunnar. And there's no way that you're going to be allowed to do that."

"I disagree. There are other major tech corporations."

"Any as big as ours?"

"As big as yours. And anyway, my company has other facets to it."

"Why would I agree to that?"

"Because the alternative is prison. You will find."

"Really. You would really have me arrested?"

"Think about it. Do you think that your father would really have had my father arrested?"

"Well. You know he would have."

"And do you think that I should spare you because you are a woman? Is that how this is going to go?"

"Yes," she said. "I'm a girl. You can't send a girl to prison."

"Last I checked, they had prisons for girls."

Olive huffed, the sound practically a hiss. "That is incredibly unkind."

He could see she did not truly believe he would do it.

"Was it unkind of you to go about snooping into my affairs when you should not? And then… Seducing me?"

"Seducing you," she said. "Ha! Seducing you. Last I checked, I wasn't the one with the entire online forums dedicated to my sexual prowess, Gunnar. So I would assume, that if anyone had done the seducing…"

"Was I the one that took my shirt off in the middle of my living room?"

"Well. No. But. Some people would consider a steady stream of chocolate cupcakes to be foreplay."

"I'm not going to deny it."

"What I wanted," she said, leaning in, "was to have it all

done. All of it. I didn't want to see you anymore. I wanted to come out on top in business, and I wanted to deal with this… This thing. It's always been there. You know it. I know it. We ignore it. We go into boardrooms and we spar, and by the time I'm done I feel like I need a cigarette and I've never even had a cigarette. It's the most… The most invigorating, infuriating thing, and I needed something to… To finish it. Because you know, Gunnar, when fighting with the man I hate most in the world excites me more than making out with a different man, something is wrong. I just wanted to… I just wanted to be done with it. That's all."

There was something about the admission that humanized her again. That tempted him to look at her and see his Olive. The one he had cared for all this time.

But she had revealed herself to be untrustworthy.

And even if not…

He might have cared, but he'd never touched her all those years and it had been for a reason.

He'd felt deep affection for her but he'd never planned on having her in his life. He didn't do romance. He didn't do love in that sense.

It was one thing to feel protective toward her from a distance, to care for her well-being, her safety. But he'd never wanted a wife or children, and he'd never thought to drag a woman into his life in that way.

So he'd never touched her, because he'd known he would only hurt her.

And she hurt you instead.

No. He was not hurt.

He was furious.

"It was a lovely speech," he said. "Are you finished?"

"I'm finished."

"We will continue speaking about this when the doctor has had his say."

She looked out the window. "Where are we?"

"The doctor."

She gave him a narrow-eyed look.

It was a plush facility. Private, and they were ushered in immediately, where Olive's vitals were taken, and her temperature checked, while she was cocooned in a blanket on a velvet couch.

"I don't need a doctor," she protested.

"You seem to be dehydrated," the intake nurse said.

Gunnar lifted a shoulder. "What did I tell you?"

"And what is this? You just can't send me to prison until you make sure I'm properly hydrated? That's very strange."

"I like my opponents to be healthy. For the same reason I don't engage in corporate espionage, Olive. I like my playing fields even. All the better to prove that I am the best. I can see how you failed on that score."

"If you proceed through the door," the nurse said. "You will find a restroom. We'll take a urine sample, and then we'll work on getting you some liquid."

"I don't want to give a urine sample," she said.

"Oh," the woman said.

And Gunnar thought… Well, he thought that he had not imagined he would be sitting in this place, listening to Olive discuss what sorts of samples she was willing to give the doctor, but it was strange to him that she did not wish to give this one.

"We are very discreet," the nurse said. "If narcotics are detected…"

"It's not… I don't do drugs," Olive said. "It's nothing like that. It's just… Invasion of privacy. And I don't want to do it. I have a phobia of lab cups. They scare me."

"Why exactly?"

And he walked his mind backward. Through all of this. Through coming into her office and finding her eating saltines. To her passing out. To her combative behavior.

And now the fact that she did not wish to give this sample. And if it was not drugs, as she was quick to state—and he believed it, because for all that Olive was a competitive and strange creature, he could not see her taking a risk with her brain, and substances—well, he could think then of only one thing.

"Olive," he said, his voice a growl. "Are you pregnant?"

CHAPTER FIVE

OLIVE FELT AS if the rich brocade walls in this very strange doctor's office had come crashing down around her. She made her eyes as round as possible. "Not that I'm aware of."

"Do you suspect?" he pressed, his voice a growl.

"I don't... I don't..."

"Go in and take the test," he said.

She did all she could to make herself sink more heavily into her seat. "You can't make me."

"Olive," he said.

"I..."

Her face drained of all color. "Do not pass out," he commanded.

"You can't tell someone not to pass out," she said. "You're unreasonable. Barking orders like that. A person doesn't choose to pass out, it just happens. And if you keep looking at me like that, all the blood is going to drain out of my head and I am actually going to do it. I'm going to faint dead away at your feet. And you just said you didn't want that, so maybe you should try being less of a scary jackass."

She was breathing hard, her hand pressed to her forehead again. "I don't... I don't... It's just that... It could be many other things."

"It likely couldn't be," the nurse said.

"There are a lot of reasons that women miss their periods."

"Mostly it's pregnancy," the nurse said.

Olive felt dizzy. She'd trained her whole life to run her father's company. She knew how to focus on that at the exclusion of everything else.

She didn't know how to be a mother.

She'd never even considered the possibility.

Facing the prospect of her whole world changing like this....

She couldn't bear it.

"It was just two periods."

"Likely pregnancy," the woman said.

"I did not ask," Olive said, directing her ire at the poor woman sitting there looking white-faced and unsure of what to do. Olive had a feeling that she was about the same color. The pallor of being confronted with her potential pregnancy—a word she had not even wanted to think—with Gunnar in the room was... Far too much.

"Though I bet if I was you wouldn't send me to prison," she said, laughing weekly. It really was a terrible joke. Then, all of it was.

"Go and take the test. Prioritize the results," he said to the nurse.

And Olive found herself obeying. All the while, she thought she would find a way to slip out the back. But there was no back. The bathroom was as beautiful and lush as the rest of the place, with pink wallpaper and a crushed velvet chaise lounge in the corner. "Great. A fainting couch. I needed one earlier."

The little lab cups seemed utterly at odds with the rest of the place. Clinical, where the rest of it wasn't. And it did not take long for her to gather a sample, and leave it in the little two-sided cabinet in the wall.

She sat down on the couch for a second, and then laid on it.

Her heart was pounding. What would she do? What would they do?

Right now, she had no idea what he would do, and that was the terrifying question in all of this.

Gunnar was furious with her. Absolutely mad with outrage. And he had every right to be, she supposed. She had found all these ways to try and justify her actions. Things that had made it all seem... Reasonable. Yes. She had found ways to make it feel reasonable. But it wasn't. And she knew that.

She had just been so... So desperate. Desperate to get away from him. Desperate to do something about the feelings that rioted through her body whenever she saw him. Desperate to please her father and set herself up as the CEO he'd trained her to be.

It had been the culmination of everything. Putting her one weakness behind her, claiming her future, her fated future.

And now it was all in doubt.

There was a soft knock on the door.

"I'm just resting," she snapped.

"It's only me," said the nurse, opening the door. And she came in, her eyes looking soft.

"Did you already talk to him about the results?"

The nurse shook her head. "No. They're your results, Olive, not his. I don't know the nature of your relationship with him..."

"Really? Do you not watch the news?"

"All right," the nurse said, holding up a conciliatory hand. "I am attempting to not know who either of you are. Because that is part of my job at a place like this. I don't make any assumptions, and I certainly don't make any judgments."

"Go ahead," said Olive. "Judge away. I judge myself."

"Too bad about privacy laws. Because there is a very large office pool that concerns whether or not the two of you are actually secretly sleeping together. And I could clearly win."

"Really?"

The woman looked at her gravely. "They worship you."

"Do they?" Olive asked. "How weird. I would've thought that… Anyway. Never mind. What are the results?"

"You already know, sweetheart," the woman said.

And immediately, tears began to slide down her cheeks, and she was so grateful that the woman had brought these results to her in confidence, because Olive didn't think she could have stomached crying like this in front of Gunnar.

And who else did she have?

What a strange, dysfunctional, lonely existence she had. Her father was gone, she'd never known her mother, and now she wanted them both so badly.

Except…

Her father would be so disappointed in her. That feeling was like a crushing weight now. He wouldn't have been happy to be a grandfather. He would question her suitability. Ask how she'd been so weak, so foolish as to get herself pregnant with the enemy's baby.

He would ask how he'd managed to fail her so badly that she had exercised no control at all.

"I don't know what I'm going to do."

"Well. The rest is up to you. He doesn't get to have the results. You can tell him whatever you want."

But she knew there was no lying to Gunnar Magnusson. He saw everything with those sharp blue eyes, and Olive well knew it.

But she needed to get herself together. She could not go out there looking like this. She could not go out there with tears running down her face. She refused to let him see her weak.

And that's all he'd seen, all day. She'd been doing her best to brazen it out, to smile through it, to banter and make jokes, but she would not show weakness now.

"Okay. I just need a minute."

She took a breath, and she steeled herself. She reminded

herself of why she had made all the choices she'd made in the last few months. They'd made sense.

And she would find sense at the end of this too. But she was not a coward, and she wouldn't hide.

She was Olive Monroe, CEO of Ambient technologies, and she had been trained to handle every single thing that was thrown at her. And Gunnar was...well, he was Gunnar. But as genetics went...

Hell, this baby was going to be a genius.

This baby... As it was a foregone conclusion that she would be having the baby.

A little voice inside of her nudged her. *You know that it is.*

Of course, she would need the baby to work for her, and not for Gunnar.

Will then. That had allowed her to put something into a category. And that felt... Reassuring. In a very strange way.

She took a deep, fortifying breath, and went back out to the room that Gunnar was in. But then, the nurse met her again. "IV," she said.

And she found herself ushered into a gloriously beautiful bedroom, where she was stuck like she was a little pincushion, and wrapped up in blankets again, as they began to feed liquid directly into her veins.

What an indignity.

And Gunnar was there for all of it, standing there looking forbidding, his arms crossed across his broad chest.

"Well," she said, attempting to find some sort of haughty manner, even if she was wrapped in an extremely fluffy blanket, her arm propped up on a stack of pillows, and her face poking out as if it was a sea of blankets and she was barely keeping her head above the surface. "I'm pregnant," she said. "So. Interesting."

"Interesting is not the word I would use," he said. His voice hard.

"Oh. Well, don't worry about it. You might not be the father."

His gaze did something terrifying then. And she was transported back to the medieval Viking books that she enjoyed reading.

He looked every inch the marauder. Ready to do something... Drastic.

"Is that so?" he asked, his voice deceptively quiet.

"I mean, it's been... Two months? It's... You never know. Things happen..."

"Do I have the right to assume then, that you have taken a string of other lovers since coming to my bed?"

"Well, you make it sound as if you're not just part of the string of lovers. The ones that came before, the ones that came after. You're acting as if you were a singular event, Gunnar."

"And you are on dangerous ground, Olive Monroe. Is this my baby?"

"I don't have a crystal ball," she said, feeling sick.

Of course it was his baby. She had never even seen another naked man, much less had sex with one. She had never wanted anyone but him. This was... This was so twisted. Such a strange expression of a girlhood fantasy gone wrong.

But she wanted to wrench back some of the control here. She didn't want to be the only one that was confused and out of sorts. She didn't want to be the one without... any power.

Her father had taught her to never go into a business deal without leverage. She needed time to find leverage.

Or even a foothold.

She was in shock.

As if it wasn't a completely logical thing that if you had unprotected sex you might find yourself pregnant.

But the first time? It just seemed… Like a bad lottery. People tried really hard to get pregnant.

She had just been trying to feel something. To feel him.

To finally give in to the experience that his eyes, his hands and his body had been promising her for all of these years, and now here she was.

CHAPTER SIX

IT WOULD'VE BEEN nearly amusing, the howl of rage that Olive let out, if he were not half so angry himself. This woman, this woman who had tied him in knots for years—when he allowed nothing to touch him, nothing to reach him—was now carrying his child.

Or not, she said.

As if there was a doubt.

And he'd have said she wasn't. That he was sure she could not be, but it turned out he didn't know her at all, and also that when it came to Olive he could not trust himself.

Few things would have outraged him half so much as that fact alone.

Add in that she was pregnant, and his rage was an Icelandic volcano.

"Your heir," she said. "Your heir. I am the owner of one of the biggest tech companies in the entire world—"

"Soon to be former owner, though, I will keep you as CEO. Your image is a very important one. It's part of the brand. I would never mess with such good branding."

She did not seem quite so concerned about being tethered to an IV when she scrambled out of the nest of blanket she was in. "I will not lose my company to you."

"Are you only just now taking me seriously?" He could see by the look in her eyes, that she was. That she hadn't truly believed he was serious before. "If you play with dragons, you must expect to be burned, Olive. Your protestations are weak. You should've thought of it before you dared cross me. This is not a game. And it never was. Chocolate cupcakes notwithstanding. People enjoyed the show of you and I, and I find you amusing. But much like a child who needs to be taken in hand, clearly, you did not understand the severity of the consequences that lay before you. I am not to be trifled with."

"Neither am I," she said, rage seeping from her every pore.

And even now, even now with her looking wretched, dressed in that black turtleneck and black pants—the only thing she ever wore, and he would change that if she were his—her brown hair tied back in a low bun, and no makeup on her face, she was delectable.

Because he could well remember exactly how she had tasted. Exactly how it had felt to slide into her tight, wet heat. She had been so tight. So glorious.

And the fact that she had other lovers since then should enrage him—he had not been able to even look at another woman since he'd been with her—but instead, he found himself hard and throbbing as ever.

What she did to him was unacceptable.

It always had been, but before he had… He had wanted to protect her. From himself, and from the world. He'd felt… in awe of her. Proud of her. He'd used that pride to explain his attraction. The ferocity of it.

Now he had to face the fact he was but a basic man who had been blinded by the needs of his body.

She was not special. She was merely good at deceit.

She was not singular.

He would not forget that again.

And he sat there, watching as the bag drained. Watching as some color returned to her face.

They did not speak. And when the cycle was through,

the nurse came in and detached her from the bag, taking the needle from her arm.

"Do you need some assistance getting her out to the car?" the nurse said.

"Oh, no need."

And he swept her up out of the bed, taking the blankets with her. "I will make sure she's comfortable."

He expected her to fight, but instead, she was suspiciously limp, and he found he did not enjoy it. He preferred her hissing. He preferred her fighting.

But she seemed suddenly exhausted.

He carried her back to the street, to his car.

"To the airport," he said.

"I don't even have anything with me," she said. "Someone needs to feed my goldfish."

"You have a goldfish?"

She seemed reinvigorated all of a sudden, and he was glad of that.

"No," she said. "But I *could*."

"You couldn't, and we both know it. And if you did, there would be some method of feeding it by way of telephone app, I assume."

"Telephone app. For all that you're a tech wizard sometimes you sound a hundred years old."

"An issue with my understanding of the language, perhaps."

"I don't think that's true."

It wasn't. He had spoken English from the time he was a boy. In fact, really, his only investment in hanging onto his accent was that he found it benefited him from time to time.

He spoke six languages. Though, he knew Olive wasn't any less accomplished on that score.

"You often travel. I imagine your apartment is perfectly set up for you to leave at a moment's notice."

Her cheeks went red, and he could see that he was correct about that. And that it infuriated her.

Good.

"I don't have time to go anywhere with you. I have a project to work on."

"Then you didn't have time to betray me."

It was a strange word, that one. Betray.

They were enemies, or rather rivals, so perhaps it wasn't a betrayal at all.

Except… It was a betrayal of what he had thought she was.

And he did not like being wrong. In fact, he found it unacceptable.

"It is the principle of the thing," she said. "This. I can't believe that you wouldn't…"

"I wouldn't. If I had a tendency toward such things you would know it by now, Olive. I would've destroyed you that way. But I didn't. Because I do not do things like this."

They were silent the rest of the drive to the jet.

It was there, prepared and waiting, sleek and well appointed. He did all of his business in major cities, but Iceland would always be his home. Even if sometimes when he breathed too deep he felt like a shard of volcanic rock had lodged itself in his chest.

Even if, he could return to his homeland, but had never returned to his true home.

The house he kept now, tucked into the craggy mountains, just above a natural hot springs was his one refuge. He did not bring people there. Not women, not business associates. No one. It was in fact, almost entirely unknown, even by the media. And that was how he liked it. It would be the perfect place to spirit Olive away to, and have no one know where she had gone.

She was in the corner of the limo, wrapped in the blanket. "Must I drag you out of the car?"

"No," she said imperiously. She got out, still wrapped in the purple blanket, and thrust her nose into the air as she walked up the steps into the plane, looking every inch an indignant Queen.

He would say one thing for Olive, she had an exceptional amount of nerve.

She settled into the far corner of the plane, a couch the opposite end from him.

"It is a quick flight," he said. "It won't take long."

Takeoff was immediate, and once they had reached altitude, he stood, and began to open up the drink cabinet. "Would you like something?"

"Obviously alcohol is off the table," she said.

"Obviously."

"I don't understand what you're doing," she said. "First of all, regardless of the paternity of the baby, you can't tell me that you actually want a kid?"

He looked at her, his blue eyes laser focused. "It is not about need. But we both need children, do we not?"

His own father had been a bastard. And as for the man who had been his father figure...

Gunnar had squandered that relationship. He had been wrong about what mattered. For it was not paternity. As for himself, he did not know how to be a father. But he did know that no child should be unwanted or uncared for.

He might not know how to show love or affection, but he had the means to care for a child.

"I suppose. To pass on the companies."

"It is why our fathers had us," he said. "Or at the very least, why my father decided to take part in raising me."

The words seemed to cut her beneath her skin. She flinched. "I suppose so."

"Anyway. I will let no child of mine go unclaimed. It is not my way."

"Oh, really? Is this not the first time for you?"

He ignored that.

"And what about you? You want a child?"

She shook her head. "I'm busy. But I have a lot of money, I imagine that nannies can... Handle everything. Otherwise, I happen to know that there's usually a good space for children to sit outside of conference rooms. And often there are snacks." Her voice wavered at the end, as if she heard the words she spoke, and realized what she was consigning a child to.

Their own childhoods. Repeating.

Neither of them spoke for a long moment, but they looked at each other, and he could feel the shared history between them. It was a strange thing. This.

For the most part, he felt connected to no one and nothing. He'd broken the happy home he'd once had with his idiotic, childish demands to be reunited with a father who hadn't loved him at all. He'd destroyed that connection. And as for his father...

Building one had never been on the table.

"Sometimes there are even cupcakes," she said, her voice a whisper now.

"Yes. I suppose there are."

They didn't speak after that. And he was perfectly fine with that. He was still volcanic with anger toward her. He had decided to ruin her, and now things were complicated. He resented this barrier to her ruination.

Ruthless? Perhaps. But he had only ever been taught one way to be. His father had taken a happy twelve-year-old boy and had broken him, remade him. Forged him in the fire of uncompromising fury, with yet one goal set before him. Winning.

Gunnar had taken all that fire and fury and used it to make his own path. Make himself his own man, apart from his father. He might be principled in a way his father never had been, but that didn't make him a man who knew how to bend.

Yet he'd grown too indulgent of Olive. He was reaping the punishment of that bad decision now.

He had seen her as soft. He had seen her as relatively harmless. He had seen her as something he wished to shield, protect. He did not need every contract in the tech market, and the fact was there were certain things that were better suited to the products that Ambient provided, than Magnum.

He was an honest man. To his core.

And perhaps that was what disappointed him so.

He had thought that she was better than her father. Better than his father. He had thought that she was…

He had respected her. He had, as far as his heart could care, cared for her.

And now, no more.

When his good opinion was destroyed, it could not be remade.

And she was potentially pregnant with his child. A fascinating and unwelcome turn of events.

And yet, the idea of her being pregnant by another man…

It ignited his blood. Made it run hot with fury.

And he did not know now which betrayal burned the worst. That she had proven herself to be dishonest in business, or that she was claiming she had given her body to another man after giving herself to him.

And he could feel the heartbeat of his ancestors in his chest as he imagined another man putting his hands on her skin.

She was looking at him, defiant.

Olive was a powerful woman. She went out of her way to never appear to be the sort of woman who used her sensuality to get ahead—and indeed, she did not use her sensuality in business.

It was a strange thing to think of other men seeing her as he did.

For he could not deny that he saw her as sensual.

And after being with her the way that he had been…

She was exquisite.

Her sexuality was a sweet, secret thing, a jewel at the heart of a steely reserve. One that you had to work to see— at least he had thought so. But she made it sound as if she gave her favors away freely.

He was surprised he had heard no rumors to that effect, but he could also imagine Olive going to great lengths to ensure that nobody knew.

To ensure that her brand of desire stayed under wraps.

For one thing he could appreciate about her. She had stepped into a man's world. All of the other CEOs of the major tech companies were men. Their fathers obviously had been.

And there was her. Groomed and trained to take over, certainly, but a woman all the same.

And he admired the way that she had fashioned for herself a niche.

She did not try to emulate the men around her. She did not wear suits. She did not try to borrow a masculine toughness.

But she had her own. Like a bright-eyed vole who kept her head down and scampered to glory.

She was…

She was a thief. Essentially. She had stolen information. She was not any of those admirable things that he had once imagined.

Just as her sexual favors clearly weren't rare or difficult to earn.

"If you think that I will be bringing you a steady supply of male concubines during your tenure at my residence, I will have to disappoint you."

"Drat. I absolutely do not know what I'll do without my concubines. I like to be fed grapes and fanned with palm fronds before I receive the evening's pleasure."

"Sadly. I am fresh out of grapes and palm fronds."

"Was that an offer of pleasure, Gunnar?"

The words held an edge, and he could see that she was attempting to mock him, but once their eyes met, heat flared there in the depths of hers, and her cheeks turned pink.

She was not as in control as she would like him to believe. And when he thought back to the entire actions of the day, from her clutching the crackers and behaving in such a ridiculous manner, to now, he could see that all of it was a wild attempt to keep him at arm's length. Because she had most certainly known that she was pregnant, whether she had taken a test or not.

And she did not want him to know.

Whatever she said, he had a feeling she was certain enough whose child she carried. He felt as if women generally did know such things. That even if they had multiple lovers, they often had suspicions. Her desperation to hide it from him gave him a fair idea of what her suspicions were.

"Was that an offer of pleasure?" She asked again, attempting to look bold.

"That all depends. I personally like a bit of pleasure with my pain. I'm not certain that you feel the same."

She shivered.

But he knew it wasn't from her lies or even fear.

Oh, yes. This was the problem. He had always sensed that little Olive was his match in a great many ways. In the bedroom, at least.

She had been asking him questions that were dangerous for him to answer with those wide beautiful eyes since she was far too young to be asking them.

After that exchange, Olive pretended to nap. She was not asleep, he was certain of that.

She was like a little kid, feigning sleep with her eyes scrunched tight.

He would've found it charming, if he were capable of finding her charming.

The plane landed on his private airfield, at the base of the mountain. The snow had begun to fall in earnest, capping craggy black rocks.

The house—made of concrete and thick glass—was nestled into the side of the mountain, all the better to shield it from the harsh weather.

The sea was to one side, the hot springs midway to the top of where the house sat.

All of it accessible only by tram.

He had one built specifically for the journey both to the hot springs, and the house.

They disembarked from the plane, and Olive looked around, her eyes wide. "Are we supposed to…walk?"

"Yes. I hope you brought your trekking poles."

"I didn't. And you well know I don't have a parka," she said, still wrapped in the blanket, standing out there with the vast expanse of snow behind her. She looked like a little drop of blood out there in the pristine wilderness, and he could not help but wonder if that were a metaphor of some kind. Certainly one he did not wish to examine too closely.

"I'm kidding."

"Are you capable of kidding?"

"Clearly. We take the tram to the top."

"What?" she asked, clearly not any more appeased by this than she was at the idea of walking.

"Yes," he said. "We take the tram to the top. It is quite nice. Beautiful view."

"I don't… That is…"

"Clearly you are not made of hearty Icelandic stock," he said.

"No. I am a city-dwelling marshmallow. This is… This is not… No."

But she was not about to freeze to death, and when he grabbed the edge of her blanket and began to tug her along, she came, taking tiny indignant steps as she endeavored to stay bundled up.

He took them to the edge of the tram platform, where the car was sitting. "It's probably cold in there," he said, not bothering to sound apologetic at all.

"Oh, gosh," she said, getting inside and shrinking into the corner.

She looked up ahead, her eyes round with worry.

"Are you afraid of heights?"

"No. I love them. It's a natural thing for human beings to love heights. What with how we are capable of gliding down safely if we fall from them."

"You're hysterical," he said, noting the genuine fear in her eyes.

He might have pitied her. But he knew her now.

"Thank you. I do try to keep some humor in these situations."

"No. That is not the kind of hysterical that I meant."

She looked up at him. "Really?"

"Do you see me laughing?"

"No. But then. I never have."

"Physically incapable," he said.

"Must be the Viking."

He shrugged. "Perhaps. Though Vikings had a particular affinity for me too. And I imagine if you get enough of it flowing through your veins a bit of pillaging seems amusing."

The car gave a jerk, and the cable began to carry them up the hill, up, up toward the mountain home.

And Olive became more and more agitated. The tram flew over the tops of the snowcapped trees, past rocky crags and waterfalls. And it was clear that at a certain point in spite of herself, Olive became too fascinated by the view to hide.

"It's beautiful," she said. "I can't believe I've never been here. Of all the places in the world that I have been, I just… It's so strange…"

"Because the kind of business we do isn't done here. It's different. That's why it's my refuge."

"I don't have a refuge," she said. "New York born and raised. Unless we were in London. Or Tokyo. Or Berlin. Or Stockholm."

"It was a transient childhood for us both, I think."

"I consider myself lucky," she said. "Very few people have had the kind of on-the-job training that I had the opportunity to receive. Coupled with my experiences traveling… It doesn't get much better, I don't think."

He could remember time he'd spent in a small house. With a woman who had cared for him. A man who taught him about life, and not just business meetings.

He could remember real birthday parties. Evenings spent reading by the fire.

Olive had never had that. It made him almost find that pity for her again.

Almost.

One thing he knew, their child would not have an identical experience to them. And he would be sure of it. Their child would have a mother and a father.

He would marry Olive, and ensure that they had…

He thought again of the small cabin he had spent the first twelve years of his life in.

No. They would not have that.

But they would have something. They could not be people they weren't. And he had concerns about Olive and what she would teach a child.

But as long as she was bound to him, he could ensure it was all right.

"No. There is nothing better," he said.

"But I am glad to have seen this."

"Even though you're not very happy with me?"

"Well. I did not exactly anticipate that I would see Iceland on a nonconsensual vacation."

"A kidnapping?"

"No. You didn't kidnap me," she said.

"I think I have."

"Absolutely not. It's nothing more than a mandatory detour."

"Kidnap."

It took ten minutes for the cable car to reach the summit, and it stopped gently, letting them out at the automatic door to a long, heated corridor.

It was all glass, the windows looking out at the view on either side. "This is sort of terrifying," she said.

"It's beautiful," he returned.

"I guess. If you love heights."

"And I obviously do."

"Sure." She looked around. "So that is your game plan? Do you have a game plan?"

"You should know me well enough to know that I do. I will be finding out from a doctor how quickly we can get a paternity test."

"Oh."

"And the minute we discover if the baby is mine, you will marry me."

CHAPTER SEVEN

THE HOUSE WAS INCREDIBLE. Made mostly of glass with black window frames, concrete everywhere else, somehow light and airy rather than heavy or industrial as you would assume. Rather it made the house appear as if it was just another piece of the landscape. The windows offered a view of the sea, and the broad expanse of snowy wilderness on the other side.

And yet, it was difficult to concentrate on the beauty of the house what with the specter of a threatened marriage looming over her head.

"You cannot really mean that."

"I do. And for your sake, Olive, you had better hope the baby is mine. For if the child is mine, I will spare you time in prison, and I will have a care with Ambient, as it will be my child's legacy. Or rather, half of it."

"If the baby isn't yours then what? Then I'm hosed?"

"Emphatically."

"How can you…" She looked at him, at those eyes that were like ice chips, and she could see how well that worked as a comparison, since she was currently surrounded by ice.

And she had no idea what she had been thinking. Because she had in some ways not truly respected exactly who Gunnar was.

She had lied to herself about the level of comfort she could have in their… Relationship. Association. She had allowed herself to fashion him into a fantasy object that had blunted some of the truths about him.

He was a Viking. And she had betrayed him. Even if she weren't pretending she didn't know who the father of the baby was, spying on him, taking secrets from his company... Of course he took a dim view.

To say the least.

She should have listened to what he'd taught her the night they'd made love.

She had tried to control it, but Gunnar pushed the limits, found her true fantasies, her true self, beneath all the slick confidence she'd tried to convey.

Yet somehow she'd lied to herself. Convinced herself it wouldn't be that way outside of that experience.

She had let cupcakes and years together soften the reality of what she was doing to him. And the reality of what he would do in return.

And she had... She had been so caught up in her victory that she had underestimated fully the manner of predator that she had gone to bed with. And she had blocked out the lesson after.

She was an idiot. She was an absolute idiot. Well, more accurately, she was a mouse. And she was trapped handily beneath the paw of a lion.

She had a feeling no matter how she scrabbled or scurried, she was going to stay exactly as she was. Trapped.

And so she would not debase herself.

"I'm tired," she said.

"Well, you are welcome to avail yourself to one of the bedrooms. Since your fake nap on the plane didn't actually gain you any rest."

"I challenge anyone to rest while you're looming about."

"I don't recall looming. I feel as if I was sitting."

"Of course. Nobody thinks that they loom."

"You say that definitively."

"I have a heavy exposure to men of all varieties, and believe me when I tell you, many of them loom, and none of them think they do."

"Go to sleep, Olive."

And she realized then that she was being left to her own devices.

She made her way down the hall, and opened a couple of different doors. All of the rooms were quite similar. Scandinavian sparse, with beds and fireplaces and sheepskin rugs. She chose the one with the purple bedspread. Simply because she had a bit of a theme going on.

And as soon as she closed the door, it was like layers upon layers of armor were peeling away from her body, and she had not given it permission to do that. She had cried at the clinic. But that had been different. It had still been controlled. She'd still been protected.

But just now, she felt as if she had been hollowed out. As if there was nothing but misery contained inside of her.

Weakness.

A weakness that she strove always to hide.

A weakness she tried to ignore, but Gunnar had started to pick away at her defenses. When he'd brought up their childhood...

She wanted to howl, but she didn't. Instead she doubled over, a silent wail forcing her lips open, no sound coming out.

What had she done? A baby? She replayed everything that she had said to Gunnar over these past hours. The child could sit outside of conference rooms. Her childhood had been wonderful. Such an education. Traveling the world.

Lonely.

Lonely.

Lonely.

The honesty that lived beneath all those words assaulted her now.

She wanted to kick something. Wanted to rage.

Her childhood hadn't been wonderful. That thought made her feel like a terrible person. Like she was betraying the father who had raised her alone, the father she loved so much.

But it had been isolation. The reason that she had all these complicated feelings for Gunnar was that he was one of the only other human beings she knew. She didn't have friends. She had a… strange relationship with a man that she had a business rivalry with. She was obsessed with him because she knew nothing and no one else.

Was this what she was consigning a child to? A life of… And what would she even have? Because Gunnar was now claiming he was going to take Ambient from her. And what would she do if she lost the company? Then all of her life, all of her childhood, all of the everything that she had ever worked for would mean nothing. Nothing.

She felt exhausted by her own misery. And she hadn't even fully given in to it yet. But it was like a living thing, digging its claws into her, and making her feel hopeless.

She didn't know who she was if she didn't have Ambient.

She didn't know who she was right now.

And she had no idea how to fix the mess that she had gotten herself into. She had never done a thing beyond what was expected of her. Not ever. Not once.

Until Gunnar. Until she had given in to the need that she felt for him, and look where she was now.

She was currently reaping a particularly awful harvest from a string of bad decisions.

The only bad decisions she had ever made.

And she had no idea how she was going to dig herself back out of this. None at all.

And so she surrendered to her misery. And she wept.

While Olive slept Gunnar was busy having items delivered for her. He also checked with the doctor who said that a blood test could ascertain the parentage of the child as soon as they could get it. And he made an appointment for the doctor to come to the top of the mountain as soon as he was able.

He also arranged to have a large spread of breakfast set out for the two of them. And then he slept for two hours.

He awoke before Olive, and just before the breakfast arrived. Baskets of breads and honey, dates and figs, and hard cheeses. The kind of breakfast you needed when you had been traveling and your body had no idea what time of day it was.

Olive's entire wardrobe arrived then as well.

He began to brew strong coffee, and it was then that Olive emerged.

In of course the same outfit she had on yesterday, her brown hair halfway released from its bun. Her eyes were swollen, her expression bleak.

"Good morning," he said.

"Good morning."

He wanted her. He realized that with a kick of lust and ferocity.

He wanted her. Even now, he wanted her. Even now, knowing how duplicitous she was.

He was a sick bastard, that there was something in that thought that actually made his desire kick up even higher.

He wanted to punish her.

Wanted to pin her down with his hand on her throat and make her beg him for mercy. And for pleasure.

There was certainly more of the old ways, and the old ancestors in his blood than he normally thought.

That, though, was nearly a comforting thought. It was the surge of tenderness on its heels that he felt desperate to deny. That he wanted to respond to her clear distress by wrapping her in a blanket, as he'd done the night of her father's funeral, and holding her close.

"Is it?"

"Morning?"

"Good," she fired back, looking angry.

He quite liked her angry. It was better than sad.

"You will be relieved to know that I have clothes for you."

"Wonderful. Did someone go and get my things?"

"No. I am tired of your self-imposed uniform. I would like to see you in some colors."

"Colors?"

"You wear all black. And I find it unbecoming."

"You found it becoming enough to screw my brains out a couple of months ago."

"Yes. But after I got you out of the clothes."

She huffed, and then looked hungrily at the spread set before them.

"This looks good."

"It isn't poisoned."

"How did you know that was the last question I was going to ask you?"

"Because smart-asses are predictable."

She wrinkled her nose. "Well, I'll get more creative then." He had a feeling that for Olive a lack of creativity was the singular greatest sin a person could commit. Which was yet another reason it was so odd that she had stolen from him the way that she had. For in his opinion it evinced an extreme lack of creativity. She must've been desperate. He wondered exactly why.

"Why did you do it?"

"What?"

"Why did you stoop so low to win that contract? It is not in your character, Olive, at least not in your character as I knew it."

She looked away. "I really needed to win that."

"And you possessed such little confidence in yourself?"

Her head snapped back, her eyes suddenly filled with

anger. "No. That isn't it at all. It isn't that I had a lack of confidence in myself. I wanted to make sure. I think I would've won either way."

"And yet, you have no way of knowing. You stole not only from me, but from yourself."

"That's excellent, Gunnar. You should be a life coach. But this isn't inspirational Internet bullshit. I had to win."

"Yes. You've yet to give me a good reason why."

"Because it mattered to my father, and if it mattered to him, it mattered to me."

"Then why prolong it? Why go back to my penthouse? Why make the game into something sexual?"

"It wasn't the same thing. I wanted to win the contract for Dad." Her voice broke. "I wanted to do what he'd set me up to do, and I couldn't take a risk. You… You're a different part of that. I wanted you, and I… I needed to be done wanting you. I needed to be done being confused by you. I needed to be rid of you."

Her voice was low, trembling.

"It was so bad that you wanted me?" His voice was rough, almost a stranger's voice.

"Yes. I needed to be above it. Better than it. I hate that when I go into meetings I spent all of my time mentally undressing you. I just wanted it done. I wanted a clean break."

She cringed when she said the words.

"You're embarrassed about this?"

"Yes. Of course I am. Are you not embarrassed?"

"I don't spend any time being embarrassed of my inclinations. Whatever they may be. In life, things can be as simple or as complicated as you make them. For me, desire is a simple thing. If I want someone, I have them."

"So you had never wanted me before that moment I took my sweater off in your penthouse?"

It was a deliciously delivered barb, one that hit its mark. Because she had in fact pegged him as a liar. She had been the one thing he had ever denied himself, and he had never really thought of it that way. He had never put it into words.

He was not a man given to self-denial or self-delusion, and the fact that he had such a blind spot there enraged him. Especially because she had called it out.

Had he ever wanted her?

It was such a complicated maelstrom of feeling. He could remember the first time he'd noticed the sweet lines of her body when she'd been eighteen, wrapped tightly in a black gown at a charity function, her lips painted red.

He could remember also, her being a sad, lonely-seeming child, and how he'd felt a strange mix of resentment and pity for her. Resentment because she was like an external echo of his own loneliness.

He could remember watching her give her first business presentation, being in opposition to her and wanting to protect her from failure all the same.

He could remember that pity and desire mingling when he'd held her after her father's funeral.

Had he ever wanted her?

It seemed so base to describe the way she'd gotten a hold on his soul all those years ago.

"I suppose," he said slowly, the words cutting his throat, "you intersect an uncomfortable line for me. I do not mix business and pleasure."

"Well, I was trying to disentangle those things. Get out from under the business, have the pleasure…"

"Why don't you sit down and eat. You look as if you're going to fall over, and I do not wish to be put in the position of having to cushion your fall again."

"What a trial for you."

But she came forward and began putting pastries on her plate. Along with honey and cheese. He brought her a mug of coffee. And when she took a sip, she smiled. "Oh, this is heaven."

"The doctor will be here today to administer a blood test," he said.

"What?"

"To determine whether or not the baby is mine."

She looked… Stricken.

"I didn't know you could do them this early."

"Yes. Blood tests have gotten very sophisticated."

"I hate getting my blood drawn. I hate it. It makes me pass out."

"Well, sadly for you, it is the way that they determine these kinds of things."

"The baby is yours," she said, staring fixedly down at her plate.

"What?"

"The baby is yours, I thought that I could… I thought I could get you to leave me alone if I told you I didn't know. I thought that I could…"

"You lied to me."

"I was freaking out," she said. "I don't know what to do. I don't know what to do. I've never slept with a man before, and I… I gave myself to you, and it was a very big mistake. I didn't think of protection, not at all, but you would think, that given that you are some kind of famed sex expert, that you would've thought to use condoms."

"Stop," he said, everything inside of him going quiet. "You've never been with a man before?"

"Well clearly I have been now," she said.

"You were a virgin." It was a roar of triumph in his blood, and he hated himself a bit for it. But he'd wanted her for so long, and to know she was his and his alone…

It made him feel every inch the conquering warrior.

"Yes," she said. "I was a virgin. Not that I care much about that kind of terminology. I knew what I was doing.

I've read a lot of… I like books that have… Look, I know how everything works. So I was pretty well… Primed on the topic by the time I actually… I needed to get you out of my system."

"You're moving too quickly for me now. You know that the child is mine because you were a virgin."

"Yes. I don't need a blood test."

And he couldn't trust her. Or far worse, couldn't trust himself.

"Sadly for you, because the story keeps changing, now I require a blood test. Because I don't know which version of you is real, Olive. I always thought that you were my rival, but I felt that you were a rival that had a sense of integrity. And now I find out you have engaged in corporate espionage, and also, that you have lied to me. Either now, or before."

"Why the hell would I lie to you now? I would just tell you that I knew for sure the baby wasn't yours if I was lying. Because that would actually benefit me. I want to get away from you."

"It actually wouldn't benefit you. As I would see you in prison under those circumstances."

"I just… I don't… You're being ridiculous," she said.

"I'm being ridiculous?"

"Yes," she said. "I wouldn't lie to you about this. Not this time. Not now."

"You need to explain more clearly what led you to this point, because I have no idea what the matter is with you."

And then, all of a sudden, steely, tough Olive burst into tears.

CHAPTER EIGHT

SHE WAS DOING IT. She was losing her mind, and she was crying in front of this man. She didn't like it. Not one bit, but she couldn't stop herself. She was weeping, wailing. It was like she had lost all ability to be… Her. She had learned to be tough and strong and hold the shield up in front of all of her emotions when she was a girl.

A leader couldn't afford to be led by their feelings, her father had taught her that. Instilled it into her so deep it was like it was carved into her soul.

And now she was just… She was falling apart. Maybe it was the hormones. Did you already have those kinds of hormones at this point in the pregnancy? She didn't know. She didn't know anything about being pregnant. In many ways, she didn't know anything about being a woman.

She had no feminine influence in her life, she didn't really have any female friends. She saved all of her feminine feelings for fiction.

She identified heavily with the women in the romances that she read, and put herself in their place, and when she did that, she felt… whole in a way that she wasn't able to feel outside of that.

Because it was just so damned difficult.

Because in her real life she had to be unflappable, she had to be hard and she had to be capable of anything.

And she did not feel capable of anything right now. In fact, she felt...

She felt like a disaster.

"I *needed* the contract," she said. "It was the one my dad wanted. It was in the portfolio as the single most important thing that he was working toward. But when I got in there and I saw the building blocks of what there was, of what he was working on a decade ago to go in these cars, once they were ready to go to market... It wasn't up to par. I had so much work to do so quickly. There was no real blueprint. But it was his white whale, and if I couldn't get it... If I couldn't get it, Gunnar, then I might as well not be in charge of the company. I might as well not be anything."

Admitting that to him made her feel so much shame. She wondered if Gunnar did anything to prove himself, or if he simply just did it. Because he wanted to. Because it was something that felt good to do.

This was the problem. It wasn't that for her. And it never could be.

"But what are you without your honor?"

"That's philosophical. A wonderful idea. You want to do things simply to prove you're the best. I wanted to do it to get the contract. It was something that mattered to my father. So how I did it didn't matter. It was just... The getting it." She squeezed her hands into fists. "It was the one thing he wanted of me Gunnar, and now it's ruined and gone. I was willing to debase myself, to violate any morals I might have to see this done, and it's for nothing anyway."

"I see. And where exactly does our passionate interlude in the penthouse come into play? Simply to get rid of me, as you've said before?"

She shook her head. "I did want that. Because you make me feel...a way I don't want to feel. But that night, I wanted something for myself. That's all. It was a mistake. Like everything else. I..." She felt small then. Utterly undone. "I'm not perfect." It cost her to say that. She looked up at him. "I'm not perfect. I don't know how to do everything. I have been trying as hard as I can to do everything that my father would've done, and sometimes I think I do better than him, and sometimes I think I... Sometimes I think I have no idea what I'm doing. And that's... That's all. But I wanted to win this. And then... I was weak, I guess. Across the board."

She watched his face as she admitted all this, tried to get a gauge for what he was thinking, feeling. She couldn't.

"You will do the blood test," he said.

"I don't..."

"You will," he said. "This is not up for debate or discussion. It is the way of things. And so, you will do as I say."

"You're such a dick," she said.

"And you have proven yourself to be duplicitous. Therefore, you will be punished for it."

"Punished with a blood test."

"With a lack of trust."

"What would I have to gain by lying now? I've ruined everything. Everything I cared about, it's all nothing, so you might as well know it all. I read Viking romance novels and fantasize about you carrying me off and ravishing me, I don't like the classics. I am in charge of this company, which I trained for all my life, and I feel unequal to it. All I wanted was to make my father proud and he died. He died and I didn't have a chance to show him, so I was trying to do it as an homage and I messed that up too, and now I'm pregnant, and yes, I lied to you. I was underhanded with the contract, I lied about being with other men, but I was trying so hard to protect myself, and now I can't so...why would I keep lying?"

She shrank beneath his withering blue gaze. And she found that she hated it. That she had earned his disdain. That she did not have his trust.

Why? Why did she feel this way for him?

He said nothing. He seemed unmoved by the way she'd just shattered, and it made her chest feel like it was too tight.

"Do you need to take everything from me, Gunnar, is that it?"

She had always known him to be steely, but he brought her cupcakes, and sometimes, it almost felt as if he were her friend as much as he was her enemy. She didn't have any others.

"If it seems I must."

In this, it he was proving that he was nothing like she had imagined.

She had thought that the hardness would give way to something else, because she felt sort of a connection to him.

But it was clear, he made it abundantly clear now, that he did not feel the same.

That underneath it all, he was the barbarian that she had fantasized about him being.

Of course, that had been in a sexual sense. And it was a lot more fun to imagine things in the bedroom, than spilling over into her actual life where there were real consequences and…

She supposed that was the issue. If you had fantasies about large, dominant men who made you feel small and beautiful and like they could scoop you up and handle everything, you had to take the negatives that came with that. Which in this case, turned out that he was a vindictive asshole.

Except… He wasn't acting like a child. He was not simply lashing out. It was all calm and measured. As if she were the child and this were the punishment that she deserved.

It got its hooks into her. Made her feel shame. Made her feel as if she were the foolish one.

As if she were the one that was small.

"Gunnar I…"

"You what? You vastly underestimated me. And that is

the problem. You thought that because you won a few contracts when we went head to head that you knew the measure of me. But that is not the case, Olive. You do not know
me. You do not know... You do not know what I thought of
you before, and how this has changed things. And now you
must face the consequences of your own actions."

"You act as if that hasn't been part of my life, all my life.
You think my father was easy on me?"

She felt disloyal speaking of her father, particularly to
Gunnar.

She loved her father. He was all she had. And she had
loved him dearly. She also knew that essentially, Gunnar
hated him, as his father had hated him. They had not had
the type of rivalry that she and Gunnar had, where there
was sniping but it was...

*It was sexually charged. And you mistook it for some-
thing else.*

*Because for all your talk of reading romance novels
and understanding the way of things, you were a silly virgin. And you did not protect yourself. At all. You are a
silly, silly girl.*

She felt silly. She felt absolutely foolish.

She felt as if she had completely ruined everything. Det-
onated a bomb in the middle of all of it.

She was so used to feeling like everything was well ordered, every risk calculated. And she had been so convinced
that she had the measure of things, that she had moved forward with the corporate espionage. That she had moved
forward with sleeping with Gunnar because she had found
a way to make it all makes sense in her head. Perhaps that
was the worst thing that her father had taught her. To trust
in her mind.

In this case, she had managed to construct for herself a
palace of nonsense.

And she couldn't live in that damned palace. No she could not. She was in Gunnar's ice palace.

But she had a feeling he was not going to let it go.

"My father expected me to be every inch the CEO that he was by the time I was twenty-two. He had all those years to become proficient at what he did, but he wanted me to step in to this company that he grew and have the lay of it. And yes, he had the skills to turn it into what it was, but he needed me to take the helm and do so with authority. I have never had another path. I've never had another option." She swallowed hard. "I had never had anyone else. I loved him, he loved me in his way, I know he did. I know he did. And all I have left is Ambient and it's the only way I can… I can keep on loving him."

"As you can see, my options were many and plentiful and laid out before me as the bounty of the earth." His tone was dry. His expression bland.

"I'm not saying you had it any differently. You are perhaps the only person in the entire world that understands exactly what it's like to be raised by a man like my father."

"I do not think that our fathers were the same."

"Don't you? I think they were. In essence. Certainly they did things differently, at least, in certain fashions. But… Don't you think… Don't you think?"

"I do not."

"Well. It doesn't matter whether you understand or not. I'm just explaining. If you want to try and find it in your concrete soul to empathize with what I was going through, you now have all the information."

"I don't do empathy."

"You did," she said. "You did when my father died."

"A mistake."

She continued eating, because it was only when she was eating that she did not feel like garbage. Either because of the pregnancy or because of the emotional duress that she was under.

And Gunnar sat unnervingly at the end of the table, palms flat, and it reminded her of the way he had stood in the penthouse that night. Regarding her, as she stripped her clothes off.

There was no way she could be feeling aroused by him. Not now. Not when he was being so… So awful.

But then, that was the way it was. Her attraction to him always and ever defied logic of any kind.

The fact that he was her most long-standing crush was just… *He is your only crush. Ever.*

And a man less deserving of a title of childhood crush, she could not think of.

He was not a pop star. No smooth boy-band member who might make a young girl comfortable. No. She had always been swinging above her weight class. Always.

Maybe that was part of what had been instilled in her. Maybe that was why she had never been able to find it in herself to be interested in a man who was less confronting.

Because it was all about Gunnar. Beginning and end of story.

Because she had been taught to be ruthless, efficient, and above all else goal oriented. And a man who seemed like he could be anything less wouldn't appeal.

She was such a mess.

And she was pregnant. With this man's baby.

And suddenly, she felt as if the entire world had shifted.

She really hadn't had time to wrap her brain about any of this. She had been caught up in trying to keep Gunnar from knowing the truth. She hadn't really examined what it meant that she was having a baby.

Was she really going to have that child sit outside of boardrooms?

She knew how to be a CEO. It had been what she was trained for.

She wanted to have a moment of knowing what it was like to be a lover. Because it had been exhilarating. Because it had been freeing in a way. To embrace her femininity in a fashion that she had never done before.

She wanted that. But then… Now she was going to be a mother.

A mother.

She hadn't even had a mother, she had no idea how to be one. She only knew how to be one thing.

And raising a child was all expansive, it required you to shift yourself, change yourself, wrap yourself around them in protection.

No one ever did that for you.

No. But the idea of bringing a little life into this world and not doing that… It seemed almost untenable. How could she? How could she give a child exactly the same life that she'd had when she stood here at twenty-six knowing how incapable she was of living in any other part of the world?

She knew her office. A corner office with a fabulous view, and she certainly had money and assets enough to take care of her basic needs. But she did not have friends, she didn't know how to be with a man… She didn't know… And he wanted to get married.

Suddenly, she wanted to cast up her accounts.

But she didn't want to do that, because it would be humiliating.

And she just couldn't bear any more humiliation. Not in front of Gunnar.

"Are you well?"

She shot him her most deadly glare. Her CEO face. "No. I'm not well. I'm pregnant."

"Silly question, perhaps."

"Let me ask you this. What are your plans for a child?"

He looked at her. "The child will be my heir."

"You certainly don't plan on arranging anything emotionally around the life of the child."

"Do you?"

"Do you expect me to? Because I'm the woman?"

"Yes," he said. "I do."

"What a relic."

"I also expect you to because your workload will be drastically reduced as acting figurehead of a company that I will now be in charge of. So it has less to do with your gender and more to do with the fact that you will be significantly reduced."

"How can you… How dare you. It isn't your company. You're not the one that built it. You're not the one that gave up… Childhood. You're not the one that gave up friendships and parties and sex, to run it."

"I think you'll find that I managed to work sex into my schedule."

"You're a man," she said. "You're a man, and people will expect it of you. People are fine with you sleeping around, but you tell me, who am I supposed to sleep with? Perhaps you're comfortable giving yourself to some empty-headed model to fill the hours, but I cannot respect a man who isn't as smart as I am. Who isn't as driven as I am. And if I can't respect a man… I don't want to sleep with him. Also, you men… You're idiots. I'm sorry. Women are the ones who must risk actual death to sleep with a stranger. Not only that, we are not guaranteed satisfaction. The risk is greater. And therefore, I find myself unwilling to take it."

"And that is why you were a virgin?"

"Yes," she said, "that's why."

Easier than admitting that he was the only man she had ever wanted, and the only man that she could imagine wanting, because that was just a horror.

"Well. We will see soon enough if that is true."

"It was true. I mean, I'm flattered that you think that I had a comprehensive enough set of skills to believe that I had a parade of lovers before you, but sadly, no parade. I am the grand marshal of my sexual parade of one. So."

"Extremely vivid. But then, you always did have a way with words."

"Indeed."

"Well, I eagerly await the news from the doctor. We shall see what his report is."

"Great."

"And then…"

"Yes. I know. Ruination. Marriage."

"In the meantime, have another doughnut."

"You know. I might as well."

And she realized then that she had been eating as if this were her last meal.

As if she were a prisoner bound for execution. She felt very like she might be.

For Gunnar was her Viking captor, and whatever lay ahead was not in her control.

CHAPTER NINE

WHEN THE DOCTOR ARRIVED, Olive swept out of her room wearing a camel-colored sweater and loose white pants that flowed with her every motion.

She looked soft, her dark hair down and framing her face. Markedly different to the woman she typically was, in her black uniform.

"I see you have rejuvenated."

"As much as possible. Though, I am a bit chagrined to see there is no black."

"None," he said grinning.

"That seems mean. Unnecessarily."

"I feel that you are mean to yourself, unnecessarily."

She mused on that. "I'm not mean. It is simplification. Also, I have never seen fit to dress for the approval of others."

She was beautiful all the same. Though he did not say so.

He found that he should be more disdainful of her than he was.

He of course had to give a blood sample as well, to determine the match. The doctor gave her a general once-over for her health as well.

"I will call you with the results," the man said.

Olive was pale and mute following the blood draw, and she curled up on one of his white couches, next to the roaring glass-backed fireplace that offered a view of the valley below.

"I'm tired," she said, resting her cheek on her forearm, which was leaned against the back of the couch.

"Yes. I can see that. How exactly do you suppose you're going to take on this business project while this exhausted."

"I have done some googling," she said. "I should only be this tired for the first trimester. Anyway, I only have four weeks left of that."

"A boon for you, then."

"Oh, yes," she said. "I'm in the middle of a huge boon. Truly, I have never been so boon to."

"Perhaps you need help. Perhaps, my acquisition of Ambient will be beneficial to you."

"Somehow, I don't think so. Somehow, I think you're trying to position a hostile takeover as a favor, and I find that to be disingenuous, and frankly, think you're better than that."

"Fine. Do you want honesty? I find you unworthy of retaining ownership of your company. After that stunt that you pulled."

"Unworthy. Gunnar finds me unworthy. Whatever shall I do?"

"Begin to make your apologies, Olive."

"Screw your apologies."

"You are unrepentant?"

"I think I've made that quite clear."

"You'll find that I am also unrepentant. Whatever happens after this."

She faced him down, her hazel eyes glittering. "Tell me this, Gunnar. Would you have brought me up here if I weren't pregnant?"

He shook his head. "No. I would have had you arrested and dealt with the fine details later. While taking over your company."

"Why did Jason tell you what I did?"

"I think he hoped that he might find himself on the receiving end of a promotion. For his honesty. He decided to manipulate you instead of me. And... That is his prerogative. Though, it did not end the way that he had hoped."

"You didn't reward him for his loyalty?"

"He was duplicitous. Both to me and to you. There is no honor among thieves, as such. At least you have loyalty, Olive. I find your moral compass to be skewed, but your loyalty is to your company. To the vision that your father laid out. That is a fixed loyalty. It makes sense. It can be tracked. Someone who is continually changing the guard as it were, is not trustworthy in any fashion."

She sniffed. "I suppose at least there's that. He's a bigger rat than I am."

"So you admit that what you did was wrong?"

"Why is it so important to you that I admit it? I'm not certain that it's wrong, if there's a weakness in your system. Again, we have different goals. Mine was to get the contract. Yours is to feel a certain way about how you go about getting the work."

"And why does it not matter to you?"

"Because I have to... Like I told you. I have nothing. I am nothing apart from this. You have this whole other company that you've built. I have this one thing. And I was willing to try and get whatever I could from you at all costs. Because it just seemed... It seemed reasonable. At the time."

And he could see, unspoken, that nothing much seemed reasonable now. Now that she was pregnant with his child.

You believe her?

He looked at the sad, waifish creature sitting before him. He would never have thought of Olive as *waifish* before. But yes. He did believe her.

Though this was just another way in which he'd failed to see Olive, when he'd been so convinced before that he had.

That she was a virgin was difficult to wrap his mind

around, because she was a beautiful woman, and confident, determined.

But there had been clues. She did not seem to care about her appearance—though he had been certain enough that she would be able to get whatever man she might wish to have.

She clearly did not think so, though. She felt that she needed to stay buried in work, and work alone.

He wondered if that was how her perspective had become so twisted.

As if yours is better?

Yes. It was better. He did not have a more emotional life than she did, but he had honor. He might not believe in things like love, and he himself might not have friends, but he lived by a specific code.

Which was why it disgusted him so when he flared in his midsection when he looked at her.

He should not find her half so compelling. Not now. Not after everything.

And yet he did.

"Are you hungry?"

"Assume that I'm hungry unless stated otherwise," she said.

"But you don't seem to feel well."

"If I'm eating it makes it bearable. Strange, I know, but I didn't know anything about this sort of thing… And I don't really know what's normal and what's not, but that seems to be the way of things for me."

He went to the fridge, and took out a large tray of meat and cheese. She looked at him with skepticism. "Why are you being nice to me?"

"Do you consider this nice?"

She blinked, and tilted her head, and she looked rather like a questioning sparrow. "I… Well, I don't really know. Maybe it isn't all that nice. I don't have a lot of interaction with people. I have employees. And I have…" She started laughing. "I have you. I have you, and we spar and fight, and you bring me cupcakes. I guess you like to feed me."

"It was a game," he said.

"Well, you are the only person that I play games with. I think I sadly misread what we were."

"What exactly did you think?"

"I would've said that you were my rival. My enemy. But sometimes I felt as if you were my only friend."

"I do not have friends," he said. She nodded slowly, the desolation in her eyes puncturing something in his chest.

"No. Of course you don't. You are… You're a Viking. A warrior in all things. A man with a code of honor, but…"

"There is no point bringing emotion into anything," he said.

"Well. That's a lie. You're entirely comfortable with anger, which as far as I can tell is essential to men."

Anger.

The truth of that was a scalding handful of ash pressed hard into his chest.

"Anger is the one emotion that can exist unfettered," he said. "Anger is clear."

"You get so angry with me for having been dishonest, but you are lying to yourself. It's just… It's an emotion loophole. You're not cold if you're angry. Not at all."

"You speak very confidently of things you do not know," he said.

She waved a hand. "I know well enough. We watched each other become who we are now."

"Yes. I suppose that is true."

"I always thought that you brought me cupcakes because you felt bad about taking that last one. Since it was my birthday."

"I didn't know it was your birthday."

"I didn't mention it."

"But you did mention the cupcake often enough."

"Well, then you started bringing them to me. So it worked."

"You started craving chocolate the minute you heard my footsteps. Which was more my aim. I found it amusing."

"Yes. You trained my body to respond to you."

Suddenly, it was as if she heard the words after they exited her mouth, and she breathed in sharply, her eyes going round.

"Indeed."

"Well. Hopefully the doctor calls soon. So we can get down to the rest of your threats."

"You are looking forward to them?"

"What other choice do I have?"

But he could see that there was calculation behind her eyes. Because she was not weak. He could not afford to get caught up in her again. She was a worthy opponent, and he had to not forget that.

CHAPTER TEN

APPARENTLY, IT TOOK a little while to get the results on a DNA test. And Olive was doing her best to pass the time until Gunnar confirmed what she suspected they both already knew.

After breakfast that morning she explored. Every room in the house was a particular sort of beige, not plain, just tranquil.

But then she opened the door at the back of the house, and was stunned by a riot of color. The shelves were lined with action figures, still in their boxes, stacks of board games and bins of… Candy.

"What?"

"What are you doing in here?"

She turned to face him, her heart pounding rapidly. "I was only… I just wanted to look around."

"And now you have."

"What is this?"

His face went hard. "It is nothing."

"It's not nothing. Look at all these toys…"

"It is a collection," he said.

"Surely candy is not part of the collection." She examined the rows of sweets. All brightly colored and very out of character.

But then, he'd eaten her cupcake.

Maybe it wasn't out of character.

"In a manner of speaking it is."

"You don't eat the candy?" she pressed.

"I do," he said.

And she might have laughed, at the discomfort she saw in him just now, except she could sense something vibrating beneath the surface, and it concerned her.

"Why?"

"It started as collecting some things I had when I was a child, and it expanded. Every billionaire must have a prescribed amount of novelty items that make no sense. I am quite a bit under the usual threshold."

"That is fair. You don't have an entire fleet of electric cars."

"Only three."

"Well, there you are. You are actually quite restrained." She moved further into the room, her hands brushing up against one of the games. "Do you play these?"

"I've never had anyone to play with."

She looked at him, and she felt…

It was such a tangle of emotions. Because he'd brought her here, and threatened her business, and turned her life upside down. And he was also…

Him. The him he'd always been. Who bewitched her and tangled her up, and made her want things she'd been certain she could never have.

Who vexed her and charmed her sometimes in equal measure. Though usually he was more vexing.

He was a cold, forbidding Viking warrior.

A man incensed by her lack of honor.

A man who had kissed her like he'd die if he didn't have her.

A man who had this room, hidden away in the back of his house.

"Gunnar. We have to play a game." She took the box off the top of the stack, one she was familiar with. A strategy game that was all about building empires with wheat and sheep and ore. "We must not pass up this opportunity to match wits with one another."

"Must we not?"

"Absolutely."

"I suppose while we are still waiting for the doctor…"

In truth, she was just desperate to have a moment with him that wasn't…well that wasn't fraught or angry.

"Yes. All right."

He took the game from her hands and walked out of the room, charging toward the kitchen. She followed. She sat across from him at the table, and it quite reminded her of times they had sparred in the boardroom. They set up their game tiles and chose their pieces.

"You should fear me. I am a master at this kind of thing," she said.

And he smiled at her. For the first time in a long while. "You should fear me. I am a Viking."

She smiled back. "Oh, I know."

They got stuck into their gameplay, and it was fearsome. And there was something about the moment, about the connection. Him smiling and laughing when he would rob her of her land, that made the time fall away. And she wished they could've done this before. She wished they could've been children together. Properly.

She wished that things could be different.

He was another side to the coin of her existence. There was no one else like him. Nobody. And she feared if she couldn't find a way to connect with him, to fix this with him, she would never have a connection with anyone.

"I'm quickly cornering the market on sheep," he said.

"I'm not sure that's something to be proud of," she said.

"I think you will find that it is."

He grinned, the way he did when he presented her with a cupcake.

"You know what you were doing with the cupcake," she said. And to his credit, he did not seem confused at the abrupt introduction of the subject. It was almost as if he had been thinking of it too.

"You mean I knew I was training you?" He shrugged. "Perhaps."

"I've never understood it, you know. What we were. Really. Before all this. Before I... Before I broke it with what I did. And I am sorry. I am. And then we made a muddle of it with sex and then... Here we are. I never understood."

"We are not like anything else," he said.

And that, she feared, was the only answer to be had. They were not like anything else.

They had not quite been friends, but never quite enemies. Rivals, but allies in some ways.

It had all gotten strained and difficult with her attraction to him. With the way the loss of her father had spurred her to behave.

She felt so much loyalty to her father, but sometimes she wasn't sure why. More and more there were cracks beginning to form, particularly if she imagined what kind of parent she might want to be. Particularly if she imagined what her life might look like going forward. And in those moments of honesty, she could realize that Gunnar had actually been the closest person in her life. The one who had been the most human on many different occasions.

"You're right," she said. "We're not like anything else."

Tension stretched between them, and what she really wanted to do was close the distance between them and kiss him. What she really wanted to do was take back so many of the things that had happened in the last couple of months. Just so she could erase the anger that he felt at her. The obvious betrayal it had created.

"Did I hurt you?" she asked.

His eyes suddenly turned into ice chips. "No. You do not have the power to do such a thing."

"Oh. It's only that… You have been very angry at me."

"Yes. I have been."

"But?"

"You do not possess the ability to hurt me, Olive."

And she could hear beneath that, a firm *no one does*.

"And so now you won't take my word. You won't take my word that the baby is yours."

"Just play the game, Olive."

"Or is waiting for the test results just a bit to punish me."

"I do not need to punish you."

"All right then, is marriage not meant to be a punishment?"

"It is meant to be a solution."

"All right. So tell me, will we ever be friends again?"

"We were never truly friends to begin with."

"So you'll tell me that I'm singular, unique. That we are like nothing, but you cannot tell me that we are friends?"

He shrugged. "I don't have friends."

She gestured to the board game. "This is a very odd way of expressing it."

"I have colleagues, I have lovers."

"And you intend to take me as a wife. I already know what the results will be. So I already know what you will demand. And so I want to know. What does it mean? Will you love the baby? Will you ever love me?"

She felt small and afraid asking that question, and she did not wish to know why it affected her so.

His expression went flat. "There is no love left in me."

"Then what's the point?"

"Sometimes the point, Olive, is to simply do the right thing."

"What if the right thing becomes the wrong thing if there's no feeling behind it?"

"It does not matter if the end result is the same."

"I think it does," she said.

"Then you are free to feel as you see fit."

"I won," she said. "And I didn't cheat." She looked at the board game and counted up her resources.

He frowned. "So you did. You're a worthy opponent."

And he got up and walked away, without speaking. And she wished, more than anything, that she could find a way to be something to him other than an opponent, worthy or not. She wished that she… She didn't wholly know what she wanted from Gunnar. Or perhaps she was simply afraid to put voice to it.

They were *them*. Like nothing else. This had reminded her of that period of their long history. Of the years that had not been this. This fraught, terrible thing. But the last few months could not be altered or changed. They had to find a new way to be.

And she ached. With wanting him. Not just physically but… She wanted to piece back together the emotions.

But tomorrow the test results are going to come back, and they are going to be positive. And he's going to marry you. That grim man who hates you now so very much.

And it was a long future that stretched before her, married to that man. One that reminded her far too much of the cold in her childhood.

She was going to have to come up with a plan, because she did not think she could bear it.

She'd already had a lifetime in offices, with no birthday parties. She could not philosophically consign herself to more of the same.

CHAPTER ELEVEN

OLIVE KNEW IF she was going to escape, it had to be tonight.

This wasn't going to work. He was so angry with her, with everything, and so convinced of his rightness. She'd tried connecting with him, tried to find their footing and he'd closed it all down.

He had said he'd never love her.

And she just needed…

She needed some control back. She'd given it all to him when she'd told him there had been no one else, no other men. That the baby was his and she'd loved her father and she was broken by his loss.

That she'd wanted Gunnar as a gift for herself. She'd told him that.

She felt unmade.

Unraveled.

Her father had told her never to fall apart like this. To never let her emotions cloud her judgment. To never let them take the lead.

And here she was.

She needed to regroup. She could not let him take control of her. She could not be…here with him, she just needed space to sort it all out.

And maybe part of her just couldn't accept allowing him to win.

He wanted her here. Wanted to marry her. Wanted her on his turf.

Or maybe you just don't want to be with someone else who looks at you like you're a disappointment...

She shut that thought down.

Yes, her father had sometimes treated her like she might disappoint him. Yes, that had hurt. But daddy issues weren't the thing here. Maybe. Probably.

Handily, in her new clothing, he had included clothes with which to make a track in this sort of weather. She still had her phone, though, and she had managed to charter herself a private jet, which would land soon enough, some distance away from his home. The airstrip there was private, and the pilot had been adamant that he could not land on it without permission from the owner, which was going to be a problem, since she needed the owner to not know that she was fleeing. It would sort of undermine her escape if he knew.

At midnight, with the snow falling softly outside, she put on the fur-lined leather pants, boots and parka that he had provided for her. And then she slipped from the bedroom, ready to make her way down the hall.

She was not going to keep him from coming after her forever, but she didn't have to be secluded in his mountain-top retreat.

She was going to get back on her own turf, get her lawyers involved, get into a position where she could attempt to defend her business.

Attempt to defend herself.

He could not force her down the aisle, after all. If he was intent on ruining her either way...

This was the thing. If he did not have her, he would have to negotiate. And she needed to put Gunnar in a position where he had to negotiate.

He would have to give a forfeit of some kind. If he

was holding her bodily against her will, then she became the token.

And she did not wish to be the token. So, she would not be.

Keeping her footsteps silent, she slipped through the living room area, and to the corridor that led to the sky tram.

Of course, it was only when she arrived at the sky tram that she had the thought that she actually had no idea how to run the sky tram.

She looked for a box and tried to figure it out. Look for controls. She couldn't see anything. It was dark, and the snow was coming down thick.

But that was okay. She was intrepid. She knew exactly how they had gotten up, it was a straight line. And so, she decided to head down on foot. She knew that it would be a bit of a long walk, but thankfully she was outfitted. She was prepared.

She moved her foot to a rocky outcropping, and slipped. She clung tightly to the ground, the frozen dirt biting into her fingertips.

No. She would be fine. She wasn't going to give in. She wasn't going to turn back. She was just going to go step by step down the mountain. Because it was the only way down.

Just step by step. And she would make it.

She had to.

For herself. For the baby.

She would.

He woke up when he heard a noise.

He got up, and dressed—he always slept naked—and went outside. He didn't see anything. And then he went to Olive's room, and found her bed abandoned.

Her phone was gone.

Of course. Whatever she was doing…

She was not trustworthy. Not on the level that he would've liked her to be.

But what did she think she was playing at? If she went out there in the dead of night she was going to die.

And the baby...

He growled, throwing on his winter clothes and grabbing a stack of blankets.

He saw that the tram was still in place, and judging by the way the snow was situated on it, it had not moved. But of course, there would be no way she could operate it.

Had the little idiot actually gone down the mountain on her own?

He growled in a fury, and began to go after her.

She could only be a few minutes ahead.

He tried to find her through the thick sleet, but didn't see her.

He hiked down in a straight line, making it halfway down the mountain without ever seeing her once. And he knew beyond a shadow of a doubt that she had not gone that far ahead. She had to be lost. She was zigzagging, or she had taken a wrong turn.

Perhaps she was parallel to him.

But he could not imagine that she had made as much progress down the mountain as he had. It was familiar to him, and he knew where he was going. She did not.

He turned and started to go back up the mountain, keeping his eyes to the left and right. And after a fashion, he simply began to call for her. "Olive," he said. "Olive."

And then he saw her. With three inches of snow built up on her coat, crouched down against the side of the mountain. Her eyes were closed, her body limp.

"No," he said, his voice rough. He went to her quickly, shaking her. Her head lolled back and forth, and her eyes opened, dazed.

"You little idiot," he said.

"You're not the pilot."

"Fool," he said.

And he began to beat a path as quickly as possible to the hot springs. It was shielded from the wind and snow, and it was much closer than the house. He needed to warm her up, and he needed to do it quickly.

When they arrived at the edge of the hot springs he set her down in the snow, and stripped himself naked with ruthless efficiency, then he picked her up, and did the same to her, carrying her into the steaming pale blue liquid. She didn't rouse when the hot water touched her skin. Her lips were tinged blue, and he cursed. He can only hope that hypothermia had not set in in truth, or she would be in much bigger trouble than a hot springs would be able to solve.

He moved the water over her skin, and ignored the stirring in his body.

She was beautiful, it was true, and he had been battling attraction for her along with his anger these past few days, but now was not the time.

Her eyelids fluttered open. "Oh," she said, thrashing suddenly in his arms.

He held her tight up against his chest, her hands splayed there. "Settle down," he said.

"What happened? Where am I?"

"You're in the hot springs."

"I'm not supposed to submerge in water over a hundred and four degrees. I read that online when I couldn't sleep the other night."

"You probably aren't supposed to freeze either. But don't worry, the water isn't even one hundred degrees."

"Where am I?"

"Three-quarters of the way down the mountain. I found you on an outcropping. Because you nearly killed yourself doing whatever the hell you were trying to do. Which makes your lectures about water temperature feel a bit empty."

Her eyes went wide. "I *did*?"

"Yes. What were you playing at?"

"Escaping, obviously. But I figured it was a straight shot down the mountain…"

"And you managed to get yourself going sideways. It doesn't matter, I don't think you would've made it to the bottom. You're small, and you don't move quick enough. I think you do not have an adequate understanding of how cold it is. You've been out here now for a couple of hours."

"I have been?"

"Yes. You might not want to believe me, but you should. I wouldn't lie to you."

"Right. Because of your honor."

"I have no need to. I have been up-front with you about who I was and what I was doing from the beginning. You know better."

She trembled in his arms, and he thought perhaps now might not be the time to yell at her. But she was an idiot. And she deserved it.

"Did I really nearly get myself killed?"

"Yes. You have got to stop acting as if you can overcome anything. You cannot overcome winter."

"I just… I've had to train to be in charge. To handle everything. I don't have the luxury of being tentative. I don't have the luxury of… You know that. You know how it is."

"You cannot wage war against temperature. It does not matter how determined you are. It does not care how brilliant you are. The weather will equalize you. To everyone else."

"I have a pilot coming."

"Stupid girl," he said. "No pilot can land in this. Even if a pilot said he was coming, he is not coming now."

"Really?"

"Yes. You might've traveled the world, but you certainly don't have an adequate respect for the kind of snow we get here. The kind of cold. Children here learn, and early, that they must have a care for the wilderness. For the turn in the weather."

His grandfather had taught him how to respect the wilderness and all the creatures in it. To love the cold, even as he respected it. He had taught him that the earth was living, and like any living being it had to be respected.

He carried that with him. Always.

"How are we going to get out of this without freezing to death?"

"Getting out will be unpleasant. But it will help that you warmed up. And I brought blankets."

"Did you know that I wouldn't make it?"

"I didn't stop to think," he said.

"I thought that I would make it," she said.

"Yes. I realize that." He snorted. "I did not think that you were suicidal over the prospect of marrying me."

"No. I wanted leverage."

And suddenly, it was as if she became conscious of the friction between their bodies. Of the fact that there was no clothing between them. Her cheeks went pink, and she wiggled slightly.

"What kind of leverage did you want?"

"What I wanted," she said, "was something. Anything. As long as you're holding me, you're holding all the cards, aren't you?"

"I have not offered you a buffet, Olive. This is not a chance for you to choose what you would like and put back what you do not. This is not an endless array of options for you. You have left yourself little choice here. You have no one to blame but yourself."

"Now, on that score you're wrong. The pregnancy was not just me. So don't be like that."

"All right. I will give you that. You are not alone in that."

"Oh. I know. I remember. I remember your…" She wiggled slightly. "Your involvement."

"A delicate way of putting it," he said.

"Well. I'm nothing if not delicate."

"Do not do anything so foolish again," he said, smoothing his thumb over her cheek. She looked improbably young, and he could remember when she had been a girl. And a wild one at that. He remembered when she had been as vulnerable as she looked now, and he wondered if anyone had ever held her then. He just wondered. He did not think they had.

And he should not feel any sympathy for her. Her choices were hers, and hers alone. As his had been. He had no sympathy for himself either. He had chosen to leave this place, to leave the people who had loved him. He had chosen to go with his father. He had been wrong about his father, and the consequences of that had been his to bear.

As her consequences were hers.

She might have felt some pressure from her father but the man was dead. He could not actually force her to do anything. He could not influence her.

At some point, everyone had to stand on their own feet and own who they were. What they were.

"You are warm," he said, his voice coming out rougher than he intended.

"Yes," she said.

"Let us get you back to the house. Do not try anything like this again."

"Not in the snowstorm."

"Never," he said.

"I'm not a kitten, Gunnar. I am not the kind of person who is simply going to lay down and accept what you have decreed. I am a woman. A woman who has been taught how to fight. I'm hardly going to let go of that now."

"The war is over. Consider yourself pillaged."

"The war isn't over until you're dead. And even then... I'm pretty sure that I would haunt your ass."

He chuckled. He couldn't help himself. It was the absurdity of it. Of her spirit. From the moment he had found her crouched behind her desk eating crackers. And she had tried to play it off. She never admitted when she didn't have the upper hand. But sadly for her. Sadly for her, she was the decisive loser in this battle.

He reached to the banks of the hot springs and laid out one of the blankets, then he lifted her from the water and set her on the blanket. She grabbed one of the folded blankets and wrapped it around her body. The dim light and her quick concealing of her curves made it so he didn't get a good look at her body. For the best, he supposed.

Then he got out of the water, his feet planted in the snow, and he dried himself quickly with the remaining blanket, before dressing quickly. Then he set about to help her get dressed without letting too much of her body be exposed to the cold.

He realized then that she was staring, wide-eyed.

"Yes?"

"Well, I'm never going to be used to just... You being naked. But also... Are you made of ice?"

"No but there is a resistance. Or perhaps I have a comfortable relationship with it."

"I have a comfortable relationship with fuzzy blankets."

"Women who are half so attached to blankets should not go taking off in the blizzards."

"Well, maybe if women who are attached to blankets were not also attached to freedom and agency, they wouldn't."

"Maybe those women who like blankets, freedom, and their agency, should not commit corporate espionage."

"Maybe men who are made of ice shouldn't be such sore losers."

"Again. Was I a loser?" he pressed. "Or did you cheat."

"Functionally immaterial to me."

"So you said."

When she was finished dressing, he looked up the side of the mountain. Thankfully, the snow had let up. "Climb on my back."

"What?"

"I'm going to carry you up."

"No. No. You don't need to do… No."

"Are you through arguing with me?"

"Yes," she said, exasperated as she hopped up onto his back, her legs resting on his lean hips, her arms around his throat. The softness of her body pressed against his sent a lick of heat through him. How was it she did this to him? After what she'd done. After running away. After all of it. How did he still want her like this?

"This is kind of dumb," she said. "Because I could strangle you if I wanted to."

"And how would you get yourself off the mountain."

"All right. That is a serious concern."

She was silent for a while.

"I really did think I could get myself out of this with sheer determination. That's what my father taught me, you know. Dad always said separating a person from greatness was their own unwillingness to be uncomfortable. That you had to work hard in order to achieve things, and… Once I realized that all of it was in my control… I've had a hard time doing things any differently. I mean, if it's just temporary discomfort… Why not push through? That was what propelled me down the mountain tonight. Cold is just temporary discomfort."

"Temporary discomfort that can kill you."

"I don't look at it that way. I didn't. I'm just trying to explain. All these things. The long work hours, the not having relationships, the… The corporate espionage even. They are unfortunate accessories to the main goal. And what my dad taught me was that the ends always justify the means. They always do. All you have to do is… Just ignore all the things that you need."

Her words tapered off on that last sentence. As if she suddenly heard what she had said. "The problem is, it never ends. You never arrive at a point where you go… Well. That's enough. It's sufficient sacrifice. No. I haven't found that yet. It's like you get to a point and you think… That wasn't so bad. I can keep going. I can do it again. I can… I can keep pushing myself. I'll catch up on sleep later. I'll make friends later. I'll have a relationship later. And you just chip away at yourself. At who you are and what you expect. At what you think you deserve. Until… Until it's only work. Until it's only work and you don't remember anymore what it's like to be something other than a robot." She tightened her grip on him. "I never set out to be a robot. I just wanted to make him proud. I just loved him and I wanted to be… what he wanted me to be."

He'd wanted that from his father once. He knew what it was like to not see. To not know.

"And I just took one little thing for myself," she whispered.

"That night in the penthouse was your indulgence?"

Except it had been his too. Whether he wished to admit it or not. She had been off-limits for a very long time, and few things were off-limits to him. He set the parameters for his life, and if he wanted something, he usually took it. But not her. For very specific reasons, not her.

He made sure to act dutifully as a better man than his father. But he'd had no confidence he could be better for her truly.

But he'd broken that rule.

And the world had come crashing down on him.

He was an Icelander to his soul. Protecting the land,

the natural resources mattered to him more than just about anything.

And he tried to have harmony in all parts of his life. His business life did not conflict with the morals he felt outside of it.

And yet, he had to wonder at the exacting symmetry of all these things.

For it was more as if he had no other life at all.

Olive seemed to be at war. With what she wanted, with who she was. With what she did.

She was a fascinating constellation of fractured stars. Little things here and there that seemed to speak of dissonance in who she was.

Not him.

He was at ease. At one accord.

Finally, they arrived at the summit. Finally they arrived back at the house.

"Go and put something else on," he said.

She looked up at him, beseeching.

"Go," he said.

She emerged a few moments later wearing sweats. "Now," he said. "You will sleep in my bed tonight."

"I will do no such thing."

"You have proven yourself to be a flight risk," he said. "And now I have to keep an eye on you. If you do not like the consequences… You have no one to blame but yourself. And I mean that for every piece of this, all the way down." He went into the bathroom and changed into a pair of athletic pants, only out of deference to the fact that he would be getting into bed with her. He was not normally so kind, but he also had no interest in terrorizing a woman in that regard.

Even if the woman in question was a holy terror herself.

She was standing there in his bedroom with a mutinous expression on her face. He ignored her, and wrapped his arm around her waist, picking her up and bringing her down into the bed with him. "As jail cells go, you must admit this is a warm one."

"But it's still a jail cell," she whispered.

"Forgive me if I do not find myself to be overly concerned with your protestations. You should've thought of that before any of this."

They lay there in darkness, her softness nestled against him, and desire bloomed in his midsection. This was an exercise in restraint, and he was not a man who normally put himself in the situations that required any.

He should hate her, this woman, for she had upended his well-ordered life.

He had not planned on taking a wife, least of all her. Especially not after what she had done.

And yet, he desired her. And there was nothing to be done about that. It simply was.

It simply was.

And in the morning, there was a phone call, telling him definitively that the child was his. And he knew that their path was now set in stone. There was no turning back now.

CHAPTER TWELVE

SHE WAS IN a dreamless sleep, cocooned in warmth. And when she woke up, the sun was shining bright in the room. She couldn't make heads or tails out of where she was, not for a moment. And then, suddenly, she remembered.

She was in Gunnar's room, and Gunnar's house. Because she had tried to run away last night, and she had nearly frozen to death and then he had dragged her naked into a hot springs. And that was now too many times that she had been unconscious in the presence of that man.

She was starting to feel like what she had never been. A wilting flower, incapable of standing on her own feet. That wasn't her. It never could be.

It wasn't her.

She was supposed to be better than that. She was supposed to be stronger. It was important that she…

She could hear herself, talking, what she had told him last night. It was the saddest admission she could think of. The way that she had said that she was basically a shadow person. The way that she seemed to think that it was acceptable.

She had never articulated those things before, and she wasn't sure why she had done it now. Hypothermia. It had to be. Because it just didn't make sense otherwise.

It was just…

It was just all a little bit too much. These last few days that she had spent in Gunnar's house were the only real vacation she'd had in years. And this was basically a kidnap. And it felt like a vacation.

She rolled over onto her back. And that was when she remembered he had slept holding her in his arms all night. But he was up now.

She flushed, thinking about it.

How could she not? She still wasn't used to all that kind of thing. She flushed even more thinking about the hot springs. About the way his hard, hot body had felt pressed up against hers.

Really, if she could be aroused thinking about a situation wherein she was maybe dying, it was really very bad.

She got out of bed, and padded out to the living area. And he was standing there, arms crossed over his broad chest. He was wearing a black sweater, and black pants, and the outfit looked like it could barely contain his muscles. But she could not ignore the fact that it was an outfit that looked alarmingly like the one that she typically liked to wear every day. The one that he had denied her.

She opened her mouth to say something, but the forbidding nature of his expression stopped her.

"What?"

"The paternity test results are back. I am the father."

"Well. I knew that already, Gunnar. I think you did too." He said nothing.

"But you said to me that…that love is hard for you and I just don't understand…" She cleared her throat. "Why are you so intent on having me? On having the baby?"

He said nothing for a moment, his eyes going so cold they made the snow outside look like it might be a retreat into summer. "Do you know, I went to live with my father when I was twelve years old."

She shook her head. "I didn't know that. I just assumed that…"

"Of course you would assume I had always been with

him. But no. Until I was twelve I was raised by my maternal grandparents. When I was older, when I wasn't a little boy, I thought I wanted to go and live with my father, you see. He sent me letters. From time to time. And I idolized him. I looked up photos of him on the Internet. I thought that he was brilliant. Exactly the sort of man I wanted to be when I grew up. I wanted to meet him more than anything in the world. I wanted to live with him. And when I was twelve I got my wish."

"Gunnar…"

"I still remember the thrill of it. He came in a helicopter. He was wearing a suit. He looked exactly like he had in the photos. And I knew… I knew that it was the right thing. He took me to where he was living in London. I had never seen a city. It was… It was incredible.

"It did not take long for me to realize that he was not the man that I had dreamed him to be. There were women. Always in the home. In various states of undress. They were… They were paid to be there. Or perhaps manipulated. I came to find out later that he had a close association with a rather infamous man who was renowned for trafficking women. I will always wonder if those women were there of their own accord or not."

"That's terrible."

"It is. Of course, I was a boy, and I did not know the meaning of those women wandering about in flimsy robes. But I could see the way that he treated them. The disdain. As if they were something beneath him." He took a breath. "I understand now, that this was his cruelest abuse. But when I was a boy I only knew the pain of what he did to me. He kept my room Spartan and spare. And that, I did have feelings about. Because I missed my toys, no matter how humble they had been. I missed… But he said that I could not have toys. He said that I could not have friends."

And at sixteen, he'd eaten her birthday cupcake, and

she'd thought him a villain. When he was a boy with a room that had nothing nice, and probably had no sweets, judging by the collection of candy he kept in that room.

The cupcake meant something else now.

Something different than it had before.

"That's awful."

"Is it so different from you? Is it so different from what your father did to you?"

"My father taught me to be hard. He taught me to win at all costs. But I had toys. He… He did treat me with some affection. It was not entirely void of those things."

"My father thought that beatings would teach me to be hard."

"Gunnar…"

"You see, Olive, I was as wrong about my father as I could've been about anyone. There was no way I could possibly have misjudged him more. We fell out finally when I was eighteen. There was a woman staying in the house, she could not have been much older than I. My father raised a hand to her. I would have none of it. I beat the hell out of him. And I regret nothing. I called the police, but she was unwilling to speak to them. I tried to help her, tried to get her to leave whatever situation she was in, but she… She was afraid. She ran before I could get her name, and I… I regret that bitterly. I have endeavored to do better than him because I have seen the destruction that a man with unchecked power can have on the world. I've seen the scars. I bear them."

Her throat was tight, with anger, sadness, all for him. But also…fear. For her child. For her future. "Let me ask you, truly. Why is it that you want to be a father to this child?"

"To protect them. It seems absurd, and yet… If they have you, and they have me… There is accountability."

"You won't let me hurt them, and I won't let you?"

"Yes. There is the possibility of course the both of us could be toxic."

"We won't be. We can make a different choice. For the baby. For us. We can make better choices."

"No child of mine will grow up without his father. And when I say that…"

"Why not? What do you care?"

"I'm not leaving it up to you," he said.

"That's offensive," she said.

"No. I will have my child, and I will have you. He will have a family that is together. That is married. I will not have…"

"Why?" She raised her hands in exasperation. "Neither of us had mothers, Gunnar. Neither of us had nuclear families. I am willing to give up Ambient. I'm willing to give it up." Her voice fractured, as she realized how true all of this was. "Because I can't have a child raised in boardrooms. Because I can't have a child be raised simply to be an afterthought. Simply to be an instrument for which to continue to carry out our bidding. It needs to be something else. We need to be something else."

"Then you may do that. If you choose. No one is forcing you to continue on as head of Ambient. But we will do this together."

"Well, make me understand what you're thinking then, because I'm the person that's having your baby, after all, and I think I ought to know what you're thinking. I think I ought to know why I have to be subject to your whim simply because you…" But the expression on his face stopped her short. There was something raw there, something ragged. Even in his anger at her he had managed to affect a sort of smoothness. An *I'm not mad I'm disappointed kind of countenance,* even though she had a feeling he was volcanic.

But this was different. This was a locked door. There

was more to what had happened with his father, and he wasn't sharing it.

"What happened to you?" she asked.

"It does no good to speak of. All you need to know is what you are expected to do. I expect that you will give me what I ask for. I expect that you will marry me. Because if you do not, it is not only the company I will take."

"Gunnar..."

"Then what will you suggest, if we don't marry? Will I take the child for six months, and you another six? Will you surrender him to me completely? How do you suppose we make this work, if not the way I've commanded."

"I'm going to carry this child. I'm going to feel it move. I'm going to... How I feel now has nothing to do with how I'll feel in a few months, and already I... When I think of the baby, I can't help but..." She felt so raw and fragile, like she was cracking apart. In her desperation she had offered up the thing that mattered most to her. The thing that she defined herself by. Mostly because she was desperate to make sure that she did not raise a child in a world where that was all that mattered. When it was the only way that they mattered. Because it just felt... Wrong. It felt wrong, and she couldn't do it.

She didn't know what that would make her. The idea of not having Ambient made her feel rootless. Adrift.

But the idea of raising a child who would feel like she did about their life, about the world, that did not seem acceptable.

Her life hadn't been happy.

She'd tried to be happy in it. She'd tried her best but there had been no softness. No real...affection. Her father had set a hurdle and she'd done her best to clear it. Then there would be another, and another and she had learned to equate the praise she got for jumping over them with...love.

And she knew he had loved her. But it had been conditional.

She'd been happy to idolize her father's memory until she'd had to think about what sort of parent she wanted to be, and that had started to erode everything.

Because she would not do this to her child.

The last eight months had been hell. What she'd gone through, what she'd stooped to to try and make her father proud…

She didn't know herself.

And as she stood there she realized that was one of her problems.

She didn't know herself.

"What I said to you last night," she said. "That was honest. I don't know who I am apart from this corporation. I don't know who I am if I'm not succeeding. If I'm not chipping away at my own comfort in order to make things happen. It's the only thing I believe in. And I want a new god, quite frankly. Because this one hasn't served me very well. It's given me money. It's given me…" She shook her head. "All I ever wanted was to make him proud. All I ever wanted was to make it so that he didn't resent the fact that he had to drag me to all those board meetings and…"

"They could've hired nannies. They were billionaires. What your father chose to do with you during the day, had nothing to do with you. Not really. That was what he was doing to try to cultivate you into what he wanted. He could've had you back at home, couldn't he? He could have made sure that you were safe and comfortable, in a playroom with lots of toys. You do not have to be there on your birthday. You could've been home with balloons and a pony ride, hell, he could have changed the day of the meeting. Because he is not a nine-to-five worker drone, he owned the company."

He was rubbing salt in her wounds and while this was

certainly the moment for honesty, this hurt, and she wanted to hit back at him.

"And if he would've showed that kind of weakness what do you think your father would've done?"

"He would've exploited it. He would've exploited the hell out of it, because you may have noticed that I was not home with nannies either. Nor was I receiving birthday parties of any kind. But still. These were choices that they made. To shape us into a very particular thing. You have nothing to make up to your father for. Nor do I."

The realization rocked her, because he wasn't wrong. He was... He spoke the truth. Her father didn't have to bring her to those meetings. She had this idea, this narrative that she had built in her mind of the single dad who had done his very best and dragged her along because he wanted to spend time with her. But they didn't spend time together. And it was thoroughly manipulative. They did not spend time together, and what he had been doing was showing her what she needed to value most. What he had been doing was teaching her that there was no such thing as a personal life.

He had been teaching her to erase boundaries. To not respect her need for a break. Leading by example, sure, but his dream didn't have to be her dream.

Now, standing there in this living room, as far as all of it had taken her, she wasn't sure what her dream was.

She was twenty-six years old, and the lone female CEO of any of the tech companies. The youngest too.

She didn't know if she wanted it. And it wasn't simply that cliché of knowing she was going to have a baby, but it had certainly done something to shake up her priorities.

As had passing out two different times in front of Gunnar. Maybe she was weak because she didn't have any stores built up. Maybe strength wasn't about how hard you could push yourself, but the restraint that you could show sometimes too.

Maybe there was a strength in saying no. One that she had certainly never found.

"I'll marry you," she said. "On one condition."

She saw it clearly now. She needed to get off the path her father had put her on.

She needed her own path.

The one that would lead her to herself. To Olive. The best person she could be, the best mother she could be.

"And what is that?"

"I want you to invest in a start-up."

"What will your start-up be?"

"I don't know. And maybe it won't end up being a start-up per se. I have no idea. Not yet. But I want you to invest in me, and what I decide I want. It won't be until a year after the baby is born, and by then I should have some ideas. I will marry you, as long as I can still figure out who I am. Because all of this is making me realize that I actually don't know. I don't feel guilty about the corporate espionage, not really. Because I know why I did it. What makes me feel strange is the fact that you know that's a hard limit for you, and I don't know what is for me. I don't know myself. I'm a hollowed-out vessel that my dad created to carry out his dreams, his ambitions. His wishes. And I don't want to be that. Not anymore. Because if I do, then I'll do the same to my child. I will carve them out and make them into something less than a person. Something less than a whole human being. And I cannot have that. I won't. It's not right or fair."

"That's a pretty speech. And if you wish, of course I will do that."

"And what will you expect. From a wife. Out of… Having a child."

"I offer protection. I offer fidelity."

Heat swept over her body, because of course. Of course to be married to him would be to sleep with him. But the idea filled her with a kind of reckless heat that she hadn't anticipated.

"What about…" Her throat suddenly felt scratchy. "Love? Not for me, obviously. Obviously not me. But the baby. Our baby."

"I offer protection. That as far as I'm concerned is an expression of something that many people might call love."

She looked at him, at that icy façade. "You don't believe in love, do you?"

"Oh, I believe in it. Many people around me have experienced it. Who am I to deny them what they feel. I just am no longer capable of it myself."

"You said that already but I don't…"

"Olive, I let you negotiate because there is no point in the two of us being miserable. But you do not get to set the terms here."

"This is isn't a business negotiation, actually, Gunnar. For the first time, we are not talking about the terms of a business deal. Were talking about a human child. Our child."

"In our experience, that is much the same thing."

"No. It doesn't matter what our experience was. It doesn't matter… We cannot do things this way."

"Our child will have two parents. That is a beginning."

But it wasn't a promise of anything fantastic or romantic. Not at all. He condemned their childhood but without love…

Without love how would their child's life be different?

How would her life be different?

He was cold, and he was remote. He was the very frozen wasteland outside.

You'll have to do it. You'll have to create enough love to cover you and the baby.

"I'm going to be putting out an announcement about our upcoming marriage."

And suddenly, she realized what that would mean.

The world was going to explode. They were the most storied business rivals in modern history, and they were getting married. Having a baby. For all the world to see, merging their companies. Beneath the umbrella of his.

It was a decisive victory for Magnum. At least, that was how it would look to everyone else.

And she decided then, that she had to let it go. That she could no longer live to serve a public performance. Because she had to worry about whether or not something was a victory for *her life*. For the child.

Nothing else could matter, nothing else could be more important.

And that meant letting go. Stripping away the things that she used to mark success. "Well then," she said. "I imagine when we go back to the real world there will be quite a show waiting for us."

"Undoubtedly. I hope you're ready."

She looked at him, her greatest boardroom rival, and now her fiancé. The father of her child. "I'm ready if you are."

He smiled, that wolfish smile. And this time she realized that when he did so, it did not go all the way up to those steely blue eyes.

There was a reason he was like this, she knew it. And she had seen glimpses of a different man. A warmer man.

But he did his best to cover it.

And she had a feeling that she would never be powerful enough to melt all that ice.

CHAPTER THIRTEEN

"I LOOK LIKE a Russian trophy wife," Olive said as she settled back into the leather armchair on the plane, one booted foot stuck out in front of her. She was wearing spiked heels in a camel color, and a long white jacket, with a furry white hat perched atop her head.

He thought she looked soft, and far more delicious than any woman had a right to. But he could also see Russian trophy wife.

"Well. As of next week you will be my trophy wife."

"The idea of being your trophy sticks in a particularly..." She made a stabbing motion with her hand. "Rough place."

"To the victor go the spoils. In this case, I suppose the public notoriety."

"Well, we're going to be notorious, all right. Have you checked all of the socials?"

"Hell no," he said, waving a hand. "I have management teams for that kind of thing, I don't concern myself with the inanity of Internet chatter."

"Oh, you should," she said. "Sometimes it's hilarious. Honestly. Some people think that we are part of the evil one percent, conspiring to take over the world with this present merger. The wedding is obviously fake. We are aliens. We don't marry."

"I admit, that is a slightly more interesting take than what I expected."

"There's more."

"I told you I don't read these kinds of things."

"But I do. Welcome to marriage."

She grabbed her phone and sat up, scrolling through something. He didn't know what. "OMG, it's like a rom-com. Enemies to lovers."

"What the hell does that mean?"

"Oh, I don't know. But somebody said it on a social media site, therefore it's news." She continued to read. "For sure she is getting the better end of the deal. I hear that his broadsword is the size of—"

"What is this garbage?"

There was something about this that worked its way deeply beneath his skin. No one knew him. He didn't allow it. And all these people were talking about him as if they could.

If he would ever have allowed anyone to know him, it might have been Olive.

"I believe broadsword is a euphemism for your—"

"I am aware of what it is a euphemism for. What I don't understand is why. Why do people concern themselves with these things. They could be living their own lives, rather than chatting about the lives of others."

His life was not a spectator sport. Not a game. It had been marked by abuse and an extreme need to fix that which his father had done to scar the world.

He was marrying Olive to right yet more wrongs, and it was sharp and filled with danger. And these people called it a rom-com.

"People chat. They like to do it. It makes them feel connected. See, this is the thing that you missed. You make technology, but you failed to see the ways in which it can make beautiful things. You like to make functional things."

"People discussing a stranger's penis is hardly beautiful."

She scooted to the edge of her seat and doubled over,

her furry hat falling into her face as she laughed. "Okay. Maybe beautiful is a stretch on this score. This is a shallow way that people use the Internet, but it's fairly harmless."

"Is it harmless? They talk about us as if they know us. They don't."

"Well, they feel like they do. And it has little reflection on our actual lives, it certainly doesn't impact us. But people connect. I think it's kind of beautiful. Something that could be cold, something that could be difficult… People have found a way to make it something different."

"Except when they decide to use it to burn down the lives of others. To hunt them down mercilessly and bring up a comment made ten years ago, and determine they're not allowed to have jobs or friends or… Even live."

"Granted," she said. "It has a dark side. Everything does. Because people do. Fundamentally, however we are expressing it, we are who we are. Isn't that the case?"

He grunted, and leaned back in his chair.

"I'm serious. Think about it. What is a public Internet shaming if not the stocks and pillories? And ostracizing of somebody for violating the way the group perceives morality. It's what we've always done. Computers don't change that. I mean, that's the thing. I understand why you think something like this is silly, or even harmful, but I just think it's human nature. We bring it with us wherever we go. And we bring it into modern technology."

"You're much more fascinated by the intricacies of human behavior than I am. I make products, and if they are useful, people will buy them. That is all. I don't need to understand the concept of public shaming to know that."

And yet he had to wonder if he was so averse to it because it felt…foreign to him in some ways. Unknowable.

"Really? I would've thought that you would find it interesting. We're always looking for the barbarian at the gate.

Even if we have to make one up. And most especially, I think we have to make one up in this modern world."

"I thought you said you didn't have any friends. You sound like a person who is interested enough in the way that people behave and communicate that you want to."

She scrunched her nose. "I observe people. And this is what I think about them. I don't know. You don't like people, do you?"

"I don't like or dislike people until I get to know one of them. You speak of humanity. I don't care."

"Why not? I would've thought that somebody who was so invested in green energy would have a lot of thoughts on human nature."

"What does that have to do with human nature?"

"For example," she said. "You're never going to get people to switch to a green energy product unless it is convenient, less expensive, or remarkably better. People are all about their own convenience. And they might philosophically care about broader things, but at the end of the day, you have to make things appealing to them. Because most people have to get what they can afford. Or what feels nice if they have money. Or what is convenient, because God knows everybody is strapped for time, and the point of technological innovation is supposed to be convenience."

"An interesting perspective," he said. And he had to admit that it was. He tended to think of things in terms of right and wrong. To him, changing things to benefit the planet was right. And he felt that comfort, convenience… None of it could possibly be more important than that one moral truth.

Obviously, Olive saw things differently.

He thought again of the corporate espionage, and the way she had justified it.

"So what then does you stealing information from me fall under? Convenience? Luxury?"

"That was about loving someone," she said softly. She met his eyes. "I loved my father so much that there was nothing quite so important as making sure that he got what he wanted. Even if he wasn't here to see it. The more emotions get tangled up in situations like these, the less black and white they are. Because it shifts what's acceptable. And what isn't. For me, acceptable is only getting the contract my father wanted. And that's… It's changing. Inside of me. All the time. As things… As they change. As I think about what kind of mother I want to be." She looked up at him, her gaze dewy. "I had a realization, or, it skimmed past me yesterday, and just now it's beginning to bloom into a full-on epiphany. My father loved his company more than he ever loved me. For me, it was about loving him. As much as Ambient has been the biggest work of my life, my motivation in making it so was to make him proud. Because his investment in my childhood was entirely related to Ambient. Because what he considered a success was entirely related to Ambient. I wanted to make him proud. But he never wanted to be proud of me half so much as he wanted me to accomplish specific things. What he wanted was the result. Not the feeling. I think he wouldn't have cared at the end of the day if it were me or somebody else who had accomplished all these things, except that if it's me, it links more directly back to him and his legacy. It's convenient for him. You understand?"

"I suppose."

"The point is, that's what got me started on letting go of this. Because that isn't why I was doing this. You're doing things for achievements, that's why the cheating seems important to you. You want to know that you're the best. I just want to know that I did what my father asked of me. That's all. I also realize that I don't want to consign any child of mine to the same sort of fate. To this desperate need to make their dad proud. To this desperate need to perform to please a parent. Because it's… It's nearly impossible. It's such a weight, such a burden. And I just can't… I just can't put them under that."

"I do not know why my father did the things he did. He was a man with more money than God. He could have lived well and been decent. I will never understand him. But I know why I wanted to take control of Magnum and turned it into something better than he ever did."

"Why?"

"To prove I'm better. To prove that he was wrong. To prove that he is nothing."

To prove I'm not the same.

"Revenge?"

"If I'd sought revenge, I would have done it while he was alive. I want more than revenge. I want to make a change. My takeover of Magnum is essentially what I'm doing to Ambient. It has become part of the thing that I made. Which is bigger. And is the way of the future. These things are simply… Assets."

"And you don't care about them."

"My father thought that to care about things was a weakness. I do not respect my father, but if there is one thing I never allowed myself to become…it's weak."

His one indulgence was the house in Iceland. A faint echo of better times. Simpler times.

"My father wanted there to be no softness in me. And he got his wish. But the fact is, the hand that sharpens the sword must be very careful that the sword is not turned upon him."

"That seems very Viking of you."

"You seem to have a preoccupation with Vikings."

Her cheeks went red.

"Well, it's just… It's just… I like… I like medieval Viking romance novels."

"You mentioned this before. I cannot believe romance stories about Vikings exist."

"I find them to be diverting."

"Vikings specifically."

"Yes."

"But they were raiders. Pillagers. More often than not, they would simply take women captive rather than marry them. How exactly can that be a romance?"

He lifted a brow and regarded her closely. He did not know why her answer seemed suddenly important.

"Wow, Gunnar, I cannot imagine why the story of a woman who is forced into a life against her will and must find softness and pleasure in it, in spite of circumstances she will never be fully in control over, would appeal to me."

And he didn't say anything, because he had to sit with that comment.

It was a strange perspective.

One he certainly had never thought of. And who did she feel trapped by? Her father?

He supposed that at the moment she felt trapped by him.

But he could not let her go.

He would not.

They would be married next week, in a wedding that was certain to be the media spectacle of the decade.

And she would simply have to continue to live in her world of romance novels and whatever else she might need.

He was not a man who could make a different choice than this.

And he could only indulge her so far.

He looked at her, all of her softness.

And he ached.

Once had not been enough.

But soon enough, she would be his bride. And then...

Then he would have her.

Raiders. Pillagers.

Was he any different?

He had not imagined that he was a Viking.

But in that moment, he felt as if he were.

The conqueror, quite eager to take the conquered.

Except he looked at the stubborn line of her jaw, and she glanced at him out of the corner of her eye.

No. Olive would never be conquered.

Instead, it would be a battle every day forever.

And he ignored the tightening of excitement in his gut at the thought of that.

CHAPTER FOURTEEN

By THE TIME they landed in New York, it felt as if the entire Internet had exploded.

Rumors about their affair and how long it had been going on, about the wedding, and who would be on the guest list.

And she realized, she would have to put that together, and quickly, so that it all looked a bit more thought out than it was.

But they should have no issues getting a raft of celebrities to attend. It was exactly the sort of thing that they loved to be seen at. Something that made them look smart and tied into a world that had nothing to do with the entertainment industry.

And something that would make her and Gunnar look even more like the illuminati. Which kind of amused her.

She was looking forward to going back to her apartment, but they didn't go there. In fact, they didn't even go into the city. Instead, she found herself in the back of a limousine, on a winding road that led… She didn't know where.

It became clear, when a large home came into view. "You have a house?"

She hadn't known that he had a place other than his New York penthouse in the States.

"I bought a house," he said.

"You… You just bought this?"

"Yes. I thought that it would make a wonderful wedding

present to you, and we could set up a nursery here. You must admit, right in the heart of downtown hardly feels the appropriate place to have a baby."

"As if you have any idea of what to do with the baby," she said.

"I didn't say that I did. However, I do feel that I can confidently say that this is a better place to raise a child."

"Well. Your cliffside home is definitely not the most child friendly. Can you imagine if a baby got outside there?"

"This is silly. In Iceland, we simply teach children…"

"Whatever. In America we put leashes on them. Anyway. You probably should've talked to me about buying a house that we're going to live in."

"Why? I wish for you to get used to exactly how this relationship is going to work."

"You think you're in charge?"

She looked at him, and she didn't feel… Trapped. She didn't even feel particularly angry. But she was… Still puzzling over the things that she had figured out about him over the last little bit. The way that he talked about emotion. The way that he talked about his father.

That he had actually hated his father. She wanted to know what happened. She wanted to understand.

She really didn't know anything about his life. She felt like she did, because she saw him in a certain setting over a number of years, but a great amount of that was witnessed with a child's understanding of things, and the rest… It was just so specific to the situation they had been in.

And she had filled in a whole lot of details about him using her own life as a guide, and that was not necessarily the most honest way to do it.

She had been certain that she knew Gunnar, and now she realized that she really didn't.

"But you need to be in charge of this," she said. "Because

it needs to be a decisive victory for you? Because this is how you prove you're better than me?"

"You make me sound like a petty child. As I said, I did not need to prove that I was better than you, I would simply not be able to rest knowing that I had not been the best, if that was my goal. I was happy always when you had the better product and won. It was fair. But if we are to have harmony in our home, then certain things must be understood. Certain things must be clear. That is the making of a good company, is it not?"

"But families aren't companies," she said. "And when you marry me, Gunnar, you are going to be my family."

He looked over at her, his blue eyes sharp. "I do not think that is a very fair characterization."

"It's just true. We are going to be a family. And I think we need to... We need to not look at it like a business."

The car pulled up to the front of the house, and Gunnar got out, rounding to her side of the vehicle and opening the door for her.

She looked up at the place, a feat of modern craftsmanship, not wholly dissimilar to the house in Iceland, though formed instead around the landscape here. She opened the door, and turned circles as she looked at the palatial entry. There was a large chandelier in the doorway, that seemed to be made entirely of tubes of glass with little sparkling drops of air illuminated inside of them.

"Wow," she said.

"Like my house in Iceland, all of it runs on green energy."

"See. You really do have the luxury part of it down. It's absolutely beautiful. And nobody could complain about not being comfortable here. That's for sure."

"Well, I'm glad you find it to your liking."

"I suppose I need to find something to my liking."

She wondered then if he wanted her. At all. Or if being married to her was going to feel like a life sentence.

She wondered if…

She wondered what he felt at all.

They had been fighting. And through all of it, she had not lost her desire for him. When he had taken her into the hot springs and held her close, in spite of the chill, she had felt rising desire for him. It had been…

It still made her hot just thinking about it.

She flushed even now, looking at him in the entryway, and felt so ashamed that she had to turn away.

"Your room is up the stairs and down at the very end of the hall."

"Are we to have separate bedrooms?"

He looked at her, his eyes molten. "Of course. I should not like to take your space from you."

Or maybe he just didn't want her. And what did she want? She wanted him, but…

He was such a complicated man. And what she knew about complicated was it was only worse when there were feelings involved. Her feelings. The feelings he claimed he didn't have. Yes. There were a whole lot of feelings here, and she had a feeling that he would deny it, but it was the truth of it.

Having her own space would probably be a necessity.

For her sanity.

"Has anyone ever told you that you're infuriating?"

"A time or ten."

"What do you want, Gunnar? What do you want from me? Do you want simply to be husband and wife and bump around this giant house together? Do you want… Do you want me? I don't understand. You seem to want to turn me into something else. And as much as I kind of love this outfit, you know it's not what I prefer to wear. Are you throwing me in these things to change me, or is it simply to get at me? This is the thing, you know me. I think you might know me better than anyone else on earth. I thought I knew you. I'm trying to know you. But I wonder if I do, even a little. Even at all."

He moved toward her then, fire in his eyes. He backed her up against the wall there in the entry. And there it was. Her Viking marauder.

It made her heart throb with desire. Made that place between her legs ache.

Yes, her soul whispered. *Take me.*

Because that would make sense. It would make sense because she wanted him. Because it was how they had gotten here. Because of the desire between them, and the two of them denying it for these past few days while all of these intense changes happened around them… It made her feel disconnected from it all. But this reminded her.

It reminded her that in a sea of uncertainty, there was this. There was him.

"You do not wish to be strangers in the house together? I should've thought that that would be to your liking. I should've thought that it would make things easier."

"Nothing makes this easier. But at least…" She didn't know if she wanted to shame herself like this. "At least if there's this…" She reached out and put her hand on his chest, and she found herself being pulled toward him.

"This is just sex."

It wasn't, though.

Because if it was only sex, it would have eased by now. Or faded slightly, but there was none of that. Instead, it came alive with an intensity that threatened to destroy everything else. Threatened to destroy all that they were. Threatened to burn her where she stood. She wanted him. She wanted to burn in this. To burn in him. She wanted desperately to get out of her head. She wanted to fracture this thing between them. To make it as undeniable for him as it was for her.

She wanted to get through that hard layer of ice in his

chest. He was in control. That was what bothered her. That he was maddeningly endlessly in control.

Everything seemed logical to him. If the baby was his, then they would get married. If not, he would send her to prison. And none of it spoke to any kind of feeling for her or for the child or anything. None of it spoke to the spark between them. None of it seemed to matter to him. And it felt astronomically and categorically unfair. That he could remain so untouched by all of this when she was upended. When she was ready to give up the pursuit of her life. The company, when she was reevaluating her entire relationship with her father. Her relationship with herself. Her relationship with everything.

But in this, she felt as if they were equalized. In this, she could feel her own power.

He wanted her. She could see that even now, even as he stood, poised as if on a knife's edge, unmoving. Like a predator. Lying in wait. Even in that, she could see how difficult it was for him to seize control. And she gloried in that. Because it made her feel like perhaps she wasn't the only one. It made her feel as if she wasn't alone.

She desperately didn't want to be alone.

But she waited. Waited for him to break. Because she needed him to. Waited for him to break, because it was the assurance that she needed. Because she needed control. She needed power. Even while she needed for him to claim her. To brand her.

It didn't matter if that made sense to anyone else, it made sense to her. She wanted. With hot reckless greed. With a deep abandon that she hadn't experienced in any other part of her life.

What she wanted for Ambient, she wanted on behalf of her father. What she wanted was to please him. And everything she did she had done with precision. But what she did, what she wanted, with Gunnar had nothing to do with precision. It had nothing to do with logic and everything to do with need. And she wanted to become that. Wanted to embrace it. She wanted to become his, and through that, become more of herself.

And maybe no one else could ever understand that, maybe if it were someone else, it wouldn't make any sense. But they were them. And even feeling like she did, even feeling like she didn't know him to the degree that she wished, to the degree that she had imagined, she knew that they were something that no one else was. The media could make proclamations about them all they wanted. The world could post about how they were this and that and something else entirely, but they weren't anything except for Gunnar and Olive. And they couldn't be. Not ever.

Nobody would ever be them. And no one would ever be him for her. He was everything. Everything and glory, and he made her want to be more. Somehow, even with all that iciness in his soul, he made her want to find her warmth. Or maybe that was why. Because she wanted so much to do something for him. To fix him.

Or maybe not even that. Just knowing him… That would be enough. That would be enough. She wondered if anyone did. And she imagined they didn't. That he kept himself as closed off as possible. The human representation of that house of his, up on the hill.

And he was the one this time who gave in. The one who growled, lowering his head to hers and claiming her lips in a searing vow.

Whatever they would say to each other in that church, this week, whatever promises they would make in front of the world, they didn't matter. Not compared to this. To this moment, with this man. He was everything, and they were incendiary. The rest of this, it would be a performance. The union for their child. But this? This was all them. Only them. A lack of control, a flaw in their personal systems.

But it could not be denied, nor could it be controlled. He gripped her face, shoving his fingers through her hair, pushing the fur hat off of her head and onto the floor. She had chosen the outfit to be deliberately ridiculous. Soft when she normally went for severe. But she had to admit she sort of loved the hat. And the boots. And the coat. But all she wanted was to get all of it off now. She wanted there to be nothing between them. No barriers. Nothing. She wanted to give herself over to him entirely. To surrender to this, him.

And he kissed her. And kissed her, as if there was no particular hurry, and a ticking clock all at once.

He kissed her, his tongue sliding against hers, his big rough hands moving over her body.

She loved the feel of him. She loved everything about him. And the real problem was, she had always loved Gunnar more than she had ever loved her company. And that realization nearly made her knees buckle. But it was true.

He fascinated her, bewitched her, beguiled her, and had shaped her every fantasy from the first moment she had begun to have them. And it wasn't simply because there had been no one else around. She could see no one else because of Gunnar. He blinded her to everything and everyone that wasn't him. He was essentially everything. And it was not a lack of opportunity, a lack of skills, a lack of beauty, that had kept her away from other men.

It was the all-consuming desire for this one man. And not simply desire. She had felt when she was a girl that she understood him. And she knew now as a woman that she did not. But whatever was behind the ice blockade, she wanted him.

And perhaps that was the real truth of it. The real deep certainty of love.

That if she kept going, if she went deeper. She would still care. That she would accept him. That he could reveal to her any sort of new truth about him and she would simply kiss him and be grateful that he trusted her enough to tell her.

He was the spark to her flame, and she knew that, and it was enough. The man who could keep up with her. Who could challenge her. She respected his mind, his drive.

He was her equal. But even better than that, he was a mystery as well. And that was fascinating, more than anything ever had been.

The way he was known and unknown. The way he was like her and yet so different all at once.

And it was more than just their physical differences, but it was highlighted even now. He was so large. So hard.

And she began to greedily strip away the layers of his clothing as he kissed her, as he licked into her mouth.

She undid the buttons on his shirt, pushed it and his jacket down onto the floor. She gloried in the broad expanse of his chest, the hair there, the sculpted muscle.

She moved her fingertips down to skim his abdominal muscles, and she whimpered.

She wanted him more now than she had the first time, because now she knew how good it felt. She had explained away how aroused she had been that first time they were together with the simple explanation that it was years of pent-up longing. But now it wasn't that.

It was simply their chemistry that threatened to consume her. And she wanted it to. She was more than happy to drown in it.

He gripped her chin, and her hair, forcing her head back and taking the kiss impossibly deep. She moaned, writhing up against his body.

He picked her up from where they stood and carried her from the entryway, into a living area where there was a plush, wide couch.

It did not look as if it was especially made for sitting, but rather it was made for something like this. Black and round, with ample space for how athletic she knew the sex was between them.

She had never really considered herself an athlete. But he made her want to endeavor to be one.

At least, he made her happy enough to exert herself where typically she found that sort of thing overrated. There was nothing overrated about this.

She could honestly say, that for all the big deal people made out of sex... She could see why. Ten out of ten. Would recommend.

And then she couldn't think anymore, because Gunnar was methodically stripping her clothes from her body, licking his way across all of her skin. Teasing her, tormenting her.

He turned her over onto her knees, and wrapped his arm around her waist, lifting her up. Then she heard the sound of his belt buckle coming undone, and she came undone along with it.

She felt the blunt head of his arousal pressed against the entrance to her body, and she moaned. He slid into her slowly from behind, the new position making things unbearably tight. Making her feel so full.

The raw sound that came from her lips was animal. Foreign.

She loved it. She loved what he did to her. The way that he took her every expectation about herself and turned it inside out. The way that he changed her into something new.

And he had. That was the most extraordinary realization of all. The woman that had agreed to marry him, the woman that had decided to try something different. To try being someone different, to try and make a life that wasn't in service to a dead man who had never loved her more than a corporation, that woman had been forged in the fires of passion with Gunnar. And yes, much of the heat and strength came from inside of her, it took two of them to create this alchemy after all.

He gripped her hips, a short curse on his lips as he began to thrust hard into her body.

She loved this. This animalistic passion that created in them something entirely new.

"Gunnar," she moaned his name, and he growled.

"Olive," he said.

And she knew that he was with her. She knew that he was as much enslaved by this as she was.

How she loved him.

And it made her cry out. Because it was a terrible thing to love him. A horrible thing. And yet it was the inevitable thing. It was fate. She couldn't deny it.

He had always, and only ever, been the one man for her.

This moment had been written for her long before she had ever picked up a romance novel.

Except the problem was, she wasn't sure she would get her happy ending. Oh, he would marry her. He was a man of integrity. He would keep his word. She knew that. And that was what scared her. He didn't love her. He didn't love her. And what was she supposed to do with the knowledge that he would not. Could not. Did she persevere. She had no choice. She knew that. She had no choice, because… Whatever was behind the wall. She wanted him.

The question was, would she ever be able to get behind it.

"Gunnar," she moaned when the large head of him scraped up against something sensitive and glorious inside of her. And she began to tremble. Began to shake.

She wasn't going to be able to hold out for much longer, her desire overwhelming her. A thunderstorm of need. He gripped her hips hard, and she hoped—she desperately hoped—that he would leave bruises behind. She wanted to be able to look at herself and see that she was as physically changed as she was emotionally.

This man.

She felt as if he had grabbed a loose thread of hers once long ago, and had been pulling it ever since, and now she was threadbare, worn, and desperately trying to cover herself up. And yet, it was the beauty of it. The utter beauty. Her brokenness. The places where she could no longer hide.

It allowed her to see herself for the first time.

And yes, it left her open to him as well. And she felt bright and scalded and new, shaking as she was, while he destroyed the version of all it that had existed before.

She lowered her head to the velvet couch and pressed her face into it, balling her hands into fists and shuddering out her pleasure, while he suddenly growled out his own.

"Yes," she whispered. She wanted it all. Everything. Everything he could ever be.

Everything they could ever be.

And when it was done, he pulled away from her, and he began straightening himself, as if it hadn't just dissolved the two of them.

"It is good that there is attraction between us," he said, his tone sounding remote.

And she felt devastated. Because it was more than attraction. It was more than chemistry. It changed her.

"Maybe we won't need separate rooms."

"I imagine it will be good for you to have your space," he said.

And what she heard, inarguably and unequivocally, was that he wanted his own space. Away from her.

And that was fine. It was. She had to accept him. And if she couldn't do that then...

Tears filled her eyes, but she turned herself away quickly to avoid allowing him to see.

"Our things have been moved in already."

"You really are efficient," she said.

"There's no point doing anything if it's not done efficiently."

"Even screwing your fiancée, I guess."

He lifted a brow. "Have you a complaint?"

"I'm not complaining. It felt wonderful."

"But?"

"Nothing."

And she would not speak to him about the fact that he clearly didn't want to show her any tenderness, or get to know her anymore than he already did. She would say nothing about the fact that she had experienced something transformative just now, and he looked as he ever did.

She would not say that she loved him. Because she had a feeling that it would be the most cardinal sin, and yet if he really felt nothing, why would it matter? She just knew that it did. She knew that it would. She knew that he would take that and reject it so violently it would leave it torn and bloodied, and it was too new for her to take a chance on that.

So she said nothing. So she kept it all in her own heart. Kept it all to herself.

Because what would be the point. Of any of it.

"I guess I'll go to my room then."

"Yes. That sounds a good idea. You are likely tired."

She really resented him telling her what she was. What she felt.

Especially in light of everything. That he had created the feelings in her, and she knew that he would do nothing to soothe them.

She went into the bedroom, and she had to laugh. Because this looked nothing like his home in Iceland.

This was completely different. This was… Her. And yes, she knew that a designer had done it, and quickly, but she imagined that he had asked them to take their inspiration from her existing apartment. To take it and find a new way to express it so that it felt like her, but also felt fresh.

Gunnar. Oh, Gunnar.

She slept fitfully, and the next morning she wandered around the massive house alone. She wasn't certain if Gunnar was even in residence.

She had a croissant and a tea for breakfast, then answered some work emails. After an hour or so she was restless.

The house was incredible. Huge. There were so many rooms, and any one of them could be the nursery. *The nursery.*

Her heart squeezed tight. She was here, committed to making a family with Gunnar. Committed to...

There was so much between them. Heat and anger and despair.

She wanted more.

She didn't know if he would ever give her more.

She started to push the doors open, looking inside. There was nothing remarkable about any of them. And there was one door, painted blue. She stopped, and pushed it open. And inside was... It was nearly identical to the room in Gunnar's home in Iceland, except there was a crib in it. But the walls were painted bright colors, and there were games, toys. She walked out of the hallway. "Gunnar?"

She heard footsteps coming up the stairs. "What is it?"

"Did you have a nursery put together for the child?"

He stopped at the top of the stairs and nodded gravely. "Yes."

"It looks like... The room in Iceland. Was that meant to be a nursery too? Except... It didn't have a crib in it... It's because your father took your toys."

"Olive..."

"It is. It's because your father took your toys, and you replaced them." Her chest went horribly tight. "Gunnar..." She moved to him, and she touched his face. "You're going to be a good father."

He turned his head away. "I choose to be a good man. I choose to do good things."

"You are a good man."

"Any man is capable of being corrupted."

"Is that an accusation directed at me?"

"I can see how you would think it might be given our history. But no. This is about me. And what I know of men. Men like my father."

"I've never seen you display a violent temper. Even when you were angry with me in my office… I fainted and you took me to the doctor."

"And yet it is complacency that could create problems. I will never be complacent."

But he had bought all these toys. It was like the only way he knew to show affection. And suddenly… She was filled with hope. Hope for their future. He had said that he could not love, but what was this if not… The very depths of his soul brought out before them. The one thing he had wanted more than anything. It was a physical representation of what he had thought a father's love might be, and what he had been denied. And here it was. Here it was.

"It's beautiful."

"It may not work for a girl," he said.

"It's perfect. It's perfect no matter what. We are not our fathers. Our child will have birthday parties here. In the yard, with friends. And there will be ponies."

"Ponies?"

"Yes. And chocolate cupcakes."

And she saw something soften in him.

"Perhaps."

"What else happened? With your father."

Gunnar shrugged. "He did not believe in spoiling me. Which to him meant not giving me any softness. He left me locked in my room for large swaths of time—primarily from the time I was twelve to fourteen, after that he began to take me to different events. If I didn't perform the way he wanted me to...there would be consequences."

"He hurt you," she said, her chest feeling like lead.

"Yes."

"But look at all this. Look at how you...you want to give different things to our child. That matters. It counts for something." She needed him to know that. He looked so bleak she just...needed him to know that.

"The past has shaped me into the man I am today, and a room full of toys and good intentions doesn't... There is only so much I can offer."

He meant that. She could see that he did. But she just didn't understand why. She could see that he cared. She could see it in this room around her.

She could feel it in his touch.

"The past doesn't matter. It doesn't have to matter."

And then something shuttered in his expression. "I wish that were so. But as far as I'm concerned... One must learn from the past. Or there was never any point to it at all."

And then he walked away. From the moment, as he always did.

But the nursery remained. A real, beautiful testament to something, to more.

What he'd wanted as a child.

What he wanted to be as a father.

Why was he like this? Why was he so infuriating. So maddening, and yet so wonderful, all at once. Why was... It seemed like they had a connection. It just seemed also like he would want to deny it.

And everything in her ached for that to not be the case.

But she could not ignore the fact that he seemed remote. That he'd said he would never love.

Well. She was beginning to think she had never really been loved before.

Her father had affection for her. He had been kind to

her—conditionally. But it wasn't the same. It certainly wasn't the same as what she wanted to give to her child.

She blinked, scrunching her eyes tight.

She would make it through this. And she would not give in to despair. She had this room, and it showed that he saw her. On some level, he saw her.

And in the dark of night when she slept in this bed alone, she would remember that, and the way he had held her in the hot springs, and she would use that to keep her warm and insulated against all the ice.

CHAPTER FIFTEEN

The LEAD-UP TO the wedding was intense, but well handled. If there was one thing that he and Olive knew, it was how to delegate, and how to formulate a plan. The two of them together setting this into motion made it seem satisfyingly easy. Watching all of the pieces work in time with each other really was incredibly satisfying.

And he… He found that he liked the way that he and Olive worked together. They had been sparring against each other for so many years, that he had not been aware of the fact the two of them could create something so spectacular when they used their gifts in tandem.

But Olive was particularly brilliant at getting the best out of people. She excelled with team management and with aesthetics. She was a hard worker, and she knew how to adjust things to make them just that much more special. Just that much more pleasing to the eye.

He was good with mechanics. With the way things ran, and how they would work. He was good at organizing tasks.

They complemented each other in a way that he could never have foreseen. He had not thought he'd had blind spots remaining in his life, and yet, this was a large one.

But he had never understood Olive and her quirkiness. The way that she behaved, or the way that she looked at things, but he could see now that it was an essential part of what she was. An essential part of who she was. Without it, she would not come up with things that she did.

Without it, she would not be Olive.

He had watched her march around the room eating saltine crackers, making suggestions to how the reception decor might be shifted slightly, that changed something from lovely to unbearably brilliant.

She was bright. And smart. She was a spark that he could not look away from.

And the day of the wedding, she made herself scarce, texting him about how it was bad luck for the groom to see the bride.

He also had not been with her again since that first day they had moved into the new house.

Their encounter on the sofa had been incendiary, and he had nearly been undone by it altogether.

The moment in the nursery had been something else entirely.

He could not quite understand, this thing that she did to him. He could not quite understand what it was she made him. For he was accustomed to having a sexual appetite, but he was not accustomed to being controlled by it. He was not accustomed to being at its mercy, but when she had stood there, looking up at him as she had, it had been outside of his power to resist. He had kissed her when they'd first arrived, because he'd had no other choice. He had kissed her, because he had been unable to stop himself. She was all things brilliant and beautiful, but it was more than that. He had had any number of beautiful women, and he could go out today and get more, even if they knew that his wedding was today. Maybe most especially if they knew.

But they would never be Olive, and they would never do to him what she did.

She fascinated him.

And if he were honest with himself, he could admit that

she always had. It had been easy to write it off as some twisted form of forbidden lust, but that would take it and oversimplify it far too much. It was not that. No. It was something without a name. Something without measure. Something that made him think of a tiny home in the middle of nowhere in Iceland. Smoke coming out of the chimney, a simple meal of fish and bread.

A life where there had not been money, but there had been a warmth that he had not felt since.

And he had been cold. Every day of his life since he had left that cabin. Cold, except for when Olive ignited within him.

He had no one standing up with him at his wedding. And neither did Olive. It spoke volumes but neither of them had another person to ask to fulfill such a duty. They could have manufactured friends out of nothing, but they had both agreed that there was no need to be performative. Not when the rest of it was such a performance.

They were marrying outdoors at a massive estate, because Olive had said it would be atmospheric, and she wished to embrace that over tradition.

And he deferred to her, because she had been right about many things all along, so why not that.

The guests were all there, seated and looking appropriately like the sort of people that should be at a wedding that united two of the largest tech moguls in the entire world.

The performance was impeccable.

And as he stood there and waited for his bride, he felt the sense of performance begin to slip away.

His parents had never married. It was one reason he felt so strongly about this.

He had never known his mother.

But her parents… They had been warm and wonderful people.

They had been the only real taste of family he'd ever had.

And yet, he could not get back to that. He did not know how to find it. The loss of them was something that had frozen him over, and he had never yet found his way back. Not to himself. Not to anything else.

Nothing that felt half so much like home.

And then Olive appeared in his vision, walking across the grass, between the chairs. And he nearly laughed. She was not wearing black. But she was wearing a white wedding dress with long sleeves and an extremely high neck. It was elegant, and perfect, like the rest of her, but also inarguably shaped like her preferred black turtlenecks.

It was essentially her, to make that reference, perhaps one that only he would understand. And she would make it slyly all the same.

She was holding a large bouquet of flowers, all in fall colors, her brown hair down and curling, swept to the side over her shoulder.

She had never looked more beautiful.

It was enough to drive him to his knees. It was enough, to harken back to his raider ancestors, make him wish to pick her up and carry her out over his shoulders so he could make love to her, rather than stand here with her in front of an audience.

But the audience was necessary.

The rest of it was not.

When she arrived at the front, she had no bridesmaids to hand her bouquet to, so she turned to the crowd and cheerfully tossed it out. There was a minor celebrity in the third row who caught it and screamed excitedly.

Oh, yes. Olive was wonderful at a spectacle.

She knew how to command attention.

She always had.

Her tech presentations where she debuted the year's new technology for Ambient had been huge events for the last few years. Building in popularity each and every time.

She was just that way. Just undeniably that way.

He was not a man given to socializing. And the truth was, he had never been to a wedding. He never had occasion to. He had certainly never attended as anyone's date, and had never felt beholden enough to somebody to have to review the spectacle himself.

And so the words of the vows were unfamiliar to him, something foreign, even though he had seen abbreviated versions of them in movies. But not many. He didn't watch a lot of movies. Occasionally one would play in the background on the plane.

How could you promise such things to another person? And how can they promise them to you and expect to keep them in any kind of fashion? He found it a daunting thing to think of. And the divorce rate was so high. And yet humans did this. And expected theirs to last.

The unbearable optimism of some people amazed him.

He had lost his own when he'd been twelve years old.

He had traded his own. Sold it. For thirty pieces of silver, as it were.

Olive was saying her vows, bright and clear and true, her eyes shining, and anyone might've thought that she meant them.

It did something to him. To hear that.

To see her pledge her loyalty to him. Her... Her love. But then, he had just promised the same thing, and he had no concept of love.

Not really.

And when it was time to kiss, it was a relief. Because he understood that. The physicality between them was undeniable, and there was a familiarity to it. It was at least the ghost of something that he had experienced before.

Except then her mouth met his, freshly scented with the words she had just spoken, and it was as if he had never been kissed before in his life.

As if she had found a way to weave the words into every pass of her mouth over his. And he was undone.

There before a crowd of people. He, Gunnar Magnusson, who had never once been undone.

Who was the undoing and ruin of many, but had never been touched by another soul.

And when it was through, the crowd cheered, and Olive put one arm in the air, and laughed, and he knew that the photos that were being taken made it look for all the world like she was a joyous bride.

There would be interviews, and they would do them. They had already agreed. It was not his favorite thing to do, but Olive was a PR machine, and she wanted to give a story, though they had told all media outlets that they would not be speaking until after the wedding, since they would be far too busy preparing to devote any time to media.

It had been true, more or less.

For all that they were doing this wedding, they were still bound to each other. And in the meantime, he was in the process of making sure that the acquisition of Ambient remained legal, and did not in fact violate antitrust laws. But it was beginning to disquiet his spirit.

He had wanted revenge on her, or so he'd told himself.

He was beginning to wonder if what he'd really wanted was her.

And now there was a farcical reception to get through, and what he wanted was to be alone with her.

What he wanted was to claim her.

That echoed through his body with ever increasing insistence as they socialized, ate cake and pretended to be amused by the shocked commentary of their guests regarding the change in their relationship.

But what it really was, was a slow burn. A smolder, a promise of what was to come.

He had a surprise for her.

Because what he had wanted, truly, was an opportunity to have her alone. To have her to himself.

They would be going back to Iceland.

And they would be spending three days in his bed, doing nothing else. He had meals prepared, and very few clothes. He would get this intense need for her out of his system. And then, things would go back to the way they had been. Because this meant nothing to him, this wedding, the first wedding he had ever been to, which happened to be his own. And she meant nothing to him. It was easy to feel a sense of affection for Olive, but that was part of who she was.

She engendered that response in everybody, he could see it here.

That she also brought it out in him was not a surprise.

And when it was done, the private jet was waiting, and he picked her up, and carried her aboard.

She was his wife now.

And suddenly, it felt altogether different.

When they arrived at the house in Iceland, everything had been positioned just so. And the table was set with a romantic dinner for the two of them.

"This is beautiful," she said.

"Yes," he agreed.

He had not noticed until she had turned away from him at the wedding, but her gown had no back.

The torment of all that bare skin when he'd had to behave himself had been… It had been impossible.

What was it about her that bewitched him so?

She was brilliant, he knew that. But he had never felt compelled to take lovers that matched his mind.

For they filled a space in his bed, and nothing more. He did not need to make conversation with them. They existed only to slake generalized lust that he felt. But the desire that Olive created in him was specific.

And it was more than sex. It was tangled up with hearth smoke and warmth, and it made him want to push it away. Made him want to deny it. But she was having his child, and perhaps that was it.

A child.

And he was bringing that child into a union that he enforced.

A union that saw him taking over the company that mattered so much to all of them.

She had explained why. Exhaustively. Also why she was willing to let it go. To try something new.

Olive seemed to turn over her own motivations endlessly. The motivations of others.

And when she spoke of them, she made him understand. In a way he had never even understood himself.

He wanted only to strip her naked now. Forget dinner.

Because all of this overthinking was beginning to get to him, and he did not have any patience for it.

"I believe we can take our dinner later," he said.

He pulled her up against him, pressing his hands flat to her bare back.

She felt like heaven. Like silk and cream and uniquely his Olive. "Little Olive," he said, biting her lower lip. She gasped, rolling her body against him in that particular way she did. He loved that about her. It was not a move born out of experience, but rather she simply did what seemed to feel good to her. And she did it with abandon.

She did it out of desire.

It soothed something in him. To know that she was as caught up in all of this as he was.

"You like my dress?" she whispered.

"It is distracting as hell," he said. "And don't think I didn't notice that it's your preferred style."

Her entire face lit up. She laughed. And she looked at him like no one else ever had. "You noticed," she said. "That delights me. I love that you noticed. I thought that you would find it both amusing, and be slightly relieved that I didn't wear black."

"I'm surprised that you didn't."

"I wanted to dress for you. I wanted you to think that I was beautiful."

And that took all of it and turned what had just happened on its head.

Maybe she wasn't telling the truth. Maybe. Because he had been convinced that it was a performance for those who had been in attendance, but she claimed that it was for him.

That she had wanted him to think she was beautiful. But why would that matter?

"Of course I think you're beautiful. The problem is, I think you are beautiful, even when you wear your black turtlenecks. I may not like them, but I am powerless against the desire that you create in my body, whatever you have on. Or off."

She flushed with pleasure, and he was pleased for having been the one to create the response in her. Such a unique little Olive. Singular and bright. And his. Irrevocably his.

He moved his hands over her body, over the bare skin on her back, and it was not food he was hungry for. Not when he held Olive in his arms.

He kissed her, all that sweetness, and he had to look away when she stared up with those beautiful eyes.

He knew what it was to be on the receiving end of her ire. But this adoration that glowed there, it was foreign. And strange.

He had to turn away from it. He had to close the distance between them and claim her sweet, soft mouth. He kissed her, claimed her. Because that was what his blood demanded that he do. Because that was what made all of this feel real.

For he had married this woman today, making vows that he had never intended to make, facing the future he had never intended to have. Or rather, one he had never truly thought of. It was one thing to think that perhaps someday he might have a child. And that the child might inherit his company. But it was another thing of having a child with Olive, to know what she knew about growing up in the environment they had.

To be offering her the exact same thing for the baby that she carried. It felt wrong. In a way that he could never have anticipated.

And so he kissed her, because that was something he knew how to do. He knew how to pleasure her. He knew how to touch her. How to kiss her. He knew how to light the match that would ignite them both.

His skin burned with her touch, but at his core, he remained ice.

She moved her hands over his chest, down to his stomach.

She kissed him like he was everything. Like they were everything.

She was bolder now, which seemed surprising, since she had been quite the forward little thing even the first time. But now she touched him with the familiarity of what was being built between them.

Like she knew just how to set him on fire.

And she did.

And it was a strange thing, the sudden urgency that gripped him, to make love to his bride.

His bride.

And this was the old ways, the old sense of possession, of having. That was what overtook him now.

He stripped his clothes off, as quickly as possible, and naked, carried her into the bedroom.

She clung to his shoulders, her lips parted, her eyes wide with pleasure.

There were furs on his bed, plush and soft, and he laid

her down there and looked his fill. He wanted to see her naked. Of course he did. But it was not what he wanted most of all. Not now.

What he wanted most of all was to have her in that gown.

He moved his hands down to where the fabric skimmed her ankles and pushed it up past her knees, up to her waist, exposing the white lace panties she wore beneath. He moved his fingertips over that flimsy fabric. And watched as her hips jerked up off of the bed.

Watched as she lost herself in the rhythm of his touch, as he devoted himself only to her pleasure. He slipped his fingertips beneath the elastic there, touched her, moved his hands over her wetness, found her slick and ready and desirable for him.

She flexed her hips along with the movement, and he thrust two fingers deep into her, glorying in that silken desire.

He pulled her panties off, leaving her bare, spread her legs wide and looked his fill. In that wedding dress. White and for him. Only him.

A virgin. His virgin bride—though she may not be a virgin now, she had been when he had taken her, and it stoked a beastly fire in him, spoke to the savage at his core that he had not fully realized existed.

That she carried his baby.

It was a thunderous instinct. A wild demand. A testosterone-fueled fury.

His woman. His. His child.

All of the things that he had sworn that he didn't want. That he had sworn he would never take for his own.

And somewhere in the center of it was that little house. That little house with smoke coming out of the chimney, surrounded by snow. This was heat, but at its center was warmth, and they were two very different things. And it was the warmth that he denied. The warmth that he pushed away as he allowed himself to be swallowed whole by the flame.

He kissed her thigh, and then her very center, meeting his fill as he embraced the intensity of his arousal. As he lost himself in the pounding, swirling, never-ending need.

Oh, but how he wanted this woman.

Most of all.

He wanted to claim her profoundly. Wanted to be skin to skin, and yet, he would deny himself that now.

Because this was his moment to have his wife on their wedding day, in that glorious symbol of her purity, while he brought her down to the depths with him. She was not an angel. She was better than that. Sharp, determined, brilliant. And his.

This intoxicating, seemingly incompatible mix of things that electrified his soul.

There was nothing easy about this, and he had to laugh at what she had said about human nature. People would always want the easy thing. But this… This threatened to peel his skin from his bones. To carve him into something entirely new.

He rose up onto his knees, and fisted his arousal, bringing it to the slick part of her, and driving home. She arched up off the bed, her silk-covered breasts heaving with the force of her desire.

He gripped her hips and pumped into her hard, fast, running away from something. Some demon, some unimaginable force that felt like it was chasing after him as the hounds of hell.

And it would catch him. Consume him.

It would destroy him. Bring him low.

And yet, it was quite possibly the only thing that would ever allow him to breathe.

In her he had found his destruction, and his renewal, and there was not a clear path ahead of him.

Except that she was his. His.

She cried out, her internal muscles pulsing around him as her orgasm overtook her, and he followed behind, roaring as if it were a great victory in battle, crying out his claiming as if there were ears to hear.

And then it was over. The storm. And yet it simply felt like the quiet of it. Not the end. Not truly. For it was only the beginning. She curled up against him, nestled in the furs, her head on his chest.

And he could see their lives entwined, bringing them to this moment, and yet, even seeing it all, it made no sense. How had they arrived here?

Inevitable winds of fate? He did not believe in such things. A man made his own path.

And yet she felt like something more than a choice.

"I'm hungry," she said softly.

And when they ate dinner, they did so naked, wrapped in furs, with her looking delightfully disheveled.

They spent the next few days like that. There was no reason to wear clothes. There was no contact with the outside world. It was simply the two of them, lost in a reality that could not be contained outside of this place.

For a media frenzy awaited them, and the demand to perform. And none of that was here. Here, there was nothing but their bodies. Nothing but their pleasure. Here, he began to feel something like comfort. Something like home.

And it felt like something close to peace for the first time since he had left the one place he had ever truly thought of as home.

Olive was beginning to realize that nothing was going to magically spark between the two of them that would prevent her from having a conversation she simply didn't want to have.

She was beginning to realize that it was different when

you had your actual emotions invested in something. It wasn't going to be clean or easy or quick. It wasn't just a business deal. It did matter how it happened. It mattered... All of it.

The things that she had done before had been out of allegiance to her father. A desire to give him exactly what he wanted, even though he wasn't here. But this was for her.

Her feelings for Gunnar were hers.

And the risk was hers.

It was such a catastrophic feeling. She felt rocked, altered. She felt afraid. Because she was going to have to risk something, not a contract. Her soul.

But she had made a decision.

He had bought her the skimpiest bathing suit of all time, as if a bathing suit were at all necessary here. But she wondered if he liked it purely for decoration. He did that sometimes. Make love to her with her clothes on. He had her naked too, but there seemed to be a particular thing he got out of leaving articles of clothing in place. She couldn't deny there was something sexy about it. When all he could manage to do was open the front of his pants and have her with all of his other items in place, it made her feel cherished, which was a funny thing, because she never would've imagined that animalistic passion could equate to feeling cherished, but it did. It made her feel special. Made her feel like she mattered.

Like she was something special to him.

She worried sometimes that she was simply a shackle. Because he had done this for the sake of their baby, and yet... They didn't talk about the baby. They didn't really... They didn't really speak of the future. It was difficult. Strange. This thing between them. It seemed wholly focused on them, and yet he would never have said that he was doing this because of her.

Or maybe he would. It was the asking, that was what she had to do.

"I have something a little bit different planned for tonight," she said.

What she had learned, being up there on the mountain, was that there were people she could call for assistance. And for the two hours a day that they were both off doing work, she had sacrificed a little bit of time planning this.

"You're going to want to bundle up," she said. "It's going to be cold."

She could have told him to bring his swimsuit, but she wanted him naked.

She wanted him to have absolutely no defenses at all when she did this.

It was dark, the northern lights visible out over the snow, green and purple and all the light. They cast beauty out onto the stark landscape, and it gave her hope.

Bundled in her parka, she took his hand in her mittened one, and began to lead him down the side of the mountain. She knew now where the path was that took them to the hot springs.

"What is this?" he asked when they arrived down there to a table set with food, and heaters placed around. "You have set us up food on the tundra."

"Yes," she said. "I have. I wished to take you on a date without entering into civilization. This seemed like a reasonable enough way to do it."

The dinner was exquisite, lamb, fish and potatoes.

Extremely Icelandic, and she could see by the look on Gunnar's face, that it tapped into something special.

She knew that this place was special to him. That no matter how much time he spent in the rest of the world, this was his home. His heart.

The scary thing was, this was an unforgiving, harsh, frozen landscape.

But there were also northern lights. There were miracles. Hot springs. Possibilities. And she had to hope that his heart reflected all those things in the same way as his homeland. She had to hope that that was true.

As soon as he finished eating she unzipped her coat, and revealed that she had nothing but a bikini top underneath.

His gaze suddenly became keen. Extremely interested.

"I had thought that we might use the hot springs."

"Indeed."

She shimmied out of her boots and pants, and stepped into the steaming, pale blue pool. He was not far behind her, stripping his clothes off, moving down into the pool and taking her into his arms.

He kissed her, her neck, on down her shoulder blades, making his way to her breasts, he clearly loved her breasts.

And she arched her back, rubbed her nipples against his hair-covered chest, gloried in the textural differences between them. In his strength.

But this was different than the other times they had come together. Those times had always been furious, intense. Growling and fighting, and she loved them.

But she wanted to show him something else. She wanted to show him her heart. And so, she swam away from him, to the corner of the pool. And he followed. But when he rejoined her, she wrapped her arms firmly around his neck, and kissed him. She made the kiss long and deep, keeping her hands firmly clasped behind his neck, preventing herself from exploring the rest of his hard, beautiful body, as much as she wanted to. And she poured everything into it. All the things that were hard for her to say. All the things that she felt with every last bit of her heart.

Finally, she broke the kiss off, and began to move her hands over his muscles, and as if he sensed that this was her moment, something she must do, he kept his hands at his sides, and allowed her unfettered access to his body.

She explored the planes of his chest, the glorious ripples in his stomach. She moved her hands to his thighs. He had a warrior's body. And that, she realized, he was. Fighting an endless battle to find victory.

But she wondered what he was trying to claim victory against. For all that they had been together, she had not been able to entice him to share.

And tonight, she realized she could not kick the ice wall down. She had to melt it.

It was all that could be done.

With an elegant lift of her body beneath the water, she brought herself down over his stiff arousal, lowering herself slowly onto his shaft. She clung to his shoulders as she took him into her body, as she reveled in this moment. She looked up, dizzy, the light swirling above, mingling with those crushed glitter stars, doing their best to light up a black velvet night.

It was them. All that velvet darkness, and never-ending hope.

Hope.

She hoped for better without even ever seeing it with her own eyes. She hoped for more for the two of them without any assurance that such a thing existed. Without a certainty that it was possible.

It was faith, at the end of the day, something she had never put a lot of thought into. But that was love. Faith, hope and love were all part of the same thing. You could not have one without desperately wanting another. Without clinging as hard as possible to another.

For this love in her heart was the substance of all that was hoped for, and she took her peace in the fact that she knew she did not have to see it for it to be there.

Love.

Oh, how she loved him.

As her body began to quake with pleasure, as she began to shatter in his arms, she whispered those words.

The words that she had been too afraid to speak all this time. "I love you."

He growled, his climax overtaking him, and she felt his surrender, and for just that moment, she let it shine within her like lights in the northern sky.

I love you.

No. This could not be borne. This could not be.

I love you.

It brought back with scalding clarity words within him that he had not thought of for years. Words that no one had said to him in so long…

I love you.

He gritted his teeth. "Let us go back to the house," he said.

"Is that all you have to say?"

"It is all there is to be said."

"That isn't true. And you know that. I said that I loved you, Gunnar, and now you're telling me you want to go back to the house. The appropriate answer is to either say that you love me in return, or tell me that you don't, but acting like the words were never spoken feels a bit like a lie."

"In all things, I have never been a liar. That is you."

"Well, that suits your narrative right now, doesn't it? That somehow what I have to say to you isn't true. But I love you. And you are being a coward."

"I don't love, I told you that."

"Why. Why? Look, I know what it's like to be hurt by the person who's supposed to love you, but during this time, these past couple months, I've been rebuilding myself. And with that, came the realization that the company isn't the most important thing to me. Not anymore. I don't want to raise our child in an environment where love is conditional. Where performance is the only thing that matters. I can't deal with that. Live like that. I want love. I've never been loved before. Not really. And I want a life, a house, a world that is filled with love. I don't think that's wrong. Is it wrong? I would hope that it's not. I would hope that it is entirely understandable that what I want is… What I want is to be cared for. But I've done all this work to break down the barriers in my soul, and I want you to do it too. I wanted to come out here. Because I know this is your heart. I want you to tell me. I want you to tell me."

"Enough," he said.

"No. I'm not going to be afraid. You married me. You're stuck with me. What are you going to do? Stay married to me for a week? Deny me, divorce me, just because I'm not doing everything that you want? I don't think that is a very reasonable move. I simply don't. So, here's what I think. I'm going to push. Because that's who I am. But you know what else… Love isn't a contract negotiation. There isn't a winner and a loser. And there are no prizes for a grudging acceptance. I want you to love me. I want you to love me because you have no other choice."

"Let me tell you what you don't know about my life," he said. "Until I was twelve I was raised here. I never left Iceland. I never left the country. I never knew my mother, she left when I was a baby. But I lived with my grandparents. Her parents. We lived in a small house out in the middle of nowhere. I spent all my days in the snow. In the wilderness. I would come home to warm dinner, and people who were there for me. Who cared. They taught me to love this land. They taught me what mattered. But I was enamored of a man who had never even come to visit me. Enamored of his money, his power. He took me and he tried to…to bend me into his image. To break me into it. Before he died, I told him that he had failed." And suddenly, his soul felt as cold as the world around him. "But he didn't. He stripped something from me that I will never be able to get back. He stole the only warmth, the only love that I ever knew."

He thought of when he'd tried to go back. He thought of it, but he could not bring himself to walk through the memory. Not now.

"Gunnar," she said. "I want that house that you're talking about. I want that love. I want to be that thing for our child. I want simple and beautiful and ours. I want it to be home. I want it to be filled with love. Your father didn't win unless you allow him to. A man chooses his own steps. I know that you believe that. You took what your grandparents taught you, and you made your company focus on the planet. Because you loved the wilderness that you grew up in. Because you took that love and you carried it out with you. It isn't gone. It had to take a different shape."

"You don't know, Olive," he said. "It does not matter. This. We have passion. And that is enough."

She shook her head. "It matters to me. It matters to me, and I cannot live in a place where I am not loved. Not again. Not ever again. Gunnar, I want our life to be different. Wholly different. I want it to be everything that we could've ever dreamed of. When we were children, when we believed everything was possible. Not now. Not as cynical adults, taking what we've been told we're allowed.

"No. What I want is a miracle. And I don't see why we can't have it."

"Because there are no miracles left in this world."

He thought of the empty cabin.

The pipe, sitting cold on the counter.

Never to be smoked again.

Two people who were gone, with Gunnar never having a chance to see them again. To say that he was sorry.

"Look at the sky," Olive said. "If that's not a miracle, then what is? Look at us. If we are not a miracle... I don't know what is."

"There are no miracles in this life. That is just science. And we're just two people who had sex, and are now dealing with the consequences."

And he could see the moment that he had lost her. And it was a moment that he knew true terror. Because he had not imagined that he could lose her. He had thought... He had thought that she would stay.

"But I love you," she said. "I love you, and I want you to love me. Why can't you trust that? Why can't you trust me?"

"Olive, I trust nothing. Nothing. I was a boy, who grew up in the safest, most loving home possible, and what did I want? More. More. I was greedy. I looked at my father, I saw his wealth and his success and I thought... I thought it would be happier with him? And for what? Because I was blinded by the trappings of all that he had, and I could not have been more wrong. And if I could be wrong about him..."

"It's why you were so angry with me, isn't it? Because you believed better about me, and I proved you wrong. And I'm sorry. I'm so sorry. But you have to understand. It didn't come from a place of wanting to hurt you. I was just trying to do what my father wanted."

"Enough. I don't care about that. Not anymore."

"You are afraid that you can't trust your judgment, and I only made that worse. I only..."

"It is not you, you fool. It is me. I do not trust myself."

"Gunnar..."

"That is the way of it. The truth of it, Olive. I *chose* to leave them. I betrayed them. I squandered the love that I had. I was a bad judge of character... But most of all... It is my own character that I have no certainty in. Because I looked around that cabin, I looked around at this frozen wasteland, and I did not love it. I did not esteem it. I wanted to go and live with my rich father. As if money might insulate me. As if money would make me happier. I knew nothing. And I will never be so complacent that I think that might've changed. Yes, I pride myself on my moral integrity that is only because I have written rules for myself that I will not compromise. I had love. And I squandered it for the shallow things in life."

"You were a boy."

"A boy who broke the hearts of the only two people who ever loved him. A boy who left them to die alone. My grandfather went first. And then my grandmother… And who was there with her, Olive? Because it was not me. Those hands that held mine when I learned to walk. Those hands that taught me to fish, taught me to cook. They were empty when she died, because I was not there. How can I ever speak of love. I had it and I squandered it. I failed when he came to get me. I had a little wooden soldier in my hand. He took it from me, and looked at it. He said that I should leave it because I could have much better with him. And so I left it. And it is… It is the one thing that you cannot get back, Olive. The simple things that you squander, thinking that you will replace them with money. You won't. You can't."

"So take this. Take it now. I can't replace what you lost, but I am here. I'm here."

"My heart was turned to stone long ago. It cannot be fixed. Not now."

"Gunnar please," she said, the words raw.

"There is nothing to be done, little Olive."

She looked bleak, cold and tired. And then, she turned her face up to him, and the stark sadness in her eyes gutted him.

"I will be setting up residence somewhere else," she said. "I will stay married to you. I will allow you full visitation of our child. As much as you like. But I need to be free. I need to be free to live my life. To feel loved. I cannot exchange one man in my life with expectations on me that come from a place that has nothing to do with how much he cares, for another. I'm sorry, Gunnar. But that's how it has to be."

"No," he said, his voice rough, the denial bursting from him.

"I'm sorry," she said. "I can't do this. I can't. I lived my whole life with a man who wanted me around only for what he could train me to be. How are you different? How are we different?"

He felt as if he was being wrenched in two.

He watched as she got out of the pool. As she dried herself and dressed herself. An entirely different woman to the one that he had brought here first.

This one would not shrink against the wind.

And she did not shrink against him.

And he had no idea what the hell he was supposed to do with that.

Go after her.

And yet, he stood frozen. As Olive hiked back up the mountain. As she took that torn piece of him with her. And it felt like a terrible metaphor. Because Olive was strong enough to hike up the mountain, and he stood frozen, in the pain of his past.

And suddenly, it was as if the frozen ice blocks inside of him began to crack. Crumble.

And he wanted to roar at the sky.

Because he had only ever loved his grandparents, and he had lost them. And then he had spent a childhood being abused by a man who hadn't loved him at all.

But Olive… Maybe it was because Olive had never known the warmth of home, that she didn't fear its loss. Because she didn't know what it was like to return to an empty cabin and find out that the people in it had died years ago.

And you would never have the chance to say goodbye.

He dressed, and he called his pilot.

There was something he needed to do. Somewhere he needed to go.

He was a man who had been all around the world, but there was one last journey he had to take.

CHAPTER SIXTEEN

OLIVE WAS WRETCHED. But she was the one who had decided to go back to the States. She began to work at making arrangements for where she might go and be with her baby.

She began to think in earnest about what kind of life she would build. What kind of mother she would be.

It all started her thinking about who she was in a way she never had before.

She was resourceful, and resilient, she wanted to be soft. She had always been trained to be afraid to be. She didn't like to ask for help, and right now it felt as if she needed a lot of help. But maybe that was better. Maybe it was training.

Because she needed to embrace some of the vulnerability inside of her so that she could soften for a baby.

She started to write a letter, one that had nothing to do with press releases or the media. One that simply felt good. A list of promises. Ones that she was determined to keep.

And she did her best not to dissolve.

But what if you did?

It was a profound question. And it was one that sent a crack down to the very depths of her soul.

What if she did?

And so she wept. Openly. With her whole body.

She wept for the little girl she'd been. Who had spent her childhood waiting outside of boardrooms. Who had been angry at Gunnar for eating her cupcake, but not at her father for giving her a birthday party where the only semblance of a treat was a cupcake that just happened to be there, not even for her specifically. One that didn't make her special. One that didn't matter at all.

She wept for her childhood. For her teenage years. For the fact that she had taken everything seriously all this time.

For the fact that Gunnar was the person she loved so very much, when what she wanted was something normal.

And she did not think they could ever have that.

She wept for so many things. And she didn't feel weaker for it. Instead, she felt like she had found something new.

She was only very sorry that she had had to break her own heart to find it.

The helicopter pilot touched down in the snowfield, and Gunnar stepped out, standing before the darkened home.

He had bought it some years ago. Just to ensure that it stayed there.

He walked across the bleak, empty snowfield and pushed open the door.

It was impossibly cold, the fire in the hearth dead for these many years.

It was strange to see the place without so much as an ember.

The pipe was still there.

He walked over and touched it.

He wasn't sure why he had left it the first time. Why he hadn't kept it for himself.

Really, it did not make sense.

And yet, if he thought of it truthfully, it did. He had spent all these years running away from how much this place hurt.

He walked into the back bedroom, where the quilt his grandmother had made was still spread over the bed.

This was the only place where he had experienced love.

A love he hadn't deserved.

A love he had squandered.

And now he had the offer of love again, the offer of a life, from Olive.

How could he accept her love? How? He was wrong about all these sorts of things. He'd had love. He had love and he had squandered it. He had seen something shinier, something that he thought was better. And he had been wrong. So desperately wrong. He had stolen from himself a life of warmth and love and simplicity. And he had exchanged it for fists of fury and barren rooms. He had exchanged it for years where he had lived with a man who had done his level best to strip the humanity from him, and he had to fight for all that he was to cling to it. To cling to that cabin. To cling to its warmth. To remember that when his temper had flared his grandfather had taught him ways to cope with it. That his grandmother had showed him softness.

He had betrayed them. The cost had been everything. Everything. And they died. They died and he had never been back. How could he accept love now? How?

Knowing what he had squandered… Knowing how…

How little he could trust his own heart.

Perhaps he needed to trust hers.

Because he had been given love once. And it had been keen and clear and bright. And it was the same sort of love that he had seen reflected in Olive's face.

His Olive. They were like nothing. He'd said that to her. And it was true.

If that's not a miracle, then what is? Look at us. If we are not a miracle… I don't know what is.

He had thought those feelings long dead in him. And he had thrown the issue of her betrayal in front of them, because it was easy. Because it was easy to tap into that old fury, that old hurt at the way he had been wrong about his father.

Far easier than admitting…

Of course he had always loved her. Of course. She was everything to him, and she had been for all this time. He had thought, not so long ago, that if he had been another man he might've loved her. But he always had.

He had just been desperate not to label it thus, because part of him knew…

If he wanted love, then he had to reckon with his past. If he wanted love, Olive was right. He had to let it go. To keep what warmed him, and to set aside what hurt him.

She had always been there. The only good thing. The only healing thing. Waiting to be ready. Waiting for him to be ready.

They were more than a miracle. They were fate. But fate was not going to chase him down.

He was going to have to do some work. No matter how hard it might be.

"I'm sorry," he said, his breath coming out in a fog, the apology lingering in the air. "I am so sorry I left you. I didn't know. I didn't understand."

He was bringing a child into this world. And perhaps that meant…perhaps that meant finding forgiveness for the boy he'd been.

The boy who had walked away from this and into a life of cold manipulation that had made him desperately unhappy.

His sin had been trust.

His sin had been loving someone undeserving of it.

Was that so unforgivable? Could he not release it?

And he suddenly knew, that he could not give his child the life he wanted without risking himself. He could not have Olive without risking himself. She was a bright, beautiful woman who showed him continually that she was his match in every way, and he was lowering himself. He was not giving her all that he could.

And he was doing it out of fear. He wanted to prove that

he was the best, he had acted as if that put him above her. That he would not cheat on something like a project. But the truth of it was, Olive had been willing to compromise everything for the love of her father. Olive had been willing to risk herself to tell him that she loved him. And he hadn't risked a damn thing for her. Olive was the brave one. She was the one that was honest.

He did not deserve her. He was not worthy of her. And suddenly, like a light in the darkness, he knew the truth.

It shone into the very depths of his soul, and kept him from being able to lie. To himself, to anyone else.

He had loved Olive for a very long time. It was only his cowardice that kept him from admitting it was so. And if he wanted to be half the man that she was a woman, he had to change everything now.

What good was being a man forged in the fires, a man whose blood cried out for battle if he could not fight for the one thing that mattered.

No matter the cost.

She was wretched. She had cried herself hoarse, and then gone to sleep in their bed.

Well, it had been their bed. What it would be next would be determined by what she did.

And she was waiting. Waiting for him to return. Waiting to see what her life would look like. She would have her child. So there was that. She had to cling to that.

"I am prepared to do this," she said.

She stood up, and when she turned around, he was standing there. In the doorway, his eyes ice blue. And something in her shifted. She felt as if they were standing in a boardroom, ready and able to have the biggest negotiation of their life.

"I cannot stay if you don't love me."

"You can't, or you won't?"

"I'm no longer willing to sacrifice myself to the needs of others. I will not do it. I want to be loved. And yes, I want all of this for my child, but I want it for myself as well. I need it for myself. I need to have this."

"I am willing," he said.

And he said it as if it was a forfeited business. And her whole heart turned to stone.

"You see, I have focused on winning to make what I did worthwhile. Leaving my grandparents for as long as I did. I could've come back, much earlier than I did. Much, much earlier. But I didn't, out of fear. I stayed away, and I kept working hard, and when I returned, they had… They had died. I waited too long. And so his success became everything. I never wanted to experience loss again. Ever. I could not face it. But what is the point of living if we are not trying, in all of our messy glory, to love? What is the purpose of it?"

"I don't know," she said.

"Neither do I. Not anymore. Not now. For I have ascended to the heights professionally, I could've had my revenge on you, but none of it fixed who I am, what I was. Nothing has come close to fixing anything. But when I was with you in the hot springs, beneath the northern lights, I could nearly believe it. In miracles. In love. In a little house out in the country."

"I love you," she said.

And she ran forward, closing the distance between them, and kissing him on the mouth.

"I need to show you something," he whispered against her lips.

"I'll follow you anywhere." She smiled. "Or you know, you could kidnap me."

"Kidnap?"

"A little pillaging, a little ravishing…"

"Later, my love, later."

Shortly after that, Olive found herself on a plane, bound for Iceland.

The cabin Gunnar brought her to was his home, she knew it, without him having to tell her.

"Oh, Gunnar…"

She walked through the little place, looking at the hand carved furniture. At the small, remaining signs of the lives that had once been here.

And then she saw something, just very small, beneath one of the little beds.

She bent down and discovered a small, wooden soldier.

"Gunnar."

She turned and he was standing in the doorway.

"I found this."

"Olive…"

"It's been here all along. Waiting for you." She looked up at him, and she smiled. "It was waiting for you to find your way home."

He took her in his arms, his voice low and fierce. "Yes, that may be true. But first… Olive first, I had to find you."

"I was there the whole time."

He kissed her then, deep and hard. "Yes, you were. You were."

"I love you."

"I love you too."

There must be, Olive thought, a German word for that unbearable feeling of caring for someone so very much you thought you might break apart. And then she realized, there were no words for it. There was only this. Only two hearts that had long stood divided on opposite sides of the board-room, that had become one over time, and would stay one, because of the miracle of love.

EPILOGUE

IT WAS CHRISTMAS, their favorite time of year. Snow fell outside, and everybody was tucked up in their little beds, beneath handmade quilts. The fire was going, and he knew from experience that smoke from the small stovepipe chimney was pouring into the frigid air.

The cabin was their Christmas tradition.

And they all loved it. Including the kids.

It was smaller than their other homes throughout the world, but it would always be the most special home. The most real.

He and Olive did not work so much these days. Delegating various tasks to other people of the company. What Olive had decided to do was not start a company at all. She had started writing children's books. Her particular brand of ridiculous humor in banter creating a series of exceedingly popular works. About a young girl who had to spend her days in office buildings while her dad had meetings, and the different shenanigans she got up to.

But he would've loved her whatever she did, because she was his.

Because she had given him his home back.

He looked at the Christmas tree in the corner, and the sleeping children in their beds.

She had given him his heart back.

* * * * *

COMING SOON!

We really hope you enjoyed reading this book.
If you're looking for more romance, be sure to
head to the shops when new books are
available on

Thursday 4th August

To see which titles are coming soon, please visit

millsandboon.co.uk/nextmonth

MILLS & BOON®

Coming next month

INNOCENT UNTIL HIS FORBIDDEN TOUCH
Carol Marinelli

"Seriously?" His deep Italian voice entered the room before he even walked in. "I do not need a PR strategist?"

"A Liason Aide, Sir," his Aide murmured.

Beatrice stood as she'd been instructed earlier, but as he entered, every assumption she'd made about him was wiped away.

Prince Julius brimmed, not just with authority but with health and energy. It was as if a forcefield had entered the room.

She had dealt with alpha males and females at the top of their game – or rather – usually when they crashing from the top.

Not he.

He was, quite literally, stunning.

He stunned.

"It's a pleasure to meet you," she said and then added. "Sir."

"Likewise," he said, even if his eyes said otherwise.

God, he was tall, Beatrice thought, it was more than just his height, he was the most immaculate man she had ever seen.

Beatrice swallowed, not wanting to pursue that line of thought. The issue was that at most interviews she had found most people were less in the flesh.

He was so, so much more.

Continue reading
INNOCENT UNTIL HIS FORBIDDEN TOUCH
Carol Marinelli

Available next month
www.millsandboon.co.uk

MILLS & BOON

THE HEART OF ROMANCE

A ROMANCE FOR EVERY READER

MODERN
Prepare to be swept off your feet by sophisticated, sexy and seductive heroes, in some of the world's most glamourous and romantic locations, where power and passion collide.

HISTORICAL
Escape with historical heroes from time gone by. Whether your passion is for wicked Regency Rakes, muscled Vikings or rugged Highlanders, awaken the romance of the past.

MEDICAL
Set your pulse racing with dedicated, delectable doctors in the high-pressure world of medicine, where emotions run high and passion, comfort and love are the best medicine.

True Love
Celebrate true love with tender stories of heartfelt romance, from the rush of falling in love to the joy a new baby can bring, and a focus on the emotional heart of a relationship.

Desire
Indulge in secrets and scandal, intense drama and plenty of sizzling hot action with powerful and passionate heroes who have it all: wealth, status, good looks…everything but the right woman.

HEROES
Experience all the excitement of a gripping thriller, with an intense romance at its heart. Resourceful, true-to-life women and strong, fearless men face danger and desire - a killer combination!

To see which titles are coming soon, please visit

millsandboon.co.uk/nextmonth

LET'S TALK
Romance

For exclusive extracts, competitions
and special offers, find us online:

f facebook.com/millsandboon

🐦 @MillsandBoon

📷 @MillsandBoonUK

Get in touch on 01413 063232

For all the latest titles coming soon, visit
millsandboon.co.uk/nextmonth